Praise for Lorelei James'
Rode Hard, Put Up Wet

Rating: 4 ½ Hearts   "This book was like having two romances in one. The dialogue was excellent... you could easily visualize the scenes and the transitions from Gemma/Cash to Carter/Macie, didn't distract from the super hot sexy romance between the couples."

~ *Lisa F., The Romance Studio*

"Rode Hard, Put Up Wet is a wonderful read. The relationships in this book are out of this world. I could tell how much care Lorelei James put into these four characters...Not only did I get two great romances I also got to read about a strained father and daughter relationship on the mend and the family dynamics of a large group... Ms. James had me on an emotional rollercoaster, but the hot sex made up for it."

~ *Jambrea, Joyfully Reviewed*

Rating: 4 Stars   "Rode Hard, Put Up Wet is a multi-generational Western saga that I found highly enjoyable. Ms. James intricately weaves all four characters into one cohesive story...plenty of steamy love scenes that will have you reaching for your own hottie! I hope that Ms. James will return to this setting, giving us more of the McKay family's stories in the future."

~ *Just Erotic Romance Reviews*

Rating: 3 Angels "...a great cowboy treat as well as being a hot story...For all who want two stories in one I would recommend this book highly."

~ *Missy, Fallen Angel Review*

Look for these titles by
Lorelei James

Now Available:

Running With the Devil
Dirty Deeds
Beginnings Anthology: Babe in the Woods

Rough Riders series
Long Hard Ride
Rode Hard, Put Up Wet
Cowgirl Up and Ride
Tied Up, Tied Down

Coming Soon:

Rough Riders series
Rough, Ready and Raw

Rode Hard, Put Up Wet

Lorelei James

A Samhain Publishing, Ltd. publication.

Samhain Publishing, Ltd.
577 Mulberry Street, Suite 1520
Macon, GA 31201
www.samhainpublishing.com

Editing by Angela James
Cover by Scott Carpenter

First Samhain Publishing, Ltd. electronic publication: October 2007
First Samhain Publishing, Ltd. print publication: August 2008

Dedication

To everyone who's found true love—no matter what stage of life.

Chapter One

"That horse nearly throwed you clean into the funeral parlor, boy."

Whoops of cowboy laughter cut through the dusty air.

Gemma Jansen hung on the edge of the trash-talking bronc riders, waiting for a break in the conversation. The rodeo announcer's voice reverberated through the arena stands as he pumped up the crowd for the next event: steer wrestling.

"I didn't break nothin', but he shore loosened my jaw so's I tasted some dirt."

Another round of male laughter.

A baby-faced kid shoved a plug of tobacco in his cheek. "I'd rather have a bucker like him than the last one I had. Shoot. That bronc couldn'ta tossed off a baby blanket."

Gemma jammed her hands in her jeans pockets and sauntered closer to prop a hip against the muddy tailgate. "Afternoon, boys."

Immediately slouched postures straightened. A couple of the younger fellas even removed their hats. Aw. Their mommas would've been proud at their show of respect. Still, it made Gemma feel...old.

Feel? Hell, she *was* old enough to be any one of these guys' mommas.

The wiry bronc buster named Jesse grinned at her. "Hey, Miz Jansen. You're lookin' purty as a picture today."

The other young buckaroos nodded and gave her an appreciative appraisal. She didn't mind. "Thanks."

"Ain't seen you around the circuit for a while. Everything

okay?"

"You know how it goes. Been busy takin' care of ranch business."

"Ain't doin' all the work alone, are you?"

"Trying not to."

"Good to hear." Jesse frowned and scratched his chin with the back of his leather glove. "Come to think of it... How come you ain't been supplyin' none of the animals this season?"

"I've been asking the same question. None of the promoters can give me a good answer."

"If you don't mind me sayin' so, that sucks." His eyes gleamed. "I'd sure like a chance to ride that ornery bronc of yours again."

"Which one?"

"Warpaint. Man. That roan could buck off a man's whiskers."

"He's itching to be rode. Maybe you'll get a shot later in the year."

"Lookin' forward to it." He gifted her with another inspection from beneath the brim of his Stetson. "So you just wanderin' around, lookin' good, showin' up them baby bunnies who're trollin' for buckles?"

What a charmer. She grinned. The kid's eyes were brown from being so full of shit. "No. Actually, I'm looking for Cash Big Crow. You seen him?"

Jesse pointed to a stoop-shouldered man perched on the tailgate of a rusted-out International pickup. "Ask Frank. He keeps tabs on all the stock handlers."

"Thanks."

She skirted the rigging bags and saddles, avoiding the gigantic potholes in the makeshift road.

When she reached the pickup, the old Indian man squinted against the cigarette smoke curling into his left eye. "Help ya, miss?"

Miss. Right. She hadn't been called that in a coon's age. "Yeah. I'm looking for Cash Big Crow."

"You ain't the only one. Last I heard he was at the first aid station."

Gemma's stomach pitched. "Was he hurt?"

"Don't rightly know."

"Thanks."

He nodded.

She paused to let the two female trick riders by, all decked out in flowing purple regalia. Once she reached the tiny room beneath the bleachers serving as the first aid station, the only person inside was a bored-looking EMT.

"Has Cash Big Crow been in here?"

The man lifted one pierced brow. "You're the second person to ask me that. No one's been in here for a coupla hours. Been a yawner today." He refocused on the girlie magazine on the exam table.

Damn. Where could Cash be? Hopefully he hadn't left.

Gemma cut through the contestants' area, steering clear of the motor home, which housed the rodeo headquarters. She'd been in and out of that rig several times in a fruitless endeavor to convince rodeo promoters to give her a shot as a rough stock contractor.

As much as Westerners claimed gender bias or prejudice no longer had a foothold in the Western way of life, it simply wasn't true. After her husband Steve died, Gemma had gradually been shut out of supplying stock for nearly every rodeo on the circuit. She was beyond frustrated with the "old boy" system but she was too stubborn to quit.

In the meantime, her ranch needed attention and she couldn't concentrate on expanding her rodeo stock operation until she fixed the problems that paid the bills.

A bank of gray clouds floated overhead, covering the sun, sending dark shadows skittering across the chalky vanilla-colored dirt. She glanced at the paddock across from the arena and noticed the stocky cowboy leaning on the white metal corrals.

Her heart slammed. She hadn't seen him for almost a year, yet she'd watched him often enough she'd memorized how he looked from behind. A braid swung against his broad shoulders, the rest of his coal black hair remained hidden beneath a beat-up cowboy hat. Tight Wranglers showcased his tight ass. The toes of his boots pointed out, as he was a little bowlegged. She knew his face was a little worn, but handsome. When she was within twenty yards an anticipatory smile bloomed.

The smile died when a shout caused Cash to turn. A young woman launched herself straight into Cash's outstretched arms. Cash kissed the woman and spun her in a circle, causing a feminine squeal of delight.

Gemma froze, unable to slink away from the intimate exchange. Cash set down the hot chickie and squeezed her curvy body tightly against his. While she talked a blue streak, he tipped her head back, tenderly smoothing away a section of her long brown hair.

Gemma's lips tingled in remembrance of when Cash had touched her that way. Reverently. Confidently. Sweetly.

She could've had that. Could've had him looking at her that way. Instead, he was grinning at the Indian princess like she'd hung the moon and the stars.

There was no fool like an old fool. Gemma backed up, preparing to retreat. But a gust of wind ripped off the young woman's straw hat and blew it directly toward her.

Cash gave chase until he caught the hat ten feet from where Gemma stood. His gaze started at the scuffed toes of Gemma's dirty ropers and traveled up her body to lock on her eyes. He blinked. "Gemma? Is that really you?"

Rather than snap off a smart answer, Gemma escaped. Cash shouted her name but she didn't slow down until she'd reached the area where she'd parked her horse trailer. She zigzagged through the maze of silver and black steel until she found hers. Leaning her forehead against the heated metal, she fumbled for her keys.

Fool fool fool. Dammit. Why had she hoped Cash would wait around for her to get her head on straight? Especially after she'd told him she didn't want to get involved with him at all? What had she expected? And why in the hell had she bolted like a spooked filly the second she'd seen him? Lord. She was *forty-*eight years old, not eight.

Dry grass crunched behind her and she wheeled around.

Cash's luminous, coffee-colored eyes stared back at her.

"Dammit, Gemma, I know you heard me yellin' at you. Why didn't you stop?"

"Because I didn't want to intrude."

"Intrude on what?"

She turned, shoving the key in the locked door. "Don't tease me, Cash."

"Tease you? I know I ain't always the brightest bulb in the box, but what the devil are you talkin' 'bout? Intrude on what?" He grabbed her shoulder and forced her to look at him.

"You and—"

Just then the gorgeous young Indian princess sidled in behind Cash. Silent. Watchful. A stunning vision of youth and beauty. A sharp reminder of everything Gemma was not.

"Me and who?" he demanded.

Her. "Never mind."

"Huh-uh. I ain't seen you in almost a year so I wanna know why you were lookin' for me."

Gemma ground her teeth together.

"If you were so hell-bent on findin' me why'd you race off without sayin' a word?"

"Because once I found you, I realized it was a bad time. I didn't mean to interrupt you...and your girlfriend. Besides, I figured I'd catch up with you later."

A sly smile lit up Cash's face. "Then why am I the one who had to chase *you* down, eh?"

Crap.

"Lemme tell you what I think." His breath tickled her ear as he whispered, "I believe you took off because you're jealous."

Jealous? More like mortified. Gemma had half a mind to crawl under the horse trailer and hide until Cash and his jailbait buckle bunny disappeared. She managed a small snort of disgust. "Jealous? Not hardly."

"Really? You want an explanation for what you saw by the corrals?"

Yes. "No."

"Or an introduction to my *girlfriend?*"

The girlfriend gasped.

"You don't owe me nothin', Cash. Just forget it."

Cash grabbed the young woman's hand, dragging her front and center. "I'd love to milk this jealous side of you for all it's worth, but I ain't that mean. Or that patient. Gemma, meet my *daughter,* Macie Honeycutt. Macie, Gemma Jansen."

Chapter Two

Relief swept through Gemma.

"Ah. She's the one you told me about," Macie said with a charming grin exactly like her father's.

"Daughter?" Gemma repeated.

Cash kept his gaze on hers. "Yep."

"I-I didn't know you had any kids."

"There's a lot you don't know about me, Gem."

A pointed silence thickened the air.

"Well, this is fun...*not*," Macie said.

"Macie, darlin', I know you just pulled in and we've got some catchin' up to do. But I'd appreciate it if you'd run along for a bit and wait for me by the main entrance until after I have a private word with Miz Jansen."

"Fine. I hate being a third wheel anyway. But don't be surprised if I make a few new friends on my own."

He shot his daughter a warning look. "Stay away from them cowboys, Macie, I mean it."

Macie rolled her eyes. "You wish. Later." She vanished around the corner.

They were alone.

"You finished with your snit?" he asked softly.

"It wasn't a snit," Gemma retorted.

"Whatever." Cash curled his big hands over her shoulders. "So, happy as I am to see you again, it pisses me off that you think I'd be knockin' boots with a woman the same age as my daughter."

The warmth of his touch sent tingles down the center of her body. "Far as I know, the young bunnies hovering around an experienced cowboy like yourself *could* be exactly your type."

"Wrong. But I don't think you tracked me down just to chew my ass for who you suspect might've been rockin' my horse trailer." His hands fell away. "So why don't you cut to the chase and tell me why you're really here, eh?"

Gemma studied him. The regal bone structure in his face highlighted the intriguing crosshatch of facial lines, courtesy of the years he'd spent working outdoors. When he smiled, the corners of his eyes crinkled and added to his rugged good looks.

"I heard you quit rodeoin' fulltime."

"Yeah? Who'd you hear that from?"

"Colby McKay." She paused. "Is that true?"

"Pretty much."

"Why? I figured you'd be chasing the gold buckle and silver spurs until you were a grizzled old man."

Cash shook his head. "Between seein' Mike Morgan's career-endin' injury and Colby bein' damn lucky to be alive after getting stomped by a bull, I decided to quit while I still had a choice. In the last two years, most days I rode I felt like a grizzled old man anyway."

"So what've you been doin' to earn a living?"

Color darkened his cheekbones and he raised his chin a notch. "Whatever I can."

"Like?"

"Like I spent the winter fixin' houses on the rez. Then I helped a buddy down by Hot Springs during calvin' season. Lately I've been wranglin' rodeo stock for the contractors. I ain't got a place of my own to maintain so I'm flexible. I can go anywhere at the drop of a hat."

Gemma overlooked his embarrassment. It was a point of pride for white-line cowboys to own a chunk of land, to have a place of their own to call home if the road to rodeo glory ever quit calling them. Now that she really thought about it, why hadn't Cash ever talked about why he didn't have a place of his own? Was that a conscious choice? "Does that mean you prefer to keep moving around rather than have a steady income?"

"No." His eyes narrowed. "Why?"

"The reason I came here is to offer you a job. I had another foreman quit on me last week."

"Tell me you ain't doin' everything by yourself."

"Most of it. Carter McKay is helping me out this summer. But he's just part-time."

"Carter McKay? One of Colby's brothers?" His eyebrows knit together. "I don't know him."

"He's the youngest. Been away at school for a number of years. He's a hard worker, but his heart ain't really in it. I need someone I can count on."

"And you think that someone is me?"

"That's what I'm asking. You know how to handle livestock. You know that ranching is hard work. And I could use an expert opinion on some of the young, untried broncs I'm hopin' to get into the circuit. Not that those smug bastards calling themselves promoters are giving me a chance."

Cash frowned.

"Plus, I've discovered I need testosterone around. Things run smoother even if a man just stands there lookin' pretty with his mouth shut while I do all the negotiating."

He stared at her without speaking for the longest time. "What?"

"I ain't pretty, and I ain't interested in standin' around with my mouth shut. That ain't who I am."

"I didn't say that you were."

Cash raised his eyebrows.

Two short horn blasts signaled the start of the wild horse race in the arena. "Anyway, I can't afford to pay more than two hundred dollars per week. But you'd get room and board. Including any horses you might want to stable. I assume you don't need a truck?"

"Nope."

"We're talking seven days a week. No days off at least until late October and haying season ends."

"I know. Ain't the first time something like this has been offered to me."

"Recently?"

"Yeah."

Damn. Was she already too late?

"'Course. I turned 'em down flat."

"Why?"

"Wasn't interested in their offers."

"So does anything *I've* offered interest you?"

Cash kicked a clod of manure under the trailer. "Depends."

"On?"

"On whether the only thing you're offerin' me is a job."

Her pulse jumped. "What else would there be?"

"Gemma, you know what else I want. What I've wanted since the first time I clapped eyes on you. And if bein' in your bed—whether or not anyone else knows I'm there—ain't part of the deal, then I'll have to pass."

No way to misinterpret that.

Lord. Was she prepared to let the past fade? She and Steve Jansen had been happily married for twenty-six years. She'd been widowed for the last three. In recent months she'd grown tired of being alone and in her heart she knew Steve wouldn't want her to mourn him forever.

But why did Cash want *her*? When he could have any woman? Young, or old, or in between? Was it a simple case of lust? She didn't kid herself she was an aging beauty queen. Neither was she a spring chicken.

What if the reality of sharing her body and her bed with Cash Big Crow didn't hold up to her fantasies? Worse, what if *she* disappointed him?

There was only one way to find out.

Gemma locked her gaze to his. "Just as long as you know that bein' in my bed doesn't change the fact that I *will* be your boss outside of it."

"Yeah? Just as long as you know I will be the boss in the bedroom, no matter if you do write my paycheck." He angled his head until they were only a breath apart. "Tell me somethin'."

Being this close to Cash sent her senses into chaos. "What?"

"What changed? Last summer when you and I fooled around a little, you stopped it cold." His brown eyes searched hers expectantly. "Why?"

"I wasn't ready to move on."

"And now?"

"I am."

"For everything that bein' with me means?"

"Meaning what, Cash?"

"I ain't some mild-mannered gentleman rancher. I've been called a savage. I have savage appetites. Think you can handle it?"

She nodded with more confidence than she felt.

"Then you know what to expect from me when that bedroom door closes?"

"Ah. Um. No. Maybe you'd better spell it out."

"Obedience. Trust." He skimmed a finger up her cheek. The casual touch held just enough of an erotic edge that she trembled. "I heard you talkin' to Channing last summer. I know there's a...wild streak inside you. I wanna be the man to tap into it. I wanna give you something he never did."

Her whole body heated as she remembered the heady feeling of surrendering all control in the name of pleasure. "Okay."

"Good." Something primal glittered in his eyes. "It's 'bout time. I've been waitin' for this day for two damn years." He hauled her against his body and settled his mouth over hers.

Gemma expected a hard, demanding kiss. But Cash merely pressed his lips to hers and held them there. One callused hand slid up her neck, his thumb tracked the pulse in the hollow of her throat, where her blood beat wildly. The other hand cupped her cheek. His firm lips indulged in little nips of her trembling mouth. From corner to corner, from top to bottom, a leisurely, teasing glide.

"Let me in," he whispered, seductively brushing his mouth back and forth against hers. "Kiss me back, Gem."

Her tongue darted out and traced the seam of his warm lips. Mmm. He tasted as tempting and hot as she'd remembered.

Cash groaned, backing her into the trailer as the gentle kiss turned ravenous.

She latched onto his belt loops and held on for dear life.

Her head spun like a windmill. The way her skin vibrated, it seemed he was touching every inch of her bare flesh, yet his hands hadn't strayed. He took his own sweet time exploring her mouth. Gauging the change in her heart rate with just a flick of his thumb as the deep kiss became wetter. Hotter. As she became wetter and hotter.

Cash backed off in increments, muttering softly spoken words against her inflamed lips.

Good thing her spine rested against the camper or she might've fallen face-first in the creeping Jenny vines covering the rocky ground. She blinked up at him.

His smile was half-cocky/half-sweet. "You sure you're ready for this?"

"You sure you're ready for a grumpy old widow set in her ways, whippersnapper?"

"That ain't funny."

"It wasn't meant to be."

Cash's grin vanished and his eyes hardened. "Is this gonna be an issue? Age is a number, Gem. I'm thirty-eight. You're not. So what?"

"But—"

"Would it matter if I was older than you?"

"No."

"Then it don't matter that you got a few years on me." He kissed her hotly, a drawn out seductive promise. "Besides, you're sexy. Kinda remind me of Madonna."

"Madonna the pop singer? But she's—"

"The same age as you." He squinted at her. "Yep, definitely. You're like Madonna in a cowgirl hat. And if I had my pick of any of the ladies—including the material girl, I'd still choose you."

"I forgot what a sweet-talker you are." She steered the conversation back to business. "I'm heading back to my ranch today. When can you be there to start?"

"Damn." He frowned and shuffled back a step. "One kiss and my mind is on a single track."

"What?"

"Macie. We'd planned to spend the summer traveling together. Since her momma died a coupla years back, she ain't got no one else. I can't just shove her aside, especially when I been doin' that to the poor kid her whole life."

Without conscious thought, she smoothed the guilt from his puckered brow. "I don't expect you to ignore her, Cash. She's welcome at my place too, if she wants to stay for awhile."

"It won't bother you that she'll know we're involved in more than a workin' relationship?"

"Maybe I should wonder if it'd bother *you*. Think you might suffer from performance anxiety if you're trying to fulfill all my wicked sexual fantasies when your daughter is sleeping under the same roof?"

Cash shuddered. "I'm thinkin' I'll offer her my camper for the time being. And we'll park it away from the main house."

"Good plan. Although, I'm still gonna assign chores for her to earn her keep if she decides to stick around."

"That won't be a problem. She's an independent cuss; she ain't one to take charity."

"Like father like daughter, huh?"

"Yep. You won't regret trackin' me down." Cash rubbed his jaw along hers. He placed a soft kiss below her ear and growled, "I've half a mind to make you crawl inside the trailer and take off every stitch of clothing right now."

Warmth pooled between her thighs.

"But as I've been itchin' to touch you forever, I ain't about to settle for a quick tumble. I wanna take my time. Make it last until the sun comes up. Make *you* come until the sun comes up." He leveled her with a hungry kiss. "Let's get loaded, track down Macie and get the hell out of here."

Gemma was only too happy to oblige.

Chapter Three

Macie Honeycutt muttered, "Watch it, Tex," as another saddle almost clipped her in the head. It sucked being short. She ducked under the fence and detoured to the beer garden.

As she stood in line, she tried not to obsess about the situation with her dad. After hearing about her epically bad month, he insisted they meet up at a rodeo. Why? Far as she knew, he'd given up chasing the gold-buckle dream last year.

So what was the first thing he'd done after she'd shown up in the middle of nowhere? He'd ditched her!

Like that should surprise you, Macie Blue. You can't count on him. Cut your losses and run.

She closed her mind to her mother's phantom voice. The woman had been dead four years and she still had an opinion. Unfortunately, it was the same bad opinion of Cash Big Crow Macie had heard her entire life.

Macie's relationship with her father was tenuous at best. He hadn't been around when she'd been growing up, though as she'd gotten older, he'd made a point to track her down.

So why did she have the perverse need to do exactly the opposite of what Daddy said? It'd serve him right if she hooked up with a hot-tempered, good-looking cowboy, as it appeared he'd done some hooking up of his own.

Yet, by the almost worshipful way he'd talked about Gemma in the last few months, it didn't surprise Macie that Gemma looked like a former rodeo beauty queen who'd horsewhip the shit out of you if you looked at her crossways. It'd take a woman like that to tame her father.

The white-haired man behind the plywood partition

interrupted her thoughts. "What can I getcha, sweetheart?"

"Bud Light. In a bottle."

"Can I see some ID?"

"Sure." Macie whipped out her driver's license, waiting for the man to make a smarmy remark about her age or her ethnicity.

But the guy smiled, popped the top and slid the bottle across the counter. "Four-fifty."

She passed him a five. "Keep the change." She snagged a seat at the back table, propping up her feet on the spare chair to discourage the group of cowboys eyeing her like a chunk of prime sirloin.

How long did her dad expect her to cool her heels?

Didn't matter. Wasn't like she had anywhere else to go. Macie tugged her hat lower on her forehead and nursed the beer.

What a jumbled mess her life was. Two months ago she'd caught her boyfriend two-timing her. She should've known with a sissy name like *Dante* that he played for both teams. She should've known since they'd dated for, oh, two months and they hadn't had sex that he was, oh, *gay.*

Still, it'd shocked her to walk in on him scoring with his racquetball partner, Dooce. They'd been so busy playing with each other's balls and making a "racquet" they hadn't noticed her.

Things went downhill from there. Her best friend Kat moved out of their apartment and in with her boyfriend. Two weeks after that, Macie'd gotten canned from her waitressing job. The jerk-off customer deserved the pitcher of iced tea she'd dumped in his lap after he'd grabbed her ass—even if management saw fit to punish *her* for the moron's happy hands. No wonder she preferred to work in the kitchen. Vegetables didn't talk back.

At her father's urging, and the looming expiration of her apartment lease, she'd packed her few belongings into her Ford Escape and left Denver. Her options were unlimited. She was free, half-white and twenty-two. She could do as she damn well pleased.

The bottle stopped halfway to her mouth.

Mmm. Mmm. And she'd do *him* in a heartbeat. He was the first guy who'd tripped her trigger since the Dante debacle. She liked hot men. She liked hot sex. She really liked the hot man/hot sex combo.

Right. Like she'd ever be bold enough to try anything kinky with any man, let alone a man who looked like him. She talked a good game but it'd taken four trips to the adult toy store before she'd finally bought a vibrator.

Whoo-ee. She wouldn't need a vibrator with him. This guy was pure hot sex on the hoof.

Her pulse skipped as the hunky man ambled into the beer garden. From a distance he was a yummy package; up close he was a gourmet meal. Tall and leanly muscular with sharply defined facial features. He had curly dark blond hair, liberally laced with streaks of brown and gold, long enough to brush his shirt collar. A little stubble on his square jaw made him look wild and sexy, like a roguish Viking raider. His mouth was drawn in a flat line. Ooh. A brooding bad boy. She wondered what color his eyes were. Blue? Green? Hazel? Even wearing a scowl he was a head-turner.

As he waited for a beer, a couple of blondes took notice of him.

Slouched in her chair, Macie watched the scene unfold. The guy didn't notice the attention he was gathering from women of all ages, shapes and sizes within his radius. He drank his beer fast, leaving as quickly as he'd arrived. The two blondes lingered a few minutes before they stalked him.

The poor bastard. Nothing was worse than buckle bunnies on the prowl for a "real" cowboy. He wasn't sporting the obvious cowboy clothing, but he owned the attitude.

Macie finished her beer, and headed toward the contestant's gate. With any luck, her dad was done screwing around. When the wind caught her hat, she wadded it up and tossed it in the closest trashcan. She hated the cheap damn thing anyway.

෨

Carter McKay perched on the split-rail fence and longed to be anywhere besides the rodeo grounds. It wasn't that he didn't fit the rural surroundings. Hell, he fit outdoor arenas with dirt-packed floors and livestock sale barns better than he had the stuffy classrooms and snooty galleries he'd been living around for the last eight years.

As the last McKay boy born and bred on the family ranch, he not only looked the part of a cowboy, he *was* a cowboy—through and through. He just wasn't dumb enough to climb on a bull or ride a wild bronc for the thrill, or for any amount of money. Not that rodeo paid diddlysquat. Not that being an artist was the most stable occupation either.

Certainly his family didn't understand his chosen profession. Sure, pride shone in his parents' eyes when he'd earned a Masters of Fine Arts—yet, they hadn't known what to do with him.

Problem was there wasn't need for a painter at the McKay Ranch, unless that meant slapping a coat of Sherwin Williams on one of the three wooden barns. Even if he'd wanted to join the family cattle business, between his father and his older brothers, Colby, Cord, Colt, and his cousins, Kade and Kane—every aspect of their growing operation was under control.

So Carter was at loose ends. He'd been on his own too long to live at home for longer than a week or two. Made him shudder to think of Mom and Dad dogging his every boot step. Or his smart-mouthed little sister, Keely, snickering and calling him a brooding "arteest". He'd taken his revenge by using her favorite silk shirt to clean up his paintbrushes. Scary, how quickly he'd reverted to juvenile behavior.

Luckily, Gemma Jansen, a family friend, needed a part-time ranch hand. He'd signed on for the summer and relocated his art supplies, welding iron and paltry possessions to a small trailer on her property with a huge barn he could use as a studio. An added bonus? Her land was vastly different from the buttes and sage-dotted hills of the McKay Ranch and it gave him a wealth of new visual material.

For the past week he'd been finishing sculptures for his gallery showing. A series of interconnected Western pieces, different styles, including clay pieces slated to become bronze statues, and welded metal works using rusted sections of discarded farm equipment. So far the only concrete images on canvas were landscapes done with oil paints.

Boring.

He needed inspiration, something new and different. The only way to find the passion that defined his quirky artistic style was to start at the source of all things Western: rodeo. The salt-of-the-earth people—spectators, families of the cowboys and cowgirls and the iron will of the competitors themselves. The livestock—angry, slobbering bulls, high-strung broncs kicking at the metal chutes, the bellow of steers, the nervous tamping of hooves behind the gates. The bawling tones of the calves in the pens. The rich scents of sweat and leather, mud and manure, the choking heat and the constant buzz of insects, hay and linament, tobacco and beer. The excitement. If he could capture the hope and desperation, the heartache and the pride of these...things, all of which made up the true experience of rodeo, well, then, he'd truly accomplish something spectacular.

Carter chalked it up to karma when Gemma asked him to ride along to the one-day event in Buffalo, South Dakota. She'd been vague about her reasons for the impromptu road trip and he hadn't pushed this issue. Their unspoken rule of "mind your own business" was why he and Gemma hit it off.

Except the outing was proving to be a bust. He'd seen nothing that'd kicked his muse in the ass. He'd rather be locked away carving a wax mold of the image that had been haunting him. Not of a breakaway horse or a defeated cowboy, but of a young woman with long, flowing hair the color of mahogany.

In his mind's eye her angular face captured the interesting juxtaposition of feminine ferocity. Her carriage was proud, yet hesitant. She was beautiful. Mysterious. Serene. And he was fixated on creating her likeness down to the most minute detail. Tawny skin. Delicate hands. A lush mouth with a confident, secretive smile.

Yeah, he needed to quit sniffing turpentine and get out more often if he was obsessed with a figment of his imagination.

The two fluffy blonde buckle bunnies approaching him with a single-minded purpose weren't imaginary. He pasted on a good ol' boy grin, wondering if it looked as fake as it felt. "Ladies. Nice afternoon."

Blonde #1 giggled. "I'll say. You done competing, cowboy?"

No reason not to cut to the chase when everyone knew the score. Or rather, when everyone *wanted* to score.

"Nah. I ain't doin' much rodeoin' these days."

Blonde #2 leaned in. "That's too bad. Is it because you were hurt?"

"Busted up my knee bulldoggin'." The incident with a breakaway calf happened during branding when he was ten years old. These women wouldn't ask specifics and he didn't offer. They wanted the illusion of a cowboy, not the reality. And he knew if any of his brothers were around, neither of these chicks would look at him twice.

Some of their admiration dimmed. Blonde #2 blatantly focused on the size and the engraving on his silver buckle. "Seems a shame. So, what're you doin' now?"

"I'm an artist."

"Really?" came Blonde #2's bored response. She tugged on Blonde #1's arm. "Come on, Jen. Let's keep lookin'."

"Hang on. Even though he ain't rodeoin' no more, he's still a hottie. I wouldn't mind takin' him for a test ride." Blonde #1 winked at him. "You've got a great smile. I bet you know how to use that mouth, doncha?"

"You aimin' to find out?"

Blonde #2 scowled. "Have at him. I'll meetcha by the truck in an hour," she said and disappeared.

"My name's Jen," Blonde #1 cooed and squeezed her curvy body between his widespread knees.

"Carter."

"So, Carter. You up for a wild, no-holds-barred rodeo?" Her hands slid up the inside of his legs. She found the bulge beneath his zipper and stroked until his dick sprang to life.

Whoa. It'd been a while since he'd played this game and apparently speed rules had been enacted in the interim.

Jen nestled her breasts against his chest, leaning on the tips of her high-heeled boots to whisper in his ear. "Mmm. You are a big one."

Carter sucked in a harsh breath as she continued to work his cock through his jeans. In public. He scooted back. "Uh. Thanks."

"Bet I can figure out what you want. 'Course, it'll take me more than eight seconds to make my guess." She giggled, "But that's okay. You'll appreciate that I am very thorough."

"Um, yeah, maybe we should—"

"This is fun, talkin' about what makes you hot and bothered. What makes you horny." She dragged her tongue up the side of his neck. "Ooh. You're awful quiet. A shy one. Big and shy. My favorite kind." She tsk tsked. "Now you know I'm just gonna have to talk dirty to loosen you up, Bashful. So...are you thinking about me blowing you? Sliding this big cock in and out of my mouth?"

His tongue stuck to the back of his teeth. He got extremely hot under the collar. But the greedy part of his brain reminded him that he hadn't been laid in months and conjured up the image of her on her knees unfastening his jeans. Watching her eager lips open and swallow his dick to the root. Seeing his cock smeared with bubblegum pink lipstick as it tunneled in and out of her swollen mouth until he exploded inside that hot, wet cavern, and pulling out to watch his come dripping down her chin.

"Ah, yeah. That'd be good."

"You'd better believe it'd be *very* good." Her tongue swirled around the shell of his ear like she was licking the head of his cock. "Me getting your cock good and wet. Your hands holding my hair as tightly as a bullrope. Your hips thrusting against my face like you was ridin' a bronc. Arching your back, keeping the strokes steady. Can't you see it? Can't you almost *feel* it?"

Carter couldn't make himself leave. And he sure as shit couldn't stop his sex from pulsing with eagerness. "Why don't you—"

She nipped his earlobe hard enough to draw blood. "Ah-ah-ah. I wouldn't let you come that fast, Bashful. I'd back off. Use my teeth as you pulled your cock out. Then I'd play with your balls. Suck them. Roll them over my tongue like hard candy. Mmm. I love candy. I'd use my hand to build you back up. Slowly."

His cock throbbed as her fingernails repeatedly scraped the full length of it. He bit back a groan, not sure if it was one of dismay or encouragement.

"Then I'd bring your cock back into my mouth and finish you off. I'd swallow every hot drop until you had nothing left."

"Sweet Jesus." This chick—was beginning to scare him.

"Does that sound good?"

"Ah—"

"I do believe I've left you tongue-tied, cowboy." Jen stepped back and licked her lips suggestively. "So what do you say we put that idle tongue of yours to better use?"

He didn't answer.

Annoyance crossed her face at his less than enthusiastic response. "I laid it all out for you. What *do* you want?"

To escape, he thought even when his dick had other ideas.

A flash of sunlight drew his awareness to a figure in front of the arena. A woman with long, shiny hair the color of burnished mahogany.

For a second the woman faltered. She seemed to sense him staring at her. She turned. Their eyes met.

Everything inside him went tight and still.

It was her, the image that'd been haunting him. Right here. Flesh and bone. He could study her. Sketch her. God, he could touch her sun-warmed tawny skin. Mold her curvaceous body with his hands so he could immortalize her perfection in clay. In wood. In steel.

Then she vanished into the crowd like an apparition.

Carter leapt off the fence and readjusted the softening bulge behind his zipper.

"Hey! Where you goin'? I thought you were up for a rodeo?"

"Sorry. Gotta see a man about a horse." He raced after the woman and didn't look back.

Chapter Four

Macie made it halfway across the rodeo grounds when the fine hair on the back of her neck stood up. She glanced over at the paddock and saw her brooding bad boy with one of the bimbos standing between his wide-spread thighs. But he wasn't paying attention to sure-thing-blondie; he stared directly at her. Intensely. Intimately. Hungrily.

Something hot and elemental passed between them. When he started for her, she hustled through the throng of people. About thirty seconds later she was spun around and found herself gazing into the bluest eyes she'd ever seen.

Sexy, brooding man said, "It *is* you." His rough hands framed her face. "My God. You're exactly—"

Flustered, she knocked his mitts away. "You can't just grab any woman—"

"You're not any woman. I grabbed you because you've been in my head for the last damn month and it's drivin' me crazy. Who are you?"

Macie snorted. "That is the worst pick up line I've ever heard."

Those blue, blue eyes narrowed. "That wasn't a pick up line."

"Good thing, because it sure as hell isn't working."

"Look. Let's start over. I'm an artist. And I'd like—"

"—to show me your etchings?" She snickered.

"Har har. I really am an artist."

"Yeah? So was the last guy I was involved with. Been there, done that, have the tie-dyed T-shirt and the roach clip to prove it. Move along, Picasso."

"You always such a smartass?"

"Better than being a dumbass. Which is what you are if you think I'm gonna fall for your line of bullshit. Move."

He cocked his head. "Interestin'."

"What?"

"That you have the face of an Indian princess and the mouth of a truck driver."

Against her better judgment, Macie smiled. "I'll admit that line was better."

"I ain't usin' a line on you." Serious once again, he stared at her steadily. "What's your name?"

"What's yours?" she countered.

"Carter."

She mimicked his posture and cocked her head. "Interestin'."

"What?"

"That you have the face of a Viking warrior and the name of a Georgia peanut farmer."

His enormous grin, with a side of deep-set dimples, nearly knocked her off her game. Damn. This Carter guy was trouble with a capital 'T'.

"You always such a smart-mouth?"

She shrugged. "It's a gift."

"Or a curse." Still smiling, he leaned closer. "So, what *is* your name?"

"Macie."

"Pretty. A little odd, a little flowery, but it fits you."

Macie frowned. "Was that an insult?"

"Not at all. Anyway, *Amazin'* Macie. You from around here?"

"No."

"Just passin' through?"

"Yep."

"With who? By yourself? Or with your family?"

"A little of both."

One dark blond brow winged up. "Meaning?"

"I came here by myself, but I'm meeting my dad. Going where the road takes us. Looking for work and adventure." Her brain urged her to walk away; her legs didn't listen. "What about you? You from around here?"

"Nope. I'm on a day trip. I live in Wyoming."

"Where you're an artist."

"Yep."

"What's your area of study?" She held up her palm. "And if you say female nudes, I'm totally out of here."

A cagey grin curled his mouth, making him look oh-so-naughty. "I'll tell you exactly what magic I can create with these hands if you let me buy you a beer."

Hell yes. Then maybe you could give me a hands-on demonstration of your magical hands.

No. Bad, bad idea, Macie.

"I'll pass."

"Whoa." His strong grip around her forearm kept her from bolting. "Just one beer. It'll give me a chance to explain why I chased..." A sound, half sigh/half groan rumbled from his chest. Then the blunt tip of his finger traced the outline of her face from her temple to her chin and down the curve of her throat. "Goddamn. You are stunning. I want to paint you like this. Fire and interest warring in your eyes."

"Carter—"

"Say it again," he growled. "I wanna hear my name on your sweet lips as I'm touchin' them." The rough pad of his thumb slowly swept her bottom lip. He stared into her eyes. "So soft. And warm. A perfect fit for mine."

The way he was looking at her made her feel like she'd suddenly developed a case of sunstroke. No man ever acted like he wanted to crawl inside her head, mark her soul his and claim her body as his own.

You just met him. No one feels that. It's a trick.

"Carter—"

"Say yes, Macie."

"Say yes to what?"

"To everything I ask you."

Her stomach cartwheeled.

"It sounds crazy, we just met, but I *know* you. I want..."

"Want what, Picasso?" she murmured.

"You're playin' with fire, askin' me that question, darlin'."

"Why's that?"

"'Cause my very explicit answer would make you blush like a virgin and run screamin' for the Black Hills."

Everything surrounding them—sunlight, tinny music from the carnival, whoops from the grandstand, the sugary, greasy scent of fried Twinkies—faded into the background.

Boldly, she said, "Try me."

Carter's shaking fingers smoothed a flyaway hair from her cheek. "Oh, I'd try you. I'd test you. I see what your eyes are offerin' me, and I'd take it all, without apology."

Totally out of your league with this man, Macie. Cut and run.

"And then?"

"Then I'd give that need, that passion, that obsession, that control, that lust—right back to you. Times ten."

Pure sexual heat overloaded her circuits. "Oh."

"Yeah, *oh.* Not what you expected?"

"No."

"Why not?"

"Because that kind of fascination isn't usually aimed my direction."

"Straightforward. I like that. I expected you to play coy." The back of his fingers continued to lightly caress her damp skin. "I want to paint you, sculpt you. Do you in every medium."

"You sure that wasn't a line?"

He shook his head. "There's a reason we both ended up here today, Macie. Don't know why, but I ain't about to argue with fate. Or question my good fortune."

A hot tongue of desire licked along her veins.

"So what's your answer?"

"Take your damn hand off my daughter."

Carter froze.

"Move it or lose it, son," Cash ordered. "Now."

Macie snapped out of her sexual stupor. "Back off, Dad."

"Like hell. Who is this joker?"

Gemma said, "Cash, wait—"

"I told you to stay away from—"

"—you." Macie stomped over and came nose to nose with her father. "Which I did. You can't blame me for not waiting around for you to ditch me." *Again.*

Cash's eyes and his voice softened. "Oh, honey-girl, I ain't gonna ditch you." He shot Carter a dark look. "But it appears you decided to ditch me with the first loser wannabe cowboy that comes along, eh?"

Gemma cleared her throat.

Macie and Cash both swiveled to look at her.

"Cash Big Crow, meet Carter McKay. Carter, Cash is the new foreman I hired for the Bar 9 Ranch. You two will be working together."

"You gotta be fuckin' kiddin' me," Carter muttered.

Macie frowned. Her dad had taken a job? What'd happened to them hitting the road this summer?

"McKay?" Cash repeated. "You're related to them slimeball McKays from up around Crook County?"

Carter's gaze hardened.

"Cash! What a thing to say," Gemma chided. "You've been friends with Colby McKay for years."

"I *am* friends with him, just as long as he and his wild brothers are far away from my only daughter."

"Macie is an adult," Carter pointed out.

"True," Gemma said.

"Jesus, Gem." He threw his hands in the air. "You know the bad reputation them McKay boys have!"

"With all due respect, sir, I'm nothin' like my brothers."

Cash whirled on Carter. "Yeah? I ain't some dumb Indian. I traveled the rodeo circuit with Colby. I know what he's like—like breeds like, so I ain't lettin' a McKay within two miles of Macie."

"Well, that's gonna be difficult, since we'll all be living together on the Bar 9 for the next few months," Gemma said dryly.

"All? Me too?" Macie asked suspiciously. Her gaze darted from Gemma to her dad and back to Gemma.

Gemma nodded. "You are welcome to stay as long as you want. Cash said he'd set up his camper for you. I'll warn you there might be some chores involved if you're living with me."

Macie's head spun. This was all happening way too fast; hooking up with her dad, him taking a new job on the spur of the moment, meeting the woman she suspected would be more than Dad's new boss, and trying to figure out what weird connection she and Carter shared, mostly whether it was real or wishful thinking on her part.

Her dad lowered his voice. "Truth is, I need this job. But I want to spend time with you, that's why I'm here. Can we try it for awhile and see how it goes? If it don't work, we can go on as planned?"

What other choice did she have? Besides, wouldn't this provide them with neutral ground? If trying to establish a father/daughter relationship wasn't working, would it be easier to place blame on outside forces? Such as the stress of a new job, or romantic relationships or an unfamiliar setting? She could leave and he wouldn't be forced to give up a good job opportunity. She briefly closed her eyes. "I guess."

"Then I guess it's unanimous," Carter said. "We'll be one big, happy family all summer."

Cash took a menacing step toward Carter. "You ain't part of the family. If I see you around I'll kick your sorry—" Gemma grabbed Cash's shirtsleeve and tugged him out of range.

While Gemma and Cash argued, Macie glanced at a grinning Carter. "Why're you smiling like that? He'd like to scalp you."

"I noticed. Your dad's a bit protective, huh?"

It was a surprise to her.

Carter moved until he loomed over her. "I am curious as to where he's keepin' your chastity belt."

"Funny."

"He won't think so when he realizes nothin' will keep me away from you this summer, Macie." The sexual heat in his eyes changed the color from sky blue to indigo. "Nothin'."

"A little sure of yourself, aren't you?"

"Yep. And I've got a few belts and ropes to keep you right where I want you, in case *you* need a little convincin'."

Sweet, hot pleasure rippled through her.

Carter's warm, firm lips grazed her ear. "I'll come to you tonight, okay?"

"That's not a good idea."

"It's the best idea I've had in a long time. Be ready."

"For what?"

"For me to be the man to give you everything you've ever wanted."

Chapter Five

Gemma and Carter were lost in their own thoughts on the way back to the Bar 9. Once they hit the sagebrush and wide-open spaces of Wyoming, Gemma sighed. "Sorry to spring this on you, Carter. I was afraid if you knew I was lookin' for another fulltime foreman—"

"—that I'd bail on you? Come on, Gemma, you know me better than that. I promised I'd be here all summer. Despite the shitty opinion Cash has of the McKays, you know we always keep our word."

"That you do."

"What's really goin' on?"

She didn't take her eyes off the gray ribbon of bumpy road. "I wasn't sure he'd say yes."

"So? It ain't like he's the only man for the job. Shoot, there's lots of guys around here more than qualified."

Gemma angled her chin from Carter's shrewd eyes so he couldn't see her blush.

"Hellfire and damnation. He *is* the only one you wanted, ain't he?"

She paused. "Yup."

Carter sighed. "I ain't gonna ask why."

She probably couldn't give him a good answer on that one even if he did ask.

"Just so you know, what happens between the two of you after the barn door closes ain't my business. You don't hafta worry 'bout me blabbin' your private business to everyone or pokin' my nose in where it don't belong."

Gemma looked at him. "Thanks."

"But that goes both ways."

"Meaning?"

"Meaning, I won't stay away from Macie just because her father wants me to."

Lord. He was just as bull-headed as the rest of his family. She waited, knowing he wasn't finished.

Carter drummed his fingers on his thigh. "Remember last week when I was cleanin' stalls like the devil possessed my soul, and you asked me what the hell was wrong with me?"

Gemma nodded.

"It was her."

"Macie?"

"Yeah."

"How's that possible? Didn't you just meet her today?"

"Yep. This is gonna sound dumb, but she's been in my head for the last month. This fuzzy image in my mind that's only partially there. Been drivin' me crazy, tryin' to capture her. I've tried painting her, sketching, working with clay. When I saw her today? Flesh and blood and real? At first I thought I'd gone completely 'round the bend."

Gemma couldn't withhold a shiver. "That's some spooky serious shit, Carter."

"Don't I know it. Normally I don't believe in that kinda karma and fate voodoo crap, but I ain't about to chalk it up to coincidence neither. Nor am I gonna let the new foreman chase me away from his daughter just 'cause he thinks he can."

"Macie is an adult, but I don't think that's gonna matter to Cash," Gemma pointed out. "He still is her father."

"That's hard for me to believe. Jesus. How old was he when she was born? Like twelve?"

She smiled. "Probably more like sixteen. He made it sound like he hadn't been around much when she was growing up."

"Probably because he was too busy growin' up himself. Where's her mother?"

"Dead, from what I understand."

Carter whistled. "Harsh. Anyway, from what I remember

Colby tellin' me, Cash knows his stuff 'bout livestock. So I ain't gonna cause problems with him while we're workin'."

"I appreciate that."

"But I expect him to do the same." Carter faced her again. "The only person with the power to tell me to get lost is Macie, agreed?"

"Agreed. But I ain't gonna get in the middle of this." Gemma figured she'd have her hands full dealing with her situation with Cash. She turned down the gravel road leading to the trailer on the outskirts of her property. "I think it's best if I show Cash the ropes for evening chores, don't you?"

"I reckon."

She circled the barn so the front end of her truck was pointed to the road. "Can I ask you one more favor?"

Carter's hand froze on the door handle. "What?"

"Can you give us—me, Cash, and Macie—a night to settle in? Macie's agreed to stay in Cash's camper, but I doubt he'll just dump her off."

For a second it appeared Carter would argue. He scrubbed the back of his neck and sighed. "I guess. I have some new ideas to sketch. I'd probably lose track of time anyway." He opened the door and hopped out. "See you bright and early, boss lady. Try and get some sleep." Carter grinned and slammed the door.

Sleep. Right. Cash seemed pretty anxious when they parted ways. The heat and promise in his eyes nearly burned her from the outside in.

Neither of them would be getting much sleep.

When Gemma ventured out of the house in the early evening, she noticed Cash had already parked his camper between the old wooden barn and the metal granary. The spot was perfect. It'd keep the aluminum camper sheltered from the oppressive dry summer heat and it was set back far enough from the main house to offer them—and Macie—privacy. The generator at the back of the camper hummed. She saw Cash carrying an armload of assorted items out of the camper, but no sign of Macie's car. Once Cash caught sight of her climbing in the truck loaded down with the horse trailer, he loped over.

"Where you parkin' that rig, eh?"

"Over behind the other barn."

"Back 'er in and I'll unhitch the trailer." He frowned. "Why'd you drag that thing along to Buffalo? It's empty, ain't it?"

"Yeah. I stopped at a ranch outside of Haroldsville to look at a couple of mares to breed. Decided not to take them, but I needed the trailer just in case."

Cash's gaze narrowed. "What was wrong with 'em?"

"Nothin'. The guy wanted too much money." It burned her ass the guy thought she was too stupid to know he'd been trying to screw her over. But Gemma doubted Cash would understand she'd been dealing with that mentality since Steve had died.

After he'd unhitched the horse trailer, Cash wiped his brow with his forearm and stared at her.

"What?"

"When we're done with chores, I expect you to show me where to put my stuff in the house."

"I-I—"

"Just so we're clear. I will be sleepin' in your room, in your bed."

Yowza. Gemma nodded and proceeded to show him around, detailing what needed to be done in the morning. She finished the tour in record time. He dragged his duffel bag up the porch steps and dumped it on the kitchen table. Before she opened the door leading upstairs, Cash pressed her against the wall and kissed the holy hell out of her.

When she could breathe again, she tipped her head back and blinked at him. "You hungry?"

"Not for food."

"Cash—"

"Point me to the shower, *winyan*. I'll not come to you the first time smellin' of a barnyard."

Feeling reckless, she nipped his chin and tugged the end of

his braid. "I wouldn't mind. The bathroom is the second door at the top of the stairs."

"Thanks."

"While you're cleaning up, should I ask Macie to supper tonight?"

"Nah. We stopped outside of Canyon River and grabbed a burger. She said after she settled in she was goin' right to bed. Been a long day on the road for her."

"I imagine."

Cash shouldered the bag and gave her a gorgeous smile. "Don't go nowhere, Gem."

Gemma stepped back and anxiously rubbed her hands over her bare arms as Cash disappeared up the stairs. Lord almighty. The man could melt her with just a look. Was she ready for this?

To make sure, she raced to the guest bath, quickly rinsed off the road grime and combed her hair. After she scrubbed her teeth, she changed into clean clothes, a low-cut tank top and a short skirt.

Dusk had fallen, sending purpled shadows across the yard and darkening the interior of the house. She sipped a beer and gazed out the kitchen window, reluctant to flip on the overhead lights. Talk about magnification of her wrinkles and her age, hell, magnification of all her flaws. Would candlelight make it too obvious she had plenty to hide?

The door creaked and she jumped. She heard the soft pad of feet across the linoleum. The scent of sandalwood soap, toothpaste and warm male skin enveloped her. Heat from his body seared her back as he brushed damp, soft kisses over her bared shoulder. She trembled and nearly dropped the beer before she upended the remainder and gulped it down.

Cash chuckled by her ear. "Nervous?"

"Yeah."

"Me too. But that ain't gonna stop me." His teeth nipped on her earlobe and she shivered as he suckled the sting. "You expectin' anybody tonight?"

"No."

"Good. C'mere, sexy lady." Cash turned her into his arms

and his soft lips nibbled up the side of her neck. "I'm dyin' to touch you." His finger traced the lace strap of her tank top. "Take off your shirt."

Gemma pulled back and looked at him. "Right here?"

"Right here, right now." When she made no move to move, he frowned. "There a problem?"

"Besides that we're in the kitchen?"

"Does that bother you?"

"Well. I thought..."

"Ah. That's the problem. You're thinkin' too much." Cash walked to the door and locked it. Then he snagged a blue bandana off the counter. He folded it crossways in a long strip.

"What's that?"

"A blindfold. Then you won't know if you're in the kitchen, the living room or the bedroom. You'll be so busy feelin' what I'm doin' to you that you won't have time to think. Now close your eyes and turn around."

Gemma knew his wasn't a request. If she refused he'd take it as a sign she wasn't ready for this intimacy, and he'd leave her house and her employ. But she was ready. It'd taken her a full year to get to this point and she wasn't about to back down now. Blood pounded a warning in her head not to be stupid. She slowly spun toward the window.

The dense cloth covered her eyes and she felt a pinch in the middle of her skull as he tied it. He turned her back around. "Can you see?"

Gemma's heart rate kicked up as she opened her eyes to complete blackness. "No."

"Good. You'll leave it on? You won't make me tie your hands too?"

A picture formed in her mind of being trussed up, naked and at his every wicked whim. The thought made her absolutely dripping wet.

He chuckled again. "From the flush on your cheeks I suspect you'd like to be tied up. I'll keep that in mind for another time." Rough palms skated down her arms. Callused, thick fingers threaded through hers. Cash pulled her forward a few steps and they stopped. "Stand still."

He released her hands. Then those same rough palms circled her ankles, slid up her shins, and over her knees. When Cash's fingers breached the hem of her denim skirt, he ran the tips across the top of her thighs several times before he tugged on the material. "Off. Now."

With shaking fingers, she shimmied the skirt down to the floor. As she stood clad in pale pink bikini panties, waiting for his reaction, she was grateful for the blindfold.

Cash's warm breath tickled her ear. "No wonder you hide such great legs. Wouldn't want to start a stampede among all them young bucks at the rodeo grounds, eh?"

His sweet-talkin' made her sigh softly.

"Damn, Gem, I can't wait to feel these thighs wrapped around me tight. So tight I can't breathe. Just lookin' at you is enough to make my heart stop and make my dick stand up and take notice." His mouth moved across her jaw in a sensual glide. Automatically her lips parted for his tongue to sneak in and tangle with hers.

She moaned. He tasted sweet. Hot. One hundred percent hungry male. God. She'd missed that scratchy feel of a man's beard rubbing against her cheek. Missed that insistent hard body crowding away her reason, just allowing her to feel feminine, not to think like a responsible ranch woman. The sensations seemed ten times stronger when she couldn't see and had to rely on other senses.

Cash continued kissing her, each movement of his velvety tongue deliberately provocative; a game of chase and retreat. Liquid pooled in her panties and she found herself pressing her legs together. Wanting him to catch a whiff of her arousal. Wanting his hand stroking her, his fingers using her wetness to plunge deep inside her.

Finally he retreated from her mouth. Soft puffs of air drifted over her temple. He clamped his hand around her hips and lifted her, eliciting a gasp when her butt and the back of her thighs connected with the cool metal rim of the kitchen table. "Whoa. Cash, wait—"

"I got you." He gently pushed her shoulders.

She resisted. "But—"

"There's other places I wanna kiss you, so lay back and let

me show you where."

"Oh." Gemma's token resistance evaporated. Her spine met the hard, flat surface of the table and her legs dangled off the edge.

Cash drew a blunt fingertip from her left hipbone to her right hipbone.

Her belly trembled and she arched.

"Easy." His fingers hooked the outside of her panties and he whisked them off.

She heard him drop to his knees. Felt his rapid breathing on her inner thigh. Sensed him staring at her blood-engorged pussy. A blush started from her cheekbones and worked down the length of her body to her curled toes. Never had she felt so exposed. She couldn't even study his face and watch his eyes to see if what he saw turned him on. She held her breath and herself rigid, wondering what he'd do first. Tease her with his hot breath and barely there kisses? Whisper dirty talk? Work her into a frenzy with his fingers?

Gemma was totally unprepared for the thorough swipe of his hot tongue straight up her creamy slit. She gasped.

Cash dragged his mouth across the inside of her right thigh, muttering, "Dammit. I know I'm supposed to take it slow, but Lord, *winyan*, you're already wet." He inhaled. "I want to taste you. Bathe in you. Suck these pretty pink lips and lick you until I feel you come against my tongue."

"Oh—" The rest of her sentence was lost on a long wail as Cash did exactly what he described.

No slow build up and then teasing withdrawal. He widened her knees and settled his mouth on her throbbing sex. Licking and sucking, focusing all his attention on her clit. Before she had time to brace herself, an orgasm rocked through her. Even as she lifted her hips for more, Cash sucked her clit harder, deeper, using his teeth and tongue until cries spilled from her throat.

As Gemma floated back to earth, a slight sense of embarrassment surfaced that she'd been so quick on the trigger. She stifled the urge to giggle when Cash's lips zigzagged up her ticklish belly. Instead, she scrambled up on her elbows, to better see him, forgetting about the blindfold. As she sat completely upright and reached for the tie at the back of her head, Cash's fingers circled her wrist.

"Leave it. We ain't close to done."

Chapter Six

Cash scooted Gemma to the end of the table. "I'm doin' this all wrong, I should be takin' my time."

"You already said that once. There's no hurry."

"Maybe not for you, but I ain't got a lotta patience left. This go around is gonna be short, to take the edge off, so to speak." Then he gently flipped her, so her stomach rested on the table and the white globes of her upthrust ass were the same level as his cock. She was pretty, and he also knew she was pretty much at his mercy. It humbled him, having this strong, fine woman at his command—right where he wanted her. He tugged the drawstring on his sweatpants and they dropped to the floor. He kicked them under the table.

"Cash?" Her voice was strangely subdued.

"I'm here, hang on." He angled across her back, kissing the lovely curve of her neck as he reached for the box of condoms he'd set on the table. He ripped a package open and rolled the latex down his stiff cock.

"Wait. I want to touch you."

"Next time. Been a long time for me, and you're so damn sexy." He noticed her body had tensed and he whispered kisses down her spine. "Come on, sweets, spread your legs for me. Yeah. Just like that. Hold tight."

Gemma's arms stretched until her fingers curled around the opposite edge of the table.

Holding her hips with one hand, he aligned his cock and slid into her slick heat an inch at a time. He closed his eyes, savoring the moment he'd been dreaming of for two long years.

When he was fully seated within her, she arched up. "Oh. That feels good. More. Don't stop."

"Yeah?" He withdrew slowly and slammed home three times. "How 'bout like this?"

She moaned. "Just like that. The harder the better."

Cash glanced down. Damn, but it was sexy as hell, watching his dick tunneling in and out of her hot pussy. As he pounded into her, he snaked his hand around, placing the heel of his palm on the rise of her pubic bone. His middle finger found her clit and he stroked in time to his thrusts.

"Yes," Gemma hissed. She pushed back into him, meeting his increased pace, flexing her hips against his finger. "Faster. I can't believe I'm gonna come again. Oh."

He rubbed her clit more rapidly and his balls drew up. Gemma gasped and he felt her clit pulse beneath his stroking finger as she came apart. Between her erotic cries and the supplicating way she was splayed before him, Cash didn't stand a chance of staving off his own orgasm. He threw back his head and groaned, lost to the greedy satisfaction of hot spurts shooting from the end of his cock, her slick walls spasming around his hardness, extending his orgasm until he felt woozy from the sheer blinding pleasure.

When the throbbing in his groin stopped, and the dots faded from his vision, he looked at her. Gemma's face was smashed into the side of the table, her cheek flushed with color and damp with sweat. A small, secret smile lifted the corner of her lips. A wave of tenderness swamped him and he leaned over to nuzzle her neck. "You okay?"

Gemma made an affirmative noise.

He pulled out. "Stay here and catch your breath, I'll be right back."

After disposing of the condom, he grabbed two more from the box and gently slapped her ass. "Roll over."

"I don't think I can move."

Cash fought a sense of unease. "Did I hurt you?"

She laughed softly. "In a good way. You wore out this old-timer, cowboy."

He slapped her ass again. Harder. When she made a

squeak of pleasure, he grinned. So Miz Gemma didn't mind his hand on her ass? Interesting. "I don't ever wanna hear talk like that because next time there will be consequences." Flipping her over, he emphasized his point with a fiery, prolonged kiss. When he released her mouth, he whispered, "Wrap them sexy legs around me. Let's find someplace a little softer for round two, eh?"

She sat up quickly. "Round two?"

"Yep. I warned you 'bout my savage appetites. Now that I've got you naked." He planned to keep her that way. He wanted her so mindless, so occupied, that she wouldn't have time to think or have time for regrets.

Or to wish he was someone else.

Gemma yelped when he picked her up and carried her into the dark living room.

Cash plopped on the couch, keeping her straddled across his lap.

"Can I take off the blindfold now?"

"No. But let's get rid of the shirt. Lift." In one quick movement her tank top disappeared. He eyed the front closure on her pink bra. Well, well. This presented an intriguing opportunity. "Lean back and put your hands on my knees."

She did so without arguing.

Cash nibbled on her lips, not quite kissing her as he unhooked her bra. The cups split and he slid the straps over her shoulders and down to her wrists. Three quick twists and he lifted his foot to step on the thicker back strap, leaving her wrists trapped in the stretchy arm bands.

Gemma froze. "What are you doing?"

"Makin' sure you can't get away. I wanna take my time tasting these." He flicked his tongue across her nipple. "And I know you're a little squirmy." He blew on the wet spot he'd created and watched the coral-colored skin tighten into a pointed tip.

She jerked back.

"See? I gotcha right where I wantcha." His hands curved around her ribcage and he swept his thumbs back and forth across her beaded nipples. "Tell me what you like."

She arched into his hands and rolled her chest closer.

"Huh-uh. Don't go shy on me. I'll do whatever you want, but you gotta tell me first."

"Suck them. Put your mouth on me, Cash. Please. It's been so long..."

While drawing lazy circles on her left breast, he bent his head and latched onto her right nipple. Suckling deep and long until she whimpered and thrashed. He used his teeth and his tongue until he smelled her creaming again. Then he switched his attention to the left nipple and started the process all over. Slowly. His cock stirred as she ground her wet pussy into him and made sexy, needy moans.

But Cash wouldn't be rushed no matter how much she pleaded. He took his time, learning every nuance of her reactions. What made her sigh. What made her clench her thighs. What made her curse and gyrate her hips. As he licked a path up her neck, she shuddered and gooseflesh appeared beneath his tongue.

"Cold?"

"God, no. Please. You're torturing me."

"What do you want?"

"Take the blindfold off. Untie my hands. I feel so helpless."

"Mmm. Ain't it a bitch to have no control?" He growled against her throat, "This is what I've been feelin' since the first time I saw you. You've had me all tied up in knots, Gem. Just thinkin' 'bout all the things I wanted to do to you. Now that you're right where I want you, I ain't inclined to let you go."

She buried her face in the curve where his collarbone met his neck, trilling her lips across his skin until he shivered. "I'll make it worth your while. Lord knows there are other places on you I wanna kiss too."

"Got a specific place in mind?"

"Uh-huh. Need a hint?" She blew in his ear.

He smiled. "Why, Gemma Jansen. You offerin' to blow me?"

"Yes." She scraped her teeth down the cord in his neck. "Please."

"No." Cash took her mouth in a consuming kiss. After he broke away, he said, "Don't get me wrong, I'm dyin' to have those sweet lips wrapped around my cock, watchin' you takin' me deep in that hot mouth, feelin' your throat tighten on the head as you swallow every drop I give you, but it ain't gonna happen tonight."

"Why not? Because you're showin' me who's boss in the bedroom?"

Her pouting attitude didn't help her cause. "Yep. I warned you I planned to be in charge. You agreed. That's all you need to remember." He reached for a condom package, ripped it open and rolled it down the length of his erection. "Scoot your knees closer."

"Why?"

"So you can ride me, cowgirl."

"Oh."

"I'll even let you take the reins—" he nipped her chin, "—this time."

Gemma kept her balance, even though the bra straps stretched more tightly around her wrists as she maneuvered in position. She canted her hips and sank down on him.

The slick feel of her pussy tightening around his cock made him grind his teeth together to stop from howling his satisfaction like a beast. "You're so wet for me. Do you know how sexy that is? You bein' so slick and hot again?"

She groaned softly in his ear.

He smoothed the hair from her cheek. "What?"

Resting her forehead to his, she said, "Kiss me while you're fucking me, Cash. I wanna be skin to skin and mouth to mouth with you when I come."

"Whatever the lady wants."

This time was slower. Sweeter. More intimate, more like making love than straight-up fucking. Keeping his mouth attached to hers, he shaped her luscious breasts with his hands, avoiding her pebbled nipples entirely. Contenting himself with tracing her lush contours, a teasing touch of his fingertips on the upper swell as his thumbs swept the side near her armpits, until she began to shake with increased desire. He caressed the strong muscles in her bare back and squeezed the delicious curve of her ass as she lifted and lowered on his cock.

They sustained the languorous kiss until the very end when the thrusts grew shorter and faster.

Her chest was slick with sweat. As was his. When she bowed backward, changing the angle so he could thrust deeper, his thumb found her clit and he brought her to the brink, keeping her there, greedily watching the pleasure cross her face, until the pivotal moment. Her internal muscles clamped down on his cock and he smashed his mouth back to hers, swallowing her cries as they sailed over the edge of insanity together.

While she slumped against him, catching her breath, Cash released her hands, rubbing them vigorously to return blood flow.

Gemma nuzzled his jaw, the coarse cotton of the blindfold catching on his cheek. "I never imagined it could be this good again."

Part of him wanted to ask if she meant their second round of sex, or whether she meant with a man other than her late husband, but a larger part of Cash couldn't stand to hear the truth.

She sighed. "You're quiet. You okay?"

"Fine. Great. Just tired."

"No round three, then?" she teased.

"We'll see."

"Speaking of seeing...could you take this off?"

"Sure. Can you stand up first? I'm getting a cramp in my leg."

"Oh sorry."

He was reluctant to remove the blindfold, though he did so, his gut clenched in fear at what he might see in her eyes. Or what she might recognize in his. Cash tenderly kissed her eyelids, her eyebrows, the corners of her eyes, the bridge of her nose, every part that'd been covered by the cloth. She didn't melt into him, rather, held herself stiff. With a sinking sensation, he whispered, "I'm gonna head upstairs." And he turned away so she couldn't see his face.

After he hit the bathroom he crawled in bed. A sick feeling settled in the pit of his stomach.

Was she staying away, wallowing in regret?

Eventually Gemma entered the room. He feigned sleep as she climbed between the cool cotton sheets. She didn't snuggle up to him. They stayed on their respective sides of the queen-sized bed, back to back. Cash had almost drifted off for real, when the bed creaked and he heard her get up. Her light footfalls stopped at the window.

He laid there in silence, in misery, pretending sleep as he listened to her soft sniffles.

Never a good sign to hear the woman you'd just spent hours making love to, crying as if her heart was breaking.

Chapter Seven

Lord it was hot.

Macie wiped the sweat from her forehead with the inside of her arm and dropped the empty bucket near the water pump. A low groan drifted out from the barn. Weird. The door was ajar. Curious about the strange noise she heard, she stepped inside and immediately was plunged from bright sunshine into darkness. She picked her way through discarded tools littering the dirt floor, the scent of hay and feed and horseflesh overwhelming her senses. She rounded the corner by the last wooden stall and stopped.

Three men were crammed in the small space. Three men, naked, except for their cowboy hats and boots. She couldn't see their faces, but at the moment it wasn't their faces she was interested in.

They were all buck-ass naked. Oh, man, it'd be a damn shame to cover up such glorious bodies under chaps, jeans and long-sleeved shirts. These hunky cowboys should be all nude, all the time.

Two men studied a man who was bound. His muscular arms were stretched above his head, his strong wrists tied together and hooked to a long rope. His feet were spread wide, though the tips of his boots scarcely touched the hay-strewn ground. His bulky thigh muscles were rigid from the strain. A single thin golden sunbeam blazed between the wooden slats, highlighting his sweat-coated skin.

Macie's eyes drank him in. Of the three, he was the most striking. Wide, defined shoulders. A hairless chest with sharply sculpted pectorals. His biceps bulged with corded muscles and thick veins. As her gaze swept down to his ribcage and his tapered waist, to the dent in his navel, the other two naked cowboys blocked her view of his groin.

Damn.

But she watched in fascination as the men murmured to him before each one latched onto a flat bronze nipple. The bound cowboy arched, but no sound emerged. The blond man suckling his right nipple reached down between the man's legs. Although Macie couldn't see specifics, by the way the bound cowboy bucked, and by the way the guy's hand moved up and down, she had a pretty good idea what was being done to him.

A fireball of heat blazed through her.

The dark-haired man on the left brought his fingers to the bound cowboy's mouth. The bound man parted his lips and sucked the offered digits to the knuckles. The man withdrew his wet fingers and reached around the bound cowboy's hip, his arm dropping below the phantom belt line.

A stuttered breath left the bound cowboy's mouth and he jerked once before a low-pitched groan escaped. Sweat beaded his upper lip. More perspiration coated his golden skin. He twisted beneath the men's ministrations and the ropes, yet his cowboy hat remained in place, covering his face.

Laughing, the two men abandoned the bound cowboy. The dark-haired man hooked his arm around the blond's neck and yanked him close. They fell on each other like long lost lovers. Hard male body slid against another hard male body. Cowboy hats hit the dirt as hungry mouths met in a ravenous kiss. The sounds of heavy breathing and of rough hands caressing even rougher skin echoed as the pungent musk of animals and sex hung in the air.

Macie's panties grew damp. She felt like a pervert but she couldn't make herself flee the sexy scene. There was something electrifying about three strong men lost in a taboo passion, no need to be gentle, doing to each other exactly what they'd like done to them.

The dark-haired man fisted one hand in the blond's hair and the other around the blond's long cock. He forcefully stroked the thick length, yanking back the blond's head to savage his throat, muttering unintelligible words against his skin.

The blond moaned.

The dark-haired cowboy released his hold on the man's hair as his open mouth skated across his lover's upper torso, his tongue tracing the dips and valleys of the musculature. He suckled the pebbled tips of the blond's pale nipples, biting down hard enough to cause the blond to gasp. Then he scraped his fingers over the taut washboard abs, flicking the tip of his tongue around the belly ring and through the thick nest of light hair before he fell to his knees.

Macie chanced a peek at the bound cowboy. His cock twitched against his stomach as he watched the two men from beneath the brim of his hat. A part of it, yet apart from it. A strange sense of déjà vu surfaced.

"Open your mouth," the blond demanded, drawing Macie's attention back to the male couple.

Shaking his head, the dark-haired cowboy lifted the blond's cock and nuzzled his low-slung balls before his tongue darted out and licked them. Thoroughly. Then that long flickering tongue disappeared behind the tight sac.

"Lick it. More. Get it wet. Yeah, push your tongue inside." He canted his hips. "Deeper. That's it. Fuck my ass with that greedy tongue. Stick it in as far as you can."

The dark-haired man's thick fingers pushed the inside of the blond's thighs as far apart as possible so he could bury his face beneath the blond's cock and balls. Wiggling his head as he dove deeper, he made wet, slurping sounds, sucking, moaning, grinding his hips and cock into the blond's shin.

The blond watched, wild-eyed as the man on his knees pulled back and brought the furry blond balls completely into his mouth again. "Like that. Yeah. Use your teeth a little. Roll them together. Now suck them. Jesus, that's so good. I love to watch you."

After the dark-haired cowboy released the globes with an audible wet pop, the blond grabbed the brunette's head and rammed his rosy meat into his lover's mouth.

The dark-haired cowboy made a choking noise and backed off, releasing the cock until just the tip remained in his mouth.

The blond thrust his hips hard, keeping his hands clamped to his lover's head. "Deeper. Come on. Take me all the way down that throat. Don't pretend you don't love it when I fuck your face."

The enthusiastic sucking sounds and the answering guttural demands mesmerized her. The blond would pull his wet cock out completely, circling the weeping purple head around the other man's swollen lips before plunging back in to the root.

Saliva dribbled down the dark-haired man's chin and neck. He kept up the frantic pace, digging his fingertips into his lover's hips with enough force to leave marks. Making greedy, happy hums that seemed to heighten the blond's pleasure.

The unbearably erotic interlude didn't last long. The blond cowboy muttered, "Fuck, here it comes," as he clutched the man's dark hair, and tipped his chin down so every inch of his cock was lodged in the man's throat, his ass muscles flexing with every spurt.

Macie was surprised at their collective stillness as the dark-haired cowboy gruffly swallowed. She glanced over at the bound cowboy, who was fighting against his restraints, his cock still hard as a railroad spike, yet, telltale wetness spread across his belly.

The blond man stumbled back as the dark-haired cowboy rose to his feet. A sexy, secret smile, followed by a gentle touch of the blond's hands. Then they exchanged a sinuous full-body hug, cock to cock, their hands stroking, caressing sweaty, bared skin as they shared a hot, long soul kiss.

Sweat trickled between her breasts and her nipples tingled as if they were touching her.

After they reluctantly broke apart, exchanging soft murmurs and soft laughter, they moved toward the bound cowboy as one unit.

"See what you've been missing?"

"We know you like to watch us," the blond said. "That's why you've been sneaking in here."

"Lucky for you we ain't done yet." They turned the bound man sideways and the dark-haired man disappeared into the shadows and returned with a sawhorse.

"And lucky for you, we'll let you participate. Isn't that what you've secretly hoped for, cowboy?" The blond circled the bound cowboy and plucked up his forgotten hat. "Have you ever been sucked off by a man?"

The bound cowboy grunted, "Fuck no."

Both men laughed. Then the dark-haired one said, "Then we'll make it memorable. No one knows how to suck cock better than another man." He positioned the sawhorse close to the bound cowboy's thighs. Then he slapped the blond hard on the butt. "You know how I want it. Bend over and spread those ass cheeks. I wanna see every inch of that hole."

Where had she heard that before?

Without argument, the blond placed his chest on the sawhorse. His mouth was directly across from the bound cowboy's straining cock. He smiled wickedly and the bound cowboy stopped squirming and seemed to hold his breath.

The dark-haired man reached into his boot and pulled out a condom and rolled it on. He moistened his fingers with his mouth, then traced them down the blond's crack and plunged them inside his ass.

The blond wiggled back. "Give me your cock or your tongue, not your fingers."

"I've already tongued you, that'll have to do for lube. It's gonna be one hard ride." The dark-haired cowboy lifted the ass in front of him higher, pulling apart the cheeks as his cock prodded the blond's dark hole. One thrust of his hips and his dick disappeared completely.

"Yes," the blond hissed. "Harder."

"Damn. No matter how many times I do this to you, you're always so fucking tight."

Macie focused on the blond circling his hands around the bound man's ass, bringing that big, straining cock to his mouth and swallowing it in one greedy gulp.

As the dark-haired man's cock reamed the blond man's asshole, each hard thrust sent the blond man's mouth further down the length of the bound man's cock, until his nose was buried in dark pubic hair. Then he'd release the cock slowly, and bring it fully back into his mouth, each hungry stroke increasing in speed and suction

The scene looked as smooth as a choreographed dance. Like these cowboys had fucked each other well and often. The blond bobbed his head. Grunts burst from the bound cowboy as he began to pump his hips into the blond's face.

But the blond retreated and nuzzled the bound man's quivering belly. "Do you want me to finish you?"

"Yes," he hissed.

"You want to come in my mouth? In a *man's* mouth?"

"Yes, goddamn you, finish it."

With a loud slurp, the bound man's distended cock was once again buried between the blond's lips. Skin slapped skin. The sawhorse squeaked with the escalating thrusts. The musky odor of sweat and sex and dirt permeated the air.

Macie was so worked up, she slid her hand down inside her underwear. She slicked up her finger with her own juices and frantically rubbed her swollen clit, aching for fast relief, sighing when the familiar throbbing began.

The dark-haired man panted, "Shit, Dooce, I can't hold back."

Dooce? Macie made a surprised noise. The dark-haired man looked over his shoulder briefly as he pounded his meat into Dooce's ass like a man possessed. At that point she realized the dark-haired man was her ex-boyfriend, Dante.

Dooce turned and glared at her. "What are you doing here? He doesn't want you. No one wants you."

The bound cowboy finally looked up and his cowboy hat slid off his head.

Her heart stopped; the man was none other than Carter McKay.

Their eyes met and he said hoarsely, "I want you, Macie, in ways no man ever has. I want to give you everything you've ever wanted."

She closed her eyes at the heat in his eyes and the perfection of his quiet declaration. She slumped against the chute, finding it soft as a pillow.

A pillow?

Macie's eyes flew open. She sat straight up and looked around. She wasn't in a darkened barn, but in a darkened camper.

Dammit. It was another dream, a variation on the dream

she'd been having the past two months. Except, it wasn't really a dream since the scenario was very close to the real one she'd walked in on in Dante's apartment. Dante on his knees, Dooce jacking off as Dante fucked Dooce's ass like a madman. It'd been rough, and raw, and unbelievably hot. She'd stayed hidden in the shadows of the hallway, ashamed she'd gotten off at the sight of Dante's sexual synchronicity with Dooce—a synchronicity she and Dante had never experienced.

No wonder. She hadn't been born with a penis.

So why did her subconscious place Carter at that scene? Because he was an artist like Dante? Because she wondered if Carter was gay? The last two times she'd experienced this dream, she was the one tied up and forced to watch the two men fuck like animals. Was Carter's presence because she was afraid the situation with him would turn out the same as every other past relationship —with her on the outside looking in?

A therapist would have a field day with that one.

She glanced at the clock. The red numbers flashed five a.m. No use going back to sleep now—the alarm would ring in another half hour anyway.

Macie cleaned up, dressed, and braided her hair before she hopped in her SUV and navigated her way to work.

Late yesterday afternoon, after she and her father finished their meal at the local diner, he'd sped off to Gemma's ranch to set up the camper. She'd sensed he needed to be alone with his thoughts and to gauge his new responsibilities without her chattering at him. So she'd lingered in the booth, thinking of her best friend Kat, wondering how she'd managed to be a third wheel again. Then she noticed the "help wanted" sign by the cash register and asked the waitress about the opening.

Velma—the sixty-something owner of the Last Chance Diner—needed a gal Friday to fill in part-time as a cook and waitress. The hours were sporadic, but the pay was decent for rural Wyoming. With Macie's experience in restaurants, Velma seemed genuinely happy to hire her on a simple handshake.

Macie was glad her first day would be spent in the kitchen. Between the bizarre dream, and her father ignoring her, beating eggs and dicing veggies would be a productive way to channel her frustrations.

Inside the restaurant, the rich scent of coffee caused her steps to quicken and she poured a mug before clocking in.

Velma grinned. "Another caffeine addict, huh?"

Macie grunted.

"Well, I've already had four cups so I've shaken off the cobwebs and started the bacon."

"What time do we open?"

"Six bells." Velma dumped two packages of frozen hashbrowns on the griddle. "Most of the early customers are construction workers. They like a big breakfast in a hurry. So I always have a bunch of potatoes and meat done ahead of time."

"Good plan." Macie donned an apron, lifted the metal press flattening the bacon to check on its doneness while downing her coffee. "Mostly egg specials?"

"Yeah. Some with pancakes, most with toast. You have any problems making omelets?"

"Nope. But I didn't check to see if there's anything fancy on the menu like eggs benedict."

Velma poured her another cup of coffee. "No. No huevos rancheros either, no matter how much Diaz begs me to add 'em." She confided, "Don't seem worth it since Diaz is the only Mexican around here. Though he threatens to bring his cousins up from Denver all the time."

"If he asks me, I might just surprise him and whip up a plate." She added more oil to the sizzling potatoes. "Most folks assume I'm Mexican anyway."

"I didn't want to be rude and ask, but are you?"

Macie smiled. "No. I'm half Lakota Sioux."

"Oh. So the man with you last night? Is he your…"

"Dad. Cash Big Crow."

"He don't look old enough to have a daughter your age."

She'd fielded this question often enough it was second nature to her. "He was sixteen when he knocked up my mom."

"I know how that goes. I had my first kid when I was seventeen." She shrugged. "It happens. What's your dad doing around here?"

"He's the new foreman for Gemma Jansen's ranch." Macie

froze. Maybe that wasn't supposed to be common knowledge.

"'Bout damn time Gemma hired somebody decent. She's been tryin' to do it all since Steve died. Be workin' herself into an early grave." Velma seemed ready to settle in for a long chat. "Do you know Gemma very well?"

"No. I just met her yesterday."

"Seems strange she didn't offer you a job on the Bar 9."

"To tell you the truth, Velma, I'm not much interested in ranching. I'm just tagging along with Dad for the summer, but I couldn't sit around and do nothing. I don't want to be accused of being lazy." Macie knew her father still struggled against that racial stereotype—of being nothing more than a lazy, freeloading, boozing injun. An attitude she'd run into a time or two herself.

Velma chuckled. "You ain't been here for more than twenty-fours hours, and you've already got a job, so I think it's safe to say you ain't lazy."

"Thanks." Macie flipped the hashbrowns. "Just so you know, I'd much rather be back here than out front."

"We'll get along just fine, Miss Macie, 'cause I've had enough years of cookin' over this hot griddle. I do believe there's more grease in my veins than blood."

Macie laughed. "Must be why you look so young, Miz Velma."

Velma snapped a dishtowel at her on the way to unlock the front door. "Yes sirree. You and I are gonna get along just fine, squirt."

Chapter Eight

Gemma woke alone. She'd gotten used to it in the last three years, but she still experienced a pang of disappointment.

Thank God Cash was conked out when she'd come to bed. But in her restless state she couldn't sleep. When she'd quietly crept out to stare out the window, the tears started. Unwanted tears, both happy and sad, as she said goodbye to her past and hello to her future.

An odd thought occurred to her. Cash hadn't overheard her crying, had he?

Pointless to worry about now. She rolled her lazy ass out of bed, realizing she'd overslept by a good hour. Did Cash think she acted the lady of the manor, lolling around between the sheets all day while he was out busting his ass?

Places were sore on her body that hadn't been sore in awhile, so she popped a couple of aspirin. She dressed in her usual attire of jeans, boots and a lightweight, long-sleeved cotton shirt to protect her skin from the blistering sun.

Cash wasn't in the kitchen. A single bowl and spoon rested in the dish rack beside the sink. No coffee was left warming; the pot was still sparkling clean. Well. Shoot. This wasn't what she'd expected. Would've been nice to share a cup before heading out to feed the cattle.

She stepped out onto the covered porch, shielding her eyes against the bright rays. Cash's pickup wasn't parked in front where he'd left it last night, and the ranch truck was in its usual spot. Then Gemma remembered Macie. After devoting last night to her, Cash was probably hanging out with his daughter.

Gemma didn't want to interfere, but she had a perverse

need to make sure Cash was all right. He seemed a more contentious sort than to take off without telling her where he was going.

Are you speaking as his lover? Or as his boss?

She ignored the voices in her head as her strides ate up the distance to the camper. She stopped between the outbuildings when she realized Macie's vehicle wasn't around either. What the heck?

As she debated on what to do next, Carter came barreling around the corner of the barn, scaring her half to death.

"Where is she?" he demanded.

"Who? Macie?"

"Yeah."

"I have no idea. Have you seen Cash?"

"I saw him headin' out to the west pasture with a load of hay in the back of his truck about an hour ago."

"By himself?"

"I guess."

"Dammit, Carter. Why weren't you with him?"

His eyes narrowed and he countered, "Why weren't you?"

She should be beyond blushing at her age. Gemma sighed. "Evidently I overslept. Which means Cash is out there doing everything on his own."

"So let him. It *is* his responsibility now."

"That don't make me feel any less guilty. This is my place. I don't know if I'll ever be able to turn over full operations to someone else."

"You'd better at least try. What's the point of hirin' someone if you ain't gonna let him do the work?"

Her mouth opened, then closed. She couldn't think of a rational rebuttal.

Tires thudded by the barn, sounding abnormally loud in the morning stillness. A drawn out squeak echoed as the gate was opened. An engine gunned and a *screech bang* followed.

Gemma hustled toward the sound. Her stomach did a little flip at seeing Cash.

He yelled, "Mornin', Gem."

Cash's smile died the second he saw Carter coming from the direction of Macie's camper. His neutral expression became a frown when Carter demanded, "Where's Macie?"

"If she would've wanted you to know, McKay, she would've told you."

"You ornery—"

"Carter," Gemma said sharply, "enough."

Cash said, "Maybe you oughta be doin' your job instead of worryin' 'bout my daughter."

"At least somebody is worried." Carter snorted. "Did you see her last night? Or ignore her? I bet you don't even know where she is."

"As a matter of fact, I do know where she is, and the chances of me tellin' you just dropped to zero, boy."

Good God. This was ridiculous. "Look. I don't have time for this stupid male posturing. Carter, what did you get done this morning while Cash was tending the livestock?"

"I moved the horses into the south pasture. I sprayed down the stalls and refilled the flytraps. Then I prepped Daisy's medicine. Didn't know if you wanted me to give it to her or if you wanted to do it. Then I took stock of the rest of the veterinary supplies and made a list for the next time someone goes to the feed store."

Cash seemed impressed. "I noticed them flytraps were lookin' ratty last night. Thanks for takin' care of it." He knocked his hat up a notch and addressed Gemma. "The stock tank out where the cattle are grazin' is bone dry. I came back to switch out trucks before I head back out to refill the water tanks."

"Is that damn pump broken again? That's twice in the last month," Carter said.

"I wondered. Thought boss lady could help me out. Show me how, or let me figure out the best way to prime the pump."

The double meaning in Cash's words caused Gemma's stomach to pitch again. "Sure."

"Did you notice if the salt licks are gone?" Carter prompted. "'Cause it was damn close to nothin' the other day when I checked on 'em."

"Completely gone. I couldn't find replacement tablets."

"She keeps them in the cellar."

"I'll know where to look next time." Cash angled his chin at Carter. "Far as I'm concerned, you done everything I thought needed doin', so there ain't no reason for you to stick around today. I'll see you bright and early tomorrow."

The two men stared at each other. "Fine. I'll go. Just as soon as you tell me where she is."

Cash laughed, a little harshly. "If Macie wants to contact you, she will."

"And when she does? What then?"

Gemma stifled a groan at Carter's surety where he stood as far as Macie was concerned, after knowing her for one day.

"*If* she does contact you, I'll abide by her wishes. Until then, you'll abide by mine. Stay away from her, McKay."

"You forgot one tiny detail. I don't think Macie wants to stay away from *me*." Carter retreated and loped to the barn. Before either of them said another word, Carter mounted his horse Deacon and galloped across the pasture, away from what probably would've been an argument as heated as the day.

Cash swore.

She tried to diffuse the situation. "What happened to you this morning? I woke up and you were gone. Was I snoring or something and chased you off?"

"No. You looked so peaceful I let you sleep in. I woke up early to hang out with my daughter, but she'd already taken off."

"Where is she?"

His eyes narrowed. "If I tell you, you gonna blab to McKay?"

"No. But if he asks me, I ain't gonna lie."

Cash sighed. "I called her cell when I couldn't find her this morning. Evidently she found work at the Last Chance Diner. She's cookin' first shift today."

"She already found work? I hope I'm not the reason she felt the need to get a job when I told her she'd have to earn her keep if she stayed here."

"Don't worry. Though your offer was mighty nice, ranch work ain't her thing."

"Glad to hear I didn't chase her away."

"Take more than that to scare either of us off."

Gemma stepped closer. She had an overwhelming compulsion to touch the smooth skin on his cheek, which was still damp from the exertion of early morning chores. She settled for curling her fingers around the window frame. "Is everything all right? You seem...I don't know...different today."

"Just tryin' to get the lay of the land, so to speak. I don't want to disappoint my new boss lady."

"Nothin' you've done to me, or for me, has disappointed me so far, Cash."

He grinned. "Good to hear. What do you say we get the rest of these morning chores done and head over to the diner for lunch? I'd like to see my girl in action."

"Sounds good. I'll grab the truck keys, and the salt, and meet you by the gate."

Something between them still didn't feel right. Rather than press the issue, she'd see if it resolved itself—or if it was unfounded paranoia on her part.

Carter tried not to fume as his horse cruised across the pasture. Problem was, he suspected he was mostly mad at himself. He should've trusted his gut feeling and gone to Macie like he'd planned last night. From the looks of it, Cash and Gemma had been so wrapped up in each other Macie probably spent the night by herself.

How often had that happened to her? Was that the reason for her reserve?

It was a detached attitude, a purposeful distance he recognized. Hell, even his own family considered him aloof. Last night, in the long hours he'd spent alone, he'd attempted to draw Macie from memory. He'd expected that seeing her in the flesh would lift the veil stifling his creativity. It'd worked at first. By the time he'd finished with the half-dozen or so sketches of her, none of them to his liking, it was nearly three in the morning. He crumpled them up and managed to nod off. His dreams weren't memorable, but on some level they'd disturbed him enough to rouse him from a light slumber.

His sole desire when he awoke was to sculpt her. Dig his hands into clay and immortalize her, then cast her likeness in bronze. But again, rather than give his muse free rein, he literally had to rein in Gemma's horses.

Normally he loved working outdoors with animals. It gave him a chance to study their movements. The come-hither toss of a filly's head. The way the stallion's nostrils flared in response. The gleaming wetness of a horse's coat after a vigorous ride. How the constant Wyoming wind stirred their long manes as they galloped, so the same horse never looked the same way twice.

He figured Macie had as many different looks and moods. No wonder he was having a hard time capturing her likeness.

Carter checked on her first thing after he'd arrived at the Bar 9 to find her camper empty and her car gone. Taking out his frustration by scooping manure had worked for a while. He knew it was a stupid move to take out the rest of his frustration on Cash. Then again, he suspected nothing he could've said or done would've convinced Cash to reveal Macie's whereabouts.

He grabbed a beer, a chunk of wood and his sharpest knife. Sometimes it helped clear his head to just have something in his hands to carve with no specific object in mind. Rather than squirrel himself away in the barn, he plugged in his boom box and perched on the front stoop in the sunshine. A mixed CD of country tunes his sister Keely selected lightened his mood. As the wood shavings fell away, he thought of families, his family in particular.

His oldest brother Cord kept himself on the brink of exhaustion since his wife had divorced him and left their son Ky in his care nearly two years ago. Colby, the second of the five McKay boys, gave up his dream of pro rodeo after a life-threatening injury. Last year Colby had settled into married life with Channing, a woman who'd softened his harsher edges. Between buying up every bit of available land around the McKay homestead, and chasing every rodeo queen within one hundred miles, his brother Colt made sure the McKay reputation for wild behavior remained intact. Although he and his older brother Cam were closest in age, since Cam had been stationed in Iraq, his visits to the ranch were infrequent. War had changed him. Cam was silent and serious; his infamous practical jokes non-existent.

How did his family see him? The quiet, laid back one? Young and stubborn? Cord and Colt bantered those words back and forth his entire life. Carter had no idea if anything he'd accomplished put him on equal footing with the brothers he idolized. Which was part of the reason he'd jumped at the chance to work for Gemma. He wouldn't be underfoot and under scrutiny as he prepared for the art show with the potential to change his future.

Carter was relieved Gemma hired Cash Big Crow. Lately, taking care of the livestock sapped his energy and his creativity suffered. He'd finished half the pieces needed for the art show. The ideas were there, but the drive wasn't. Now that time wouldn't be an issue, could he focus on completing projects? Or would meeting his beautifully haunting muse prove an even bigger distraction?

Just thinking about the sweet temptation of Macie...

The knife slipped and he swore. He wiped the blood on his jeans and dumped a splash of beer on the cut. Wasn't whiskey, but it seemed to do the trick. Disgusted the blob of wood in his hand was still a blob, Carter drained the beer and headed into the barn.

Muse or no muse, he needed to get back to work.

Chapter Nine

Dog tired after a busy day at the diner, Macie crawled out of a cool shower and flopped on her tiny couch. Not two minutes later two raps sounded on the camper door. She shouted, "Come in," over the din of the air conditioner.

Maybe Carter deigned to stop by. Not that she'd been holding her breath for his appearance last night, but she was a tiny bit disappointed he hadn't shown.

Typical man. The sweet words were no more than sweet lies, Macie.

Shut up, Mom.

The door opened and her father stepped inside.

She couldn't hold back a smile. "Hey, Dad."

"*Hoka hey*, Macie. What's up? Is this a bad time?"

"No."

He paused on the threshold, looking...nervous?

"Bet it's weird knockin' on your own door, huh?"

"That it is."

"Come on in. I appreciate you letting me crash here. It would be uncomfortable staying in Gemma's house," she added hastily, "not that she's not nice or anything."

"True. Plus, I imagine you're used to your independence."

"Also true." Macie was glad he understood. "You want a beer?"

He grinned. "You drinkin' my beer?"

She grinned back. "Yep."

"Glad to see it ain't goin' to waste."

Macie pulled two bottles from the small fridge. A *pop hiss* echoed as she twisted the caps off and handed him a cold one.

Her father slid into the bench seat of the folding table. She scooted in across from him.

"So how was your first day on the job as foreman?"

"All right I guess. Foreman's a fancy title considerin' I'm the only one workin' fulltime for her. Gemma's runnin' less cattle than I assumed. There's more broken equipment than what I expected. Lucky thing I'm a jack-of-all-trades, eh?" He lifted his bottle in a mock toast.

Macie clinked her beer to his. "Very lucky."

He sipped. She sipped.

"Speakin' of jobs. You found something pretty damn quick."

"Yeah, I know. I wasn't planning to work, but when I saw the help wanted sign, it seemed like a sign. And I knew you'd be busy and I didn't want to sit around taking up space, waiting for you to pay attention to me."

A lengthy pause hung in the air before he sighed. "That's how you feel?"

"Sometimes."

"I didn't mean—"

"I am a big girl. I'm perfectly capable of seeing to my own needs and taking care of myself."

"This ain't goin' the way you wanted, is it?"

She dropped her gaze to the bottle and her fingers picked at the soggy label. "Dad, nothing ever goes the way it's supposed to when it comes to us. Something always comes up and changes our plans. No biggie. I'm used to it."

Silence hummed as loud as the air conditioning.

"I'm sorry."

More silence.

"I'm always sayin' that to you, ain't I?"

Macie shrugged.

After a while he laughed. "Well, this is fun. I sure know how to kill a conversation. This wasn't what I had in mind when I came here."

She looked up at him. "Why are you here?"

"Here as in, here in this camper? Or here as in, here on Gemma's ranch?"

"Both I guess."

With a drawn out sigh, Cash took off his hat. He tossed it on the seat beside him and scratched his head. "Mostly, I'm here in the camper because I wanted to explain some things." His gaze caught hers. "Or as your mother used to say to me, to give you an excuse on why I'm disappointin' you once again."

She looked away, but she couldn't help but listen.

"When I talked to you last week, hell, for the whole last couple of months, you sounded so down. I thought I could be the one to cheer you up for a change. That's why I invited you to hit the road with me. But the truth is, I didn't think beyond that, which has always been my downfall. I tend to live in the moment." He gestured to the inside of the camper. "As evidenced by my lack of foresight for my future. Since I ain't got much of anything. Hell, I still ain't got much to offer you, Macie—"

"Dad—"

"Dammit, you have every right to be pissed off. Why you bein' so nice to me? Here you are, in the wilds of Wyoming, stuck in a crappy camper, forcin' yourself to get a job, and probably feelin' ignored by the person who brung you here in the first place." He chugged his beer. "Am I close to right?"

"Partially." She scraped the gummy residue from the glass bottle. "But I can't help being nice. It's the way I was raised."

The way he went motionless, Macie knew he was thinking he hadn't had a hand in that either.

"You takin' the foreman's job did surprise me."

"Surprised me too. Especially since other ranch folks have asked me to go to work for them, but..."

"But they weren't her." Macie took a big drink. "You have been talkin' about her a lot for the last year. So what is it about her? Besides she's a hot lookin', tough actin' cowgirl with a big Ford truck?"

He smiled slightly. "*Shee.* I could give you some bullshit answer, but the truth is, I don't know. Been askin' myself the same question. Why, after I'd 'bout given up on her, that I'd drop everything the minute she asked me to."

71

"Maybe it's because she asked. She seems like the type of person who'd prefer to do everything herself. Which I understand."

"Me too."

"So, on a basic level if she has to ask, she really is in need of help. Your help alone, apparently."

"True." He shot her a silly grin. "Inherited your smarts from your momma, that's for damn sure."

The ensuing silence wasn't uncomfortable for a change.

Macie finished her beer and pointed at his empty bottle. "You want another?"

"Nah. I'm good. So tell me about *your* day flippin' cakes and bacon."

"It's always weird starting a new job. My first thought was, sleepy little diner in a sleepy little town. How busy can it be? Man, was I in for a rude awakening. Damn place is hoppin' for breakfast. I kept up." She smiled. "Barely. Velma was happy, so that's all that mattered."

"Didn't seem overly busy over the noon hour."

It'd shocked her when he and Gemma strolled in for lunch. It'd shocked her even more that her dad seemed...proud of her. For being a fast cook? Not that there was anything wrong with cooking in a greasy spoon, but for most parents, having their kid working in a diner wouldn't be a proud parent moment.

"It stayed steady. I think it creates a shorter lunch rush because people know Velma shuts down the grill at two and doesn't reopen until five. Day after tomorrow I'll be working the late shift. Waitressing. Ugh. Not my favorite."

When her dad didn't comment, and kept his face aimed at the table, Macie leaned forward and said, "What?"

"You waitressing." Cash burst out laughing. "I would've loved to see you dumpin' cold tea on the guy grabbin' you. Least of what he deserved. I'da clocked him."

Her lips twitched. "Wasn't funny at the time, but I don't regret it."

"Good." He glanced around the small space. "You're okay stayin' here in the travelin' tipi?"

"Yep."

"It's kinda small. Kinda out of date. Probably not what you're used to, eh?"

"It's fine."

"You sure there isn't anything else you need?"

Just time with you. "No, really, Dad, this is great. I like this place a lot better than my last apartment." There was something oddly comforting about living in a place he'd lived, since they hadn't ever inhabited the same space. Oddly enough, it felt like home.

His frown lines deepened. He looked away.

"What?"

"I just realized I ain't been to any of your apartments. Sweet Jesus. Talk about bein' a bad father—"

"Stop. You had other things occupying your mind." Macie took a chance, reached for his hand and squeezed.

He squeezed back. "Things change, honey-girl. I want things to change between us. I'll try my damndest to make it so."

"Me too."

"Good. Tomorrow night after I'm done with chores, you wanna go ridin'?"

"Nothing you can say, Dad, will ever get me on a bull."

He chuckled. "Horseback ridin', not bull ridin'."

"Oh. Umm. Sure. I just hope I don't make a fool of myself in front of Gemma. It's been awhile since I've been on a horse."

He paused. "I thought maybe it could just be...you and me."

"Really?"

No, not really, a little voice reminded her, *something will come up and he'll have to cancel.*

"Really."

Macie told the voice to shut up. "Cool. I'd like that."

"It's a date." He wiggled his hat on his head and stood. "You need anything at all, just call my cell."

Why couldn't she just go up to the house and ask him in person? "What are you and Gemma up to tonight?"

When he glanced away quickly, she understood there were certain things she did not need to know about her father—or how he and his boss spent their idle hours. "Never mind. You don't have to answer that."

"Gemma and I are goin' to check out a couple of buckin' horses over by Beulah. We'll be back tonight, but it'll probably be late tonight."

"Then drive safe and I'll see you tomorrow."

He wrapped an arm around her shoulder, giving her a quick peck on the forehead. "Later."

The familiar scent of horses and leather and sun-baked cotton surrounded her. Maybe she'd be doomed to disappointment, but Macie was happy her dad was at least trying to reach out to her. And she'd be damned if she'd slap his hand away.

Chapter Ten

Later that night another rumble of thunder rattled Macie's teeth. Lightning flashes seared her eyes. Wind gusts made the camper shake like an aluminum can. Rain pelted the steel siding.

The electricity had crapped out hours ago. She had no clue how the backup generator on the camper worked. Her cell phone was completely dead. She couldn't call her dad—not that she would've ventured outside in a raging freakin' thunderstorm by herself even if she'd had explicit instructions on how to fix the damn generator.

So Macie cowered in the dark, alone, completely freaked out and feeling stupid for being such a scaredy cat. God. She should be over this irrational fear of storms by now. Still, she knew if her dad and Gemma were around, she would've hightailed it into Gemma's house. As far as she knew, they hadn't made it home. She'd like to think her father would've checked on her to make sure she was all right.

He'd sooner check on his horses and cows than on you.

Stop it. All of it—the recriminations, the neediness, the overpowering fear.

Yet, her subconscious reminded her in every horror movie she'd ever watched gruesome scenes took place during a thunderstorm—when the female victim was alone.

Every noise spooked her. She'd tried to block them out by singing "Redneck Woman" at the top of her lungs. Didn't help. When a crash sounded outside her window, she'd managed not to scream, but panic kept her wide awake.

The wind whistled and a new fear arose. Were there

tornados in Wyoming? Here she was stuck in a small camper—aka a tornado magnet. Gemma's house had a cellar. She'd be safe there. Should she make a run for it? But...what if there were electrical wires on the ground? What if she stepped outside onto a live line? Was it worth it to take a chance she might be electrocuted? As she debated, the door to the camper blew open.

She screamed. She screamed even louder when she saw the hulking, dark figure blocking the doorway. Blindly she reached on the counter for a weapon—hoping for a frying pan, a flyswatter, a can of nonstick cooking spray...anything.

"Macie? Where are you?"

She had to be hearing things. Why would he be here now?

The deep voice became louder. "Macie? It's me. Carter. Carter McKay."

"Carter?"

"Yeah. Where are you?" *Ooof* exploded from his lungs as she tackled him. She wrapped her arms around his neck and her legs clamped his waist like visegrips. She'd didn't care he was sopping wet; she didn't care that she immediately burst into tears.

"Hey, now. Ssh. It's okay. I'm here, darlin'. I've got you. Ssh. Take a deep breath." He slammed the door shut with his foot, and walked sideways through the galley-style kitchen. He cursed when his knee hit the edge of the mattress and they half-fell on the bed.

Macie clung to him.

Carter shifted her body. He settled her on his lap, not attempting to disentangle the death grip her limbs had on him. His hands stroked her back, soothing her. He rested his chin on her head.

Her breath stuttered. She buried her face in his solid warmth. After she'd regained some semblance of calm, she sighed.

"Better?" he murmured.

"A little."

"Pleased as I am to have you in my arms, can I ask why you're actin' so..."

Please, don't say childish.

"...skittish?"

Although thankful he wasn't making fun of her, she couldn't find the guts to answer.

"Macie?"

She wasn't surprised he kept prodding her. But it was his gentle tone that made her whisper, "Because I hate storms."

"I kinda guessed that."

Rain beat on the roof in the silence, mocking her fear.

"I've been terrified of them since I was a kid."

"Why?"

She didn't answer.

"It might help if you tell me what happened."

Macie suspected he wouldn't quit pestering her until she told him the truth. "When I was about four, I woke up in the middle of the night during a bad thunderstorm. We were living in a two-bedroom trailer in Texas. I went into my mom's room, only to find she wasn't there. So I crawled in her bed and waited for her. Scared out of my mind that someone had broken in and kidnapped her. I hid under a blanket, but I couldn't even cry because I thought maybe the bad guys would hear me and come back. The lightning was so close I remember the hair on my arms and the back of my neck standing straight up.

"Then a hailstorm blew through and hailstones the size of baseballs pounded the roof, and beat on the side of the trailer hard enough the bedroom windows broke. Glass covered the floor. Everything was soaking wet from the rain. I remember it was so dark and I was alone and I couldn't move. For hours. It seemed like I spent a solid lifetime in that bed. Whenever it storms it reminds me of being helpless and alone—"

"Ssh. Macie, darlin', I'm here. You're not alone now." Carter rocked her.

She released another shuddering sigh. "My mom never understood why I was afraid, so I've never told anyone else."

"I'm glad you told me."

"Yeah, well, it seems kind of embarrassing not to have outgrown that childhood fear."

"It seems perfectly justified to me. Besides, we all have fears we try to hide."

"Even you?"

He laughed softly. "Even me."

Macie lifted her head and peered in his eyes. "You know mine, it's only fair you tell me yours."

"Promise you won't laugh?"

She nodded.

Absentmindedly, he brushed the damp hair from her cheek. "See, I'm way worse off than you because I have two. The first one is, I'm petrified of dancin'."

"You're afraid of dancing?"

"Stupid, huh?"

"Why? Did you have a cowgirl spurn you at a junior high dance or something?"

"No. I'm afraid I'll look like a fool. It is a bone-deep fear that keeps me far, far away from weddin' dances and the dance floor in honky-tonks."

"You've never two-stepped?"

"Nope."

"Slow danced?"

"Nope."

"So, your high school prom?"

"Skipped it, but I went to the kegger afterward."

"Huh." She fingered the collar on his T-shirt. "No woman in your life has tried to teach you?"

"Not a lot of women in my life, Macie." He laughed softly. "Besides my mom. And to further emasculate myself, I have a fear of monkeys."

"Why?"

"I think it stems from *The Wizard of Oz* and those damn flyin' monkeys. My brothers found out my fear and used to torture me, tyin' me to a chair and replayin' those scenes with the flyin' monkeys over and over. Same goes for *Planet of the Apes*. Then when I was older I read a short story about a possessed toy monkey—you know the kind that you wind up and it plays the cymbals?—this monkey had the power to make people kill and go crazy." He shuddered. "Not cute and cuddly creatures. Hairy overgrown rats, that's what they are."

A crack of lightning flashed outside the window, followed by a booming crash of thunder. Macie jumped and hid her face against his chest.

"Easy."

A couple of beats passed as rain pounded on the roof.

"You okay?"

No. "I'm better than I was."

"Glad I'm good for something."

"I just don't understand why you're here. Or how you knew..."

"Gemma called me to tell me she wasn't gonna spook the new horses and drag them through the storm. She and Cash would be stayin' overnight in Spearfish. I figured that meant you were here alone. When the electricity went off, I thought I'd better check on you."

Gemma had called him? Not her dad? Rather than analyze that, she said, "Thanks."

"No problem. Plus, I wanted to apologize for not showin' up last night." His thumb swept the top of her ear, causing gooseflesh to break out on her neck. "Gemma said you probably needed time to settle in. I should've ignored her and listened to my gut and come here like I planned."

"I wondered what happened. I figured maybe it'd all been—"

"—a line? What I said to you at the rodeo grounds wasn't a line, Macie. I'll keep tellin' you that until you believe it." His mouth grazed her temple. "So, you wanna pack your stuff and come home with me?"

Macie didn't respond. Despite the fact Carter was being sweet and thoughtful, she didn't want to be away from everything familiar.

Right. Nothing about this situation was familiar. But it smacked of trouble to just let Carter swoop in and take care of her. She knew better than to rely on anyone besides herself.

"Macie?"

"Thanks, but I think I'd rather stay here."

"Is it because you're afraid of leavin' and goin' out into the storm?" He paused and leaned back to look at her. "Or just afraid of me?"

"Maybe a little of both."

Carter considered her for a moment. "Well, I didn't bring my toothbrush, so you'll have to share yours."

"You're staying here? Why?"

"And miss my chance to show off my cowboy manners by helpin' a little lady in distress?" Carter grinned. "Not on your life, darlin'."

"But. That doesn't mean I'm gonna—"

"I have nothin' else in mind for tonight, I swear."

Macie gave him a skeptical look.

"That doesn't mean things won't change in a heartbeat after you're not lookin' at me like a scared rabbit." He traced her cheek with the back of his hand. "Fear is the last thing I wanna see in these beautiful brown eyes when I take you the first time."

Not make love to her. *Take* her. Despite her lingering fear of the storm, his words sent a thrill through her.

"Although, I ain't chivalrous enough to sleep on the couch."

"If you didn't bring a toothbrush, I don't suppose you brought pajamas either?"

A slow smile lit his face. "I've never been overly fond of pajamas."

The thought of sleeping all night next to a naked Carter...Lord. You'd think she was bone-cold from the sheer amount of shivers racking her body.

Lightning spiked nearby, accompanied by a deafening crack of thunder. She gasped and threw herself against him again.

"Hey. It's okay."

After she quit shaking, he stood. "Maybe we should crawl in, pull the covers over our heads and try to forget about the storm." Carter peeled back the denim comforter and smoothed the rumpled sheet. "You first."

Macie heard rustling sounds as Carter stripped down to

nothing.

The camper shook from another gust of wind. The covers were lifted, the bed dipped and a hot, hard male pressed against her.

Carter swore under his breath. "Darlin', your skin is clammy and you're freezin'. Come here and let me warm you up."

"Carter—"

"Innocent warmin' this time, Macie, I promise." His hands drifted up and down her back, and he tucked her against his chest.

She relaxed and let him calm her. She began to block out the sounds of the storm and synchronized her breathing to his.

After awhile he murmured, "Better?"

"Mmm."

Carter kept his caresses light, but constant. Another few minutes passed and he said, "Can I ask you something?"

"Yeah, I guess."

"Does your dad know what happened to you when you were a kid? About your mom leavin' you alone and your fear of storms?"

"No."

"Why not?"

Yeah, why not? That same smarmy voice persisted.

She ignored it. "Because he wasn't around much."

"Yeah? How come?"

"My mom was older than my dad by ten years. When she found out she was pregnant, she thought he'd be a lousy parent, so she did the mature thing and took off. I saw him maybe once a year. Seems pointless to tell him about this now, especially when he never knew some of the other crazy things my mom did."

"Like?"

"She'd keep me out of school so I could experience 'life lessons' not math lessons. We lived all over the country. The year I turned twelve, Dad wanted me to spend summers on the reservation. My mom believed he'd take me on the rodeo circuit;

she refused to leave me with him. When I was old enough to contact him on my own, I did. Right after my eighteenth birthday, Mom was diagnosed with liver cancer. She died quickly, which was a blessing for her. Her death immediately thrust me into the adult world, but truth was, growing up I was more the adult than Mom ever was, so it wasn't really that big of a change for me."

Talk about spilling your guts, Macie. She stiffened, full of self-recrimination for baring all of her pitiful past, and braced herself for his pity or for more questions.

But Carter said, "That flat out sucks," and his arms gathered her close as he kissed the top of her head. "Get some sleep, sweet darlin'."

And for the first time in hours, she thought sleep was a possibility.

Carter wanted to punch something, namely Macie's clueless father. As Macie curled into him, he thought back to his own childhood. It hadn't been perfect, but it'd been damn near idyllic compared to hers.

He'd never been a pawn between his parents, never worried about waking up scared and alone. A large part of that was because he'd shared a room with Cam. And he had three other brothers down the hall.

Another bout of fury washed over him and he ground his teeth together. Jesus. Who was Cash Big Crow to warn him about staying away from Macie for her own good? It appeared Cash had stayed away from her plenty. It also appeared Cash didn't know squat about what was best for his daughter, or what she needed. Macie's combination of independence and neediness made perfect sense now.

Macie made a sexy, contented sound between a sigh and a moan, snuggling deeply against his chest. Carter held his breath and clenched his thighs together, trying—and failing—to fight off an erection.

This was so not the way he'd envisioned the first night with Macie in his arms. But he'd take what he could get. After another kiss on the top of her head, he closed his eyes and tried to sleep.

Chapter Eleven

A loud snort burst in Macie's ear, startling her. A hard male body spooned hers. Strong, male arms snaked around her waist. A steady stream of air drifted over her temple.

Where was she?

Her father's camper. Then she remembered the storm and Carter showing up.

She was in bed with Carter McKay. Oh man. She squirmed. The arms tightened. And something nestled firmly against her ass tightened too.

Macie's pulse spiked.

Carter groaned, but made no move to release her. Instead, his right hand swept her belly to span the area between her hipbones. Just the very tips of his work-roughened fingers stroked the skin where the top and bottom of her pjs left a gap.

The continual, sensuous, rhythmic touch heated her blood. Tingles raced over her flesh, from her neck to her thighs, sending a rush of moisture between her legs. A man's simple touch on her skin never caused this intense reaction.

She waited, expecting him to stir. Her mouth opened. Then closed. Did she really want to wake him? Did she really want him to stop touching her, whether it was conscious or not?

No.

His breathing didn't change even when his hand dipped beneath the stretchy waistband of her pajama bottoms. The tip of his long middle finger breached the curls on her mound, and slid right between her pussy lips.

And stopped.

Macie bit her tongue to keep from crying out. Before she chickened out, she widened her thighs slightly.

Immediately Carter's fingers slipped further down. Another soft groan rumbled from his throat as he found her wet. He rubbed his fingers through the juices gathering at her entrance and glided them back up.

At the first contact with her clit, she nearly shot straight up in bed.

He drew light circles, drawing out that elusive little nub of pleasure until she whimpered.

Then Carter's first two fingers slid back across her swollen sex and slipped inside her.

This time she couldn't help it; she gasped.

His husky voice whispered, "That's right, darlin', let me hear you." Carter scraped his teeth across the cord straining in the back of her neck. "Let me make you feel good."

As his fingers moved in and out of her, the base of his palm pressed her clit, creating the perfect amount of friction. Her eyes nearly rolled back in her head from the burst of pleasure. Still, she was afraid to speak, fearing if she did, he would stop. Or she'd wake up.

"Don't be shy. You want this." His fingers plunged deep. "I can't wait until it's my cock pushin' inside you. Hearin' my name as I make you come."

His words, coupled with his hot breath and kisses dampening her skin, made her pump her hips harder into his hand.

"Let go. Let it happen." Carter curled his fingers and stroked the magic spot on the inside of her pussy. The heel of his hand ground into her clit and the combination set her off.

Macie turned her head and opened her mouth to cry out, only to have Carter's lips covering hers in a soul-stealing kiss. The pulses throbbed; inside her sex, outside under his hand, in her blood, in her head, in her mouth. The spasms multiplied in intensity with every searing stroke of his velvety tongue across hers.

Then he slowed and sweetened their first kiss as her orgasm ebbed to a faint, but steady throb.

Carter removed his hand, allowing a leisurely caress up the trembling center of her body. His damp lips drifted to her ear. "Good mornin', darlin'."

She felt so pliant she couldn't find the strength to stretch her arms. She murmured, "That wasn't a dream this time, was it?"

"No." A soft kiss teased the nape of her neck. "What's 'this time' mean? You been dreamin' about me?"

"Will you get cocky if I say yes?"

He chuckled against her shoulder. "I'm already cocky." He shifted his pelvis. The unabashed male hardness caused her belly to clench with want. "In more ways than one."

Carter rolled Macie flat on her back. Leaving his bare leg draped over hers and their dark gazes locked, he brought his fingers—those long, clever fingers that had driven her over the edge—to his mouth and sucked them clean.

This time Macie's pussy clenched, not her belly.

"Mmm. My favorite breakfast. But one sweet taste of you leaves me cravin' more, Macie."

"Carter—"

He fastened his mouth to hers and his hot tongue swept inside to thoroughly share her taste.

She clutched his shoulders, yanking his full body weight onto hers. Macie jammed her hands through his hair and arched her hips against his erection.

The kiss grew desperate. Hungry.

Carter rocked his pelvis from side to side, rebuilding her sharp ache of desire. She raked her nails down his naked back, gripping the firm butt cheeks to do a little grinding of her own.

He broke the kiss on a soft, frustrated moan. "Macie." He whispered, "Touch me. I'm dyin' to feel your hand around me."

Macie said, "Yes." Just as she reached between them, three thunderous raps sounded on the camper door.

Carter went absolutely rigid above her.

"Macie?" was shouted outside the window.

"Shit. It's my dad." She tried to shove Carter aside, but he wouldn't budge. "Okay, don't panic. We'll pretend we were sleeping."

The lust cleared from his blue eyes. "Why? There was nothin' wrong with what we were doin', when we both wanted to do it. Besides, you are an adult and—"

"—and he's still my father. Catching us sleeping is a lot better than catching us dry humping, don't you think?"

"Good point." Carter jerked the covers over both of them and spooned against her.

"Macie? It's me. I'm comin' in." A gleaming ray of sun cut through the camper walls and disappeared into shadow as the door shut.

Bootsteps thumped as loud as her heart.

"Honey-girl? Sorry 'bout leavin' you alone last night. I tried callin' you..." Then, "Christ Almighty, what in the *hell* are you doin' in my daughter's bed, McKay?"

Macie and Carter both sat up. "Carter came to check on me last night during the storm because the electricity was off. I asked him to stay."

"Why?"

"I didn't want to be alone."

Cash frowned. "But—"

"That's all you need to know, Dad." She watched his braid swing as he automatically retreated a step. "Did you and Gemma run into any problems on your way back?"

"Yeah. Lots of trees are down. I think the electricity is still off, but I'll fire up the generator for the camper." He directed his glower to Carter. "Soon as you're decent I need your help in the barn." With that, he left.

Macie slumped back in bed as Carter used her toothbrush at the tiny bathroom sink. He didn't bother to glance in the mirror or comb his hair. She admitted the curls looked cute all mussed up from her fingers.

He faced her. "Duty calls."

"I heard."

"If I'm lucky he won't line up all the shitty jobs for me, after findin' me in your bed."

"Don't count on it."

He smiled. "So, when I'm done with chores today, will you come to my place?"

"To do what? Finish what we started before my dad interrupted?"

Carter lifted his eyebrows. "Don't pretend it was one-sided."

"I'm not."

"Good. But the main reason I want you to come over is because I need you to pose for me."

Not the answer she'd expected. "Seriously?"

Carter pulled on his jeans and she couldn't help but stare at his ripped abs. Damn. She'd been so close to letting her fingers do the walking down that yummy muscled torso and beyond.

"Seriously. I never kid when it comes to art."

Her gaze flew to his. He'd gone from playful to deadly serious. "I suppose. I'm not scheduled to work today anyway."

"Work here on the Bar 9? That could be fun. You and me—"

"I'm not working here on the ranch."

"Then where?"

Would a polite look of distaste cross his face when he discovered she was just a cook? "I took a job as a cook and a waitress at the Last Chance Diner."

Carter's eyebrows lifted again. "When did you do that?"

"The day we met at the rodeo. Dad and I stopped for supper and I saw the help wanted sign."

"Ah. So are you any good?"

"At what?"

His hot gaze lingered on her mouth before a mischievous smiled curled his lips. "At cookin' of course, what did you think I meant?"

"Can you blame me for being suspicious? Especially after all the innuendos dripping from your silver tongue?"

"Baby, those aren't innuendos, but the gospel truth. And I can't wait to show you all the tricks my silver tongue has in store for you." The tight black T-shirt went over his head, covering up his abs of steel. Dressed, he grinned and leaned over her. "I'll be back as quick as I can. Be ready."

He brushed his lips across hers and vanished out the door.

༖

Carter had to remind himself no matter what went on with Macie, Cash was still essentially his boss. Surprisingly enough, he and Cash worked well together—albeit in complete silence. They unloaded the new mares and helped Gemma pick up the debris from the storm.

The morning was muggy. The wisps of clouds didn't stifle the heat. Luckily the night's rainfall kept the dust to a minimum. With three of them working, it didn't take long to clean up the broken tree branches. By the time they finished, the electricity was back on.

After Gemma and Cash drove off to check cattle, Carter moved his truck from the ditch where he'd been forced to leave it during the storm. Before he climbed out, Macie emerged from the camper, twirling her car keys in her hand. It pleased him to think she'd been waiting for him.

He smiled and let his eyes roam over her. "Darlin', you look—" *good enough to eat* "—great."

Macie fussed with the straps on the long gauzy white dress. "Is this all right? I didn't know what to wear."

"It doesn't matter."

Her gaze snapped to his. "No nudes. If this is where you tell me I'm supposed to get naked—"

"No. I'll be workin' on portraits. Pen and ink or charcoal; I haven't decided which. I'll wait to see how the light is today." She'd look stunning in any light. As he studied the angles and lines of her beautiful face, that intriguing expression appeared again.

"What? You're staring at me."

"Get used to it, 'cause I'll be doin' it a lot." His comment seemed to make her more uncomfortable so he backtracked. "Doesn't look like you're ridin' with me."

"I'll follow you in my car, that way I can leave when I want."

He didn't like it, but he managed a bland, "Fair enough."

Carter's place was a couple of miles up the road—shorter on horseback. Driving the potholed gravel road on autopilot, he imagined Macie riding bareback, a beaded buckskin dress sliding up her slender thighs, her curtain of silky hair flowing behind her as she rode wild and free across the Wyoming prairie.

The image froze in his mind. It would work as a still life as well as a medium-sized sculpture. He'd need to capture the texture of the fringe and the beads, the smooth line of her leg, the flexing muscles of the racing horse and the proud set to her chin.

So intent was his brain on cataloging the minute details that he jumped when a loud knocking echoed next to his head. The fog lifted and he saw Macie frowning at him through the driver's side window. Carter glanced around. Whoa. He hadn't realized he'd stopped the pickup.

Carter offered her a guilty smile before he hopped out of the truck. "Sorry. I lose track of time when I get to thinkin'. Come on. The studio is in the barn."

Macie trailed after him without comment.

He gathered his supplies and attempted to create professional distance. "I want to take advantage of this light. So we'll start outside." He threaded the strap to his camera over his head and caught her staring at it.

"Are you going to take pictures of me?"

"Yeah."

"So once I'm done posing for them I can leave?"

"Technically...yes." His eyes searched hers. "But I want you to stay. Will you?"

After a moment she nodded.

"Good. Grab that stool." By the time he'd arranged her, gazing across the field comprised of red dirt, gray rocks and acres of sagebrush, he'd entered the zone where everything boiled down to light and shadow. Nothing existed but curves, lines, and angles used to fill the blank white space on his sketchpad.

Carter expected her nervous chatter. But she may as well have been a statue. She didn't speak. She scarcely moved. A couple of times while she'd been lost in thought he quietly snapped pictures. He'd managed a good outline when her soft sigh drifted to him on the wind.

Absentmindedly he asked, "Need something?"

"Yeah. To use the bathroom."

He glanced at the timer clipped to his bag and cursed. Three hours had passed. "Sorry. We can take a break."

Macie slid off the stool and ambled toward him. Automatically he closed his sketchbook—a move that wasn't lost on her.

She frowned. "I'm beyond a break, Carter. I'm tired. I think I'm gonna head back to the ranch."

"You can't."

She gave him a droll stare. "What do you mean I 'can't'?"

"I need you here. I'm behind on this portion of the show. I told you earlier I need you to stick around and you agreed to stay."

"Not indefinitely."

After witnessing her meltdown last night he knew it wouldn't take much to spook her, and he'd never been particularly even-tempered. "I'm just askin' for today."

"Yeah, but I didn't realize you meant *all* day."

"You should have." He stood. "Look. How about if you take a nap while I finish up some other things in the barn?"

"I suppose I'll be napping in your bed?"

"Would that be so bad?" He couldn't look at her as he waited for her response. It'd be just like him to screw this up from the get-go.

"Yes. No. I don't know. What am I doing here, Carter? Even you have to admit this whole situation is just plain...weird."

"I ain't gonna admit any such thing. This feels right. I can't explain it but on some level you must feel it too or you wouldn't be here." Vowing to keep it light and easy, he hefted the bag over his shoulder and gave her a cheeky grin. "Come on. I'll tuck you in. Maybe after your nap you won't be such a cranky pants."

"Was that a crack at my age, McKay?"

"If I promise you milk and cookies afterward will you stop

pouting?"

A frustrated noise left her throat. A swish of lace brushed his calf as Macie pushed past him.

He snagged her arm. "Hey. I was kiddin'."

"It wasn't funny. Do you know how many people look at me and then treat me like I'm twelve? I thought you were different."

"I am."

"Never mind. Let me go."

Carter felt the air whomp from his lungs. "I'm sorry. I was bein' an ass. It won't happen again."

"Forget it. Just let me go."

"No."

"Please."

"Please what?" Carter dropped his bag and crowded her against the trailer. "Please you? That I can do." She fought him until he cupped her face in his hands and kissed her.

Jesus. Her mouth was so warm and soft. Her opposition evaporated when his tongue breached her lips and slid inside. Lord almighty he loved the way she responded to him. He allowed the kiss to stay just a shade shy of demanding. He kept his hands on her head, rather than making a play for the breasts he'd been dying to touch.

Macie broke the kiss and his grasp. "Stop."

"Why?" he whispered against her lips.

"I won't have you blaming me because you didn't get any work done today." She ducked under his arm. "I'm sure I can find the bed on my own."

He watched as she scooted inside and slammed the door in his face.

Well, hell, she'd certainly put him in his place. Maybe he didn't have to treat his muse with kid gloves after all.

Chapter Twelve

"All accounted for," Gemma said.

"Were you worried?"

"Yeah. Some of the new mommas bolt with the herd during thunderstorms and leave their babies alone to fend for themselves. Usually I find at least one dead calf. Then I gotta listen to those mommas bawling in the pasture and calling for their baby. Never get used to that sad sound, so I'm glad not to be dealing with that today. Got plenty of other stuff going on."

Cash punched the clutch and shifted. "I'd planned on cuttin' hay this afternoon, but it'll be too wet. Not that I'm complainin' 'bout the moisture. It'll have to wait at least a couple of days."

"So what are you going to do?"

"Thought about workin' with that two-year-old. Is he halter broke?"

"Barely. Ornery thing runs whenever he sees me with a halter. And I've been so busy this year I haven't had time to work with him." She expected him to wince. Not training a horse was as bad as not taking proper care of one.

"I'd sure like to take a crack at him."

"By all means."

Cash stopped the pickup and Gemma hopped out to open and close the gate. He parked in front of the house and sauntered back to where she waited by the water pump for the bucket to fill.

"What are you doin' today?" he asked.

"Thought I'd clean the horse trailer. Why? Did you need me

for something else?" She hoped he'd say yes, that he needed her naked. Right now.

"Nah. I'm gonna round up that roan." He unlatched the door to the horse trailer, which housed the saddles, blankets, halters, bridles and other horse paraphernalia. Whistling, he unhooked a blue nylon halter and draped it over his shoulder. "See you in a bit."

Hiding her disappointment, Gemma focused on sweeping and scrubbing. But while she was cleaning, she couldn't help but obsess on what had happened last night.

Or rather, what hadn't happened.

Cash had been quiet on the drive to Beulah. They'd left right after he'd talked to Macie, and Gemma didn't know if that was the reason for his introspective mood. She didn't push, figuring if he wanted to talk to her about it he would.

Once they'd arrived at the Nelson ranch to look at the bucking horses, Cash stepped up and handled every bit of the financial negotiations. The crusty old rancher even dropped his price by a couple of hundred bucks. Gemma knew she wouldn't have had the same results if she'd come alone.

As Gemma was writing out the check, the man's wife came outside to warn them severe thunderstorms were headed their way. Several areas in Wyoming were already without power due to windstorms, and state Highway 23 was temporarily closed because of excessive hail.

Since the horses were essentially wild, they decided to wait out the storm and leave them in the pasture and come back in the morning. They hadn't planned to stay overnight and Gemma hadn't packed any household supplies in the living quarters of the horse trailer.

On the drive to Spearfish to find a motel, Cash tried to call Macie several times but got no answer. Gemma snuck in a call to Carter and explained the situation while Cash checked them into the room.

After a nearly silent dinner, they returned to the motel. Gemma's hopes sunk a little when she noticed two double beds. It didn't help matters Cash was glued to The Weather Channel. And Gemma knew better than to tell him not to worry about his daughter. Telling him she'd asked Carter to check on Macie would set him off big time.

Frustrated, Gemma flopped on the opposite bed. She woke up the next morning fully clothed.

When Cash didn't offer up an explanation on why he hadn't touched her, the paranoid part of her psyche supplied reasons.

Regret.

Disappointment.

Disgust.

The situation between them didn't improve after they'd loaded the horses and were on the road. Once again, Cash insisted on driving, leaving Gemma lost in thoughts she didn't want.

Finding Macie all right—albeit with Carter in her bed—seemed to alleviate some of the tension between them. Cash almost seemed normal while they were checking cows.

But what was normal with him? What was normal with them?

Forget it. He's doing what you hired him to do.

Gemma managed to block the past twenty-four hours from her brain. By the time she finished cleaning up, her shirt and boots were sopping wet and her jeans were damp. She needed a shower in a bad way. She dragged the bucket and brooms to the barn. Nothing happened when she tugged on the string to the light bulb. Probably the fuse blew in last night's storm.

The outer door opened and a sliver of light briefly permeated the darkness like a flash bulb.

"Gemma?" Cash called. "Where are you?"

"By the tack room. None of the lights seem to be working."

She didn't hear him come up behind her so she jumped when he placed his hands on her shoulders.

"You scared me."

Cash didn't answer. He didn't move either.

"What?"

"Your shirt is wet."

"Yeah, I know. Don't stand too close. I probably smell bad."

"You smell good to me." He inhaled deeply. "Really good."

"Anything is bound to smell good when you've been in the pen and around wild horses for a few hours."

"Your shirt is wet."

"We already established that."

His warm breath ruffled the hair by her ear. "Take it off."

"What?"

"You heard me. Take off your shirt. Now."

"But—"

"Don't argue with me. I think I'd enjoy punishin' you too much today."

Her fingers froze around his when they breached the first snap. "You wouldn't."

"I would. Without apology and you'll take what I dish out without complaint."

"Cash—"

"Gemma." His voice was a low-pitched growl. "I ain't jokin'. Do what I tell you."

She tried a different tack. "Wouldn't you rather go inside?"

"No. Take. Off. The. Damn. Shirt. Now."

A kernel of excitement unfurled from the tips of her boots to the end of her ponytail.

Pop pop pop pop went the pearl snaps and the shirt hung open. She slipped it off her shoulders and Cash took it.

"Now the bra."

The front clasp popped and the bra hit the dirt.

"Unfasten your jeans."

Gemma tugged on the button on her Wranglers. The release of the zipper tine by tine sounded incredibly erotic in the heated stillness. "Now what?"

"Pull them down to your knees. Panties too."

She shimmied the denim to the tops of her boots.

"Turn around."

Soon as she faced him his hands were on her breasts and his teeth closed over her left nipple. Her breath caught at the sensation of his hot mouth on her cool skin. Then he nipped the very tip as he kissed a path to her right breast. No sweet nuzzling; Cash suckled hard and deep. He lifted the globes together, and growled against her flesh as his hungry mouth moved back and forth. Licking. Biting. Sucking.

She almost came from the sexy feel of his tongue rasping over her nipples. Giving every inch the attention she craved until she was dizzy and wet with want.

Cash placed hot kisses up her throat. "Touch yourself."

Flustered, she stuttered, "What do you mean?"

"You've gotten yourself off when you haven't had a man to do it." His tongue slicked across her bottom lip. "Show me how you make yourself come."

"Um. It's too dark. You can't see."

"Don't matter. I got a great imagination. I hear you breathin' fast. I feel your heart poundin' against my mouth. I smell that sweet cream. I know you want to get off, Gemma doll. Show me how your pretty pussy responds to your touch."

Cash rubbed his stubbled cheek along her jaw. "While you finger yourself, I'll suck these tits deep and hard. I know I can make you moan, but wanna see if I can make you scream."

She had difficulty swallowing and she knew he heard it. "And if I'm feeling shy?"

"You aren't. You want to prove your wild side. Knowin' you're touchin' yourself will drive me insane. It excites you to drive me crazy with lust without even touchin' me."

He plucked her hand off his shoulder. Kissing her first two fingers delicately, he sucked them into his hot mouth.

A flash of heat speared between her legs.

Cash ran his tongue between the digits, getting them good and wet before he released them. "Show me." He covered her hand with his, placing it between her shaking legs.

Gemma felt her wetness ease the way as four fingers pushed inside her. Her head fell back against the stalls as he helped move their joined hands in and out of her pussy.

"Like that?"

"Usually I just..."

"Just what?" he demanded.

"I go straight for my clit."

"Why?"

"It's the fastest way to get me off."

He chuckled. "Greedy wench. Show me more. Show me everything." Cash bent his head and worked her nipples.

She thrust the fingers into her pussy twice before sliding them up to her mound. She centered the pad of her middle finger right over her clit and she rubbed. Not ever-widening circles. Not side to side. No teasing. Just up and down, directly over that needy nub. A moan escaped when she realized the added weight of his finger intensified the pressure.

Cash blew a stream of air across her wet nipples. "Faster?"

"Not yet." She thrust their joined fingers back inside her core, secretly loving the way he made her lead. Made her teach him what she liked.

She liked it all. If his labored breathing and the way his pelvis bumped her hip was any indication, he liked it all too.

Her middle finger returned to the aching spot. "Faster would be good now."

"Show me."

She kept the strokes short and fast. So close. She was so damn close. The pressure built and she lost her mind when Cash sucked her nipple in perfect timing to the pulsating in her clit.

"Oh shit that feels so..." An intense rush of pleasure overwhelmed her senses. The scent of his hot skin. The complete darkness. The sharp nip of his teeth. The wet lash of his tongue on the swell of her breast. The throbbing in her sex. The sensations were too potent, too raw. Almost there...

He knocked her hand away. Then his mouth was on hers and she heard a metallic clank as he unbuckled his belt, followed by the sound of his jeans sliding down his flanks.

Blindly she reached for the hardest part of him, but his fingers circled her wrist.

He ripped his mouth free. "Don't."

"But, why—"

"Because I'm about two seconds away from coming. And I don't want to come in your hand." He put his mouth on the pulse pounding in her throat. "Although, I want to fuck every part of you. Your hand. Your mouth. Your tits. Your ass. Say you'll let me do whatever I want." He hissed against her ear. "Say it and I'll let you come."

"Yes, whatever you want."

"Right now I'll take this warm, tight pussy since it is wet and ready for me. Turn, bend over and grab the slats."

Gemma thought she couldn't get hotter. But his hot words and hot breath and the wicked hot things he planned to do to her blanked her mind to everything but sexual greed. She spun around and curled her fingers through the space separating the wooden boards of the stalls.

His boots nudged the inside of hers. "Wider."

She kicked her heels out as far as they would go with her jeans stuck around the middle of her calves.

He nuzzled the back of her head. "You trust me, sweets?"

"Yes."

"You'll let me do whatever I want to you, right?"

Her stomach swooped—excitement laced with fear. "As long as it feels good."

"It'll feel good." He sank his teeth into the nape of her neck and gooseflesh broke out across her back. "But maybe not at first."

Before she could demand specifics, Cash's big, rough hand smoothed down her spine and over her butt. He slapped her ass. Hard. Twice.

She gasped.

He did it again on the other side. *Smack smack.*

"Cash!"

"Hush."

Four more sharp smacks landed on each one of her butt cheeks. The sting morphed into a burning sensation that wasn't unpleasant...just a hot reminder of who was in charge.

"Cash?"

"I love it when you say my name," he growled.

"Why are you—"

"Because you like it." *Whack whack whack whack.* "You like it because you've never had that bite of pain and you've

98

always wondered what it'd be like, didn't you?" *Whack whack whack whack.*

"I-I—oh God. Don't—"

"Don't lie to me. You are drippin' wet, *winyan.*" He inhaled. "I can smell it." He spanked the same spot three times. And repeated on her left side. "You need a reminder that I ain't a gentleman, Gemma."

How had he known she craved a taste of kink? She moaned loudly when two hard slaps close to her anus made it clench.

"Do you want me to stop?" he asked, peppering her butt with little swats.

Her skin tingled and burned. She cried out even as her pussy wept for more. "No." The cheeks on her face and on her backside were inflamed.

He spanked her until every inch of her butt bore the mark of his hand.

His harsh breathing reverberated in the humid space as a lover's whisper. She felt his fingers circling her opening, spreading her wide for him, and finally the hot blunt tip of his cock was poised at her entrance.

Gemma held her breath for that first hard, deep thrust.

She wasn't expecting the icy cold water he dumped over her burning ass. She screamed.

And Cash slammed into her cunt to the hilt and began to ride her. His fingertips curved into her waist as he kept her in place to take his thrusts.

Water dripped down the outside of her thighs. Her juices coated the inside of her thighs. Her butt cheeks were on fire, yet chilled. She couldn't see him. She could scarcely suck air into her lungs that wasn't filled with his scent.

But she could feel him. Lord. There wasn't a single part of her body that wasn't intensely aware of every inch of him.

"Touch yourself." His voice was little more than a hoarse rasp. "Come when I'm inside you. Take me there."

Although he was fucking her hard and she needed both hands for balance, she managed to reach between her legs long enough to coax another orgasm from her swollen clit, feeling her internal muscles clamp down on his cock.

He plunged into her three more times and stopped, letting loose a guttural groan as semen burst forth in hot spurts. She actually felt his heat. Her inner walls pulsed, keeping that supreme male hardness buried deep inside her.

After the sexual haze cleared from her mind, his legs twitched behind hers. Then his hot tongue zigzagged up her spine causing her to shiver anew.

"See? I think you smell good. You taste good too. Sorta like my own personal salt lick, eh?"

Gemma was too stunned to speak.

"You okay?"

"Mmm-hmm."

Cash pulled out and swore. "Shit. I forgot a condom."

"I doubt I can get pregnant at my ripe old age." She pushed herself off the stall into an upright position. "You know I haven't been with anyone since Steve. I sort of missed the whole AIDS scare. What about you?"

He laughed softly. "Last time I had sex without a condom was the summer Macie was conceived. That's why I ain't got any more kids, a case of the clap, or anything else."

"Good to know."

Cash spun her and tugged her into his arms for a sweet, intense, exhaustive kiss.

"What was that for?" she murmured against his chest.

"For lettin' me be bold and bawdy. For bein' the hottest, sexiest *winyan* I've ever put my hands on. You drive me wild, Gemma Jansen. There's a million things that need to be done around here and the only thing I can think about is doin' you. Over and over."

"You sweet talker." Gemma kissed his Adam's apple. "I'm starved. Let's go inside and get cleaned up before we eat. Where are my clothes?"

"Who cares? I prefer you half-naked. Or all naked."

"Well, no matter what you prefer, I ain't struttin' across the yard wearing nothin' but my pants around my boots and a big-ass smile."

"At least you ain't cryin' this time."

Gemma froze. "What?"

"Don't try to pretend it didn't happen. I heard you that first night. Up in your room."

"You did?"

"Yeah. Even though part of me understands why you were bawlin', another part of me felt like you kicked me in the balls."

"It wasn't about you."

"I know. Don't mean that it changes the way it made me feel." He kissed her forehead and draped her shirt and bra around her neck. "Get dressed. I'll meet you up at the house." And he was gone.

Cash was wrong. Gemma felt like crying all over again.

Chapter Thirteen

Macie woke up and didn't know where she was.

Seemed like that had happened to her a lot lately. Right. She was such a wild child.

She sat up and looked around. Ah. She was in Carter's trailer.

But where was Carter?

Out in that run-down barn he called a studio? She called out, "Carter?"

No answer.

As she stood and stretched, she squinted at the clock. Five thirty? She'd slept for three hours? Dammit. Why hadn't Carter woken her up?

Macie remade the bed and noticed nothing else was out of place. No dirty clothes scattered across the carpet. No dog-eared skin magazines stacked on the nightstand. The ceiling fan was even dust-free.

Talk about being a neat freak.

She made a pit stop in the bathroom and wandered into the living area. Not the bachelor pad she expected with leather couches, a big screen TV and neon beer signs. He'd shoved an ugly green and orange plaid sofa beneath the windows. A brown corduroy recliner sporting several silver patches of duct tape was kitty-corner to the door. The pressed wood coffee table didn't host a pile of remote controls. Or an empty beer can. Or a discarded newspaper. No personal objects covered the scarred surface.

The temporary feel to the place made her sad. Mostly

because it reminded her of every place she'd ever lived.

As she walked to the kitchen she realized the trailer wasn't completely devoid of decoration; an entire wall was devoted to pictures. Family pictures.

In the largest one, eight smiling faces stared back at her. The infamous McKay family. Five men, one girl and a couple who didn't look old enough to have so many kids. By looking at younger Carter, she realized the picture was several years old. She scrutinized each person. All of the men were tall, with broad chests and shoulders. Three of the sons resembled their father: dark brown hair, rugged features and indigo eyes. Carter and another brother looked more like their mother: curly, lighter hair made up of every shade from red to blond, eyes as blue as the Wyoming sky, and their bone structure ran more to chiseled than rugged. The only girl inherited the best from each of her parents: her father's dark hair and eyes and her mother's angular face and blindingly beautiful smile.

Macie inched closer to scrutinize the dozens of snapshots. A picture of a young Carter and his dad dressed in camouflage, sitting next to a dead buck. A photo of one brother on the back of an enormous bucking bull. Another pic of a man in Army fatigues, squinting into the desert sun. A studio picture of his sister in a formal pink ball gown. A McKay man holding a baby and grinning proudly at the camera. A shot of a two-year-old boy standing beside a Christmas tree wearing brand new cowboy boots and a diaper. A dark-haired brother waving from the seat of a John Deere tractor with jagged mountain peaks towering in the background. Carter wearing a cap and gown sandwiched between his parents. A photo of all five McKay sons mounted on horses.

There were more. The McKays fishing. The McKays hunting. The McKays working in the garden, the fields, the barn. The McKays kicking up their bootheels at a pig roast. The McKays gathered around a table piled high with food—laughing, smiling, happy. Normal pictures of a normal family with fond memories.

Something like jealousy twisted in Macie's gut. She didn't have any pictures like that. She had a few happy memories from her childhood, but no documentation.

What would it be like to have that connection? To people?

To a single place? To have a history?

Someone like Carter would never understand that even as she craved that kind of bond, the idea of permanence scared her to death.

As she studied the second row of pictures, her face burned like she'd peeked into a forbidden window to the subject's soul. She knew without a doubt Carter had snapped these photos.

The first one was a close-up of his parents. His mother's hand rested on his father's weathered cheek. An intense love was apparent on their faces and they seemed unaware of anything but each other.

The second photo was of a dark-haired brother, wearing the duds of a rodeo cowboy. He hung on a metal fence watching the action in the arena, a far-away look in his eyes. The next one was of the man with the baby, except he was alone, exhaustion lining his face as he threw a hay bale from the bed of a beat-up truck, oblivious to the beautiful pearly orange glow of the sunset behind him. The black and white picture of his sister showed her grinning in pigtail braids, not yet woman, not quite girl, innocence and deviltry mixed with an innate sensuality. The last snapshot was of the brother who was probably the source of the bad McKay reputation, given he had a gorgeous blonde stripper perched on each knee, a big cigar clamped between his teeth and a bottle of Jack Daniels in his hand.

No other pictures of the soldier. No intimate glimpses into Carter either. She wondered if any members of his family had such introspective pictures of him? Or did he hide behind his art? Use the camera and his sketch pad as a shield? Was there a deeper reason for the distance she glimpsed in him when others were around?

So what would the pictures he'd taken of her reveal? Would her face, her heart, her soul, be an open book?

Did he intend to showcase her frailties and failings as part of his art? What would she do if he did? Although Carter claimed to know her, how much did she really know of him? She shoved the paranoid thoughts in the back of her mind.

Macie exited the trailer. The air was muggy and humid, heavy with the promise of rain. A light mist created banks of fog, hiding the beautiful landscape and the enormous sky. She'd forgotten her shoes, so she picked her way to the barn across the pea-sized gravel, one barefooted step at a time. She stopped when she saw the barn door was ajar and she heard a strange noise from inside.

Déjà vu.

Or a repeat of the sexy dream she'd had of a trio of hot cowboys?

Dammit. The blurry line between reality and fantasy was making her nuts. To ensure she was fully awake, she pinched the inside of her forearm. Hard.

Damn that hurt. But at least she knew she wasn't dreaming. Macie took a deep breath and quietly slipped inside.

Artificial light shone in the main room from a large metal cone-shaped fixture. Soft, twangy music drifted from an unseen boom box. An explosion of art supplies—jars, paints, brushes, jumbo rolls of paper, machinery, long pieces of wood, sticks— covered every available flat surface. Carter might keep his living area immaculate, but his workspace resembled a pigsty. The irony wasn't lost on her, as the man had set up shop in a barn.

She allowed her gaze to focus on him. Good God. The man was nearly naked. A ratty cowboy hat on his head was about the extent of his attire. He'd changed out of jeans and wore a stained pair of sweatpants hacked off above the knee. Few men looked better out of clothes than in them, and Carter McKay was one of those lucky men.

Lucky her. She swallowed the puddle of drool forming in her mouth.

Carter hadn't noticed her. He was working an enormous chunk of greenish clay, adding smaller blobs. She couldn't see his face, but she could hear him singing along with the radio. She smiled. Who would've thought he could carry a tune? Keith Urban had nothing to worry about, but Velma might have a new contender for the open mic contest next Friday night.

Macie was strangely content just to watch Carter, fascinated by his controlled body movements. The muscles in his shoulders bunched as he lifted his arms. As he pushed and pulled the clay, corded muscles popped up on his forearms. A thin line of sweat trickled down his spine and disappeared into his low-slung sweatpants. She wished she could see his hands. Those long, clever fingers smoothing and shaping, plunging deep.

Outside the mist morphed into a steady, soft rainfall. The clean scent of rain wafted through the open door, but did nothing to cool her off. Seemed nothing could make her take her eyes off him, either.

She'd thought Carter was sexy when they'd first met, but it was nothing compared to the way she felt when she looked at him now. Despite his overwhelming intensity, he was sweet and thoughtful and had a body made for pure sin. She wanted him. Wanted his clay-covered hands on her. Molding her breasts. Leaving a muddy trail down her belly. Leaving moon-shaped clay marks from his fingernails digging into her hips. Seeing his big handprints on the inside of her thighs.

Tasting clay and passion on his lips. Scraping her nails down his sweat-coated back. Clutching his ass. Watching lust fire in his eyes as he took everything she offered him.

Right then she knew she wouldn't deny him a damn thing.

Thunder cracked outside.

Macie gasped at the intrusion of reality into her little fantasy world.

Carter spun to glare at her. "Jesus, Macie, what are you doin' in here?"

"I-I woke up a little while ago—"

"And you just snuck in to spy on me in my private studio?"

His angry look doused her steamy thoughts. "No!"

"Then what the hell—" He paced toward her, then back. "Fuck." Angrily he wiped his hands on a towel. "Never mind. My own damn fault. Shoulda put a lock on that goddamn door."

"I-I'm sorry. I'll go."

The gentle rain changed to a torrential downpour. More thunder boomed. The wind howled and the door smacked shut.

"No. That's okay. Hang on. Just let me—"

The last thing she saw before she fled was Carter flinging a sheet over the globs of clay and mysterious shape on the table.

Macie couldn't blame the way she trembled solely on the change in the weather. The change in Carter had a lot to do with it.

Stupid girl. Stupid to hope he'd be different. When would she learn nothing ever changed for her when it came to her relationships with men?

Water splashed up to her ankles, as she couldn't avoid mud puddles. Had she left her keys in her car?

He'd glared at her like a disobedient child.

A sharp rock tore at the skin on the bottom of her foot and she stumbled. She righted herself and kept limping along in the downpour. Why in the hell had she parked so far away?

Maybe it was a cosmic sign she should drive far away and never look back. Good plan.

"Macie!"

Don't look back. He'll convince you to stay—only temporarily—and you need to keep running.

She'd counted to ten when a hand landed on her shoulder and jerked her to a stop.

A BOOM of thunder nearly burst her eardrums.

She screamed.

Strong male arms wrapped her against a warm bare chest. "Hey. It's okay. I've got you."

"No! Let me go." Being wet and mad made it easy for her to slither out of his grasp. Her hair hung in her eyes, obscuring her vision, her dress was sopping wet and stuck to her calves like plastic wrap.

Still, Macie ran.

Until two steel bands immobilized her completely. She'd only taken three steps that time.

"Macie. Calm down."

She thrashed and shrieked.

He put his mouth directly on her ear. "It's me. Carter."

"I know who you are, dumbass, why do you think I'm trying to get away?"

Carter spun her to face him, keeping his hands gripping her upper arms. "What is wrong with you?"

"You won't let me go. You're keeping me here against my will. I just want to go home."

The clouds rumbled and she went absolutely still.

Silence.

"You're soakin' wet, scared out of your mind and in no shape to drive."

"I have to get out of here."

"No, you don't. You need to take a deep breath and calm down."

"Don't tell me what to do!"

The threat of thunder gave way to another loud boom and before the noise quit, Macie screamed again.

Carter cupped her face in his hands. "Look at me. Jesus, Macie, you're scarin' me."

"And you're pissing me off. Let. Me. Go!" She knocked his hands away, dodged sideways and ran.

This time she made it about ten steps when she heard— *Riiiippppp.* Carter had caught her by the back of her dress.

She whirled around, leading with her fists, losing her footing as she yelled, "You bastard."

He lunged for her as she slipped in the mud and they both fell to the soggy earth.

She scrambled to her hands and knees and tried to crawl away from him.

He snagged her ankle, rolled her on her back and pinned her to the ground.

Macie thrashed and bucked like a penned wild animal. She was scared by the storm, mad at Carter for treating her as callously as every other man in her life, but mostly mad at herself for acting like a child in the face of a thunderstorm. Again. Breathing hard, she closed her eyes and managed not to scream at another deafening roar of thunder.

Carter locked her wrists in one of his hands and pressed them above her head, while his hard body trapped hers.

"Look at me."

She shook her head.

"Please. Macie. Let me help you."

"It'll help me if you let me go."

"No."

"You can't do this to me. First you snap—"

"I'm sorry I yelled at you."

She squirmed.

"And now seein' you so upset, knowin' it's my fault. It's killin' me. Please. Let me make it right."

"You can't."

"Let me try."

Macie didn't move.

When he eased up, she finally looked in those blue, blue eyes. She lost her will to fight when she witnessed the misery on his face.

"I'm an asshole sometimes."

She nodded.

"But I'd never do anything to intentionally hurt you. You have to know I ain't that kinda man."

"What kind of man are you, Carter?"

"A sorry son of a bitch right about now."

Rain fell as they studied each other.

"I wasn't spying on you."

"On some level I know that. But I'm so used to keepin' people away from my work until it's finished. I force everyone away from me when I'm workin' because I'm not always nice. When I saw you standin' there, starin' at my piece of shit work in progress... But it ain't your fault. Sorry I lashed out at you."

"I wasn't staring at what you were working on, I was staring at you." Crap. That hadn't come out right. "What I meant was—"

"I see in your eyes exactly what you meant."

The gray clouds above them clashed like cymbals. Before she had a chance to scream, Carter slanted his mouth over hers and kissed her.

And kissed her.

And kissed her some more, until he'd thoroughly scrambled her brain to anything beyond the way he tasted and the sexy sounds he made as his mouth dominated hers.

"Macie," he mumbled against her damp cheek. "God, Macie. Let me have you. All of you." He released her wrists and levered himself over her, trailing his lips down her throat. When he reached her chest, he yanked the stretchy bodice of her dress aside and his warm mouth engulfed her breast.

"Oh. Man. No fair," she whispered.

Carter rolled to his side, taking her with him. Mud splattered his face. He flicked his tongue over the tip of her nipple while his other hand kneaded her left breast. "Goddamn you're perfect. Just like I knew you'd be." His gaze hooked hers. He vigorously sucked her left nipple through the wet fabric until she couldn't lie still but wiggled like a worm.

"Carter—"

"I want you like this. Right now. Wet. Raw. Dirty."

"Yes. Oh. Yes."

He returned to her mouth, kissing her stupid. She felt him sliding her sodden, mud-caked dress up her trembling thighs. When it was bunched around her waist, he knelt between her legs. He pulled aside her thong and fingered her where she was slick.

"Lift up." He tapped her butt. In the split second she raised her hips, he grabbed her thighs to slide her closer to his torso and draped her knees over his shoulders.

Carter raised her ass high in his hands at an angle as he buried his face in her pussy.

"Omigod." The only parts of her still touching the ground were her shoulder blades and the back of her head.

"Hold still. Jesus, let me have more than a taste before I drop you." He licked up her slit. Alternating the flat of his tongue with just the flickering tip. Then he fastened his mouth to her clit and began to suck. When her whole body shook, he slapped her ass and growled, "Hold still, goddammit. I've been dyin' to get my mouth on you."

"But your mouth is so hot."

"Macie—"

"And I'm already so close."

"I know. Next time I'll make you wait. I might even tie you up and make you beg. Lord, you are so warm and sweet..." He suckled her pussy lips and scraped his teeth over her clit.

She gasped. "Oh. You're good at that."

He grunted but didn't stop licking. Sucking. Driving her to

the brink of insanity.

Rain poured down on them. She'd probably feel cold if her body wasn't on fire. Heck, she was so hot her clothes were steaming.

The sky rumbled a warning.

For the first time in several minutes Macie realized they were out in the open in the thick of a thunder and rainstorm.

Carter sensed the moment she froze up. "Look at me, not the sky. Think about how crazy it's makin' me to taste you. Think about how hard I'm gonna fuck you right after you come all over my face. It's right there, darlin', take it." He did some different nibbling thing on her clit that made her hips buck like she was riding a wild bronc.

He didn't move his mouth when he growled at her, and the buzzing sensation of his lips on her clit set her off.

"Oh. Like that. Don't stop. Please. Yes!" She screamed as the orgasm hit, as thunder exploded above her, reverberated inside her and she felt as if a thousand bolts of lightning struck her body.

Carter didn't remove his lips or his tongue or his hands from her throbbing sex until she twitched one last time. Her legs became boneless and slipped from his shoulders.

Hot, open-mouthed kisses seared the cool skin on her thighs, rousing her. Making her arch into his body and he kissed his way to her throat.

"Macie."

"Please, Carter. More. All. Give me all of you."

His breath tickled her ear. "Shit. I don't have a condom—"

"Where are they?"

"Inside."

Macie rolled and stood. She grabbed his hand and tugged until he was on his feet. "Hurry. What the hell are you waiting for?"

Chapter Fourteen

Carter stared at Macie, his eyes eating up the frantic, sexy look on her face as the little spitfire attempted to drag all two hundred pounds of him through the mud.

So she could fuck him.

Senseless.

Mindless.

Too late.

She'd already blown his mind.

He grinned, hefted Macie over his shoulder amidst her surprised shrieks and raced to the trailer, his bare feet skidding through the muck.

Once he had the door open, he set her down and clamped his mouth over hers. Ripping off the tattered, muddy remains of her flimsy cotton dress, he pushed her back toward his bed.

Then she was naked. She untied the drawstring on his sweatpants and then he was naked. He groaned and filled his hands with her tits. Her ass. Her hips. He pulled her hair back so he could ravage her throat without obstruction.

"Condom," she said hoarsely.

Carter bit her shoulder, then followed a wayward rivulet of water between her breasts with his tongue.

"Carter."

"Yeah? Damn, you taste good everywhere."

"We need a condom."

His fingertip traced the upper swell of her breast, as he watched, transfixed by the color of her skin tone. "You're so pretty here. Delicate, but sexy. I don't know if I'm talented enough that will come through."

"Are the condoms in the bathroom?"

"No." His dick stayed stuck against his belly and he grunted with pain as he bent forward and placed his mouth against the hollow of her throat. "I want to kiss every spot where I can see your pulse poundin'. I know where my favorite spot to feel throbbin' against my tongue is."

Macie grabbed his hair and yanked his head back to meet the fire flashing in her eyes. "Find. A. Condom. Right. Now."

Carter rubbed his cheek over her mouth to hide his laugh. He kissed her. Very softly. Very sweetly. He kissed her mostly to hear her frustrated groan rumbling over his lips because she wanted more.

Without warning, he intensified the kiss, heating her up so she squirmed and rubbed her mound over his thigh. He sucked on her tongue, then sank his teeth into her full bottom lip. When she gasped at the hint of pain, he licked the warm, wet cavern of her mouth like he'd licked her pussy. Grinding his cock into the cradle of her thighs, he reached for the unopened box of condoms on the dresser and tore the plastic packaging off with shaking fingers.

She broke away to drag kisses down his chest. "You have the most lickable pecs and abs and you haven't let me touch you."

"Do whatever you want. You don't even hafta ask."

He hissed when the very tip of her tongue lapped circles around his nipple. His cock jerked, reminding him of the box he was crushing in his hand. Damn factories, over-packaging everything. He used his teeth to rip the seal on the cardboard box and had extracted a single foil-wrapped condom, when a hot, wet, hungry mouth enclosed his dick.

"Christ, Macie, give me a heart attack why doncha?"

"Do you want me—" she sucked him deep and didn't release him until he yelped, "—to stop?"

"No. Yes. Jesus, woman, wait!" Carter lifted her off her knees and gently tossed her on the bed.

He already had the condom on as he settled between her legs. He spread her thighs wide to watch the alignment of his cock and he slammed to the root on the first push.

She bowed and gasped his name.

Carter closed his eyes briefly to savor being buried in his sweet, sexy, fierce Macie. His body urged him on—hell, he wanted to fuck her raw. But they'd only have one first time, and he wouldn't blow it for either of them because of sexual greed—hers or his.

"Carter?"

He let his body shadow hers as he looked into her eyes.

"Is everything okay? You stopped."

"It's perfect. You're beautiful." He brushed his lips across her mouth. "You're my beautiful, perfect muse."

"Please. I don't need sweet—"

"Oh, it ain't gonna be sweet. Give me your hands."

Macie smoothed her palms down his arms to his wrists. He threaded their fingers together and slid their joined hands up above her head.

Her breath caught as she bore his full weight and he pressed her deeper into the mattress.

Carter kissed her, grinding his pelvis side to side over her clit, feeling cocky about the way her pussy muscles clenched to keep his hardened sex inside her. Then he released her hands and curled her fingers around the metal bars on the headboard.

He whispered, "Hang on, darlin'," and pulled completely out and plunged back in to the hilt.

Carter fucked her hard. Too hard to kiss her. Too hard for this turbulent mating to last very long.

But she didn't seem to mind. Her sexy whimpering moans filled his ears. He told her how good she felt. Wet. Tight. How many different ways he planned to fuck her. He'd never been good at dirty talk in bed but it drove her crazy.

She arched off the bed, clamped her hands on his ass and cried out as she came again. Sending him right along behind her.

He pumped harder. Deeper. He wanted to rip off the condom and feel her slick walls bathed in his come. He wanted to watch his seed dripping down her leg, knowing he'd put it there.

He'd never felt so...possessive.

Carter groaned when the pulsing in his cock didn't stop. It'd been a long time since he'd had sex, but no sex had ever been like this.

He came so goddamn hard he swore a blood vessel burst in his brain. He came so goddamn hard he swore he actually came twice. He collapsed on her. Not lightly either.

Macie sighed.

Neither one made an attempt to move and break their connection.

Thunder cracked outside the trailer and Macie didn't freeze up.

He smiled against her temple. Looks like he had figured out a cure for her fear of thunderstorms after all.

Carter pushed up on his elbows to kiss her. He couldn't get enough of the feel of her mouth welcoming his. He flustered her with the lazy, sweet kiss. He whispered, "Amazin' Macie. I had no idea how true that was."

"Carter. You're squishing me."

"I ain't exactly a featherweight and you are a little slip of a thing." He pulled out and rolled to his side. He reached for a box of tissues and got rid of the condom. "I'm sorry I snapped at you, but that's sort of a lie because it did lead to you endin' up tangled in my sheets. I'm damn glad you're in my bed."

Macie smiled. "Mud and all?"

"Mud and all."

"No regrets?"

"Just that I hurt your feelings."

"You made up for it with hot sex."

"Mmm, really?"

"But with you I'd even take lukewarm sex."

"Yeah?"

"Shoot. I'd settle for cool sex. Yeah. Lots of cool, kinky sex."

"You know that's not what I meant, Macie."

"So this isn't just about sex?"

Not on your life, kitten. Carter flopped back on a pillow and strove to keep things light. "Fine. It ain't all about sex. If you insist, I'll let you cook and clean for me. All summer. Whenever the urge strikes you."

"I'll strike you, you jackass." She pounced on him and held a pillow over his face.

He tore the pillow away and kissed her until she couldn't breathe.

"No fair," she panted. "Your kisses distract me."

"All's fair, since just lookin' at you distracts me, my sweet darlin'." He dragged his fingers up and down her spine and she practically purred. "Stay with me tonight, Macie."

"I can't."

Or won't? Disappointed, he said, "Okay."

"I'm not cooking for you either. However, I will let you wash my back in the shower." She yawned. "Later. When I'm not so tired."

"Deal. Anything else?"

"No."

After a minute he said, "Hey. The rain stopped."

"Ssh. Stop yapping. I'm trying to sleep so I can get to those wickedly explicit dreams."

"What kind of dreams? Am I in them?"

"Sort of."

"*Sort of?* What the hell does that mean?"

"Well, you're *one* of the sexy cowboys in my dreams."

"One of? As in plural?"

"Yep."

Block it out. Ah hell. He couldn't. "I don't suppose in your wicked dreams you and these sexy cowboys are just sittin' around playin' pinochle?"

"I don't suppose we are."

Carter paused and twirled a section of her hair around his index finger. "Sometime will you tell me what you are doin' with these cowboys in your dreams?"

"I'd rather show you. But we'd need a third player in our game...of pinochle. I don't suppose you've got a hot guy friend

116

who's up for a rodeo?"

Hell yeah, his buddy Jack would totally be up for that. "Lord, you're killin' me, woman, teasin' me 'bout your fantasies. You are gonna share those details, right?"

"Yes. But I'm too tired to do the fantasy justice right now. Maybe we can act out some of the...more challenging parts later. I vaguely remember a scene with ropes."

An image of a sexy, saucy Macie naked, at his mercy, blindfolded, tied up spread-eagled on his bed, every red-gold inch exposed and bound for his pleasure alone...yeah, his dick stirred with interest.

"I'll remind you as a ranch kid I'm wicked good with ropes." He squeezed her ass. "You already know I'm good with my hands."

"Thinking about your talented hands isn't lulling me to sleep, Carter."

"That's what I'm countin' on."

Macie tried to scoot away from him.

He laughed and nestled her against his body again. "I'll behave. For now. Sweet dreams, sweet darlin'."

After a while she murmured, "I feel like I'm forgetting something important I'm supposed to be doing."

You are doing it, Carter thought. Rather than answer her, he kissed the top of her head and drifted away.

Chapter Fifteen

Cash sipped his beer and stared out across the field beyond the barn. The rain had quit a few hours ago. The gloomy gray clouds cleared and the pink rays of the setting sun reflected on the tan grasses as a golden orange. It would've been a perfect evening for a horseback ride.

Except Macie hadn't shown up.

Was it intentional on her part? He'd disappointed her so many times that she'd decided to give him a taste of his own medicine? It was no less than what he deserved.

Yet, it seemed out of character for her. Macie had always been forthright even when she was a little girl. If she'd changed her mind, she would've come right out and told him.

Would it feel worse if she'd just plain forgotten about their plans? No. The worst thing would be if Macie had blown him off because she'd gotten a better offer.

From that damn Carter McKay.

He'd felt so guilty last night after he and Gemma hit the road, when he realized not only had he left Macie alone in a strange place, he hadn't even asked her if she'd wanted to ride along with them to Beulah. Then, when he'd heard about the nasty storms rolling across Wyoming, it'd made him stir-crazy not being able to reach her, especially after calling her for hours.

So he had to sit in a motel room twiddling his thumbs, wondering if his daughter was all right, letting that goddamn guilt gnaw through him. Keeping Gemma at arm's length so she wouldn't see how badly he'd fucked up again.

It should've pleased him to learn that Carter McKay had

the wherewithal to check on Macie. Instead, it burned his ass. Oh, not because he'd found Carter in his daughter's bed early this morning, but because *he* should've been there for her, her father, not some heart breakin' wild goddamn cowboy.

Yeah. He was some great man. He could drown in the sea of regret of all the things he hadn't done for his daughter. Hell, he'd been trying, bobbing along, swimming, mostly sinking, in that cesspool of remorse for a dozen years. He'd spent a few years shame-faced and shit-faced. Compacting his bad behavior with bad decisions. He'd spent a few more years wallowing in sex with any woman who'd crossed his path. All the while he cursed his bad luck and Macie's mother. Blaming everyone but himself for his lack of parenting skills.

He'd finally wised up.

Cash supposed it'd make a more interesting story if he credited the change in himself to a vision, or because he'd received ancient wise words from a Lakota holy man. But the truth was, when Macie turned sixteen—the same age he was when he'd fathered her, the same age his father had been when he'd fathered him—he realized not only wasn't he ready to be a grandfather, he'd never learned how to be a father.

That was just plain fucking sad. At that point, Cash knew he had to change and be the one to break the ugly cycle.

Luckily, Macie had her head screwed on straight, no thanks to him. She was a bright, kind, sweet, funny, beautiful young woman.

A young woman. He couldn't help but think of her as a child. Cash took another swallow of beer. Was it because he hadn't been around during her childhood and he'd always see her as a kid? Or did all parents see their offspring that way? Macie was mature and wise in so many ways...yet in others...she seemed so damn young.

So were you.

At her age, he'd had a six-year-old child, not a six-year-old car. The autumn Cash turned twenty-two, he'd won his first championship gold buckle and his first big payout.

That same fall, Macie would've entered first grade. He didn't even know the name of her elementary school. Or where she'd lived. A brief memory of her sweet face and big brown eyes flashed in his mind. Had she cried and gripped her mother's hand? Did she think of him and wonder for the millionth time why her daddy wasn't around?

God. How did he ask Macie any of this shit without sounding like a dolt? Without reminding her of all he'd *never* been to her?

Would they ever figure out this father/daughter relationship? When it appeared they'd both find excuses to let it remain the same fucked up way it'd been for years?

"Cash?"

He jumped at the sound of Gemma's voice behind him.

"Sorry. I didn't mean to interrupt you."

"You're not. It's okay. Just sittin' here thinkin'."

Gemma scooted next to him on the cement step. "Macie's not back yet?"

"Nope."

"Maybe she got called in to work."

"Be a little hard for Velma to reach her when Macie's cell phone is dead and in the camper."

"Oh."

"Yeah. I checked." He set aside the empty bottle and sighed. "Go ahead and remind me she's an adult."

Gemma didn't say a word.

The sweet, low tones of mourning doves rose and fell in the early twilight. A bull roared in the north pasture. The humid air seemed to amplify the normal sounds and every breath he sucked into his lungs was heavy. Oppressive.

Cash took off his cowboy hat and hung it on the metal railing so he could rub the knot at the base of his skull.

"You okay?"

"Just a headache."

"Probably from tension. Want me to rub your neck?"

He glanced at her. "You wouldn't mind?"

"No. I like touching you, Cash. It doesn't always have to lead to the bedroom."

Gemma's sweetness soothed him somewhat.

"Come on. Scoot down on the next step and lean back." Once she'd settled him between her thighs, she asked, "Can I unbraid your hair?"

"Sure. Why?"

"I could claim a too-tight braid as the source of your headache, but the truth is, I've been dying to get it loose so I can run my hands through it. Been afraid to ask you if I could."

Cash looked at her over his shoulder. "Why? Do I scare you?"

"Sometimes."

"Is this about what happened in the barn?"

Her cheeks flushed and she dropped her gaze. "No."

"That wasn't a real convincin' *no*, Gem."

"Fine. I like everything you do to me. But that's why...oh, never mind."

"No. Tell me."

"I want equal time to do things to you."

That was all? He relaxed. "Okay. I'm listenin'."

"So far this relationship has been pretty one-sided."

"You think?"

"Yeah."

"It's been two days, Gemma."

"Oh. Seems longer, doesn't it?"

Cash didn't know how to take that comment so he let it go.

Gemma loosened his hair and massaged his scalp, derailing his train of thought. He groaned with appreciation at her magic touch.

She dug her thumbs into the base of his neck.

"God that feels good."

"There are other things I can do to you that will feel this good. Or better."

His cock perked up. "Like?"

"Like, I don't wanna give you a play-by-play, Cash. I'm more of a doer than a talker."

"That a fact?"

"Yep."

"I gotta remind *you* of a fact, sweets. You agreed to let me be in charge when it comes to sex."

"I didn't think that meant all the time."

"It did."

Her fingers quit kneading.

"What?"

"Nothin'."

Cash faced her. "If you ain't enjoyin' bein' with me, just say so."

"See? That's not what this is about. You're just like Steve, taking everything so personal to the point we can't talk about it."

They stared at each other. It was the first time she'd brought up her husband's name in front of him. It didn't feel as awkward as he imagined it would. Maybe it was a good reminder to him that they both had a past.

"Maybe you oughta explain that comment."

A gust of wind caught Cash's unbound hair and it lashed Gemma in the face. Before he could yank it back into a ponytail, she grabbed a handful and pulled him close. "Let me take the lead once in awhile. That don't mean you're doing anything wrong, it just lets me be on the giving end. Much as I like being on the receiving end, sometimes I just need to know you don't mind when I'm aggressive and I don't want to wait for you to take charge."

Cash watched her eyes. She had no idea how much her confession meant to him. He hadn't been kidding when he'd warned her of his savage appetites, or of his secret taste for a little kink. So, not only hadn't he scared her off, she was letting him know she might even go him one better.

He whispered, "Show me."

Gemma slammed her lips to his. After ravaging his mouth, she jerked his head back by the hair and sank her teeth into the skin above his collarbone.

And sucked like a vampire. He knew she'd left a mark and he didn't give a damn. Her show of force made his dick hard even when it softened his heart.

She licked the stinging spot. "I like to bite."

"I'll keep that in mind when my cock is near those sharp teeth."

Gemma laughed softly. "Let me finish your neck rub. No teeth, I promise."

Cash relaxed into her once again.

"Tell me about Macie's mom. And how Macie came to be." When he stiffened, she chided, "You had to expect I'd ask sometime."

"Yeah, well, you'd think I'd be used to it by now."

He wished he had another beer. "Macie's mom, Jorgen Honeycutt, came to Pine Ridge on some kind of mission trip one summer. She embodied a gypsy, which appealed to a kid like me, bein's I was stuck on the rez. Probably for the rest of my life."

"How old were you?"

"Sixteen. I lied and told her I was eighteen. When she mentioned she'd just graduated, I figured her to be twenty-two. Later, I found out she'd meant from grad school, which made her twenty-six.

"I ain't gonna lie. Jorgen was blonde, beautiful, rich, sexy and I talked my way into her bed."

"I'll bet in your teens you were one of those cocky, slow-eyed, good-lookin' Indian cowboys, weren't you?"

"Yeah. Me and Jorgen had nothin' in common. She wanted to be with a 'real' Indian cowboy. We screwed around that summer and I knocked her up. Wasn't a doubt the kid was mine as we were together all the time. She wouldn't consider an abortion." Cash still winced when he thought about how hard he'd argued for that option.

Gemma kissed the top of his head. "Sucks that sometimes those things from the past can still hurt us even when we didn't make that choice."

Soothed by her again, he continued. "Jorgen had some family money, and wanderin' feet so she took off. Called me six months later to tell me I was a father. I didn't see Macie for the first time until she was two.

"I was such a bastard, Gem. I didn't care. Thought I'd

skated by easy 'cause I didn't have to pay child support. Jorgen would call me, drunk usually, and tell me about my child. I dreaded those damn phone calls.

"I wasn't interested in bein' a father until my friends started havin' kids. I suppose Macie was about eight when I began to see her once a year. We had fun together, but it wasn't any kind of relationship. Mostly because Jorgen made sure she had all the control. *She'd* decide when I could talk to Macie. Or see her. They moved all over the damn place so I had no choice. I never knew where they were, which drove me nuts."

"Doesn't sound like your lack of a relationship with your daughter is entirely your fault, Cash."

"Maybe not. I don't remember how it happened, but the year Macie turned twelve she called me. We talked for hours. I realized I wanted to get to know my child so I asked Jorgen if Macie could spend the summer with me on the rez."

Gemma gently worked his left shoulder muscle in silence.

"Jorgen refused. I was travelin' the rodeo circuit so it was easier for me to get to wherever Macie was. I went hundreds of miles out of my way to see my girl whenever I could."

Cash took a break, not sure if he was doing the right thing telling Gemma all this nasty shit about himself.

"Can I ask you something?"

"I guess."

"Is Macie like her mother?"

"In some ways."

"Like?"

"Like I suspect she's got itchy feet. Macie doesn't seem inclined to put down roots anywhere."

"Maybe she gets that from you. You've traveled around plenty yourself, Cash."

He grunted.

"Or maybe she doesn't know how to settle down because no one has shown her," Gemma offered.

"True. But it ain't like she's gonna learn it from me. I should be happy that she's like Jorgen in that material things don't mean nothin' to her."

"I thought you said Jorgen was rich."

Cash laughed without humor. "Every white person seems rich to a rez kid who's livin' ten or twelve to a house and dependin' on government commodities to eat. She had enough money to get by, and that's more than I ever had."

"That doesn't tell me what Jorgen was like."

"Sounds stupid, but Jorgen was the type who collected life experiences and checked them off her life list and moved on."

"Meaning?"

"She had a list of things she wanted to accomplish. Live in Europe. Check. Get a graduate degree. Check. Live on the rez with indigenous people. Check. Have a child. Check. Live in the desert. Check. Live in the mountains. Check. Live by the ocean. Check. Work in a cowboy bar. Check. Work in a casino. Check. Work on a cruise ship. Check. She went where she wanted to go, did what she wanted to do and didn't care about anybody else."

"Including Macie?"

"I suspect that's the case. Macie doesn't wanna talk about her childhood too much. I don't know if it's to spare my feelin's 'cause I wasn't around or because they ain't the best memories for her." Thinking about poor little Macie fending for herself made his gut clench and his heart hurt. "I know Jorgen loved Macie, as much as Jorgen could love anyone."

"Did you love Jorgen?"

"No."

"Still, you were so young when all that happened. I'm surprised you never married and had more kids."

"After the shit I've told you, you think I'd subject a kid to havin' me as a father?" *Or a woman who'd want me as a husband.* He didn't say it; he just shifted his weight on the hard cement. "What about you and Steve?"

"What about us?"

"You never had kids. On purpose?"

"We would've welcomed a baby. Just didn't happen. And Steve was old-fashioned. He didn't want fertility tests to figure out the problem. Nor did he warm to the idea of adoption. I know some folks look at me with pity because I'm childless. But you can't miss what you've never had."

"True. What would you do if you ended up pregnant now?"

Gemma choked. "What? Lord, Cash, I'm forty-eight—"

"You ain't been through menopause yet, have you?"

"No. Have the symptoms, though."

"Don't matter. My *unci* had her last baby when she was fifty-one. She thought it was menopause. So, I guess that means we'd better make sure we're usin' condoms, much as I hate it."

"I hate it too but I guess you're right."

Darkness had fallen. The yard light clicked on. Pretty soon bugs would be out in full force. Cash was tired of talking. Spilling his guts hadn't alleviated the ache in his heart or his head. Gemma seemed to sense his mood change.

She smoothed his hair away from his face. "How's your head?"

"Still hurts."

"Want me to keep going?"

"Nah. Thanks for the offer though. I think I might just pop a couple aspirin and crawl in bed." He stood and grabbed his empty beer bottle. "Probably be best if I slept in the guest bedroom tonight so I don't disturb you."

"But that's not necessary—"

"'Night, Gem."

He didn't look back. He couldn't take her look of pity.

And he knew she wasn't ready to see what he couldn't hide in his eyes.

Chapter Sixteen

Headlights swept the windows above the sink. Water splashed in the mud puddles and the red taillights disappeared.

Macie was back.

Gemma didn't move from the kitchen table where she'd been working on the ranch books. She glanced at the clock. Cash had been in bed for two hours. She'd resisted checking on him, more worried she'd find him awake and avoiding her than sleeping off his headache.

Things had taken a strange turn today. Not only because he'd fucked her senseless in the barn, but because he'd opened up to her. She suspected he was filled with regret about showing her that tender side of himself and the guilt he carried.

Did Macie know? Did she care?

How did Gemma reconcile wanting to be with Cash outside of the workday, when she knew he felt guilty that he wasn't spending that time with his daughter?

She jumped at the four solid knocks on the glass window of the screen door. She said, "Come in," and Macie slipped inside and hesitated by the wall.

"Hey, Gemma. How's it going?"

"Good. How are you?"

"Okay." She glanced at the doorway to the living room. "Umm. Is my dad around?"

"Yeah. But he had a bad headache and he's in bed."

Macie's eyes filled with concern. "Is he all right?"

"I hope so." Gemma expected Macie to say a quick goodbye and disappear back to the camper. It surprised her when Macie pulled out a chair and plopped down.

"Is he mad at me?"

"Why would he be mad at you?"

"Because he and I were supposed to go horseback riding tonight. I fell asleep at Carter's. When I woke up it was already dark."

Ah. No wonder Cash acted so melancholy. "He didn't act like he was mad. Maybe a little disappointed."

"Crap. I never meant...I just lost track of time." Macie sighed. "Story of my life. Story of our life actually. Seems like our plans are always interrupted."

Macie left her as good an opening as any to broach the subject. "Does it bother you that your dad is here working for me rather than hitting the backroads with you? That was your plan, right?"

"Yeah, but I'd never put any stock into it beyond getting to hang out with him. We talk on the phone at least once a week, but it's not the same. It's been a rough year for him."

"How so?"

"Realizing he's too old to rodeo fulltime. Having to take shit jobs just to make ends meet." She shot Gemma a sheepish look. "No offense intended."

"None taken." Gemma sipped her cold coffee. "What about you? Are you taking a shit job just to hang out here?"

Macie grinned. "No. I was thrilled to find work in a restaurant. Mucking out stalls would be my idea of a shit job."

"You working a lot?"

"We'll see. I think Velma is testing me. Or punishing me. I'm waitressing some. I'd rather be in the kitchen." She pointed to Gemma's cup. "Got any more coffee?"

"In the pot."

She stood. "You want a reheat?"

"Sure."

Gemma watched while Macie made herself completely at home. It was weird to think this beautiful young woman was Cash's daughter. It was probably equally weird for Macie to sit down with her father's boss.

And her father's lover.

Yeah. They weren't ready to go there yet.

"So, you're doing some modeling for Carter?"

"I guess. He's been pretty mum on what it'll turn out like."

Gemma frowned at Macie's baggy black sweats. "Those seem a little informal for the kind of art Carter does."

"Let's just say there was an incident with my clothes today, and Carter lent me these." Casually, Macie said, "It's pretty cool you're letting Carter live here this summer."

"It works, since he's willing to help me out."

"How long have you known him?"

"Since he was about ten. Technically, that's how long I've known the whole McKay clan."

"So what's his family like?"

"His folks are nice. His brothers are sweet-talkin' hell raisers. The youngest, his sister Keely? She's hell on horseback. They're a close bunch. All the boys except for Cam live around the McKay ranch." She blew on her coffee and looked at Macie. "Why?"

"Just curious. Dad doesn't seem to have a high opinion of them."

"Yes, he does. He just don't like the fact Carter is sniffin' around you."

When Macie didn't respond, Gemma said, "You thought of how to break it to your dad you're doin' more than posin' for Carter?"

"It's that obvious?"

"No. But wearing Carter's clothes and the love bites on your neck might tip him off."

"Crap."

Gemma waited and hid a smile behind her cup.

"I know I just met him, but he's so...intense. I don't know if he's feeding me lines about his art or what. And I sure don't want my dad to say—"

"—I told you so?" Gemma supplied.

"No. I don't want Dad to think I'm a fool. Especially when I've yet to see a single thing Carter has drawn or painted or

Lorelei James

sculpted or whatever he does with clay. And I'm not just talking about when he's supposedly using me as a subject. Wouldn't you think he'd have something that he made where he lives?"

Gemma set down her cup and stood. "Follow me. I want to show you something." In the living room she unhooked an 8 X 10 frame from the wall next to the china cabinet and passed it to Macie. "Carter drew that for me."

"Holy cow. It's beautiful. This was your husband?"

"Yeah." She let her gaze skim over the pencil and charcoal portrait of Steve. "Carter gave that to me about a year after Steve died. Somehow he managed to capture not only Steve's personality, but his soul."

After a solid minute passed, Macie slowly raised her eyes. "That's what I'm afraid of, Gemma. That he'll see too much."

Gemma's heart lurched. Macie was so like Cash in so many ways. "I wish I knew what to say to that, Macie, but I don't."

"That's okay. Thanks for not spewing a buncha bullshit. I'd rather have the truth."

"Me too."

Once they were back in the kitchen, Macie glanced at the papers strewn across the table and said, "It's late. I didn't mean to interrupt."

"You didn't. Honestly? I was glad for the company. You do know you're welcome here—both in the house and on the ranch. If I hadn't made that clear, I meant to."

"Thanks. I should go." Macie stopped and turned around. "If my dad wakes up will you tell him I was here and I'll see him tomorrow?"

"Sure."

"'Night, Gemma."

"'Night."

Gemma watched the flashlight bobbing across the yard. Only when the lights in the camper were flicked off and she knew Macie was safe did she head for bed.

130

Chapter Seventeen

"Medium well. Baked potato with sour cream and a side of...what is the vegetable tonight?"

"Creamed corn."

The man scowled. "Disgusting. Give me the salad with Thousand Island dressing. On the side. No onions. No tomatoes. No carrots. Light on the bacon bits and cheese. No croutons."

Macie expected him to say "light on the lettuce". She waited for more instructions and the customer stared at her like she was an idiot. She pasted on a smile. "Got it. Your salad will be right out."

The diner was busy enough for the next hour she didn't have time to wish she was slaving over a hot grill instead of bringing Clem, a regular with a sweet tooth and a toothless smile, his tenth cup of coffee.

"Order up, Macie," TJ yelled from the kitchen.

"Thanks." She tossed a sprig of parsley on top of the plate and delivered it to her customer. Hopefully he was her last customer of the night. She was ready to go home and knock back a beer or six.

"What's wrong?" Velma asked as she dumped two ladles of French dressing on a bowl of iceberg lettuce.

"I don't know. I'm just cranky." And horny. Which made her even more cranky. She was never horny. Or she'd never been until Carter McKay sent her hormones into overdrive.

Why were her hormones causing problems now? Simply because it'd been a week since she'd seen or heard from Carter?

Yeah, she knew he was working. Although, she hadn't heard that from him directly, but from Gemma. Luckily her father hadn't chimed in about Carter's absence a couple of days after finding him in her bed. Evidently there hadn't been any projects around the Bar 9 that required Carter's help either. Which meant her dad had plenty of time to spend with her. Which was great. They'd gone horseback riding twice, and she'd spent her free mornings watching him work with Gemma's horses.

So why was she so cranky?

Instead of taking out her frustrations on customers, Macie snuck into the kitchen and chopped celery and green peppers for the Western-style potato salad for tomorrow's lunch special. Dicing onions always made her cry. She'd leave that task for the morning.

Unless she needed another reason to hide out in the kitchen. And cry.

She'd restocked the dry goods and was rolling silverware when the wind chimes clanked behind her, signaling more customers.

Macie groaned. "Velma, can you take the next table? I forgot to—" *drink all the cooking sherry in the pantry*, "—check the apples for worms—"

"—don't worry, I got it handled. Mmm. Mmm. Lord, I wouldn't mind handling him."

"What?"

"Nothin'." Macie heard the *spritz spritz* of Velma's breath spray and then Velma cooed, "Howdy there, sugar. Why don't you rest them fine legs, sit and take a load off?"

Sugar? Macie turned and saw Carter standing in the middle of the diner. Ignoring Velma, ignoring everyone, just staring at her.

Still feeling cranky, she demanded, "What are you doing here?"

Without a word, without taking his eyes off hers, Carter stalked behind the counter. When he stood in front of her, he curled his hands around her head and slanted his mouth over hers. He kissed her like she was air, like she was food, like she was everything.

Damn him.

The diner was dead quiet except for the sound of heavy breathing. Hers mostly.

Carter pulled back scarcely a millimeter and whispered, "*That* is what I'm doin' here. Oh. And *this* is why I'm here too." He kissed her again. Like she was naked.

"Can I get some more coffee back here?"

"Hush up, Clem," Velma snapped. "This is better than the dinner theater down in Lingle."

But Clem's whiny voice brought Macie back to reality. She retreated from Carter's irresistible kisses.

He crowded her again. "I want to talk to you. I need to talk to you."

"Sit down. You're not supposed to be back here."

"It's okay with me," Velma said cheerily.

"You're not helping. He already thinks rules don't apply to him."

Carter grinned.

Macie pointed at the counter. "Sit."

"I missed you."

"Carter—"

"I missed you something fierce, Macie. Don't be mad at me."

"Aw. See? The man is here to apologize."

"Stay out of it, Velma."

Macie snagged the coffee pot and dodged Carter's wandering hands. When she returned from refilling Clem's cup, Carter was seated safely behind the counter studying the menu.

"What's good?"

Velma answered, "Well, the New York strip is on special. But you oughta try the chicken breast in lemon vodka sauce. It'll knock your boots off. It's Macie's recipe."

Carter shot Macie a sly smile. "Is that the secret sauce you used to poach my eggs the other mornin'?"

Velma choked on her coffee.

Macie sputtered, "B-but I never—"

"—have time to cook for me when we roll out of bed, so I sure appreciate it when you do, darlin'."

She leaned over the counter. "I am *so* going to kick your ass, McKay."

Carter scooted closer so they were practically nose to nose. "Did you say kiss?"

"No, you smug bast—"

He pressed his lips to hers once. Twice. Then he whispered, "Play nice, or I'll be forced to show you what I do to naughty girls."

"Back off, or I'll be forced to show *you* how the bucket of rocky mountain oysters in the cooler came to be earlier this morning."

"Ouch."

Clem waved her down and Macie headed to the cash register. She chatted with Clem, ignoring Velma and Carter's whispers and laughter. Only after Velma had taken Carter's order and disappeared into the kitchen, did she return to the counter where Carter sat, watching her like a hawk.

"Are you really mad at me?" he asked quietly.

She fiddled with the water pitcher. "No."

"Good. So. When do you get off?"

Whenever I think of you.

Dammit. Her stupid hormones were a menace. No. This stupid man was a menace to her normally well-behaved hormones.

"Macie?"

She refocused. "Umm. In about an hour."

"Cool. I'll hang around and wait for you."

"Don't bother. I'm sure you have plenty of other things to do."

His eyes narrowed. "You *are* mad."

Before she could deny it, Velma burst through the swinging doors holding a gigantic ice cream concoction decorated with whipped cream and two cherries. "Here's your root beer float, hon."

"Thanks."

"Extra whipped cream, just like you asked."

Carter smirked at Macie. "You know how much I like sweet, thick cream."

Heat flashed between her legs. Bad, bad hormones.

No. Bad, bad man.

"This is pure artistry, Miz Velma. Mmm. Mmm."

"You would know." Velma cocked her head at Macie. "Carter here is an artist."

"So he says."

The spoon stopped halfway to Carter's mouth. His blue eyes went as cold as the ice cream in his float. "What's that supposed to mean?"

Macie addressed her comments to Velma. "He tells me he's an artist, and says he's 'working' but the truth is, I've never seen a damn thing he's supposedly created." She shrugged. "So I'm just wondering if his whole 'I'm an artist' line is just that." Macie locked her gaze to Carter's. "A line. Now if you'll excuse me, I have onions to chop."

She half-expected Carter to sneak in after her offering all sorts of sweet-talkin' excuses, or for Velma to butt in, but no one bothered her. The knife thwacked into the acrylic cutting board, cleaving the onion in two. Her tears fell unchecked until she swiped them away with her shirtsleeve. Stupid onions always made her cry.

What she'd said to Carter was true and it bugged the crap out of her that he hadn't shown her a single thing he'd drawn or molded or carved. Him calling her his beautiful muse in that sexy, low voice of his while he fucked her unconscious didn't count. It didn't count when he whispered promises about immortalizing her likeness in clay either. She wanted to see actual, physical proof. Of something.

Macie frowned. Was that why he'd freaked out when he caught her in his studio? Because he didn't want her to find out he wasn't working? Maybe he was blocked. She'd heard artists got blocked just like writers. Maybe that's why he claimed he needed a muse. She'd be even more skeptical of his motives if she hadn't seen the stunning portrait Carter created of Gemma's husband.

But he'd drawn that one years ago. What had he been

doing recently?

Irritating the hell out of her damn hormones.

She put the situation out of her mind as she cleaned up and changed clothes. When she returned up front, she wasn't surprised Carter wasn't waiting for her, but his absence did cause her a tiny pang of disappointment.

Velma said, "You ready to go?"

"Yeah."

Before Velma hit the lights, she said, "He left something for you on the counter."

"What?"

"Take a look."

Macie spied a cheap placemat on the spot where Carter had eaten. She picked it up and stared in disbelief.

It was a pencil drawing of her. A close-up. Specifically of her brooding, in the diner's kitchen, her face half hidden in shadow as she gazed longingly at something beyond the white edge of the paper.

Her eyes met Velma's. "Do I really look like this?"

"Like what, sweetheart?"

Lost.

Velma shuffled over and peered at the drawing. "Well, you do look sad in this picture. But you've been kinda mopin' around the last week, so I think it's a pretty accurate depiction of your mood. No denyin' the man has talent. That's for damn sure." She looked at Macie and smiled. "No denyin' the man also has it bad for you."

"But—"

"No buts. Swallow your pride, squirt. He might've hurt your feelin's over something this week, but remember: *He* came lookin' for *you* tonight." Velma patted her cheek. "Make sure the door is locked when you leave, eh?"

Macie rolled up the picture and carefully inserted it in a cardboard paper towel tube so it wouldn't get crushed in her backpack. She slammed the back door and rounded the side of the brick building, her guilty footsteps loud in the gravel and the muted night air. She was so lost in thought that she didn't notice him until she'd reached her vehicle.

Carter lounged against the passenger door, his cowboy hat pushed back off his forehead. His arms were folded over his broad chest; his legs were crossed at his ankles. If she hadn't focused on his eyes, she'd bristle at his defensive posture. But there wasn't a defensive, macho, self-righteous glint there—just wariness.

Or was it hope?

What if she was projecting what was in her eyes into his?

Did it matter?

No.

"He came lookin' for you tonight."

She set her backpack on the ground and launched herself at him before she ruined the moment with what-ifs.

Chapter Eighteen

Carter caught her with a grunt that morphed into a laugh after she squeezed him tight and knocked his hat off.

"Hey, hey. What's all this?"

She scattered kisses on his face. "My way of saying I missed you, dumbass."

"Ah. By all means, darlin', keep up with the sweet-talkin'. I'm hopin' it'll lead to dirty talk."

"Thanks for drawing me that picture. Sorry I was a jerk."

"Apology accepted. Just so you know...I have been workin'. Time got away from me and before I knew it, I realized I hadn't seen the real you in a week."

She pulled back to look at him. "The real me?"

"I've been paintin' pictures of you. But retouching you on canvas ain't nothin' like touchin' you in the flesh." His frustrated growl was a balm to her pride. "Jesus, Macie, enough talkin'. Kiss me already."

Her mouth trapped his. She forced her tongue between his warm lips and poured herself into him. A hot, drawn-out opened-mouthed kiss that left her wet with need, and had him grinding his hard cock into the soft notch between her thighs.

"The things you do to me make me think of all the nasty things I wanna do to you." Carter scraped his teeth down her throat. "I ain't feelin' very gentlemanly. I want to fuck you right fuckin' now. I don't think I can wait until we find the closest bed." He growled, "How daring are you feelin'?"

"Not very. But you make me want to be daring."

"That's music to my ears."

"Yeah?"

"Yeah. Ever done it on the hood of a car?"

She'd never done it *in* a car. She imagined hot metal on her back; hot man on her front. Whoo-ee. She could be down with that. "Do you have a condom?"

"Sweet darlin', I've got a whole pocketful."

Chills broke out across every inch of her flesh as he nibbled her neck. She moaned. Loudly. "Like that, do you?"

"Yes. Your mouth feels like liquid fire."

"Funny. That's the way my cock feels too."

Laughing, Macie pushed away. "You gonna take off your pants before the crotch catches fire? Before you get in my car?"

"Oh, so Miz Daring decides we're doin' this *in* the car, as opposed to against it?"

"Yep."

"Works for me." Carter kept his eyes on hers as he kicked off his boots and shucked off his Wranglers. His cock bobbed against his bellybutton and he grinned at her wide-eyed expression. "Commando all the way for you, darlin'. Your turn. Strip."

Macie had changed out of her ugly polyester uniform before clocking out, but she hoped her skin didn't reek like grease. In a flash her denim shorts and her panties were at her feet and her T-shirt dangled from the hood.

"Bra too."

"Nope. You still have your shirt on."

Carter tugged and the pearl snaps gave way, showing just a sliver of his golden flesh from his collar to where the hem brushed his balls.

"Enough."

He lifted a brow. "Enough? I thought you wanted me to take it off?"

"Well, I don't want to make it too easy for you."

"Easy?"

"I think I wanna test you, see how good you are at removing my bra in the dark, in the car, while I'm bouncing on your lap. You might get a little flustered."

"You issuin' me a challenge?"

"Yep."

"What do I get if I pass your challenge?"

Just say it. Be daring. But it sounded too crude, a little slutty, and a lot naughty in her head no matter how she phrased it.

"Macie? What do I get?"

"Whatever you want."

Carter's eyes narrowed. "We're talkin' whatever I want sexually, right?"

"Yep."

"What if I want something you ain't never given another man?"

"Then it would be yours to take."

The air between them turned thick with need.

"Remember you said that. Get in the fuckin' car, before I throw you on the goddamn ground and fuck you in the gravel and weeds."

"We've already done that once."

He growled.

"Slip on a condom, cowboy, slide your fine butt in the seat and wait for me. I need to get something out of the back."

"What?"

"You'll see."

Crickets chirped in the darkness but she scarcely heard them over the blood rushing in her ears. The weight of the car shifted as Carter climbed inside. Macie grabbed the case from under the seat and skirted the front end. She hesitated when she saw the raw, hungry look on Carter's face through the windshield.

"Don't make me come out there and get you," he warned.

Before she lost her nerve, she crawled on his lap. As she set the case on the driver's seat, her knee smacked into his groin.

He sucked in a sharp breath. Then, "Jesus-Christ-Almighty-oh-holy-mother-of-god-oh-fuck-oh-shit-oh-*goddamn* that hurts."

"Oh, sorry sorry sorry. I didn't mean to."

"I know."

"Sorry, Carter, oh, what can I do?"

"Give me a sec, okay?"

"Sorry."

He expelled a slow breath.

"Are you okay?"

"Normally I'd say after rackin' me you need to get on your knees and kiss my poor abused boys and make 'em all better, but there ain't enough room in here for you to do 'em justice."

"Will you take a rain check?"

"Hell yeah." Carter nestled her soft thighs along the outside of his muscular legs. "Gimme this mouth." His talented lips toyed with hers as he danced his callused fingertips up and down her spine.

Then he really kissed her. A full body kiss. A carnal thrusting of his tongue, his mouth gliding back and forth to find the best angle to take the soul kiss even deeper. Wetter. Hotter. His hips pressed up, his cock searching for her feminine heat. Nimble fingers unhooked her bra and tugged the satiny straps down her arms.

Hey. Wait a minute.

Macie eased back to look at him. Glare at him really.

An extremely cocky grin spread across his sexy face.

"Don't challenge me, darlin', you can't win." He fastened his teeth to the spot on her neck that made her melt. "I know what I want. I'll let you think on when you're prepared to give it up to me, 'cause I won it fair and square. But for now...tell me what's in the box."

Her hands were flat against his chest, her fingers flexing into the rippling muscles. God. He was so strong. So smooth. So perfect. She leaned forward, buried her nose against his collarbone and inhaled. "You smell so damn good. All the time. Your scent drives me out of my freakin' mind. I want to lick every bulge and vein and line from your neck on down to your hipbones. And then I want to do it all over again so I can double-check that I didn't miss any good spots."

"Macie—"

"Let me touch you, Carter, please."

The heat in the car made his pecs slick with sweat. The constant stroking of her thumbs over his nipples made the tips rock hard. His belly muscles quivered beneath her fingertips.

But Carter wasn't about to be distracted. He thrust a hand through her hair and tugged her head back so he could peer in her eyes. "You can suck and lick me to your heart's content later. Right now I wanna know: What's in the goddamn box?"

She nipped his chin. "You taste like whipped cream here."

"Macie," he warned.

"Fine. My vibrator."

He froze. "You have a vibrator?"

"Yep."

"Why?"

"Because I've never been able to count on a man for anything, so I take care of *all* matters myself."

"You keep your vibrator in the car?"

"It's safer than keeping it in my dad's camper where he could find it. Plus, it's portable. Which is handy for us right about now. So, do you want to use it on me? Or should I use it on you first?"

"Christ Almighty. I may not survive you."

"Toughen up, tough guy. Or are you scared? I thought you were daring?"

"Hah. I ain't skeered 'a nuthin'. Hand it over."

Macie reached for it and slapped the soft purple plastic phallus in his palm. "Need instructions?"

"Nope." Carter grinned and turned it to high. Over the constant buzzing noise, he said, "Spread your legs and hold on."

"But—"

"You started it. Lean closer. I wanna suck your tits while I'm doing...this."

He slid the vibrator right between her pussy lips and left it there.

Macie shrieked.

Then he shaped and squeezed her left breast, sucking her right nipple until it felt like her whole breast was in his hot mouth. He sucked and groaned against her skin while he let the vibrator rest directly on her clit.

She'd be lucky if she lasted a minute.

Or thirty seconds.

She gyrated her hips, arching her spine, wanting him to suck her harder until her nipple hit the back of his throat.

Carter moved his mouth and the vibrator away.

"Hey, don't stop!"

"I'm not. Scoot back."

She did and he slid his butt toward the dash.

"You ain't gonna last long. I wanna be ready to slide deep." Carter brushed soft kisses over the tops of her breasts and he repositioned the vibrator right where she needed it.

Macie threw back her head and moaned.

"Come for me, darlin'."

Four strokes, four sucks, that's all it took.

She exploded.

Carter bit down on her nipple as her clit pulsed against the soft rubber. Before she could find her sanity, Carter's mouth was on hers and he'd impaled her, even as her pussy still throbbed from the tail end of her orgasm.

"Jesus, Macie. You are so wet."

"It's your fault. The way you touch me, the way you look at me. You make me wet."

"I ain't complainin', knowin' I can heat you up."

"Oh GOD that feels good."

"Come again for me. I like watchin' you come."

Another orgasm ruptured inside her.

Carter rammed in and out, each thrust deeper. Harder. Prolonging her climax until she couldn't breathe and white dots appeared in front of her eyes.

The sound of skin slapping on skin drifted far away. Was she having an out of body experience? Or was this just another damn dream?

Pinch yourself.

But she couldn't move. Her arms shook. Her legs were numb. She was sweating. She was on fire. Goosebumps broke out across her flesh. She was chilled to the bone. Her head was full of white fluffy cotton and then everything was fading to black.

All movement quit. Even the sweet stroking of Carter's velvety tongue against hers. He broke the kiss completely. She tried to chase his mouth for more of his intoxicating taste, but ended up smacking her face into his chin.

"Macie? Darlin'? What's wrong?"

"I think I'm gonna pass out."

"Shit. Hold on."

"Okay. I am."

"Let me pull out—"

"No. Don't move."

"I should—"

"Carter."

"I'm here."

"Don't. Move."

"But—"

"Just hold me."

"No, baby, we need to stop."

"It's okay."

"I can't believe—"

"Please. It'll pass."

He didn't say a word.

"Just give me...a minute."

"Take however long you need."

Finally, sanity began to reassert itself. After her head quit spinning, Macie became aware of several things. Carter's cock was still rock hard, still seated fully inside her. His skin was damp. His short, broken breaths stirred her hair. His pulse pounded against her chest. His body was going haywire with the need to finish this frenzied mating, yet, he held her in utter stillness.

With gentleness. With protection. With...care.

Crap. That felt a whole lot scarier than passing out.

This man was *so* dangerous to her heart.

Slowly she lifted her head. Smiled at him. "Whoa. That's the first time I've nearly passed out from an orgasm."

"*Two* orgasms. That's the first time my spectacular love makin' has nearly caused a woman to pass out." He kissed her clammy forehead and whispered, "You really okay?"

"Yeah. But can we take it slow from here on out?"

"You don't want to quit?"

"No, I don't want to quit." She rubbed her cheek against the stubble on his jaw. "I want you to finish the rest of your spectacular love makin'."

"Smartass."

Still, he didn't budge. For what seemed like an hour.

Macie sighed. "You afraid to ride the horse that threw you, Daring McKay?"

"Hell yes. I don't want to hurt you."

"Fine." She slid her hands down to his shoulders, dug her nails in and lifted until only the very tip of his cock remained inside her. "I'll hurt you. I'll make it hurt so good." Then she lowered back down.

"Macie!"

"I dare you, Carter." She locked her gaze on his wild blue eyes as she rode him. "Fuck me. I won't break."

"You are a crazy woman. Fine. You win. I ain't got a lot of willpower left anyway." He cradled her face in his hands and kissed her with such gentleness, she wanted to weep.

They created a steady, slow rhythm. The windows fogged over. The air was heavy, a sultry scent of sex and moist heat.

Macie felt her need for release rebuild, but Carter didn't hurry to get her there like he did before.

He reached between them. Shifted his position slightly. Then his wide, hot palms slid down around her back until he had a butt cheek in each hand. His fingers squeezed her ass as he steadily pumped into her pussy. His thumbs swept closer and closer to her butt crack.

Just the pad of his thumb brushed the tightly puckered opening. She went rigid. Several seconds passed before he did it again. The third time his thumb stayed right there, and drew wet circles over that sensitive knot of nerves.

Carter placed his mouth on her ear. "I want you here."

Macie swallowed hard.

"Ever had a man in your ass, darlin'?"

"No."

He growled. "That'll make me the first."

"Carter—"

"When I fuck you here," he slipped just the tip of his thumb past the muscled ring and her breath hitched, "it'll be without a condom. So you can feel me comin' inside you. Heatin' you up where no other man has ever been before."

Her head began to buzz again.

Wait. The buzzing sound got louder. Then she felt it. Carter pressed the pointed end of the vibrator against her anus. She couldn't help it; she clenched.

"Wait—"

"Relax. This piece of plastic ain't gonna be the first thing you feel up this virgin ass. I'm just messin' around. Primin' the pump, so to speak. How does that feel? Raunchy?"

"Uh-huh."

"Dirty girl. I like you dirty. Raunchy. Nasty. My dirty raunchy nasty muse."

He managed to hold the vibrator against her even as he thrust into her pussy with steady sure strokes.

He groaned. "Shit. That buzzin' feels good on my balls. No wonder you like that damn thing so much and have it handy. Hang tight. Christ, Macie. I never thought I'd—" He bucked, grunted and started to come.

Macie canted her hips, grinding her clit against his pubic bone. He pumped hard and accidentally pushed the vibrator in a bit further, just deep enough to send a shock wave of pleasure cascading through her and setting off her third orgasm.

Utterly spent, she slumped against him as he slumped against the seat.

Neither one spoke for a long time.

Finally, she said, "Maybe I was wrong."

"About?"

"Maybe you *can* break me."

He chuckled. "Or maybe, you'll be the one to break me, darlin'."

She shook off the sense of unease. "I need to get some sleep, Carter."

"Come home with me."

"I said *sleep*. We don't seem to do a whole lot of that when we're in a bed. Or in an SUV, apparently."

"If I let you go home tonight, will you come by when you're done workin' tomorrow?"

"Maybe. Dad said something about taking me riding after supper."

"That don't take all damn night, does it?"

"No. Why?"

"'Cause I gotta burn some brush piles. I'd sure like to study your face in the firelight. I'll bet the shadows and angles and color are amazin' on your bone structure."

"So if I come by to see you, you'd be working?"

He paused and she sensed his struggle to say the right thing.

"Carter?"

"Yeah, I'd be workin'. But it doesn't seem like work when you're the subject." He slapped her butt. "You need to get on home. We'll talk more about this tomorrow."

They dressed separately and silently. He kissed her hastily and she watched his red taillights disappear down the gravel road.

Why did she feel the overwhelming urge to cry?

Macie blamed it on the damn hormones and headed home.

Chapter Nineteen

"You so totally did *not* nail her."

"I did too."

"Miss Montana?" Carter said skeptically.

"No, Miss *Rodeo* Montana."

"Right. Maybe a rodeo goat named Montana, but a rodeo queen? Come on, Colt, you're full of shit."

"No, I ain't."

"So when *did* you polish Miss Montana's crown, stud?"

"Last weekend. After the Jackson County Rodeo dance."

Dance. Never catch him at a damn dance. Carter dabbed cerulean on the canvas and dragged his brush through it before he shifted the receiver. "Where?"

"In Elk City."

"That's where your dreams are takin' place now? Elk City?"

"Asshole. No. I was *in* Kane's horse trailer *in* Elk City, Montana."

"Ah. So Kane was there when you rode Miss Montana hard and put her up wet? He can back you up on this tall tale?"

"No. I borrowed his horse trailer last weekend because we were bringin' that mare home from Missoula."

"You know it don't count if no one saw you with her."

"Cord saw me with her. He can back me up."

"Cord." Carter paused. "As in our brother Cord?"

"You know any other Cord?"

"No, but now I know you're lyin'. Cord doesn't go nowhere,

especially a dance where there's wicked women who can lead him into temptation away from his beloved ranch."

Colt laughed. "True. But Dad sent him with me to get the horse. We stopped for the night, saw a street dance goin' on and decided we'd have a beer and check it out. A couple hours later me and Mindy—"

"Mindy?"

"Mindy Sue LaRue, Miss Rodeo Montana. She rode me like a Pony Express rider. Shoot, we rocked the horse trailer so hard we busted an axle."

Carter snorted.

"We did it two times before she bailed. Cord walked in as she was walkin' out. Then he asked me if her tits were implants. I was surprised he'd noticed them. Though, I gotta admit they *were* pretty hard to miss."

"Damn. I take it back. You did nail her. Congrats." Carter wiped another streak of blue across the top. "So were they fake?"

"Yep. Who cares? They were just the way I like 'em: big and round and bouncy and then they were gone."

Carter laughed.

"What about you, bro? Getting any in that godforsaken part of Wyoming?"

Carter glanced down at the canvas. A serene Macie stared at him from the back of a dappled gray mare. Definitely not the image of his wild Macie from last night. With her sexy legs clamped around his waist, his hat sliding off her head, him swallowing her cries as she came from him fucking her against the wall. Man. She'd hardly made it inside the trailer and he was on her. In her.

The last three weeks had pretty much gone along those lines. She'd work. He'd work. They'd hook up a couple of times a week to fuck like animals. Then she'd go home and he'd go to bed. Alone.

The ideal set-up, right? No promises. No hurt feelings. Just lots of hot sweaty sex.

He was fucking sick and tired of...well, just fucking and didn't know what the hell to do about it. The first week he and

Macie spent together seemed different. Real. Like something special. Now they didn't talk. They didn't fight. They didn't tease each other, or get to know each other, or even eat a damn meal together. They just screwed and that was the extent of it.

He scowled at the shitty picture on the easel, and resisted shredding it to ribbons with his exacto knife. Even his attempts at art were a screwed-up mess. Nothing was working in his life.

"Carter? You still there?"

"Yeah. Sorry."

"So? Since there ain't no women around...who's your favorite sheep this week?"

"Fuck off."

A soft rustling filled the phone lines, followed by a heavy pause. Then he heard, "...Carter, why? Really? I ain't surprised. He is kinda rude. Self-centered too."

"Who are you talkin' to?"

"Mom. She says you haven't called her lately. And you don't answer your cell."

"Shit. Do NOT hand the phone to Mom, Colt."

"Yeah? There's been no problems with the phone line to Gemma's house as far as I know."

"Hey, fuckface. I mean it. I don't want to talk to her."

"No, that's cool. We were done anyway."

"Colt, you fuckin' loser, don't you dare pass me off to... Hey, Ma." Colt was dead the next time he saw him. Dead and buried. With a boot up his ass.

"If it isn't my long lost son, Carter West McKay. Why don't you get the excuses on why you haven't called me out of the way first thing?"

Carter heard Colt laughing. He closed his eyes. He really did feel guilty. Especially since his mother was one of the few people he could really talk to. Yeah. Like his brothers didn't tease him enough for being a momma's boy.

"Sorry. I'm a terrible son. I know how much you hate it when you don't hear from any of us, me in particular. Would it help my cause if I took you out for supper, tossed in some flowers and rubbed your feet when I get back to the ranch?"

"More like a recitation than an actual apology but I suppose that'll do."

Carter smiled. He'd still be groveling if his dad were near the phone. If Carolyn McKay was unhappy, Carson McKay knocked heads together to get answers as to why his beloved wasn't beaming rainbows. Those heads mainly belonged to him and his brothers since they were the usual source of her angst.

"So...how are things? You about done with the pieces for your show?"

"Not really. I'm pluggin' away. Day by day. Seems to be getting harder."

"Have you talked to your agent about it?"

"No."

"Gemma working you too much?"

"Actually, she hired a foreman about a month back and so I'm not doin' a whole lot of work for her."

"Who'd she hire?"

"Cash Big Crow."

"Really? Colby's friend?" Surprise laced her voice. "I wonder if he knows about that."

"Probably. How is Colby?"

"Busy. And before you steer the conversation away from asking more about you, I'll give you the rundown on the rest of the McKays: Keely is running wild. Cord is working too hard, as usual. Ky is growing like a weed. Cam won't be home for Thanksgiving again. Keely is driving your father insane. And Channing is turning out to be quite the little gardener. Am I missing anyone?"

"Dad."

"Did I mention Keely was making him crazy?"

He grinned. "Once or twice. So, how are *you*, Ma?"

"You are all a bunch of sweet-talkin' boys, just like your father. Lord. It's a wonder I don't have a dozen grandchildren spread across a dozen counties. I'm fine. I miss you."

"I'm two hours away. I'm closer than I was when I lived in Colorado."

"Well, I hoped you'd been around more now that you're

done with school."

Carter didn't know what to say to that. Mostly because he didn't know what would happen after he finished the art show.

A door slammed in the background. "Okay, I shooed Colt out so we can talk freely. Honey, what's wrong? And don't say nothin', 'cause I can tell something is bothering you."

No sense lying to her or himself. "I'm in a rut."

"With your art? Afraid I won't be much help with that—"

"No, Ma. In a rut with a woman."

Silence. "Oh. Do I know her?"

"No. I met her this summer."

"Where?"

"Here. She's Cash's daughter."

"Lord, son, she isn't underage? When I remember what we went through with Keely when she lied about her age to that bull rider from Oklahoma..."

"Macie is twenty-two. Why would you think she was underage?"

"Because Cash isn't much older than Cord." Pause. "Cash has a daughter that old?"

"Yeah, fatherhood visited him early. Anyway, Macie and I are spendin' time together, it's just lately...it's hard to explain. It's different than it was at first."

"You really like this girl?"

"Yeah."

"Does she make you happy?"

"When she's not makin' me crazy."

"I assume you're knockin' boots with her?"

"Ma!"

"Oh pooh. If I can listen to Colt brag about bagging a rodeo queen ad nauseam, I can listen to anything."

True.

"So the boot scootin' is...?"

"Amazing."

"And that's a problem, why?"

"Because I'm afraid that's all there is."

Another moment of silence.

"I'm still waitin' for your sage advice," he said dryly.

"Hold your horses. I'm thinking." Then, "Have you and Macie spent much time with her father?"

"Cash? No. He hates my guts."

His mom laughed. "I imagine he does."

"Real nice that you're takin' his side, Ma."

"I'm not. How important is family to her?"

"She doesn't have anyone besides Cash so I don't think she has a frame of reference."

"Ah. There's your answer."

Carter scowled at the phone. "Where? I missed something."

"No. She isn't used to making connections on any level. Show her how. Good sex is a good start. But every girl needs a little romance. Make her feel special. Do something for her no one else has. Your job as a man is to show her you appreciate her brain as well as her body."

"I cannot believe I'm havin' this conversation with my mother."

She laughed again. "You are so naïve when it comes to what I know and what I've done. I was young once."

"Is this where you warn me to be careful because Macie is so young?"

"Young? At twenty-two? Please. At that age I had a two-year-old son, I was pregnant again, I had a ranch to help run and your brawlin' father to deal with."

"Not the same."

"True. But I will caution you not to confuse her age with her experience. There is a difference."

"Thanks."

"Anytime. Love you, darlin' boy. If I don't hear from you soon, I'm sending Keely to live with you for the rest of the summer, understand?"

"Now that's just plain mean." But he hung up with his first real smile in days.

Romance, huh? He could do romance.

ço

Two hours later the phone rang in Gemma's kitchen.

"Hello?"

An angry voice demanded, "Why is it that I have to hear from my mother-in-law that Cash Big Crow is working for you as your ranch foreman?"

Gemma smiled. "Hey, Channing."

"Are you sleeping with him too?"

"Yep."

"I have half a mind to come to the Bar 9 and kick your ass."

"Gonna have to grow a bit, Mrs. McKay."

"I can't believe you didn't call me, Gem. So spill the details, woman."

"Huh-uh. I ain't telling you nothin' over the phone."

"How about just a small hint?"

"Nope."

"You're getting mean in your old age, Gemma."

"Damn. I've missed your smart mouth. I'd take a chance on you whipping my butt if it meant you were comin' for a visit."

"Funny you should mention that."

"Yeah? What's up?"

"Well, we were cleaning out the big barn on Colby's folks' place last week and I saw Colby has all this bull ridin' stuff, which he'll never use again. Round about that time Amy Jo Foster and a couple of her young male admirers pulled up. Those boys are hardcore rodeo kids, and when they saw the mechanical bull? They immediately wanted Colby to give them bull ridin' lessons."

"Oh Lord. He didn't, did he?"

"Over my dead body will that man *ever* get on another bull. Anyway, Colby has an attachment to that stuff and he won't sell it outright, so we wondered if Cash might be interested in teaching some of these boys how to ride bulls. Since Cash is one of the few who wouldn't feed them full of crap about how great it is chasing the rodeo dream. And he was a good rider. The bonus is they are willing to pay. Good money, I guess."

"Really?"

"Really. There isn't a true rodeo school around here, and I think these boys would like a taste of it before they pony up any money and head off to California or Florida or Texas for one of the real schools."

Gemma began to pace. How could she keep Cash away from an opportunity like that? She'd been watching him with Macie and he had more patience than she'd imagined. He *would* be a great teacher.

"Gemma?"

"Yeah, sorry. So you'd want him there at the McKay place teachin' these kids?"

"Hell no. I want the bull ridin' paraphernalia as far away from Colby as I can get it. I thought maybe since you have an extra empty barn and extra corrals that we could give—*lend*—the equipment to you, and Cash could set it up there. Then we could start funneling kids his direction."

"I can't speak for Cash, but I'm sure he'd consider it. You want me to talk to him?"

"That's the other thing." Channing's voice dropped to a whisper. "Colby doesn't know I'm calling you. He wanted to talk to Cash about it first before we contacted you. Some stupid male pride thing. But since the Bar 9 is your ranch, I figured you should be the first to know. I didn't want you to be caught off guard."

"I appreciate it."

"Plus, if you do say yes, Colby and I will personally deliver the equipment, and we'll need a place to stay, so you will get to see me. And then we can drink whiskey into the wee hours, and you can tell me all about the hot monkey sex you're having with that very sexy Indian man."

Gemma laughed. "For that, I'm all in. When would you be comin' by?"

"Next week at the earliest."

"Let me know when to get the guest room ready."

Chapter Twenty

"Dad. I'm never gonna get this."

"Yes, you will."

"No. I suck. See? I totally missed again."

"It just takes practice." He peered at the unmarked orange circle. "I think live targets would've been easier. I know I'm a better shot with them."

Macie gave him a sardonic look. "Shot a lot of people, have you?"

"Just a man in Reno. Just to watch him die."

Macie laughed. "Came by your name honestly, didn't you?"

"Yep." Cash grinned. He loved the sound of her laughter. "Come on. You can do this, honey-girl. Try again." He watched as she lifted the gun. He studied her form and her stance. Her aim. She jerked her arm before she pulled the trigger and the bullet went high into the field behind the hay bale.

"See?"

"Yep. I know what you're doin' wrong." He stood behind her as she flipped the safety back on and kept the gun pointed at the target. Then his arms came around her and he repositioned her slightly. "Keep your elbows loose. Like this. Straight-armin' it is makin' you flinch at the last second, which is jerkin' the muzzle higher, which is why you're seein' puffs of dust behind the bale, instead of makin' holes in the target. Try again. Look through the sights. Keep your eye on that center dot. This time, don't think about it, just empty the clip."

Macie inhaled a deep breath. She flicked the safety off. Moved her finger from the barrel to the trigger and pulled in rapid succession: *pop pop pop pop pop*—followed by an empty click as the slide kicked back. Methodically she thumbed the safety, ejected the empty magazine into her palm and lowered the gun by her thigh.

Just like he'd taught her. Might've been silly, but Cash had a proud parent moment. He hadn't been around to experience many of them in Macie's life, so he swore he'd soak up even the littlest ones whenever given the chance.

She ran up to the target, whooped and turned around to beam at him. "I hit two! Dead center."

"I see that."

"Can we shoot some more?"

"As much as you want."

"Cool." Her eyes danced. "What other guns do you have hidden in your truck? Rifles? Shotguns? Bazookas?"

"Settle down, Annie Oakley."

"But I want to shoot something besides this little plinker."

"The Walther P22 is plenty for you to handle right now." Cash scratched his chin. "Although, next time I might let you try the Colt revolver. It's heavier, with a little more kick, but since you're shootin' high, you might have better luck with something that weighs more."

Macie opened the box of bullets and started loading clips. "How do you know so much about guns?"

"Been around them all my life. Wasn't a lot to do for fun on the rez. My *tunkasila* used to take me shootin' when I was a kid."

"What's that word mean?"

"Grandfather."

"You don't speak Lakota very often."

"Don't remember a whole helluva lot. It's a use it or lose it thing. I never spoke it fluently anyway, though I mostly understood what my *tunkasila* said to me. 'Course, purposely misunderstandin' him or my *unci*, my grandmother, worked to my advantage on occasion too."

"Know what sucks? I don't know anything about your— our—family. Mom didn't tell me stuff like that."

"I know you don't wanna believe it, but that's probably a good thing you don't know nothin' about that side."

"Why not?"

"It ain't pretty and it ain't happy."

Slide click slide click echoed as she slipped bullets in the steel clip. "So? I still deserve to know. And I'm gonna be a total pain in the butt until you talk to me about it."

Cash directed his gaze away from her. "Macie, it ain't like the Big Crow family has anything to be proud of in recent years. We're not like some of them families, keepin' with Lakota traditions. Talkin' 'bout our glorious past. I never much cared about my Indian heritage."

"Why's that?"

"There's so much wrong I don't even know where to start."

"Start with your parents."

When he hesitated, she used a sad, doe-eyed look that would net her anything she wanted. He'd've been putty if she'd done that as a little girl.

"Please?"

"Fine. My mom died from alcohol poisoning when I was nine. My dad ended up in the state pen long before that."

"Then where'd you live when you were growin' up?"

"With my mom's parents until I lit out on my own." Right after he found out about Jorgen's pregnancy. There was a proud moment in his life, running from his responsibilities.

"What happened to your dad when he got out of jail?"

"Died in a drunk drivin' accident."

Thick, uncomfortable silence weighted the air.

"So you're like me, basically alone?"

"Basically. Why?"

"I guess I'd always heard Indians had big families. You don't have brothers or sisters, aunts, uncles and a billion cousins?"

"I only have one brother, Levon. And he's repeatin' the family history."

"How so?"

"He's in the pen on narcotics charges. Long story."

The lift in her eyebrow reminded him of Gemma for some odd reason. "Have some place to be that you can't tell me now?"

I don't want to tell you now. Or ever.

Cash sighed. "Long story short: I felt sorry for him after his wife kicked him out, so while I was off rodeoin', I let him live on the ranch our grandparents deeded to me. Stupid son of a bitch was makin' meth in the barn. So when the DEA caught him, the state of South Dakota confiscated the ranch and sold it at auction to pay legal fees, and the hazardous waste clean up bill, and the back property taxes. Nothin' I could do. I lost the only thing that was ever really mine."

"I had no idea." She studied his face. "When did that happen?"

"Four years ago." Cash finally found the guts to look at his daughter. Comprehension dawned in her big brown eyes, before those same beautiful, wise eyes filled with tears.

Shit. He'd never dealt well with tears.

"Oh Dad. That was right around the time mom died, wasn't it?"

He nodded.

"Why didn't you tell me?"

"Because you had enough shit to deal with, Macie, without me addin' to it. I've never given you anything—"

Macie threw herself at him, wrapping her arms around his neck and sobbing like her heart was breaking.

Cash held her tightly, offering her comfort she'd never sought from him. Soothing her. Holding her. His child. Feeling like a total selfish prick because on some level, he was happy, *happy*, that she'd turned to him for something.

Macie's cries slowed to the occasional hiccupping stutter. Still she didn't release her grip on him. He had the good sense not to let go of her either.

Finally he murmured, "Better, honey-girl?"

"No. I hate this. I've always hated it."

Cash's stomach plummeted to the toes of his cowboy boots. "Hate what? Me?"

"No, I hate that I don't know you. Hate that it's so goddamn awkward to get to know you. I want everything to be butterflies and rainbows in my life, just once. I want us to finally make that connection and be, I don't know, like a real family. Instead of polite strangers."

She started crying again and this time, he cried silently right along with her. Holding the best mistake he'd ever made.

"You probably think I'm a bawl baby, huh?" she asked after a time.

"No."

"What then?"

"I never thought I'd be so happy to be wearin' your tears on my shirt." He squeezed her hard and kissed the top of her head. "We're gonna make this work, Macie. We're gonna be a family, 'cause Lord knows, we both need one."

She nodded against his chest. Still making no move to leave him.

"Can I ask you something?"

"Anything."

"Why didn't you ever get married and have another family?"

That question surprised him for the second time. "I guess I never found a woman who would put up with me."

"I'm serious."

"I am too. I'm set in my ways, Macie."

"My way or the highway, huh?"

"Yep."

"But what about when you were younger? Before you got so set in your ways?"

"I figured there was no rush. That I'd have plenty of time to settle down when I was older." Cash didn't want to muddy the waters and discuss his relationship with Gemma and all that he wanted from her now that he'd found a woman who would put up with his wicked ways. "The same holds true for you too. You're young. I'm sure there are things you wanna do. Travel. See the world."

Macie snorted.

"What?"

"My mom was the gypsy type, not me."

Cash leaned back to look at her. "You want to settle down?"

"Maybe."

"Here?"

"Maybe."

He kept his tone casual. "With Carter McKay?"

"No. I like it here because you're here, Dad. But if you're talking about me and him? I don't know. Probably wouldn't work anyway."

Cash wanted to tell her it probably wouldn't and encourage her to nip the relationship in the bud. But he bit his tongue and listened.

"He and I are so different. He's smart."

"So are you. You passed your GED when you were fourteen."

"Hah. He's got a Masters of Fine Arts."

"So?"

"That's not all. He has ties to the land and to his family and I don't know what that's like."

"Is he messin' with your head? Tellin' you what you have and what you've accomplished in your life isn't good enough? Makin' promises that you know he ain't gonna keep?"

Her eyes narrowed and he recognized that challenging look: He'd seen it staring back at him in the mirror. It gave him a spark of pride that she did have something of him in her after all.

"Can I talk to you about this? Rationally? Or are you gonna run off half-cocked?"

Cash grimaced and pointed to the four clips on the tailgate. "Half-cocked? I'm fully loaded."

"Dad!"

"Kiddin'. I ain't gonna shoot him." *Yet.* "Go on."

"It's like he runs hot and cold. He treats me like I'm everything and then the next day, it's like I don't exist."

"He's an idiot."

"Yeah." She smiled and wiped the tears from her face.

161

"Never mind. I'm babbling. It's my stupid hormones."

"When you realize it ain't you, and it is his fault for how he's makin' you feel—"

"I'll keep it to myself."

Cash opened his mouth. Shut it.

"But thanks. So when we're done cleaning up, you want to come and try a piece of caramel apple pie?"

"With whipped cream?"

"I don't have any in the camper."

"Gemma has some in the fridge. I'll grab it and be right back."

Shooting guns and having pie with his daughter. It was turning out to be a damn fine day.

৶

Three hours later Cash's cell phone rang while he filled water tanks in the south pasture.

"Yeah?"

"Cash? It's Colby McKay."

"Colby, you old dog. How's it goin'?"

"Good. You?"

"Good. How's Channing?"

"As beautiful and docile as ever."

"That'll be the day. She's got you pussy whipped."

"True, but I ain't complainin'."

"She wouldn't let you. So, what's up?"

"You ever thought about teachin' bull ridin'?"

Talk about from out of left field. But he and Colby never had time for small talk.

"No, but you've caught my interest." He listened as Colby gave him a brief rundown.

"Sure. I'll take a crack at it. I probably oughta clear it with Gem first. But I don't see it bein' a problem with her. Those boys interested in anything else? Bronc or bareback ridin'?

'Cause she has some rough stock she'd like to test out."

"I'm sure them boys would love anything you throw at 'em."

"Our kinda kids, eh?"

"Yep. Though, I don't think they make 'em as tough as us anymore."

"We always thought we were way tougher than we actually were."

"No lie there. We'll see you next week sometime. I'll give you a jingle before we head your way."

"You ain't comin' here to take home your brother Carter, by chance?"

"Carter? No. Why? He causin' problems?"

"If that boy breaks my daughter's heart, I'll be sendin' him home to the McKay Ranch in a casket."

"You have a daughter?"

"Yeah."

"Shit. Sounds like we have a lot of catchin' up to do, Cash."

"And some splittin' up to do. I'm inclined to start with his fool head."

"Hang tight. If I pass along what you just said, the whole McKay family will be there in two hours with horses and ropes—not necessarily for him. So, I'm gonna ask you not to kill him just yet."

"Fair enough, but no guarantees."

Chapter Twenty-One

"Cash? You want another beer?"

He'd been sitting in the darkened living room for over an hour. He shoved aside his thoughts about his conversation with Macie and focused on Gemma. "Nah. I'm good."

"You're pretty quiet tonight. Everything okay?"

"Actually, everything would be great if you'd come over here and give me a little sugar."

"Yeah?" She sauntered over and plopped herself on his lap. "I was beginning to feel neglected." She kissed his throat. "Lonely." She kissed his chin. "Horny." She kissed his mouth in that sexy teasing way that gave him an instant erection. "Very, very horny."

"I've heard about you horny widow types. Always thinkin' 'bout..."

"About what?"

"You tell me, horny Widow Jansen. What's that gleam in your eye mean for me tonight?"

"It's so damn dark in here I'm surprised you can even see my eyes."

"*Shee.* It's my Indian scout night vision. Wait. I'm getting something else from that vision. I'm sensin' you want to—" he let his tongue dip into her ear, "—blow me."

"You *are* good. Let's go upstairs where I can spread you out on the bed and work you over real good."

"I'm comfy right here."

"But—"

"What's the rule about arguin' with me?"

"Don't."

"Good answer." Cash trailed his lips along the long, tasty line of her neck. "Unbuckle my britches and put your hands on me, Gem."

"You wear your jeans so damn tight I won't be able to get them—or you—off unless you stand up and take 'em off."

"Whatever makes it easier for you." Cash put her back on her feet and stood beside her. Gemma kissed him while she unbuckled his belt. She kissed him as she unbuttoned and unzipped him. She kept kissing him as she shimmied his jeans and boxers to his knees.

Anticipation made him crazy. Waiting for her cool, strong hand to circle his cock. Followed by her hot, wet mouth and wicked little tongue.

"Cash? Up against the bookcase."

Zero argument from him. He shuffled sideways until his ass met cold wood. She dropped to her knees.

"Spread those legs wider."

"Yes'm."

"Now, see here, cowboy. I won't have you knocking off my knickknacks on the bookshelves. You're gonna have to hold still. No buckin' your hips. Got it?"

"I can move someplace sturdier. Maybe we oughta do this by a wall?"

"No." Gemma slapped his thigh.

Shit. That was sexy, her taking charge and acting all bossy. His dick jerked against his belly.

"I will stop if you don't obey me, Cash."

"I'll obey."

"Good boy. Hands by your sides."

He clenched his fists by his clenched thighs.

She nuzzled the hair covering his sac. "How is it you smell so...sweet right here? When you're all hard, tough male?" Her hand slipped up the inside of his leg. Then she cupped his balls and rolled them between her clever fingers.

Cash didn't move, but his cock twitched again.

Gemma sucked both balls into her mouth and made an, "Mmm. Mmm. Mmm," noise. Her tongue flicked over the globes, between, and she sucked again. The very tip of her wet finger lazily stroked the sensitive strip of skin behind his sac. Then it slowly slipped back to the puckered hole. Drawing ever-deeper circles into that sensitive knot of nerves. One push and her finger breached the tightly muscled ring and was inside his back channel.

"Goddammit I shouldn't like that but I do."

She made another, "Mmm," vibrating noise with his balls in her mouth as she pumped her finger and stroked another hot spot deep inside his ass.

He groaned.

By the time she released his nuts, they were drawn up tight against the base of his cock, hard as walnuts. She zigzagged the tip of her tongue up the vein throbbing in the center of his cock. Warm, wet flicks bathed the head. She stroked his interior walls and her finger thrust hard one last time before it slid out. Then she moved his shaft aside with her chin so she could nuzzle his groin.

"I love, love, love the way you smell. I've barely started tasting you and my panties are already soaked."

"Gemma—"

She slapped his other thigh. "Are you supposed to be talking?"

He shook his head, but he knew she couldn't see him in the inky blackness.

"I'm tired of talking too. Especially when my mouth can do things to you, and to this bad boy, that will make you my love slave. Forever."

His heart shot into his throat as she deep-throated him.

Man. He'd never get used to that silky wet heat. A cool rush of air. Another warm wave as she pulled his cock in deep again. And again.

Fuck. It was like being in heaven and hell. He never wanted that sublime sucking to end as much as he couldn't wait until he reached the glorious end.

He felt Gemma's hands clamped around his hips. Her

thumbs stroked his hipbones, in a gentle erotic arc, an opposite sensation of the hard and fast and—Christ almighty—wet, wet, wet feel of her mouth bobbing on the entire rigid length. And the occasional scrape of her teeth as she released his cock an inch at a time, the little tease.

She slowed her rapid strokes to suckle just the knob. Her lips tightened around the head of his cock and that nasty, sexy tongue flicked his glans until his legs threatened to give out. He bumped his groin into her face, urging her to take in more of him.

"What did I tell you about trying to bang your hips closer?"

"Please."

"So you *do* know the magic word," she murmured against his abdomen. Once again she sucked and licked and drove him to the brink, then retreated to lap at the crease of his thigh. "You taste all musky and yummy here."

"Gemma, doll, please. Finish me off."

"I love making you squirm."

"Goddamn, you're good at it too. But I can't stand much longer."

"Then come in my mouth this time."

When she'd given him head in the past month, he'd always pulled out at the moment of truth and come on her tits or her belly or in her pussy.

Thinking of his cock pumping his seed over her tongue and feeling her swallowing part of him seemed more intimate that the act itself. He usually avoided that portion of blowjobs and the women he'd been with hadn't cared.

Until now.

"Cash?"

"Okay. But I'm gonna need to put my hands on your head."

"Whatever you want." Then her greedy lips parted and she took him in all the way.

He grabbed her hair. "Open wider."

She did.

"Get me wet with that hot fuckin' mouth."

She made slurping sounds and sexy moans as his cock

tunneled in and out.

"Suck harder, JESUS, just like that. Fuck, Gemma. I'm close. Tilt your head. Hold on." He shoved the last couple inches until he felt the tip of his cock hit her soft palette. He roared as his balls lifted, and streams of come poured down her throat as he kept her firmly in place and pumped his pelvis.

Even through the dull roar in his ears Cash heard Gemma gulping. After the last spasm, she slowly released him from the haven that was her mouth.

She stood and pushed him back, because he lost the ability to stand.

Maybe his knees were buckling in shame.

Yeah. Bet her late husband never grabbed her by the hair and fucked her face like a savage beast. He didn't know what the hell had gotten into him.

The tangy lemony scent of her shampoo drifted up. He kissed the top of her head then reached down and yanked up his pants.

"Why don't you hop up on the couch and let me return the favor, eh?"

Without responding, Gemma took his hand and led him through the darkened house and upstairs to her bedroom.

He braced himself, expecting she'd turn on the lights. Had she noticed that every time they'd made love, no matter the position, no matter the time of day, it'd been dark? Or she'd worn the blindfold?

Yes. But so far she hadn't mentioned it.

He heard the click of the door shutting.

She said, "Take off your clothes and lay on the bed. Facing up."

"I like the sound of that." He stripped. "You have some kinda wicked games planned, Gem?"

No answer. Then her nakedness pressed him into the mattress. She was warm. Soft. Willing. She smelled like heaven and her body felt like sin. Her lips sought his and she kissed him with tenderness that set his alarm bells ringing.

"Hey. What do you say we get this party started?" He slapped her butt. "Slide on up here and let me taste that pussy."

"No."

"Why? I know you didn't get off when you were blowin' my mind. You too tired or something?"

"No. Cash. I want you."

"And luckily I'm right here."

She rubbed her cheek over his bare chest. "I love the way you touch me. I love how you push me to the limit. I love how you've bulldozed through whatever sexual boundaries I might've thought I had. I love every single thing we've done together."

"But?"

"But it doesn't always have to be bawdy. Sometimes it can be...sweet."

He froze.

"Let me show you sweet. Let me make love to you. No lights. No sex toys. No games. No dirty talk. Just you and me and the potential of what it can be between us, Cash."

For once, he wished he could see her face. He reached for her anyway. "Is this because you need sweetness tonight?"

"No." Gemma's lips clung to his after she kissed him. "It's because you do."

Her words undid him. Because he couldn't speak, Cash surrendered to her, in body, mind and soul. The night was the sweetest he'd ever known.

Chapter Twenty-Two

Carter McKay wasn't feeling very sweet at all.

The night was so dark it was like swimming in an inkwell. Only a half moon remained. Clouds obscured it and the stars. So much for his plan to take Macie for a romantic horseback ride.

He reined Deacon to a stop beside Gemma's barn. Then he dismounted, removed the saddle, blanket and bridle, and led his horse into the last stall. He shoveled a bucketful of oats in the trough and stepped from the dim barn outside into the warm night air with a nearly moonless sky.

Instead of working on plan B and deciding which sweet, romantic words to use on Macie, he found himself irritated he had to be thinking of that kind of shit at all. Why was he sneaking in on horseback? Why couldn't he just drive his damn truck right up to Macie's door? Who cared what her father thought?

Evidently Macie did. Which meant he had to care too.

Dammit. Carter glanced at Gemma's house. Pitch black. He walked toward the faint light glowing from Macie's camper and put his boot on the pullout step. Should he have brought flowers? A bottle of wine? She probably wouldn't consider a handful of rainbow-colored condoms and a bottle of lube very damn romantic.

He rapped on the door. The music inside ended abruptly. A curtain fluttered and the door swung outward.

"Dad?"

"No. It's me. Carter."

"Carter?"

Was that disappointment in her voice?

She peered behind him, squinting at the darkness. "What are you doing here? Where's your truck?"

"I didn't drive. I rode my horse."

"Oh. Do you want to come in?"

"Yes."

He'd forgotten how cramped it was in her camper. Especially since they were avoiding touching. He sat on the bench next to the foldout kitchen table.

"How are the projects going? Sculptures this week, right?" she asked.

Carter looked at her. Really looked at her. And was struck dumb by his stupidity and pride. He couldn't believe he'd grumbled about having to romance her. She was beautiful and sweet and funny; he was the luckiest guy on the planet for getting a chance to woo her.

"I miss you, Macie."

"What?" Her hand flew to her throat. A nervous gesture? From stand-offish Macie?

"I miss you."

"Carter—"

"I miss you."

"You already said that."

"It bears repeatin'."

Talk to her. Ask her questions. Show her you're interested in her mind, not just her body.

"So what were you doin' before I barged in?"

She pointed to the tin on the table next to him. "I was just about to have a piece of pie. You hungry?"

For you. I want to savor you. I want to devour you.

"Carter?"

"No."

"You sure? It's a new recipe and I have whipped cream. Not fresh, it's the canned kind—"

"Have you even been listenin' to me, Macie?" He stood and

171

crowded her against the small refrigerator imbedded in the wall. "I said I miss you."

"How can that be? It's only been two days since we—"

"—fucked? Yeah, I know. But it's been a couple of weeks since we talked. Really sat down and talked. Or fought. Or did anything but fuck like wild rabbits then disappear into our separate little hidey holes."

"Sorry to be such a disappointment to you."

"There ain't a single goddamn thing about you that disappoints me, that's what I'm tryin' to tell you. I miss you."

"Then why are you here scowling at me?" She held up a hand and he automatically stepped back. "Besides the 'missing me' thing you keep bringing up?"

Carter smiled. "Because I wanted to see you. Can we just hang out and talk? Act like a normal couple?"

Her hazel eyes turned shrewd. "Are we a couple?"

"Hell yes, we're a couple. A normal couple, doin' normal couple things. Talkin' an' shit."

"Fine." Macie cocked her head. "A normal couple would sit down and have pie."

"Then dish it up, darlin'. Extra whipped cream on mine."

Once they were seated across from one another, Carter took a bite. He groaned. "That's the best pie I've ever tasted." Another quick bite elicited another heartfelt groan of delight. "My mother would wash my mouth out for sayin' that to anybody but her."

Macie finally smiled at him. "Yeah?"

"Yeah. Where'd you learn to cook?"

"Self-taught out of self-preservation."

Another bite of ambrosia. He moaned again. "Meaning?"

"My mom didn't cook. I needed to eat. My first job was in a restaurant. I like to experiment with food. I'd still rather cook than waitress, but the money is better waiting tables."

"Ever thought about goin' to cookin' school?"

"Now and again, but I wasn't the best student. I don't want to study in a specific area like French, Italian, European or vegetarian dishes. Being a fulltime sous chef would be boring.

Same goes for a pastry chef. Or a baker. I don't think I'd do well with people telling me what I don't know, or telling me what to do all the time."

"No? I'm shocked."

She swatted at him. "Plus, I like mixing it up and doing it all myself. I've heard some of those specialized schools suck the creativity right out of you." She gave him a sheepish look. "I wasn't talking about the kind of stuff you do. Art."

"But it's true there too. The instructors make you learn how to do it the 'right' way so you can eventually do it your own way." He shoveled in the last chunk of flaky crust and chewed slowly, drawing out the taste. "Then when you do the kind of art that makes you happy, no one thinks it's real art. It gets called 'folk' or 'rural' or something that belittles it."

"That's happened to you?"

"Every damn day." Whoa. He'd finished his dessert in record time. He looked over at her full plate; she'd scarcely eaten a bite. Shrugging, he helped himself to a taste of her pie. "Then there's the whole all 'artists are gay' mentality. I'm constantly getting hit on."

"Never in a million years would I look at you and peg you as gay."

"Which is why I'm the perfect foil, darlin'."

"The last guy I dated? He was an artist and I found out in a rude fashion he was gay."

"Yeah? If anyone could turn a man from the dark side, it'd be you." He scooped in two more heaping forkfuls of caramelly goodness and sighed. "A couple of the bolder ones thought I was playin' hard to get, so they tried to convert me."

"How'd that go for them?"

"I think the one guy from New York is probably still pickin' up his teeth." Carter plucked up the last chunk of pie from Macie's plate, rammed it in his mouth with a happy little moan.

He froze. Lord. Was he smacking? Would it be bad manners to lick the plate?

Yes.

Would it be rude to offer to lick her?

Yes.

Focus. Romance. Normal couple things.

He licked the tines on his fork. "I don't have nothin' against gays."

"Carter."

He dabbed up every single sugared crumb of the delicious piecrust from the pie tin, sucking the sweetness of the apple filling from the pad of his thumb, lost in thought. "Although, I think it would've killed Dad to have a gay son. I'm pretty sure he developed an ulcer when I switched my major from ag to art. My brothers joked about it—until I told them how much I get paid for a sculpture."

"Carter."

"But it's feast or famine in the art world. I could bomb and be broke as easily as I could be touted as the next best thing."

"McKay."

"I just don't know how this show'll go over. It's a mix of styles. There's some pressure from my agent and I need it to do well financially so I'll have options. The thought of spongin' off my folks indefinitely... Don't get me wrong. I love them. I love the rest of my family and where I grew up." He brooded and fiddled with his utensil. Thinking about this stuff made him crazy. "I don't want to go far, Wyoming is in my blood, but there's no place for me on the home place if I'm not ranchin'. I've always been a bit of a loner and it appeals to me to be on my own. Even if no one understands."

"Carter. Shut up."

He froze again. Had he been yappin' like an unwanted dog? He shot her a covert glance.

And lust kicked him right in the balls.

"Macie. Darlin', don't look at me like that. We're supposed to be hangin' out. Talkin'. Actin' like a normal couple."

"Fuck being normal. I'd rather have you fucking me." She lunged across the table. The pie plates skidded and crashed to the floor. He barely caught the can of whipped cream before it rolled off the table.

Macie smashed her mouth to his and he fell into heaven.

Yeah. Fuck normal.

He scooted from the bench and took the four short steps to

the bedroom with her clinging to him like a vine. Kissing her. Lord. It'd been a lifetime since he'd kissed her.

They half-landed on the bed. She ripped open his shirt and scraped her nails down his torso to his belt buckle.

Buttons flew as he tugged on the lapels of her pajama top.

"Hurry. Did you bring condoms?"

He didn't answer. He'd seem like a selfish prick whether he said yes or no. Add in the tiny bottle of lube...

No use hiding them now. He tossed the whole shootin' match by the pile of floral pillows.

Macie demanded, "Lose the jeans."

Why was she always in such a damn hurry? He still had his boots on. She jammed her hands in his boxers and grabbed his dick. "Hey, hey. Let's start at the bottom and work our way up. I gotta get rid of these shitkickers."

"I don't care if you leave the damn boots on as long as the damn pants come off. Now." Macie pulled his lips to hers as her fingers worked his Wranglers down his legs.

Carter realized the rut they'd fallen into wasn't entirely his fault. In fact, *she'd* taken the lead when it came to sex in the last few weeks. *She'd* decided where (his place usually) and when (right after work) and how long (only long enough for both of them to get off).

Well, he was taking charge tonight. Taking what she'd promised him. Taking what would be his alone.

Screw romance. She'd had him tied up in knots for weeks. It was time for him to return the favor.

He gradually broke the frantic kiss. "Not so fast. There ain't room in here for both of us to strip. Get naked. I'll be right back."

"Hurry."

While Carter doffed his clothes, his gaze swept the kitchen/living area for an item he could use. He spied the frayed nylon rope poking out of Cash's rigging bag.

Perfect. Tied up. Heh heh.

He grabbed the rope and the can of whipped cream.

Chapter Twenty-Three

"You ready?" Carter asked.

"Ready, willing and able, cowboy, come on in."

"Remember you said that, darlin'." He set the can on the floor out of sight, but let the rope dangle in his hand as he stepped in front of her. His gaze took her in; she was stunning. Macie lay sideways on the bed, her head propped on her palm. Her glossy mahogany hair pooled on the white sheet by her shoulder. The sexy position emphasized the feminine bend in her waist, the womanly curves of her hip and belly. The tips of her breasts were hardened and her chest rose and fell with her rapid breathing. Her eyes. Man. Her eyes were black with desire. Until they noticed the item in his hand, then a flash of fear showed.

"What's that?"

"What's it look like?"

"A rope."

"You'd be right. Stretch out across the bed and put your wrists together above your head."

"Why?"

"Because I said so."

"I thought we were beyond games, Carter."

"You thought wrong."

"But—"

"Don't argue with me. Just do it."

"Or what?"

"Or I'll leave."

She stared at him. Defiantly. Warily.

"I ain't kiddin', Macie. My way or no way."

Something shifted in her eyes and she nodded. She rolled on her back, knocked the pillows aside and pressed her palms to the paneled wall.

"Good girl." Carter climbed on the bed and straddled her pelvis, ignoring the questions in her eyes as he bound her. After he was satisfied she couldn't get loose, he knelt between her widespread thighs. He snatched the pillows and said, "Lift," so he could slide them beneath her ass.

Then he dragged the tips of his fingers, oh-so-slowly, over the sensitive skin on the inside of her arms, until his palms rested on her ribs. "The rope will burn your wrists if you wiggle too much, so my advice is to stay still. No matter what I do to you."

"Carter—"

He cut off her protest with a scorching kiss. As his mouth moved on hers, he touched her. Everywhere. Memorizing her from the beautiful curve in her neck to the hidden curves beneath her breasts. He contented himself by playing with her nipples for as long as he liked, since she was helpless to rush him. Pinching. Pulling. Drawing soft circles around the areola until it disappeared into a tempting tip. He stroked her silky hair, bunching it in his fist, rubbing it on his face, releasing the minty scent of her shampoo. Caressing her flat belly with his whole hand. Teasing her belly button with his thumb. Arcing the ragged edges of his knuckles over the delicate skin between her hipbones, feeling her abdomen quiver as she whimpered in his mouth.

He slid his lips to her ear and whispered, "I'm makin' you wet."

"Yes."

"You want me to touch you where you're wet?"

"Yes. Please."

Carter nuzzled the sweet spot below her jaw. "You want my fingers? Or my mouth?"

"Your mouth. Please. Put your mouth on me."

"I will. But you gotta do one thing for me first."

"Anything."

"Close your eyes and keep 'em closed."

She did.

He licked a line straight down her torso. He reached for the can of whipped cream on the floor, distracting her by keeping his tongue busy on her clit.

She moaned, muffling the sound of him thumbing the cap and shaking the can. He rested the long white plastic tip against her opening, then pushed it in and depressed the nozzle, filling her hot pussy with cold whipped cream.

Macie screamed and jerked upright.

Carter placed his hand on her chest and pushed her flat as he began to lap and suck and eat every drop of cream—hers and the sweet white stuff from the can—from every hidden crevice. He jammed his tongue in her cunt as far as it would go. Licking her deepest recesses, wiggling his tongue inside her until she moaned again.

She came in a wet rush, bucking and moaning.

He wasn't close to done.

He lifted her hips higher, burying his sticky face in her essence. Drowning in her. Feeding his need by losing himself in hers. His fingers spread her wide, opening every part of her sex to him completely. He let his greedy tongue travel from her small puckered hole up through her engorged pussy lips and back down. Over and over. Faster and faster. While rimming her anus with his thumb, he latched onto her clit and sucked relentlessly until she came again.

After the last spasm became a faint throb against his lips, he rubbed his face on her thighs and her belly, marking her as *his*. He lowered her hips, stretching himself over her supine form. Her body was hot and soft against his coarser skin, and she smelled so damn tempting. He unearthed the bottle of lube and bent to taste her hard nipples, murmuring, "Flip onto your stomach."

"Carter—"

"Don't sass me, Macie."

"Umm. I can't really move with you on top of me."

He rolled her flat, and then hiked her butt into the air.

Carter studied her position, not as an artist, but as a man. Gauging if his lover was ready for him, for something new. Macie's flushed cheek rested on the bed between her outstretched arms. Her knees were wider apart than her hips, creating a solid foundation to take his thrusts. Man, what a pretty picture she made.

His heart hammered as he squeezed lube onto his fingers and moved in behind her, bending forward to lick a path from her tailbone, up her spine, to the base of her skull. Carter closed his eyes and buried his face in her mint-scented hair, tasting the sweat on her skin. Seeping himself in the taste, the feel, the scent of her.

Macie shuddered.

"I'm takin' what you told me I could have." He fingered the little rosette. "Plunging my cock into a place no man has been. Makin' this ass *mine*." He sank his teeth into her nape the same time his slick fingers breached her anus.

Her whole body stiffened up and her breath caught.

"Relax." Carter nuzzled the curve of her shoulder. "It might hurt at first. But don't fight me, let me all the way in. Don't clench." He pumped his fingers in and out of her hole, getting her ready to accept more. To take it all. "It feels dirty, doesn't it?"

"Yes."

"Raunchy, nasty, and wrong."

"Yes."

"But you still want it, don't you?"

"God, yes."

"Good girl. I've got plenty of lube, but no guarantee I can fuck you slow once I'm buried balls deep in this sweet untried ass, understand?"

She swallowed and appeared to nod.

"No condom either, remember? I'm clean. I want you to feel the heat when I come inside you. Sweet darlin', I wanna make this good for you." He whispered, "So good. Will you let me?"

"Okay."

Carter squirted lube on his hand, making a fist as he coated his cock. He slicked up her hole, squeezing gel inside that dark entrance. His hands shook. Sweat dripped into his eye. He blinked it back as he spread her ass cheeks and placed the tip of his cock at the virgin opening. "You're so pretty here. Every part of you is so beautiful. I wish you could see…"

He held back and tried to level his breathing and his anticipation. Concentrating on the sexy line in the reverse arch of her spine. Inhaling the sweet aroma of the whipping cream laced with the scent of her juices. An underlying hint of apples and caramel and sugar. A faint whiff of his own musk.

Macie gyrated her hips and pushed back. "Just do it."

Didn't need to ask him twice. One solid push and he was past that ring of muscle and buried in that tight, tight, hot channel.

His head fell back in awe at how damn good it felt.

"Shit. That hurts."

"Relax."

"Don't move."

"Breathe, darlin'. Come on. It'll feel good if you let me move." More sweat tracked his chest as he waited for her to calm down.

"Okay. Go slow."

Carter eased completely out. She sucked in a harsh breath as he slid back in. And out. And in. And out. Slow.

Faster faster faster. Ream her. Grind into her hard and deep. Show her who's in charge.

She whimpered.

"Christ on a crutch this feels so goddamn good it's killin' me. I gotta go just a little faster. Shit. Hang on." In. Out. In. Out. Hot, wet and tight as he sank in to the root. A hot suctioning pull as he withdrew slowly until that ring of muscles clenched around his glans.

"Carter. Please. Hold on a second."

His stomach jumped and he froze with just the plump head of his cock in her ass. "You want me to stop?"

"No. I changed my mind. Don't go slow. Don't hold back. Fuck me. Fuck me hard. Make me burn. Make me scream. Make me yours." Macie drove back and impaled herself on his cock.

Carter slapped her ass and let loose the animal inside him. He shuttled in and out of her ass, ramming harder and harder. Loving the way she accepted this harsher edge of lust, of him. Gripping her hips to keep her in place. Leaving finger-shaped bruises on her beautiful tawny skin. Stretching her to take every inch of him. Marking her. Owning her.

"Oh. Yes. The pillow...is rubbing my...clit. Faster. Faster, damn you!"

He went a little insane at her sexy pleas and reamed her, rode her hard. Lost his mind in her heat, increasing the friction on her clit, rushing her toward the climax she was chasing.

Macie shrieked.

The sensations—hot, tight, slick, coupled with her orgasm—were too much. He arched, plunged his cock as deep as it would go and stopped, blowing his seed inside her with a hoarse shout as her muscles clamped down and milked him dry.

Carter stayed still, humbled, spent, and breathless in body and soul.

He slumped across her sweat-covered back, keeping that intimate, heady connection as long as possible. When he could function again, he scattered kisses over her shoulders. "You drive me out of my fuckin' mind with wantin' you, Macie. I can't hold back nothin'. I want every damn thing with you, want to give you everything you've ever wanted. I have since the moment I met you."

She went absolutely rigid beneath him.

"What, sweet darlin?"

"I can't feel my arms."

"Shit." He sat up, memorizing the sweet way those muscles yielded to his cock as he eased out. Then he gently rolled her over and undid the ropes. She was breathing hard and her eyes were squeezed shut. He brushed soft kisses across her mouth and over the red marks on her wrists. "Be right back." He cleaned himself up and brought back a warm washrag to do the same for her.

Macie was still sprawled on her back. Using tender, soft strokes, he wiped her belly and thighs. Rinsed, and cleaned the stickiness from between her legs. Then he crawled in bed beside her, giving her no choice but to let him hold her.

Carter knew her silence was an attempt to put distance between them. Not a chance in hell of that happening. He kissed the top of her head. "So, I guess me fuckin' you in the ass tonight went beyond normal couple stuff, huh?"

Macie burst out laughing. "You are a dumbass, McKay."

"I love it when you sweet talk me, Amazin' Macie." He growled, "That was the hottest sex I've ever had."

"Was pretty hot on my end too."

"You okay?"

"Might be a little sore. But it was worth it."

"I'm glad. I'd never do anything to hurt you."

"You'd be the first."

He closed his eyes and breathed her in. "What changed earlier tonight? We were talkin', getting along just fine with our clothes on and then, wham, you were on me like a bear on honey."

"It was watching you eat my pie. You tried to be polite and savor it, but in the end, you devoured every bite. Then went back for seconds. You moaned, smacked your lips and would've licked the plate clean if your momma's good manners hadn't been so ingrained in you."

Carter chuckled.

"You flat out enjoyed it to the fullest extent." She paused. "That's the way you make me feel sometimes, Carter. Like you wanna be all polite and gentlemanly, but in truth, you'd rather swallow me whole. And you don't give a damn whether or not I like it."

"That doesn't bother you?"

"A little. But when I saw that side of you tonight, I didn't think. I just reacted."

And it didn't scare her? "Well, it might not be the best side of me, but it is there. And you're the first one who's seen it."

"I'm glad to be your first at something, too." She snuggled into him. "I'm tired."

"Sleep. But I am gonna wake you up and make love to you later. A couple of times maybe."

"Remember the sore comment?"

"I'll be gentle." His hands swept down her lithe, pliant body, curled against his. "You never know, I may even be sweet and romantic."

Chapter Twenty-Four

A week later, Gemma said, "Macie, can I talk to you for a sec?"

Macie stood and wiped the dirt from the bunch of leaves. "Am I in trouble? I saw the patches of mint and just started picking—"

"It's okay. I'd forgotten all about this part of the garden." Gemma leaned on the fence and peered at the wild tangle of vegetation. "Seemed pointless to plant a garden after Steve died. No reason to can vegetables for one. Looks like the herbs have taken over."

"There's no shortage of sage in Wyoming, that's for sure."

Gemma chuckled.

An awkward pause lingered as the sun beat down on them and the gnats swarmed.

Macie wiped sweat from her brow and slapped away the bugs. "So, what did you need, Gemma?"

"Help. Colby and Channing McKay will be here tomorrow morning. Cash and I are headed over to Meeteetse to look at a couple of bulls tonight and won't be back until late."

"What needs done?"

"The house is cleaned and ready, but I haven't had time to cook anything."

Macie relaxed. Cooking, she could handle. Cleaning the barns? Yuck. "You have a menu planned?"

Gemma shook her head. "But the freezer and the pantry are both full so there's plenty of food to choose from."

"Will I be working around dietary restrictions? Is Channing

184

a vegetarian or anything?"

"No. I think it's illegal to be a vegetarian in Wyoming."

She smiled at Gemma's teasing tone. Things were getting easier between them. It was an odd balancing act, with Gemma being her dad's boss and lover—Macie was never sure when one role was more predominant for him or for her. And Gemma made a point not to intrude on time Macie spent with her dad. So they were both careful not to offend or overextend themselves or their opinions.

"So you won't mind helping out?"

"Not at all. Might not be politically correct not to aspire to be a world-class chef, but I like to cook. I like to cook for lots of people."

"That makes one of us. How are things going at the diner?"

"Slow."

"That stinks. Unless you like havin' time on your hands?"

"Not really. I like to stay busy, though I do have more time to try out recipes when I'm not flipping burgers. Sitting around drives me crazy." She shot Gemma a sideways glance as they started toward the house. "Would it be all right if I weeded that garden spot? Clem promised me a few tomato and pepper plants. I'd like to try my hand at gardening."

Gemma didn't hide her shock. "You've never had a garden?"

"Mom and I didn't stay in one place very long. Certainly not long enough to see the fruits of my labors."

"You can do whatever you want, Macie. I want you to think of this as your home for as long as you're here, okay?"

"Okay."

"You have time to come up to the house right now and hash this cooking business out?"

"Sure."

"What were you gonna do with the mint?"

"Dry it. Maybe sprinkle some in a batch of brownies."

"See? You're creative. I never would've thought of that."

An engine revved in the machine shed, then sputtered and died. Metal clanged on metal.

Gemma frowned. "Damn old tractor. Something's always broken around here. I wish your dad would just forget about it."

"Not a chance. I never knew that Dad loves to tinker with engines. My Escape is running like a champ now, thanks to him. He has some kind of magic hands."

"I'll second that," Gemma muttered. Then she stopped in her tracks and looked up, her mouth open in shock.

Macie laughed. "Not touching that one, Gemma."

"Foot in mouth disease runs in my family."

"Carter's too. So the McKays are descending on us. What is his brother Colby like?"

"Charming. Candid. Generous. He and Channing are great. You'll like them."

But will they like me? Rather than dwell on that, or if Carter was going to present them as the couple he insisted they were, she focused on the jobs at hand. Inside the kitchen, Macie made lists and took notes of where assorted pots and utensils were kept.

Gemma said, "I know it's only a little after noon, but do you want a beer? I sure could use one."

"That'd be great."

"Pull up a chair."

They sat at the table, drinking in silence. Finally Macie said, "Why are you looking at bulls?"

"For breeding bucking bulls."

"Once everything is squared away on the Bar 9, are you gonna try to get back into the stock contractor business?"

Gemma looked surprised that Macie remembered. "Good question. That's what I'd planned."

"And now?"

"I'm wondering if I'm doin' it only because it's what Steve would've wanted. Being a contractor is a lot of work and a lot of travel. Which wasn't so bad right after Steve died, when I didn't wanna be alone here, where every damn thing reminded me of him and the hole in my life.

"It was fun for a couple of years. Getting to know the cowboys and their families. Changing things up from town to town, a different rodeo every week. It felt like an extended family, appealing thought to me since I'm low on family."

Macie bit back *me too* and listened.

Gemma cleared the huskiness from her throat. "But then things went downhill fast. Mike Morgan had a career-ending injury courtesy of one of my steers. Colby was almost killed by a bull in Cheyenne. Some of the other cowboys I'd been friends with for years dropped out 'cause they couldn't make a living rodeoin'. After I quit seeing Cash around the circuit, I realized he was a big part of why I'd liked it so much in the first place."

After that personal admission, Macie waited in vain for a look of dismay to cross Gemma's face.

"It was my damn pride that kept me away from him. That and fear." She laughed. "And my age."

"Gemma, you're hardly teetering toward the grave."

"Part of me knows that. The other part, the skeptical part that looks in the mirror every morning? That part sees wrinkles, gray hair, and luggage under my eyes, and seems to have the upper hand, calling me an old hag."

"Ageism sucks on either end."

Gemma gave her a thoughtful look. "Meaning?"

"You think you're too old to do what really makes you happy; everyone thinks I'm too young to know my own mind."

"I've never thought of you that way."

"That makes one of you."

"Even your dad?"

"He made mistakes when he was young and wants to make damn sure I don't repeat them. Although I appreciate the fact he wants to protect me, I am an adult. Sometimes I feel like I never was a kid."

"Cash keeps reminding me age is only a number."

"I agree. But that means I'm a very old twenty-two."

"What does that make me? A very young forty-eight?"

"Yep." Macie winked. "Why, we're practically the same age."

Gemma grinned and clinked her bottle to Macie's. "I'll drink to that."

Her dad walked in as she swallowed the toast. "My two

favorite ladies." He kissed the top of Macie's head, then stood behind Gemma and squeezed her shoulders.

For some reason Macie was pleased he'd acknowledged her first.

"Whatcha ladies doin'?"

"Celebrating Macie volunteering to pull my ass out of the fire. She's gonna cook up a storm today before the McKays arrive tomorrow."

"Really? Honey-girl, that's awesome."

"No biggie." Though it was, because she could see how happy it made him.

"You gonna wow them with your special caramel apple pie, eh?" He frowned. "Hey, didja ever bring back that can of whipped cream you borrowed?"

Macie choked on her beer, and waved off her father as he started toward her with a worried look on his face.

Gemma's eyes narrowed, then widened with comprehension. She hid a grin behind her beer bottle.

"You ready, sweets?" Cash said to Gemma. "We need to hit the road."

"Soon as I hit the bathroom." Gemma stood and smiled at Macie. "Thanks again for helping out. I enjoy talking with you. Don't be a stranger." She disappeared up the stairs.

"You'll be okay here alone tonight?" her dad asked. "Last time we left there was a storm—"

"I'll be fine."

"Is Carter comin' over?"

"I'm not sure."

He fiddled with his cowboy hat. "Call him. I'd feel better if he was around."

Macie lifted her eyebrows. Dad wanted Carter here? That was a first. "Why?"

"Yeah, well, because I want him to check the cattle before supper. He needs to take care of what's important."

Right. The cattle. Instead of that horses-and-cows-and-everything-else-are-more-important-than-me sinking sensation, she knew her dad had meant her. She was important. Macie hid a teary smile and turned away.

↬

Later that night, Macie was exhausted when Carter barged into Gemma's kitchen.

After he kissed her thoroughly, he said, "Come on. I want to show you something."

"Can't it wait until tomorrow? I'm tired and I have to be up early."

"It'll be worth your while, I promise."

"Then will you tuck me in bed?"

"Uh-huh. I'll even let you sleep tonight."

They weren't getting a lot of sleep the nights they were together. If she'd thought the man was dynamic in bed before the whipped cream incident. Whew. It was nothing compared to the stamina with which he made love to her at every opportunity. Just a few hours back he'd wrestled her to the floor in Gemma's living room and screwed her silly.

She still couldn't figure out what'd changed him. In addition to the smokin' hot sex, they talked into the wee hours. And laughed, Lord, they'd laughed until they cried. They had pillow fights and water wars. They'd crawl in bed and feed each other ice cream. Or snuggle up by the campfire. Sometimes they played cards, although neither of them knew how to play pinochle. They were truly acting like a couple.

Macie couldn't remember ever being so happy. Or exhausted.

She sighed.

"Please? Come on, darlin', be daring."

"Okay. But you better not be taking me snipe hunting."

"Never. Close your eyes." He slipped something soft over her head. Everything went dark.

"A blindfold? Why?"

"You'll see. Trust me." He clasped her hand in his and led her outside. "It's just a short drive." He helped her into his truck. They rode down the gravel road in silence.

Macie was a little unnerved, not knowing where they were or what they were doing. They got out of the truck and walked a ways before they stopped.

"Hang on." She heard a rustling noise and then Carter picked her up and laid her on something soft flat on the ground.

"Carter—"

"Ssh. Don't be scared. I'm here. Keep your eyes closed until I tell you to open them." He nibbled around the edges of her lips as he slid off the blindfold. One last sweet kiss and he moved away.

She felt him lay down beside her.

"Okay, darlin', you can open them now."

Macie blinked her eyes open and stared at the sky above her, which was a magnificent swath of pitch black, punctuated with silver stars. Stars so big she could almost reach out and touch them. Stars bursting with light so bright it was as if she were part of the Milky Way.

"Omigod. It is beautiful."

"Isn't it?"

"I've never seen anything like it." That wasn't a lie. She was absolutely floored.

"There's no moon tonight and no clouds. No streetlights or air pollution to diffuse the pure blackness of the sky."

"Is it always like this in Wyoming?"

"No. Maybe once or twice every couple of years. I've seen it in the summer when it's hot as hell, and in the dead of winter when it's ice cold. I have to admit I like layin' on a blanket much better than bein' wrapped up in a parka."

"Me too. Thank you for sharing this, it's spectacular."

Carter reached for her hand. He swept his thumb over her wrist; he always had to be touching her. It wasn't annoying; it was soothing, and becoming a familiar and welcome quirk.

They stargazed in awestruck silence. She had no idea how much time passed. Her mind blanked to everything but the majesty stretched out before them and the sweetness of the man laying beside her.

She blinked and Carter was above her.

"I didn't bring you out here to have my wicked way with you, believe it or not."

He ran his fingers down the line of her jaw and she shivered.

"But I want you. I want to make love to you like this. With starlight on your face. With warm sage-scented night air around us and a soft blanket below us. No one around for miles. Just you and me, Macie. As alone as we've ever been."

They undressed each other slowly and rolled over the blanket, skin to skin. Exchanging soft kisses, gentle caresses. A whispered word, a low moan. No hurry. The sexual heat between them simmered, rather than boiled.

In the breathtaking moment beneath the shimmering stars when Carter slipped inside her body, Macie also felt him slip into her heart.

Chapter Twenty-Five

Colby and Channing McKay arrived with four pickup loads of bull riding equipment and half the population of Crook County, Wyoming.

Or so it seemed to Gemma.

Happy as she was to see wild child Keely McKay, her quiet friend/nemesis Amy Jo Foster, four teenage boys, and a dog named Shithead, Gemma wondered if she and Channing would get a chance to talk privately. Lord knew she needed it.

She wanted to know if she was acting like an old fool because she'd fallen head over heels in love with Cash Big Crow.

Macie had overtaken the kitchen and shooed her out. Cash loitered in the paddock setting up the mechanical bull, while Colby and two teenage boys tied one of the practice barrels between two trees. The other boys were hauling more stuff out of the vehicles and carrying it into the barn. Keely and Amy Jo were arguing while they dragged piles of brush for the evening bonfire.

Where there were cowboys, there were campfires.

Didn't take long for the heated argument between the girls to reach her ears.

"He won't let you, Keely, and it'll just piss him off if you ask him, so drop it."

Gemma's brows lifted. Sweet Amy Jo cursed now? Didn't take long for Keely McKay to corrupt her.

"Why are you acting like my mother?"

"Because I'm trying to keep you from getting killed."

"Puh-lease. Do you *know* how many times I've watched—"

"Watching isn't the same thing as participating."

Keely let loose a sultry laugh. "That's what I've been trying to tell you for months, but do you listen to me? No."

"We are not talking about...*that* kind of stuff. We're talking about you wanting to climb on that stupid mechanical bull. Colby won't let you."

"Maybe I can sweet talk Cash."

Amy Jo released a disgusted sigh.

"Or Carter would let me do it."

"Wrong. Carter won't let you get away with half the shit that Colby does. So give it up."

"If they don't let me try it, I'll sneak out on my own and do it."

"Oh, no you won't. I'll tell."

"You are supposed to be my friend and back me up on this."

"I am your friend. And if you wind up dead, who will I room with in Denver? We already paid the deposit. We're finally gonna whoop it up, away from—"

"How's it goin', girls?" Gemma asked.

Amy Jo gasped and whirled around guiltily.

Keely jumped. "What are you doin' sneakin' up on us, Gemma?"

"Seein' if you were up to no good."

"She's always up to no good," Amy Jo grumbled.

"Don't I know it." Gemma smiled. "I couldn't help but overhear you talkin'. You two movin' someplace?"

"Yep. We're getting the hell out of Dodge and starting massage therapy school in Denver in September."

"It's a temporary move," Amy Jo amended. "The school has an accelerated program, so we'll be living there for a year."

"Both of you? Together? In an apartment? With no supervision? Sounds like a disaster."

"Sounds like an episode of Sex in the City: Wild Wyoming Women."

"Keely!"

"You should've seen the look on Dad's face when I told him I wanted to open a massage parlor."

"Good Lord, Keely."

Keely smiled cheekily. "Well, I'm glad you're here. We were just talkin' about a...man versus woman situation. Men always havin' the upper hand, tellin' us what we can and can't do. You think you could ask Cash if—"

"No. And if I see you anywhere around that mechanical bull, Miz McKay, I'll tell your dad what I saw you doin' in Cheyenne last year. That oughta get you grounded, oh, for *life.*"

"Grounded? Need I remind you I'm twenty, not ten?"

Gemma lifted her eyebrows. "Need I remind you the legal drinkin' age is twenty-one, and you doin' a half-nekkid—"

"Fine. I'll shut up now."

"Good. Besides, that thing is not one of them wussy bulls they use in cowboy bars and charge you five bucks to try. That one of Colby's is a nasty piece of machinery and the closest to getting on the back of a real bull. It's dangerous."

"Told ya so," Amy Jo said.

"Why don't you try to stay out of trouble and see if Cash's daughter needs any help in the kitchen?"

"Her name's Macie, right?" Amy Jo inquired politely. "She seems nice."

"She seems young." Keely demanded, "Hey, are you using her as free slave labor just because she's too young to know better and because Cash is working for you?"

"No. She's a professional cook and she's older than you, smarty." Gemma debated on mentioning Macie's relationship with Carter, but Keely would find out soon enough.

"No way. How old is she?"

"Twenty-two."

Keely and Amy Jo exchanged a look. And a grin. Then they ran to the house.

Gemma yelled, "No askin' her to buy you guys booze. You ain't old enough to drink!"

"Well, I am. Let's get shitfaced."

Gemma turned and smiled at Channing. "Macie's camper is empty and I know she's got beer."

"You're on."

Once they each had a cold one, Gemma said, "Married life agrees with you, Mrs. McKay."

"Does it ever. Colby makes me ecstatically happy. I thank my lucky stars every day that we found each other."

"You should. How you getting along with the McKays?"

Channing swigged her beer. "Great. Carolyn is awesome. Don't see much of Cord or Colt. You know what Keely is like. Carson would like me more if I was knocked up. And before you ask, *no*, I'm not pregnant, and since we've been married less than a year, *no*, we aren't actively trying to populate the world with more wild McKay boys." She smirked. "We are practicing a lot though."

"Some things never change."

"Speaking of pregnant...how is it that I never knew Cash had a daughter?"

"No one knew." Gemma shared what she'd learned. "So, he's workin' for me, but he's also tryin' to have a relationship with Macie."

"What's she like?"

"She's a good kid. Hard worker. Sweet, but not a pushover. Wise beyond her years." Gemma shot Channing a sly look. "And she's doin' some serious *practicin'* with your brother-in-law Carter."

"No way."

"Yep. Though they pretty much keep to themselves."

"Colby is *so* going to pay for not telling me that bit of family gossip." She paused. "Cash doesn't have a problem with Carter and Macie doing the nasty right under his nose?"

"He has a big problem with it. Not a lot he can do; they're both adults."

"True. So, tell me about you and Cash doing the nasty. He finally wear you down?"

"Nope. I finally swallowed my pride and tracked him down."

"And?"

Gemma downed her Coors. "And I am so in love with that man it's not funny."

"'Bout damn time you realized that."

"But it didn't start out that way. I've always liked him even when that weird connection between us scared me to death. When he agreed to take over the Bar 9 foreman duties with certain personal stipulations, I didn't know what to expect. Cash has always been a loner. He's set in his ways. He can be a little ornery. A little distant."

"Now why does that sound so familiar? Hmm. Do I know anyone else who fits that description?"

Gemma swatted at Channing. "Smarty pants."

"I couldn't resist."

"Then he introduced me to Macie and I saw a side of him that broke my heart. He feels so much emotion, the only way he can contain it is to fall back on what he knows and act the part of a stoic Indian. But again, when he's with me, whether we're workin' or playin', he lets his guard down, and I see the true Cash Big Crow. The great, humble man who's been knocked around by life, who's learning from his mistakes and is still standing proud and tall. He wants to be a better father, a better worker, a better lover, a better man. He ain't got no quit in him, Channing. And it makes me love him even more."

"Does he know how you feel?"

Gemma shook her head.

"Why not? You aren't still worried about your age difference?"

"No."

"Then why haven't you told him?"

"It's complicated. There's Macie and his guilt about her. He works for me. And I don't want to do anything that will put a damper on the sex that absolutely blows my fucking mind."

Channing leaned forward. "Dish the details."

"It's hot and spontaneous and fun." She hesitated and blurted, "And dark."

"Dark like kinky dark?"

"No dark as in: We always have sex in complete darkness. Or he makes me wear a blindfold. I've never seen his body completely nude."

"Whoa."

"Yeah. So I have to wonder: Is it a shyness thing?"

A calculating look entered Channing's eyes. "I doubt it. Those circuit cowboys are used to stripping down to their underwear in a whole room full of strangers."

"That don't make me feel better, Channing."

"Sorry. Go on."

"Then I wonder: Is he weirded out by *my* body? I sag in spots. Maybe he's noticed the pockets of fat and wrinkles, but he's okay touching it if he doesn't have to see it?"

Channing choked. "That's the most ridiculous thing I've ever heard you say, Gemma Jansen."

"You wouldn't think it was ridiculous if it was you in the damn dark all the time."

"There has to be a reason he insists on darkness. He's not burned or physically scarred?"

"No."

"Some weird secret tribal tattoos?"

"I don't think so."

"Then it has to be emotional. Maybe a woman laughed at him once and he swore he'd keep all sexual activity hidden in the dark."

"He ain't got nothin' to be ashamed of."

"Is it a different kind of Indian thing?"

Gemma's beer stopped halfway to her mouth. "I don't know. Maybe."

"Shoot. Then I'm out of ideas. But I think you need to force the issue so you can tell him how you feel. Being in *luuurrrrve* and all?"

"Right. He's only been here two months and I'm gonna confess my love for him? He'd hit the South Dakota state line in record time."

She rolled her eyes. "Give him a little credit. And yourself too. He probably feels exactly the same way."

A bunch of male whoops echoed from the yard.

"Sounds like the mechanical bull is functioning."

Channing scrambled to her feet. "I better make sure Colby isn't showing those boys how it's done."

At the paddock, Gemma sidled up to Macie. "You sick of cookin' yet?"

"Nope. Thanks for sending Keely and Amy Jo in to help me." She gave Gemma a mocking sideways glance. "I managed to accomplish absolutely nothing, but I sure had fun."

"Good. You deserve fun. I'd forgotten Keely was close to your age."

"Whenever Carter's mentioned her he makes her sound about twelve."

"Where is Carter?"

"No clue. I thought he'd be here by now." Macie sighed. "He tends to lose track of time when he's working. That's all he's been doing lately."

"Any idea on how his pieces are coming? I know last time I talked to him he was a little behind schedule."

"Carter sort of mumbles about it when I ask. I've never seen a single finished piece. Yesterday he was disassembling an old tractor for parts for some kind of sculpture. Said he needed to weld so he shooed me home."

Gemma sensed a problem but opted not to press Macie to talk about it.

They focused their attention on the men standing next to the mechanical bull. Colby explained something, complete with hand gestures. A round of laughter broke out. Then Cash stepped up; the crowd stepped back.

"You ever seen your dad ride?"

"A couple of times. I know he's pretty good but I still think he's crazy for doing it."

"Amen."

When Cash climbed on the back of the machine, Gemma's stomach clenched. Colby turned the machine on high. Barely two seconds passed before Cash was on his ass on the ground.

Macie gasped.

"Easy, hon. He's fine. Just watch."

Sure enough. Cash stood, put his hat on his head and climbed back on. He nodded at Colby. Four seconds later Cash was on his hands and knees in the dirt. A minute later he was back on the bull.

"He's gonna keep doing it, isn't he?" Macie said. "He'll keep doing it until he gets it right, or until he figures out what he's been doing wrong."

"I reckon. He don't know the meaning of the word quit. When it comes to anything."

"I'm glad. It makes me hopeful."

"Me too, Macie. Me too."

Chapter Twenty-Six

Firelight skittered across the ground, cutting through the shadows. Wood crackled, sending a shower of orange sparks skyward. The air was temperate, reminiscent of bathwater. His family was here. The food was good. The beer was cold. The soft twang of Western music drifted in the background. Nights didn't get any better than this.

So what was wrong with him?

Loneliness?

Invisibility?

Hell if he could pinpoint it.

Somehow Carter managed to keep his sour mood hidden from the rowdy bunch. He smiled and listened to the conversations. He was part of the crowd, but set apart. No one seemed to notice his detachment. Not even Macie.

Especially not since she'd gotten so chummy with his little sister and Amy Jo Foster. Lord, the three of them yapped like a pack of poodles.

It just served to remind him about the gap between him and Macie. Not necessarily their ages, but...

But what? But nothing. You're looking for excuses because you're pissed off she's not sitting by your side like a well-trained poodle. You're pissed off she's paying more attention to your family than to you.

Like that should be a big fuckin' surprise in his life. He'd always been the McKay in the background. How many times had he heard: *Who's that one again? What's his name? I don't remember him. He's so quiet.*

Carter wasn't a rancher or a rodeo star or a special ops soldier or the county stud or the baby girl. Eight years away at school hadn't helped him stand out in the McKay family and ensured his spot at the bottom of the McKay pecking order.

It wasn't as if he burned to be the center of attention tonight or any other night. But between Colby regaling the greenhorns with his rodeo exploits, Gemma chatting up a storm with Channing, Cash scowling at him and Macie ignoring him, he felt the urge to get really really drunk.

Damn, he wished his buddy Jack was here. Jack wouldn't put up with this shit attitude. Jack's motto was: "Be a man. Find some pussy, get fucked up, pick some fights and pass out." Jack swore the only way to get out of a funk was to suffer through a debilitating day-long hangover. "Feelin' like shit makes you appreciate the shit you've got," was Jack's other mantra.

Man. He'd welcome an ass kicking from Jack. Feeling sorry for himself was an indication he'd spent too much time alone. Might make him a pussy, but he realized he missed his pal. It'd been a couple of months since they'd talked, longer since they'd hung out. After spending damn near two years together in graduate school, they'd parted ways after graduation. Work had taken them in different directions.

Work. That's what he should be doing anyway. Maybe he was just feeling guilty for leaving stuff undone. It'd be best all around if he slipped away and returned to work.

Not that anyone believed being an artist was work. His family hinted that Carter the "arteest" sat around staring into space, waiting for inspiration to strike him. Then he'd paint furiously, finish the piece and wait for another visit from the muse.

Right-o.

He wished that damn elusive muse would hurry up; he was sweating this deadline big time. It didn't help his time management issues that he'd taken two fairly substantial commissions, on the sly, strictly for the money. Yeah, he'd justified it by telling himself it was still art, *his* art, and he had a truck payment to make. Hopefully the next time the muse visited she'd bring him a bucketful of cash. That'd inspire the hell out of him.

Macie giggled. Carter's head snapped up and his gut clenched from the potency of her smile. When had he seen her so happy? Was his tendency to brood wearing off on her? Or had she been drawn to him because she had that same dark intensity and she understood it? Neither of them could be accused of a happy-go-lucky personality. Except when they were together.

When was the last time he'd witnessed that side of her?

She'd acted pretty damn playful that night in the car when she'd whipped out her vibrator.

Not helping, thinking about what you want but can't have right now.

Carter eased out of the lawn chair and snagged a beer from the cooler. He kept his back to the fire and stared off into the darkness. Bits of conversations floated to him.

Gemma said, "I did not."

"You used to flirt with him shamelessly, Gem. I saw you."

"With Trevor? Lord, Cash, you need glasses."

Keely piped in, "Trevor Glanzer is a total hottie. I flirt with him every chance I get. I'd do him in a heartbeat."

Choking sounds came from where Channing sat.

Amy Jo said, "Keely! Omigod I can't believe you said that."

"Well, it's true. I think every woman here would take a crack at him, am I right, ladies?"

Silence.

"Fine. You're all lying to yourselves."

"Keely, I'm havin' Dad tie you up in the chicken coop when we get home," Colby said dryly.

"He tried once, said it was for my own good to save me from myself. Didn't work. He shouldn't have made sure I know my way around ropes if he'd intended to use them on me."

"I'd save you," one of the greenhorns said. "Ain't nothin' wrong with speakin' your mind."

"Oh, Marky-mark, you are sweeter than ten pounds of sugar," Keely cooed. "You remember you said that to me when I look you up in a few years, when you're a world-famous bull rider, fendin' off all them hot buckle bunnies. You probably won't have the time of day for a little ol' country cowgirl like me."

"Aw shoot, Keely, that'd never happen."

Carter snorted. Keely the cowboy conqueror had struck again.

He heard the cooler lid open and slam shut. Macie sidled up to him. "Hey."

"Hey."

"You're awful quiet tonight."

He grunted.

"You okay?"

"Fine."

Laughter erupted behind them. Conversations rose and fell.

Carter looked up at the sky. "Hard to believe it was just last night we were layin' on a blanket lookin' at the stars." He drained his beer. "Seems a lifetime ago."

She put her hand on his arm.

He faced her. There was that punch in his gut again. "You look beautiful by firelight, Macie. So goddamn beautiful you make me ache."

"Carter—"

"I want so much to...shit. I can't be here right now." He spun on his heel and pitched his beer bottle in the trashcan.

He said, "See ya'll tomorrow," and half-heard the shouted goodbyes as he let dust devils and bad memories chase him home.

Chapter Twenty-Seven

Feeling stung by Carter's behavior, Macie returned to her chair by the fire, anxiety replacing her earlier relaxation.

The discussions among the group were less raucous. The four bull rider wannabes stumbled to their tent on the other side of the house. People were starting to yawn. The campfire burned to a pile of red embers.

Suddenly Colby grabbed Channing's hand and jerked her to her feet. "We're goin' to bed. 'Night."

Keely snickered. "Didja notice he didn't say they were going to *sleep*?"

"I heard that," Colby shouted over his shoulder.

"Yeah, well remember we can all hear *you*. Keep it down tonight, Tarzan and Jane. Those two, I swear. Everyone in three counties knows when they're doin' it."

"I heard that too, Keely McKay," he barked again. "Get your smart butt in the camper before I whip it."

"Fine. But I will remind you I am an adult." Keely and Amy Jo argued all the way to the horse trailer.

Cash and Gemma doused the fire, said goodnight and disappeared into the house.

Macie remained outside alone, but she wasn't tired. She tilted her head and studied the night sky. It was as beautiful as always, something she'd taken for granted. She knew she'd never look at the stars the same.

Carter. It'd surprised her he hadn't shown up right away to welcome his family. She hadn't seen him until supper. Even then he hadn't said much. He drifted into the background. No one seemed to notice his withdrawn behavior.

Unless...that was his normal behavior with his family. The distant one. The quiet one.

Now that she thought about it, it was kind of weird, Carter living on Gemma's ranch, when the McKays owned tens of thousands of acres. Surely they could've found someplace for him to live and work. He had family there. Roots there.

But were those roots strangling him?

His words, *I'm nothing like my brothers,* echoed in the back of her mind.

Along with, *there's no place for me on the home place.*

Even with all his family surrounding him, having a shared history, and a constant connection, did Carter suffer from the same sense of displacement she did?

She never felt displaced when she was with him. She suspected he felt the same. But she hadn't really been with him tonight, not like she'd wanted. Not like he'd wanted, apparently, since he'd left.

Macie climbed in her car and drove to his place.

The lights were off in his trailer, a glow spilled through the cracks in the wooden slats of the barn.

He was working. Big surprise. He was always working.

Well, the time had come for a little play.

Rather than sneak inside his sanctuary, she shouted, "Carter?"

No answer.

"Carter, are you in there?"

"Macie?"

"Uh. Yeah. Can I come in?"

"No! Shit. Hang on. Just a second." Unfamiliar shuffling, creaking, and crashing noises sounded, followed by, "It's clear. You can come in now."

Macie skirted piles in the darkened walkway and didn't look up until she'd reached the main portion of the barn.

When she saw Carter, her heart skipped a beat. He looked so...raw. A powerful male, his sweaty chest bared. Ripped

205

sweatpants hanging from his hips, drawing her attention to his ripped abs. His hair was damp and curlier than normal. His lips were full, a little pouty, his jaw rigid, and his eyes...his eyes.

Lord God almighty his eyes were absolutely savage.

She couldn't think straight.

"Why are you here, Macie?"

The guarded look on his face said he expected her to say *I'm here for hot sex, baby cakes, strip.*

And seeing him standing there, all tough and masculine and yummy—it was tempting to be flip and reduce this...*need* to be here for him tonight into nothing more than a physical act. But at some point in the last few days, things between them had gone beyond physical. So, she simply said, "I missed you."

The energy drink in his hand stopped halfway to his mouth. "What?"

"I missed you." She took a step toward him. "Surprised?"

"Yeah."

"Me too. Look. I know you were upset tonight. I don't know why, and I'm sorry I didn't notice until right before you left." Another step. "But I'm here now, in case you want to talk about it or something."

Carter's eyes devoured her. Then he threw the drink can over his shoulder and charged. A hand dove into her hair and his mouth slammed down on hers. Hot. Hungry. Greedy. Achingly familiar.

During the consuming kiss, Carter's body was plastered against hers, yet as he ate at her mouth, his fingertips softly caressed her face.

She moved her lips a fraction of an inch. "Carter."

"I'm not done kissing you." And he absolutely destroyed her with the ferocity of his need. Finally, he gentled his kiss. "I can't believe you're here."

"I can't believe you left early. I thought you'd be happy that your family was here."

"I am. But I know my place in the McKay clan."

"Which is?"

Carter rubbed his cheek along her hairline. "I'm the quiet one."

She considered that. "I'm the last person who knows anything about family dynamics. But I'm glad you're not the quiet one with me."

"Why?"

"I never have to guess how you feel. Granted, I don't always like it, but you don't hold back anything."

"That's the first time anyone has ever said that to me."

"It's true. So tell me what's wrong."

Carter sighed. "When I'm with you, I feel like I'm really me. I don't have anything to prove. You just let me be who I am. That's not always the case with my family. And tonight, maybe it was childish, but I hated that I couldn't show them..."

"What?"

"Show them who I am when I'm with you."

"Oh yeah? A bossy sexual deviant?"

She felt him smile against her temple. "Maybe. But I couldn't. Then I got really selfish and didn't want to share you with them either. You're mine, and I know even sayin' that is just plain wrong."

Wrong or not, his words sent a thrill through her. "Since they're not here, how about if you show me instead? Remind me of who *I* am when I'm with you."

"Of my bossy sexual deviance?"

She brushed her lips over his collarbone, tasting sweat and mineral spirits on his hot skin. "If that's what you want. I didn't come here for sex, Carter. I just wanted to be here if you needed me."

His hoarse laugh vibrated on the top of her head. "Oh, I need you, all right."

"For?"

"Never mind. You're not here for my sexual deviance, remember?"

"But I am if that's what you need from me tonight." She placed another tender kiss on his pec. "Show me who you are with me. I'm yours tonight to do or be whatever you want. You already know I can't say no to you. I don't want to say no. When I'm with you, I feel like I'm really me too. Tell me what you want."

Carter sought her mouth, kissing her, toying with her lips. Then his breath tickled her ear. "What I want? Well, I don't want to talk; I want to feel. You. Me. Us. Nothing matters beyond what we are together. I want your mouth on me, Macie. I want to see my cock slippin' between these sweet, sweet lips. I want to wrap my hands in your hair and feel you suckin' me deep, suckin' me hard. And when I can't stand how good it feels, when I'm about to explode, I wanna come on your tits."

A flood of moisture burst in her panties. "Oh wow."

"You rethinkin' that 'whatever' comment?"

"No." Macie placed her hands on his head. She looked directly into his eyes and repeated, "Whatever you want."

Carter growled.

In one fast movement she yanked her camisole tank up until it disappeared over her head. Her shorts hit the dirt and she was buck-assed naked before him.

Macie licked her way down his torso, stopping to taste his belly button as she slid his sweatpants to his ankles. She dropped to her knees and gripped his muscular ass. She let her tongue tease his plump cockhead, until his cock jerked and clear fluid leaked out. She lapped at it like candy.

Carter rifled his fingers through her hair and sighed.

She opened wide and sucked that delicious male hardness halfway. Released it, and sucked it all the way in.

A strangled groan echoed above her.

She took her cue from Carter on how fast he needed her mouth moving. If he started to thrust his hips into her face, she increased the pace. She lost herself in his clean, salty taste. The erotic pull of that hard silken skin over her tongue and lips. The slick feel of her saliva coating his shaft and the excess running down to glaze her face and neck. His heady masculine scent enveloped her in a musky cloud of need as she reveled in this closeness. The tantalizing sounds of his unrestrained pleasure as she gave him this intimate kiss.

"Macie. You have no idea how fuckin' fantastic it feels."

She looked up at him. Carter's neck was arched; his head thrown back in abandon. Those blue eyes were squeezed shut and he was slack-jawed. The muscles in his stomach quivered as his chest rose and fell rapidly. His arms shook from the effort to hold her head gently.

He was stunningly beautiful lost in passion. She'd never seen anything so powerful. She'd never felt so powerful.

Macie was wet everywhere, her mouth, her chin, her neck. Especially between her thighs.

Carter pumped a little faster. She increased the suction. He groaned, pulled out completely and fisted his hand around his cock, keeping one hand tightly clutching her hair. "Ah. Shit. Yes. There it is."

She watched as white spurts arced in the air and splashed on her chest. Warm at first, then the fluid cooled as it slid down her sweat-coated skin. She looked up at Carter, who was watching everything with heavy lidded eyes: his hand slowly pumping his spent cock, his come splattering on her breasts and dripping off her nipples.

Macie licked her chafed lips.

"Don't move." He sidestepped her, and she heard clanking, fabric rustling. Then from behind her he said: "Lay back. I put a blanket down."

Macie's heart raced as he propped himself on his elbow next to her. The lust-filled look in his eyes hadn't dimmed one iota. "Carter—"

"Ssh, sweet darlin'. Whatever I want, remember? And right now I want to paint you." A small brush appeared and he swirled it through the sticky spots he'd left on her chest. "I've been paintin' you a lot. But never like this. Because this time, I'm paintin' you with me."

The soft bristles and his sexy words sent shivers racing over her bared flesh.

Carter zigzagged the paintbrush through the wetness around her nipples and down her belly. Straight to her clit. He flicked the brush over the distended nub and she gasped at the ticklish sensation. He swept the bristles side to side over her slit, inserting the brush a few inches to make circles inside her pussy.

"Now I'm on you." He kissed her. "And in you." He used the brush to paint two lines on his chest over his heart. "Now you're on me." He brought the paintbrush to her eye level and traced his lips with the wetness, before sucking the tip into his mouth. "And in me."

When she gasped again, he smashed his mouth to hers, rubbing her lips against his. He whispered, "Taste us, taste what we are together," before plunging his tongue between her teeth.

Macie had never been so hot in her life. She jerked on Carter's shoulders and attempted to roll him on top of her. He crashed into a table and open jars and tubes of paint rained down around them. Blue splotted her chest. Yellow on her arm. Black on her shoulder. In trying to wipe it away, Carter smeared it more thoroughly into her skin. Cursing, he grabbed random tubes and squeezed, his fingers leaving random trails of color on her body.

She threw her arms above her head. "Put your hands on me. I need—"

Then his paint-coated hands were tracking the hypersensitive skin from her wrists down to her armpits, making her skin a mass of gooseflesh.

She writhed and arched beneath him, whimpering, craving this side of him, knowing this was who he was to *her*.

"Here?" Carter's hands plumped her breasts and his thumbs swept her nipples.

"Yes. More."

His sticky palms raced over her ribs, smearing blue paint across her belly. His mouth was busy on her throat.

"Please. I want...Carter. I'm on fire. I need—"

"—to come. I know, darlin', I'm there." Hands covered in black paint slapped the inside of her thighs and pushed them out. He buried his face in her pussy and ate at her like he'd eaten the pie.

"Oh. Yes!" Macie grabbed his head and ground her throbbing sex into his face. When she started to come, Carter kept her clit captive between his teeth and flicked his tongue back and forth until she screamed.

Rough fingers scraped the outside of her calves while the

pleasure receptors in her brain detonated. His hot breath burned her ear. "I want to fuck you from behind. Get on your hands and knees."

She vaguely heard the crackle of a condom package.

Somehow she flopped to her belly. Carter jacked her hips in the air and slammed into her. It didn't matter as she was so wet and so ready to take him.

He fucked her hard. Not fast. Methodically. Each stroke deep. When she knew he was close, she gyrated her hips. He leaned over her back and hissed, "This is my art show. You will not rush me. You will stay still and taking every fuckin' stroke I give you, Macie."

"Carter—"

He whacked her butt.

She whimpered.

He smacked his hand into her behind again. Harder.

She whimpered louder.

"Interestin'. I think you like it. Next time maybe I'll spank this ass good and red before I fuck it."

Why didn't the thought of that absolutely humiliate her?

Because he could do any damn thing he pleased to her body and she'd ask for more. It gave her a sense of security because she knew he'd never ask for—or take from her—what she wasn't willing to offer.

"If I had a bottle or a candle or a dildo I'd slide it in your ass. Let you feel being fucked both places at once. By me. Would you like that, dirty girl?"

"Yes."

Carter dug his fingers into her hips and came with a snarl, her name on his lips. Macie's orgasm exploded on the heels of his, her greedy vaginal walls keeping him buried deep as he pulsed and throbbed and lost his fucking mind in her heat and passion.

They fell to the ground, Carter on top of her and inside her. Breathing heavily.

Her cheek was pressed into the canvas. She cracked one eye open and noticed yellow and blue streaks. "Whoa. How much paint is on my arm?"

"Not as much as other places."

How had she not noticed? Right. She'd been a little distracted by his mouth on her clit.

"You're covered in it. Sorry, I got a little carried away. It was just so damn sexy, getting to use my hands to paint you. To spread colors on your beautiful curves, especially since I can't seem to get them to look right on canvas." He sighed. "Lord, woman, you just fulfilled my top fantasy."

"Mmm. Remember that when it comes time to fill mine, cowboy."

"Don't you mean *cowboys*?"

She changed the subject. "The paint washes off, right?"

"Nope. It's oil paint. We'll have to use turpentine."

"Oh my darlin', oh my darlin', oh my darlin', turpentine..."

He snickered. "You're singin'? I think the paint fumes have affected your brain."

"You would know all about that."

"Mean," Carter whispered against the nape of her neck. "You are mean as a snake sometimes, Amazin' Macie."

"You just told me I fulfilled your ultimate fantasy and now you're calling me mean?"

"Sorry. You've blown my mind to the point I ain't thinkin' straight."

"You think you could think straight long enough to get your dick out of me before the paint fuses it there?"

"Aw, sugar pie, honey bun, would that be so bad?" His tongue swiped the shell of her ear and she trembled. "I seem to remember a certain hot Indian chick beggin' me to put that dick in that very spot."

"Very ungentlemanly of you to bring it up, McKay."

"Fine." He pulled out and rested his head in the middle of her back. "Stay with me tonight. I want you sleepin' in my bed."

"But—"

"But nothin'. You said I could have whatever I want, right?"

"Right." She muttered, "I knew that statement would come around to bite me in the ass."

He slithered down and chomped her left butt cheek.

"Carter!"

"You shouldn't give a man ideas, darlin'."

"I was hoping you'd get the idea to get off of me. Soon."

"Only if you promise you'll stay with me."

It made her heart hitch to hear the pride battling with the need in his voice. "Okay. I promise."

"Good." He stood and helped her to her feet. Carter spun her into his arms for a long, sweet kiss and a bone-crushing hug. He rested his chin on the top of her head. "Thank you, Macie."

"For?"

"For knowin' what I needed when I didn't know myself."

"You didn't know you needed a blowjob?"

Carter slapped her butt. "I'm not talkin' 'bout sex. I'm talkin' about... Never mind. Just forget it."

He tried to squirm away but Macie held fast. "I'm sorry for being flip. Tell me what you meant."

That seemed to mollify him. "For lettin' me show you my intensity. For seein' me. The real me. You seem to know what I need. No one else ever has. No one has ever cared. You make me feel...whole."

They stayed locked together in a silence weighted with both spoken and unspoken words.

Chapter Twenty-Eight

"No. Keep yourself centered. That's it. Keep that free arm wavin' high. Use them spurs! You're off—" Shit.

And the kid hit the dirt with a loud grunt. The lanky boy stood and threw his cowboy hat in disgust. "I ain't ever gonna get it."

Cash said, "Walk it off, son. Take a coupla minutes to cool down then come back and try'er again. That's the only way you're gonna get better."

The kid jammed his hat back on his head and limped off.

"You're pretty good with these kids, Cash."

He angled his head to look at Colby, who'd hopped up on the fence. "You sound surprised."

"I am. Speaking of kids...how come I didn't know you had one?"

"Subtle as a freight train, ain't ya?"

Colby shrugged. "It fits, since I'm more than a little steamed at you. Why didn't you tell me about her?"

"I didn't tell anyone. Trevor found out a couple of years ago when Macie came to see me rodeo. He hit on her; I hit him. He's kept his mouth shut since then. He's good at keepin' secrets."

"I'll say," Colby muttered. "So are you. We traveled together for what? Three years? And you never once mentioned her?"

"Can you blame me? With the way she looks and the way you went through women? I didn't want her nowhere near McKay cowboys or the rodeo circuit."

"That ain't workin' out so well for you, now, is it?"

"Fuck off."

He chuckled. "So what *is* goin' on between your beautiful daughter and my brother Carter?"

"He's paintin' her or some damn thing."

"That's it?"

"No, but it ain't like I'm gonna ask either of them for particulars. They are spendin' time together, whatever that means. I just know something he did upset her last week. And that upset me. You had the misfortune of callin' me right after I got done talkin' to her."

"Well, I ain't talked to Carter about it, but I do know he's a good guy. He's way more a gentleman than the rest of us. Educated. He's laid back. I doubt he's playin' her, he just ain't that type."

Cash snorted.

"Besides, does it really matter? They're both young. They ain't gonna settle down and set up housekeepin'. This is probably just a summer fling. They'll fight and fuck and move on."

"Is that supposed to make me feel better?"

"No. But I don't want your newfound parental instincts to cloud your judgment, Cash. Yes, Macie is your daughter, and you're lookin' out for her. Truth is, she and Carter are both adults and they gotta work out whatever is goin' on between them, themselves."

"Basically you're tellin' me to butt out."

"Yep."

Cash believed Colby was right on some level. But it also made him wonder how well Colby knew his brother. Carter McKay wasn't the love 'em and leave 'em type, which was why Cash was so worried about Macie.

You can't have it both ways. You're afraid she'll settle down with him; yet, you're afraid he'll leave her high and dry.

No. Cash was afraid that no matter what happened with Carter, Macie would leave him.

"So as long as I left my subtlety at home, how's it goin' with you and Gemma?"

"Good."

Silence.

Colby sighed. "That's it?"

"Married life has made you gossipy as an old hen, McKay."

"Come on. You and Gemma have been circlin' each other for damn near two years. Now you're workin' on her ranch and sleepin' in her bed?"

"I know you sent her my direction because you knew I was lookin' for work, and I appreciate that. But that don't mean I'll be spillin' my guts to you or anyone about what happens behind closed doors."

"Fair enough. Then tell me what's happening with her stock contracting business."

"It's pretty much dead. Appears no promoters wanna give her a chance."

"This ain't because of what happened with Mike Morgan last summer?"

"Not entirely. The last guy she had helpin' bad-mouthed her to everyone in five states. Evidently he was pissed off she wasn't payin' him more. He took a job with one of the bigger stock contractors and even the little rodeos won't return her calls."

"That sucks. What're you doin' to help her get back in the game?"

Cash scratched his chin. "Honestly? Nothin'. I don't know why she'd want to travel when she's got this beautiful chunk of land to call home. Hell. I'd never wanna leave here."

Colby nodded in understanding.

"She finally let me look at the books last month. Even during the busiest month last summer when she supplied stock for two rodeos a week, she was barely breakin' even. Add in the fact she has to hire an overseer for the Bar 9 when she's gone, and she's flat out losin' money. I told her she'd be better off breedin' the stock and sellin' it off. Let some other fool take on the headache of draggin' animals to rodeos all over the damn country."

"Makes sense."

"She'd come to the same realization right before she hired me. She wants to focus on buildin' a breedin' program, with both broncs and bulls. She's smart. She runs a damn fine operation and I'm lucky to be a part of it."

"She's lucky to have you helpin' her, Cash. You know your shit and aren't gonna feed her full of none. Which was one of the reasons I recommended you."

Embarrassed by Colby's praise, Cash changed the subject. "How's your leg?"

"Hurts like a sonuvabitch most days." Colby gave Cash a cool look. "You repeat that to Channing and I'll kick your ass."

Cash laughed, mostly because he figured Channing already knew. "I noticed her watchin' you like a hawk yesterday around that buckin' bull. She's afraid you're gonna get on and show us all how it's done, eh?"

"Yeah. Well. She don't understand why I can't sell the whole shootin' match outright." Colby stared off into the distance. After a while he said, "Do you miss it?"

Cash knew *it* meant all that went along with rodeoin' and being a professional rodeo cowboy. "Sometimes. I don't miss the bruises and the constant body aches."

"Or all the boring hours spent in the truck on the road between events," Colby added.

"Or the bad food."

"Or the bad draws."

"Or the low scores."

"Or the low payouts."

Silence.

"Hell yeah, I miss it," Colby said with a laugh.

"Me too." Now was as good a time as any for Cash to broach the subject he'd been wrestling with all morning. With any luck it wouldn't tip Colby off. "You keep in touch with many of the guys on the circuit?"

"A few. Why?"

"Just wonderin' what Trevor's up to these days."

"He's still chasin' the Finals dream. Though, he had a pretty serious fallin' out with his dad about it. I'm surprised you haven't seen him this year."

"He ain't been competin' in the rinky-dink rodeos I'd been

workin'. You have his number? I accidentally tossed it. Thought I might give him a call. I need to ask him a favor."

"Sure. This favor anything I can help with?"

He nearly choked. "Nope."

Colby sat up taller and grinned from ear to ear. "Hey, shug, you lookin' for me?"

Cash turned around and watched Channing crook her little finger at her husband.

Colby jumped off the fence like it'd suddenly caught fire.

Cash grinned. Maybe someday soon, if he played his cards right, Gemma would look at him like that.

Gemma. Lord, thinking about the smokin' hot sex last night still made his dick hard.

He'd figured once they'd retired to their room, she'd be too worn out to make love. Or she'd be worried about having sex with other people staying in the house.

Had he been wrong.

They'd started messing around, and the need between them flared as hot and urgent as it always did. He'd gone down on her—man did he *love* going down on her, the sweet noises she made were music to his ears, but she'd literally turned the tables on him. She'd flipped around so she could suck his cock while he ate her pussy. He'd never been especially fond of sixty-nine until last night when the law of averages caught up with them and they'd actually come at the same time. Explosively. Feeling his cock throb hot spurts in her suctioning mouth while she came, undulating against his face... Well, he'd have to rethink his position on that particular position.

But Gemma hadn't been satisfied. She wanted to make love face to face. With the lights on.

He'd said no. She'd insisted. When he offered a compromise of making love with her blindfolding him, she offered a new threat: One of these nights she'd wait until he fell asleep, then she'd hog-tie him, turn the lights on and fuck him exactly how she wanted. For as long as she wanted. In the position she wanted. She haughtily informed him there wouldn't be a damn thing he could do about it.

Cash knew she'd follow through with the threat. And he

wasn't ready for her to see the truth of how he felt about her. So he pretended to laugh it off and waited until she fell asleep.

He snuck out of bed and cut an old T-shirt of Steve's into one long strip. Making sure the bottle of lube was nearby, he murmured instructions in her ear.

She didn't protest, just sleepily rolled to her stomach. As he bound her wrists behind her back, she woke up.

Spitting mad.

Her fury lasted about a minute until she felt his slippery thumb stroking her clit and his fingers snaking up inside her, bringing her to a fast orgasm. While she recovered, he hiked her hips in the air and squirted more lube on his fingers and his straining cock.

Gemma gasped when he squeezed a dollop on her anus.

"Cash—"

"Did he have you here?" He inserted two fingers in her ass.

She sucked in a breath and released it on a moan, nodding.

"Good. Then you'll know what to expect." He scissored his fingers inside that dark hole, stretching her to fit him. He angled over her arched spine to whisper in her ear. "You didn't expect I'd stay out of this gorgeous ass forever, did you?"

"No."

"See, this is the way *I* deal with threats, sweets, call it a pre-emptive strike."

"But—"

"Who's hog-tied now, Gem?"

"Umm. Me."

"And I'm gonna fuck you exactly where I want, and how I want, as long as I want, exactly as I've fantasized and there ain't a damn thing you can do about it, is there?"

"No."

He growled, "If I knew where your vibrator was I'd shove it up your pussy while I ream this tight hole. You fantasize about having two men at once. Two men fucking you in every way imaginable."

"Cash."

"Do you want that, Gemma?"

"Ah. Yes."

"Another time. Right now, I'm gonna fuck you so hard that you remember who makes the decisions in the bedroom. I'm gonna fuck and use this ass to the absolute limit and you're gonna love it, aren't you?"

"Please. Oh—"

Cash impaled her to the root on the first stroke. He reached between her thighs and rubbed her clit while he tunneled in and out of her ass. Faster. Harder. Each thrust had enough force to send her knees sliding toward the headboard. He wrapped his hands around her waist and jerked her back to the end of the bed and started over.

She smelled good. She felt good too. As much as he wanted to stay buried in that hot, tight channel, Cash couldn't hold back.

Neither could Gemma. She came, muffling her cries into the pillow as his cock pumped and jerked and finally shot his load high and hard into that hot, tight portal.

Gemma flopped to her stomach after he eased out of her. He was half afraid he'd been too rough. But after he loosened the bindings and spooned against her, she murmured, "I'll have to threaten you more often."

Two shouts sounded from the tent bringing Cash back to reality. The boys returned for their riding lessons and all thoughts beyond rodeo disappeared.

Chapter Twenty-Nine

Later Cash was taking a breather, enjoying the serenity of the ranch when he heard footsteps behind him. When he turned to see his daughter approaching, his heart lightened. They hadn't spent much time together recently, and he was afraid it wouldn't take much to snap the tentative connection they'd established.

"Hey, Dad."

"*Hoka hey*, honey-girl." Poor thing looked tired. "Gemma finally parole you from kitchen duty?"

"How many times do I have to tell you cooking is not a chore?"

"I suppose it is different when you're good at it." He hesitated. "If I've forgotten to tell you, the food's been mighty tasty the last coupla days. I know everyone's been talkin' about it. I'm proud of you for pitchin' in."

Macie blushed. "Thanks."

The scent of hot dirt permeated the air as they gazed across the paddock. A pair of crows circled the turquoise sky, their *caw caw* lost in the breeze blowing through the stand of cedar trees.

"It's so beautiful here."

"That it is. I was just thinkin' the same thing."

"We haven't been riding for a couple of days." She picked at a loose chunk of wood on the fence. "But I suppose you're pretty busy, huh?"

"Not too busy for you. Wanna go out right after supper?"

"Sure. Is Gemma tired of me taking her horse all the time?"

"No. She's glad. Daisy needs the exercise and she's been swamped catchin' up on ranch paperwork."

A truck whizzed by on the gravel road, sending clouds of chalky dust across the rocky field.

Macie angled her chin toward the empty mechanical bull. "What was the toss off rate today?"

"Eighty-five percent."

"Not good."

"Better than the ninety-nine percent from yesterday."

"True. So how many times did you have to demonstrate?"

"None."

"Really?"

"Yeah. Why?"

"So you're not all beat up?"

"No." But the truth was, all damn day he had been feeling some of those old aches and pains from previous rodeo injuries.

"Huh. That gives you no excuse not to give me a personal demonstration on your bull ridin' expertise."

"What?"

She smiled and teased, "Come on, Dad. Show me how an old pro does it. Every time I saw you yesterday you were eatin' dirt."

Cash bit back a grin. "Think your old man ain't got it in him anymore?"

"Didn't appear you had it in you yesterday."

"It's a new day."

"Five bucks says you land on your butt before the buzzer sounds."

"You're on, girlie." He strode toward the piece of equipment and whirled around to remind her, "Hit the switch when I nod my head. Then sit back and prepare to be awed."

Macie's laughter filled something inside him he hadn't realized was empty. He hopped on the machine and jerked on his riding glove. He wrapped the bull rope. Unwrapped it and rewrapped it.

"Are you stalling?"

"You wish. Get ready to pay up." Cash adjusted his hat over his eyes. Moved his hips from side to side. Threw his free arm up in the air and nodded.

The bull kicked on. It spun right; Cash readjusted his knees when the movement blew his feet out and up. The front end lifted, slamming him back, but he didn't fight it and stayed on. Another jumping right spin. Two hard lefts, one last buck and the eight seconds were history and he was still on.

He whooped and jumped off, surprised by how much he'd wanted Macie to see him succeed.

She grinned as he approached. "Nice ridin', Dad."

"Thanks. Pay up."

"Will you take a personal check?"

"Nope. Cash only."

She snickered. "You should have that tattooed somewhere."

A calf bawled in the distance.

Cash quietly tried to restore his breathing.

"So, can I sit on that thing?"

He frowned. "I remember you tellin' me you'd never ride a bull."

"I don't want to ride it; I just want to know what it feels like to be on a big, bad bull substitute, which is the closest I will ever get to one of those nasty creatures."

"Sure. Come on."

Cash lifted her on the back of the apparatus. He showed her how to wrap the rope, how to spur, how the free arm was the key to achieving balance. He was happy she'd taken an interest in something he'd spent years of his life learning to perfect.

The lesson in bull riding was about over when he heard, "What the *hell* do you think you're doin'?"

He turned and saw Carter storming toward them. The fence wasn't an impediment to the angry young man; he put one arm on the railing and jumped sideways over it.

"Get off that thing right now, Macie."

"Carter—"

"I cannot fuckin' *believe* you put her on the back of a

goddamn mechanical bull."

"Wait just a minute. I can explain—"

"Explain what?" Carter shouted. "How damn dangerous it is? That's a little hard to explain to her when she's dead. Christ, she could've broken her neck."

"She wasn't—"

"Jesus, Cash, what were you thinkin'?"

"Stop right there, McKay."

"I ain't kiddin', Macie, get off that death trap or I'll drag you off."

"You can't talk to her like that."

"I can talk to her any damn way I please since it appears I'm the only one who cares about her!"

"Shut your mouth, McKay, and listen up."

"No, you listen."

"Carter!"

"Do you really think I'd put my daughter in danger?" Cash kept his hands clenched in fists by his sides in an effort not to take a swing at this self-righteous punk.

Carter didn't answer; he just glared with his hands curled on his hips, looking ready to do some swinging himself.

"Well, *do* you?"

"No. But I think she'd do whatever it took to get your attention, including puttin' herself at risk by climbin' on the back of a bull."

Ugly silence hung in the air.

"Ain't got nothin' to say to that do you, 'cause you know it's the truth."

"That's it, boy, you went too far."

"Not nearly far enough. If you want to fight, bring it, old man."

"I don't give a shit who you—"

Macie stepped between them. "Stop. Both of you." She whirled on Carter and snapped, "Walk it off. I mean it, Carter."

He didn't budge.

By that time Cash noticed they'd drawn a crowd, including

Gemma, Colby and Channing, Keely, Amy Jo and the boys he'd been teaching. Great.

Cash turned and walked away.

Macie moved in front of him and grabbed his hand. "Thank you. I had fun. Don't listen to him."

Cash reached out and stroked his free hand down her soft hair. "I wasn't. I'd never do nothin' to hurt you, Macie."

"I know."

"And in case you're wonderin' 'bout some of the crap he was throwin' out, don't listen to him either. You *do* have my attention. You're smarter than to do something stupid to get it."

"I know that too." Macie stood on her tiptoes and kissed his cheek. She whispered, "I'll go double or nothing with you on that bet. Same time tomorrow. Bring your money."

Cash smiled as he watched her walk away from him...and from Carter McKay.

Chapter Thirty

"Dumbass. Get away from me."

"Macie—"

"Don't. Talk. To. Me."

"Please."

"No. Go." She slammed the camper door in his face and locked it. Then she cranked Dwight Yoakam to a million decibels, effectively cutting off all communication.

Damn. Carter kicked a dirt clod as he lumbered back to his pickup. How had everything gotten out of control? One second he'd been striding across the yard, looking forward to seeing Macie's smiling face. Looking forward to showing his family what they were together. The next second he'd seen her perched on the back of that bucking bull and his heart just...stopped. He didn't think; he just reacted.

Badly.

No shit. Now he'd pissed off Macie and her father.

But he knew what he'd said hadn't been totally out of line, merely bad timing. Macie was so eager for any kind of family connection, especially with Cash, Carter suspected she would do anything. Or listen to whatever free or bad advice her dad offered. Yeah, Carter could just hear that conversation:

Forget about McKay. He's proven he's an insensitive prick, just like the rest of the goddamn McKays. Besides, you're young. Don't make the same mistakes I did when I was young. There's no need for you to settle down. Or to settle for a hothead like him.

Then the son of a bitch would probably hand over the keys to his camper and encourage her to hit the road—allowing Cash uninterrupted time with Gemma. If and when Macie returned, Carter McKay would be long gone. Which is exactly what Cash Big Crow wanted.

"Fuck." He could totally see that scenario happening, since he knew Macie had no intention of sticking around here beyond summer's end.

How could he make her stay?

He couldn't. Not today, anyway. His only other option was to skulk around her door like some...whipped dog. Begging for scraps of her attention.

Like that would work.

Or he could go home and work.

On pictures of her.

Great.

He wondered if his day could get any worse.

"Hey, bro, when did you turn into such a macho jerk? That was quite the display of testosterone."

Keely. Carter thunked his head on his hood. The universe fucking hated him today.

"Yeah, well, I wanted to prove I was a true McKay, asshole behavior and all."

"Now that you mention it, you sorta were actin' like Dad."

"Great, Keely, just what I wanted to hear."

"At any rate, I brought you a beer."

He looked up.

She waggled a bottle of Bud Light at him. "I thought you could use one."

"Thanks." He popped the cap off and drank. "What're you doin' out here?"

"Hidin' from the bull rider wannabes and lettin' Amy Jo deal with them."

"Meanin', you ditched her and you were sneakin' off to drink a beer and you were afraid I'd caught you."

Keely grinned. "I knew there was a reason you're my favorite brother."

"Favorite. Right." Why wasn't he surprised his sister hadn't really come looking for him? No one else had either.

Maybe it's because you're acting like a shithead who deserves to be alone.

Keely blithely continued, "Besides, Amy Jo will probably come barreling over to Macie's camper to listen to her rant and rave about you."

"Why would Amy Jo care?"

"She and Macie hit it off like gangbusters. And let's just say Amy Jo is well-versed on dealing with a hot-headed McKay male who can't see the forest for the trees."

Carter frowned. "Who are you talkin' about? She got a thing for Colt?" Lord help the girl if she did. Colt would charm her, bed her, and leave her. And feel no guilt about it whatsoever.

"No. Cord."

That was worse for poor sweet Amy Jo. Way worse.

"So, how long have you been with Macie?"

He said nothing.

"Puh-lease. Even before your he-man tactics today, your eyes devoured *her* while you were supposed to be eatin' supper last night. And I noticed this morning she had a streak of paint—yellow umber to be exact, *your* favorite color to be even more exact—on her neck. So, I figured you'd been doin' a little finger painting after the bonfire."

Carter sighed.

Softly, Keely said, "You have it bad for her, don't you?"

His head snapped up. "What makes you say that?"

"Because you didn't bother with niceties today. You were scared, you were pissed, and you didn't hide it from anyone, least of all her."

He clamped his teeth together.

"You work really hard at disguising your intense side, Carter. Almost everyone believes you are this calm, cool, laid-back kinda guy." She plucked the beer from him and drank. "I've spent more time with you than the rest of our brothers have, so you've never fooled me. I know what you're really like. Macie knows that side of you too. Or, if she didn't, she got a taste of it today. But she knew before, didn't she?"

"Yeah."

"And it hasn't scared her off?"

"Not yet."

"She's exactly like you, which means she's perfect for you because she will make your life a living hell. Or heaven on earth. Depending on the day and your collective brooding moods."

Carter was stunned into silence by Keely's comments.

"So, no matter what anyone tells you, bro, fight for her. She's worth it. And I'll lie through my teeth if you *ever* tell anybody I said this, but you are worth it too." She sauntered off and vanished in the copse of scrub oak trees.

He'd underestimated his sister on many levels. When had she become so insightful? Or had he automatically discounted her lack of understanding about anything important because of her age?

Was he doing the same thing with Macie?

Either way, Carter realized everything she'd said was exactly on the nose.

He also realized Keely had taken off with his beer.

Happy as Gemma had been to see Channing and Colby, she breathed a sigh of relief after the rowdy crew returned to Campbell County.

Cash and Carter hadn't come to a resolution after the blow up over Macie. Far as she knew, Carter hadn't been back to the Bar 9. Rather than ask Carter to help Cash with chores, it was easier all around if she did it.

Things hadn't returned to normal. Since the primary cook had quit at the diner, Macie warned them she'd be working tons more hours. Gemma knew Cash worried about Macie, but she also knew something had changed significantly between father and daughter in the past few days. Not that Cash confided in her, he was determined to figure this out with Macie on his own. Still, she sensed an acceptance, which hadn't been there.

Like they'd both let down their guards a little.

She wished Cash would let down his guard with her. From a purely professional standpoint, they worked well together. They'd spent hours out in the field, fixing fences, tending cattle, watching for wildfires. She'd learned why he didn't have a place to call his own, and it broke her heart. They'd sat at the table after supper, mountains of paperwork strewn across the table as they discussed the pros and cons of various breeding programs. When the stock contracting issue came up, he'd bluntly told her to let it go and to focus on other areas of the cattle business. She'd literally felt the weight of that burden leaving her soul.

Was that because it'd been one of her final ties to her life with Steve? The Bar 9 might've been Steve's when she'd moved in years ago, but it was as much hers now as it'd been his.

The door between the upstairs and main floor slammed. Pine-scented aftershave wafted into the living room and she automatically smiled.

Cash plopped next to her on the couch, grabbed her hand and kissed her knuckles. "You need help with the laundry?"

"Nah. I've got it covered. But thanks."

"No problem."

Sometimes the ease with which he'd inserted himself into her life astounded her. But times like these, it seemed Cash had always been here. Helping her. Loving her.

Whoa. She loved him. The jury was out on how he felt about her.

Why don't you ask him? What do you have to lose?

Him. She couldn't stand the thought of losing him. Ever. She'd already waited a year to sort out her own feelings, now was willing to wait as long as it took until he was ready to sort out his.

"I'm thinkin' of surprisin' Macie and buyin' her a horse."

"Yeah? Is this some guilty throwback to 'Daddy, will you buy me a pony for my birthday?' portion of her life that you missed?"

He nudged her with his shoulder. "No, smarty. She likes to ride. It'd be good for her to learn to train a horse from the get-go. It might also be an incentive for her to stick around here at the end of the summer."

"Things are going well between you two?"

"Better than I'd hoped, which is why I don't want her to leave. Selfish, huh?"

"No."

"Are you okay with it?"

"Yes, but you know she can't live in that camper indefinitely."

"I thought once McKay left she could live in the trailer. It even has a barn."

So Cash had already written off Carter McKay. Gemma wasn't so sure Carter had cashed in his chips with Macie—more like Carter was regrouping. She kept her opinion to herself. "A barn, which would be perfect for her new horse."

"Yep." He fiddled with the remote. "By the way, I heard from Trevor Glanzer today. He's on his way through tomorrow night. Is it all right if he crashes here?"

"Sure. But that's odd. He just called you out of the blue?"

Cash aimed the remote. "Wanna see what's on TV tonight?"

Gemma heaved a dramatic sigh. "We're watching TV? The romance has already worn off."

"Can we just veg? I'm bushed, Gem. I know I passed out last night, but you plum wore me out two nights ago."

"You ain't the one with the sore ass, cowboy."

"Complainin'?"

"A little." She smirked. "Okay, not much. It was hot as hell, waking up tied up. You having your wicked way with me. Telling me precisely all the kinky things you planned—"

"This ain't relaxin' me none."

"Knowing I couldn't make too much noise, even when your thrusts felt so good I wanted to scream. So hard I could feel your cock all the way in my throat—"

Groaning, Cash picked her up and tossed her over his shoulder.

"What are you doin'?"

"Takin' you to bed, *winyan*."

"But I thought you were too tired?"

"Lucky for you I just got my second wind and a new rope to break in." He spanked her butt and she shrieked. "Keep up that dirty talk and I'll have to try out the gag too."

Chapter Thirty-One

"Hey, squirt, when you're done in there can I talk to you?" Velma said in front of the pass-through window.

"Sure. It'll cost you a beer, though." Macie tossed the metal-bristled scrub brush aside. She used a clean white towel to wipe down the grill and admired the sparkling surface before she shut the lights off in the kitchen and shuffled out front.

Velma sat at the counter with a ten-key calculator. Long curls of white tape spilled everywhere. Without looking up, she said, "I put a six-pack of Bud in the small cooler. Grab me one too, while you're at it."

Macie popped the tops on the cans and waited, thankful not to be on her feet. Man. She was exhausted. She'd been working split shifts the last two days. And with the way Velma was frowning, she figured it wasn't going to get better any time soon.

Why stay here? It's time to move on anyway. You don't owe anybody anything but yourself.

It'd been a couple of weeks since her mom's advice made an appearance. She hadn't missed it.

Velma chugged half the beer. "It sucks that TJ up and quit. I don't know if he was threatened by you or what, but it's actually a good thing."

"Why would he be threatened by me?"

"Because you are a damn good cook. And not just the usual diner fare. You're bringin' something new and fresh. Something classy."

Macie squirmed.

"Local folks who hardly ever came in have taken notice. And the changes ain't drivin' away my regular customers, which is a plus. The bottom line is my business has more than doubled in the last two months and I am attributing it to you."

"But hey, no pressure," Macie muttered and swigged her beer.

Velma stared at her thoughtfully.

"What?"

"What are your future plans, Macie? Is the Last Chance Diner a blip on the roadmap to somewhere else?"

Macie really squirmed.

When she didn't answer, Velma looked away and said softly, "I'm sure workin' in a greasy spoon in Wyoming ain't your life goal. Probably have loftier ambitions."

Macie placed her hand on Velma's arm. "Don't. You've built a great business here. And as flattered as I am that you think I've had something to do with business picking up in recent months, it still is *your* place, Velma."

"True. But you still didn't answer my question, squirt."

"I don't know if I can. You knew I'd only be around a few months. I do like working here better than anywhere else I've punched a clock lately. But you should know I've just never worked anywhere longer than four months."

"Why?"

"Honestly? I get bored. Or I get fired. I've never had a reason to stick around anyplace and put down roots or whatever."

"But your dad is here, ain't he? Things are workin' out with him at Gemma's place?"

"Yeah."

"Are things workin' out between the two of you?"

Macie smiled. "Better than I'd hoped actually."

"I'm glad."

The clock ticked. The walk-in freezer hummed.

Velma sighed. "How are things goin' with you and that good-lookin' artist feller?"

Her stomach pitched when she thought of Carter. She

hadn't seen him since the day he'd squared off with her father. Which was why laboring excessive hours at the diner hadn't bothered her. She needed distance and time to think about what'd happened.

Contrary to what other people thought, she hadn't been mad at Carter for what he'd done. She'd been upset by the fact he'd cared enough about her welfare to challenge her father. In front of everyone, his family, his friends. Carter had been worried about her getting hurt. Or dying.

Dying.

She'd never had a man worry about her for any reason, let alone for her personal safety. It was cool. It was weird.

It was confusing as hell.

So, Macie didn't know if she was supposed to throw herself at Carter in gratitude for his protective instincts. Or take her father's side for his.

Talk about riding the mental merry-go-round 'til it made her dizzy.

And that didn't even take into consideration the L-word.

Macie was pretty sure she loved Carter. But how did she really know for sure? She had absolutely nothing in her life to gauge it by.

Loving her mother didn't count. Neither did the idea she was starting to love her dad.

The skeptic reminded her she'd known Carter McKay for a little over two months. How could she possibly love him?

Didn't love take time to build? Did she *think* she loved Carter because of the incredible sex? Because he understood her? Because he calmed her fears? Because he made her feel daring? Because he went out of his way to share silly and sweet things with her? Because he showed her sides of himself no one else knew? Because he thought she was beautiful and worthy of his art?

Or did she think she loved him strictly because he'd paid attention to her? When he'd made that same accusation to her father, it caused a ricochet effect, and the opposite reaction from what Carter probably expected. Instead of questioning her motives and actions regarding her dad, Macie questioned her motives and actions where Carter was concerned.

Which always led back to the "Do I love him?" question. Or a scarier scenario: What would she do if Carter told her he loved her? What would he expect? That she'd follow him while he lived his dream? What about her dreams? Would Carter be ready to make the same sacrifices for her?

The most troubling question? Was she prepared to give up the relationship she was establishing with her dad for the ups and downs of romantic love? Would her father do the same thing for her?

"Macie?"

Her head snapped up and she looked at Velma. "Sorry. I've had a lot on my mind lately."

"I imagine. Well, I don't want to add to that burden, but I'm afraid I have no choice."

Whoa. Was Velma going to fire her?

"Don't look at me like that, squirt. It ain't nothin' bad. I've been crunching some numbers, and I think I can afford to hire another part-time cook."

"Okay."

"You're probably thinking; how's that affect me? I'm just gonna say this straight out: I want you to stay in Canyon River. Part of the reason—well, most of it actually—is pure selfishness on my part. I like you. I like what you've done for this place on a number of levels. The other part is: I think you like it here—at the diner and in Canyon River—and you need an excuse to put down roots. Or at least you need a reason to *try* to put down roots." Velma's eyes softened beneath her glasses. "You ain't never had what most of us have taken for granted. I know you're curious on whether it's worth it, or if it'd be just another heartache. I look in those pretty hazel eyes and I see wisdom beyond your years."

Macie managed to swallow the last of her beer over the lump growing in her throat.

"Here's what I propose: I'll pay you a decent salary. You'll be the head cook, and we'll mix it up so you're working all shifts."

"You want me working breakfast, lunch and dinner?"

"No, I'm sayin' it'd be smart to sprinkle your good recipes and sunny personality around all the main meals. On my days off, I'd want you out front doin' my job."

"Schmoozing the regulars and belittling the help? I'm so all over that."

Velma smiled. "See? We're on the same page. I think it's some kinda cosmic sign. Besides, you are young enough that if after a year it don't work out, you can move on. What do you have to lose?"

"Nothing, apparently. But I need to think about it. Not just a couple of days, but a couple of weeks, okay?"

"Sure thing. You'll still be workin' here while you're tryin' to make a decision?"

"Yeah. And I'd appreciate it if we could keep this between us. Just us. There's already a million pros and cons in my head. I don't need anyone else adding their opinion."

"Consider it done. And remember, I always close down for ten days at the end of this month. Gives me time to regroup after the summer months and gear up for the fall."

As Macie drove back to the Bar 9, she knew Velma's offer complicated matters in her life, rather than providing a clear solution.

When she reached for the door handle to the camper, she noticed a piece of paper taped by the window. Her heart beat hard as she unrolled the scroll.

At the top was a sketch of a rodeo clown. Crying as a bull, which looked suspiciously like a caricature of her father, gored him in the butt. The words *I'M SORRY* took up the entire middle of the page. Below that, he'd written:

I miss you. Come see me when you get home, doesn't matter what time. We'll talk. Do normal couple things. And have pie. A helping of humble pie for me, darlin' ~ C ~

Macie stared at the paper for the longest time. She whispered, "Carter McKay, you are such a dumbass." And right then, she had no doubts that she was indeed, completely, madly in love with him.

Chapter Thirty-Two

"Excuse me. Is this the studio of famous Wyoming artist in residence, Carter 'shoulda been a cowboy' McKay?"

Carter spun around and grinned. "Jack! You bastard. 'Bout goddamn time you got here."

"You do realize I'm not living in Denver anymore and I had to fly in? I've been stuck in the rental car for five hours. Without satellite radio." He dropped his duffel bag and scowled. "Can you please tell me why every single station around these parts plays nothing but that goat yodeling crap?"

"Hey, some of us like Western music."

"Yeah, well, you're a hick, so I expected that much from you." Jack stalked over and grabbed him in a bear hug. "Good to see you, man, you look like shit."

"Gee, thanks." Carter gave Jack—all six-foot-four, two hundred odd pounds of him—a quick inspection. "You look a little tight-assed yourself. Wearin' pinstriped underwear under your pinstriped suits these days?"

"Fuck off. Where's the beer?"

"In the cooler by the door."

"Cool. You care if we sit outside? I've been cooped up all damn day. Need some of that fresh mountain air."

"Nope. I need a break anyway."

Once they'd settled in lawn chairs with the cooler between them, and a cold beer in each hand, Jack sighed. "So where's the fire?"

"What'd you mean?"

"Why was it so damn urgent I haul balls up here?"

238

Carter didn't say anything for several minutes.

"If it's anything less than you telling me you're dying, I'm going to beat your sorry ass into the dirt, McKay."

Carter kept staring off into space, lost in the vast prairie and his guilty thoughts.

"Shit. I was kidding. You aren't dying, are you?"

"No."

"Then what?" Recognition dawned on Jack's face. "It's about a woman, isn't it?"

"Yep."

"You knock her up?"

Carter tossed his beer can off to the side of his chair and cracked a fresh one. "Nope." He downed half the contents. "I'm crazy about her. So crazy about her in fact, that I want you to do something for me."

"What? Be your best man?"

"No. I want you to fuck her."

Beer spewed out of Jack's mouth. "Jesus Christ, Carter!"

"What?"

"You can't just blurt out something like that...dammit."

He waited.

"I don't even know what the hell to say."

"Simple. Say yes. It ain't like we've never had a threesome, Jack."

Jack stared at him. "True. But it's been a few years and we were usually drunk. And neither of us gave a crap about the women who were bold enough to take us both on. That last time, hell, we didn't even bother to learn her name."

Man. Had he really been that callous?

Yes. Maybe Carter was more like his wild brothers than he cared to admit.

"What's really going on here, McKay?"

"Honestly?"

Jack nodded.

"You laugh and I'll kick your ass, former linebacker or not." Carter fiddled with the tab on the beer can. "This woman? I had impressions about her, almost like cognitive daydreams, before I ever met her. Drove me crazy, I kept tryin' to work her likeness into clay, and wood, or on paper. Nothin' worked. Then I actually, physically met her. Yeah. I was a little freaked out about it. And she's better in real life than in those dreams."

"What's her name?"

"Macie."

"How long have you known her?"

"Seems like forever."

Jack frowned. "She a cowgirl?"

"What makes you ask that?"

"You've always had a thing for sweet little country girls." Jack scowled again. "Personally, I don't understand the attraction. And I can guarantee you'll *never* see me with a cowgirl. Never."

Carter kept drinking.

"So. Is she from around here?"

"Sort of. Not really."

"Okay, that's vague. What's she like?"

"She's...damn. She's everything. But she's also damn young."

"Like Jerry Lee Lewis young? Great balls of fire, you jonesin' for a thirteen-year-old girl, McKay?"

"No, you fuckin' pervert. She's twenty-two."

Jack looked at him. And laughed. Hard.

"What?"

"You're all of twenty-six. How does that make *her* young?"

"I don't know. It just does." Carter drained his beer and reached for another. Now, why in the hell hadn't he thought of that before now? Because most days he felt so much older than his chronological age?

"So let me get this straight: You called me, in a panic, dragged me to Wyoming, because you need me to fuck your new, young girlfriend?"

"It ain't that crude."

"Details, man."

"Fine. Macie has this fantasy of bein' with more than one guy. She's told me she's had dreams about it. And I wanted to make her fantasy, her dream come true, since she made mine... Shit. I sound stupid. Like a fuckin' sap. Never mind."

Jack waited a beat. "Because she is your dream come true, isn't she?"

Carter didn't answer. He just drank steadily. Finally, he said, "Yeah. I'm thinkin' she probably is."

"Dude. You are so totally fucked."

"Yes I am." He passed out another round of beer. "So will you do it?"

Jack shrugged.

"She's beautiful."

No response.

"Sexy. Killer body."

Jack shrugged again.

"She's very adventurous in bed."

He lifted a brow without comment.

"Anyway, I have an extra pair of boots and a hat around here somewhere. I can't see you fittin' into my chaps, but maybe that won't matter to her."

"She wants me to dress up like a *redneck*? With shitkickers and a big belt buckle and a stupid hat and a syrupy 'Hey howdy, pretty little lady, can I ride you hard' drawl? Oh *hell* no."

Carter smiled. Spitefully. "Pretend you're a sophisticated city-boy all you want, Donohue. But we both know you're just a South Dakota plowboy with a fancy degree."

"Insulting me isn't helping your cause, Carter."

Carter pretended not to notice when Jack changed the subject. He'd let it go. For now.

As darkness fell, they caught up and talked about Jack's job with the architectural firm in Chicago and Carter's upcoming art show. More and more beer cans piled up by his chair. Why was he getting drunk?

Liquid courage, man. You didn't want to ask Jack for this favor because the thought of any man—even your best buddy Jack—ever touching Macie, makes you mad as a bucking bull.

*But you love her so goddamn much you'll do whatever Amazin'
Macie wants to make her happy.*

Love?

Her?

Whoa.

Did he love Macie?

He'd have to close his eyes and think about that one.

"Hey, McKay. Wake up. A car just pulled in the drive."

Dammit, if he could just grasp these important thoughts
that kept spinning inside in his brain...before they spun away.

Carter had company.

Macie tamped down her disappointment. She hesitated as
she climbed out of her vehicle, studying the two forms in the
lawn chairs in front of a dwindling campfire.

"Carter?"

"Hey, shweet darlin', howsh's it hangin'?"

Sexy, low male laughter drifted from the other lawn chair.

Macie took another couple of steps and noticed the beer
cans. A whole lot of empty beer cans. Beside Carter.

The man stood and thrust his hand out. "Hi. You must be
Macie. I'm Jack Donohue."

"Jacksh's my beshtesht bud from college."

Macie looked up at the man. Good God, he was a god.
Firelight glowed behind him, making him look as if he'd been
forged from steel. He was huge. Muscular. With a brawny chest,
ripped biceps, big hands, and never-ending legs thick as tree
trunks. Longish coal-black hair framed his square face. He had
a roguish smile boasting brilliant white teeth; a deep cleft in his
chin, and eyes the color of green grass. Those same eyes were
highly amused.

"Nice to meet you, Jack."

"Ain't she beautiful in firelight?"

"Yes, she is. Hang on. I'll get you a chair." Jack
disappeared into the barn.

Whoo-ee. The beefcake was a gentleman to boot.

"Come over here and give me shome shugar, shugar."

Macie skirted the fire and looked into Carter's face. He had a silly smile. And glassy eyes. She bit back a grin. He was unbelievably adorable. "Hey."

"Hey. I misshed you, my shweet darlin'."

"I missed you too." She brushed the springy curls from his damp forehead. "What are you celebrating?"

Carter frowned. "I don't remember. You probably." He cupped his hands around her face and brought her mouth to his for a deep, wet, beer-flavored kiss. Even drunk the man knew how to melt her with his kisses.

She gradually removed her lips from his. "I won't stay, since you have company, but I wanted to tell you thanks for the apology and the picture."

"An apology for what? The pictures I'm paintin' of you?"

"What are you talking about?"

From behind her Jack said, "He's babbling because he's been drinking for hours. Hate to say it, but he probably won't remember you were even here."

"Doesn't matter. I'll remember."

Jack said nothing.

Carter's head drooped to his chest.

"Carter?"

No answer.

"Maybe we'd better get him in the house before he passes out," Macie suggested.

"If you insist. Or we could just drag him into the barn."

"So you claim you're a *good* friend of his?"

Jack chuckled. "Don't kid yourself, he would've done the same thing to me had the situations been reversed. In fact, he has."

They tried to rouse the party animal but he wouldn't budge. Carter wasn't a small guy by any means, and Macie wouldn't have been able to move him by herself. Luckily for Carter, Jack was strong enough to carry him in a fireman's hold and deposit him on the sofa in the trailer.

Macie managed to get Carter's boots off before he started to snore. She stripped him down to his boxers, tucked a blanket around him. On her way outside, she noticed he'd added a picture to his family collection. She peered at it and her breath caught. It was one he'd taken of her the first day she'd posed for him, a profile shot. The light turned her skin a stunning shade of red-gold. Her lips were parted, almost in a smirk. She looked mysterious and...beautiful. Was this the way he saw her? Would his paintings reflect the same mood? Shaking such crazy, hopeful thoughts from her head, she returned outside.

Jack sat by the fire. "Got a minute before you need to take off?"

"I suppose."

"Want a beer?"

Macie wrinkled her nose.

Jack smiled. "There's Diet Pepsi in the cooler too, which is why I'm not in the same sad shape as McKay."

She grabbed one and sat. "It's the first time I've seen him drunk."

"Wish I could say the same."

"How long have you known him?"

"Three years. We met in Denver while we were in grad school."

"Oh. Are you an artist too?"

"No. I'm an architect."

"Sounds interesting."

"Carter tells me you're posing for a couple of pieces for his art show."

"I guess. I haven't actually *seen* anything yet."

"That's nothing new. He's usually pretty secretive about his work."

Awkward silence followed. His eyes seemed to be following her closely too.

"How long have you known him?" Jack asked.

"Seems like forever, but since the beginning of summer."

Jack frowned.

Crickets chirped. The fire crackled. A gentle breeze blew. The uncomfortable quiet lingered.

"Carter was right. You really are beautiful by firelight. I suspect you'd even be more dangerously beautiful in the dark."

Macie froze.

"How serious are you about him?"

Her heart beat faster. "Why?"

"Just curious." Jack granted her body a visual examination that burned her skin hotter than the bonfire. "Just wondering if it's an exclusive thing. Or if maybe you and I..."

This guy was Carter's best friend? He was a total letch. Macie scrambled to her feet. "No way. Not interested." She stomped to her SUV.

"Macie. Wait. Sorry. I had to do that."

She whirled on him. "Do what? Hit on me? When your friend is passed out not more than twenty feet away?"

"Yes."

"Why?"

"Because Carter is head over heels for you. I've never seen him like this and I had to make sure... Sit down and let me explain. I'm not going to make a pass at you, okay?"

She sat.

More sticky silence.

Macie said, "So, if I would've jumped at the chance at, well, jumping you, would you have told him?"

"In a fucking heartbeat."

She waited.

"Can I be blunt?"

"I don't know, Jack. You've been pretty subtle so far."

Jack grinned. "You bust his balls all the time, don't you?"

Macie shrugged.

"Do you know why I'm here?"

"No."

"Carter called me in a panic yesterday. He's never done that. So, I changed my schedule, flew in, expecting to hear he's dying or something. But no. He sits me down, tells me about you, how crazy he is about you, and then he asks me...shit. I need another beer." He snagged one out of the cooler and drank.

Impatiently, she demanded, "He asked you what, Jack?"

Jack locked his gaze to hers. "He asked me to be the third player in a threesome with you and him."

All the blood drained from Macie's face. "Omigod. Why would he do that?"

"He said you have some fantasy about being with two guys at one time, or two cowboys or some ménage thing. Anyway, he wanted to give you that fantasy, and he asked me here because, well, to be blunt again, he and I have done this type of thing before—granted, it was a couple of years ago. But the bottom line is he asked me because he trusts me. And he trusts me with you. Which says a whole helluva lot to me, about how he feels about you."

Macie stared at Jack, absolutely dumbfounded.

When she made no effort to speak, Jack said, "So was McKay on crack, or what? Did you, or did you not, tell him you had a fantasy like that?"

"I *joked* about it. After he and I met I had this bizarre dream that Freud would've had a field day with, and Carter was in it. I didn't give him particulars, because it would've weirded him out. And I was glad I'd spared him the details after I found out about his slight homophobia."

Jack lifted an eyebrow.

"If I didn't tell him the gory details, I won't tell you. So it was probably stupid and childish, but I kept it going like a running gag. I never believed he'd take me serious!" She gazed into the fire, feeling like an absolute idiot. "After all we've done, doesn't he know I don't need anyone else, I don't want anyone else, and I can't imagine being in bed with someone else when I'm equally crazy about him?"

"No, it appears he doesn't know."

Macie looked up and blushed. Crap. She'd forgotten about Jack.

"So why don't you tell him?"

"Oh I will, just as soon as I kick his sorry butt."

"That, I'd like to see."

"I should teach him a lesson. Thank him in the morning for

the most spectacular sex of my life, and the awesome threesome we had with you." She toed a beer can toward the fire. "But I couldn't do that."

"Might be good for him."

"I couldn't hurt him. Not on purpose." She sensed Jack's hesitation and her gaze zoomed to him. "What?"

"Can I give you some advice, Macie?"

"Sure."

"Carter is a great guy. But his artistic nature sometimes causes him to do stupid things that make sense to him at the time."

Macie thought of Carter's over-the-top reaction to her sitting on the back of a mechanical bull. Yeah. That made sense.

"He eventually sees the error of his skewed thinking, but not right away. He wouldn't do anything to hurt you on purpose either...but accidentally?" Jack shook his head. "It'll happen. More likely than not."

Even if she didn't understand what Jack meant, his words were a little disturbing. She stood. "I should go. Thanks for not hitting on me for real and for being a good friend to Carter."

"McKay is a lucky man. Make sure you send me an invitation to the wedding."

"Or an announcement for his funeral."

Chapter Thirty-Three

Carter woke at two in the afternoon with a hellacious hangover.

Shit. What'd happened last night?

He remembered Jack showing up. And drinking. Talking about seeing if Jack was up for a rodeo with Macie. More drinking.

Macie. She'd been here.

What had gone down after that?

Carter lurched up on the couch. Goddamn, that hurt his head. He looked down. At least he was wearing his boxers.

"Jack?"

No answer.

He stood. Ooh. That was worse than lying down. He stumbled past the guest bedroom and froze. The bed hadn't been slept in.

So where had Jack slept?

With Macie.

Not possible. Jack wouldn't...

Unless Carter gave him the okay. And he'd bypassed "okay" and gone straight to "what are you waiting for?" when he asked—no—*demanded* that Jack fuck Macie.

Damn.

Carter shuffled to his bedroom. The sheets and the mattress pad were stripped and rolled in a ball. What the hell? Why?

Because they are damp and stained from being well used last night.

His gaze swept the room, searching for condom wrappers, used Kleenex, a bottle of lube.

Nothing. Except Macie's sweater hung off the dresser and the scent of her skin hung in the air.

He sat on the bed. Hard.

Images flashed in his mind like a movie on fast forward. Jack and Macie kissing. Deeply. Hungrily. Jack unbuttoning Macie's shirt, feasting on her dark nipples. Macie arching her neck, moaning, demanding more. Macie shoving Jack's hand down her pants. Jack tearing off her shorts, leaving her naked.

Jack falling to his knees as he kissed the sweet curve of her belly. And down, over the dark hair covering her mound and down, zeroing in on her pussy. Spreading her pouty lips wide to reach her clit. Sucking. Licking. Making Macie cry out in ecstasy. Jack stood and whispered in her ear while plunging three fingers in and out of her wet slit until she came screaming his name.

Macie stretched out on the bed, watching as Jack whipped off his jeans. Then Jack straddled her, burying his face in her sopping cunt as his cock rammed in and out of Macie's mouth. The slow, easy rhythm built into a rush to the finish. Jack's hips pumped faster into her face. Macie ground her sex harder into his. They climaxed simultaneously. Macie sucked him deep and swallowed, but some of Jack's come dribbled out the side of her mouth as she smiled. When Jack lifted his head, his face was shiny wet with her juices.

Jack flipped her on her belly and rammed his cock in her cunt as his fingers dallied with her asshole. After they'd both come again, he lubed up Macie's tits and fucked her there, while Macie's vibrator was buried in her pussy.

She screamed Jack's name again as her orgasm hit and he came on her face.

Then Jack took her ass. Twice. First with his cock. Then with the vibrator as he gave it to Macie from behind.

But that wasn't the end. Jack tenderly cleaned Macie up, kissing her. Caressing her. Sweet-talking her. Making Macie purr beneath his roving hands. And when she was heated up again, he fucked her slowly, face-to-face, whispering in her ear. Making love to her mouth as his body made love to hers. Then they fell asleep curled in each other's arms, smiles of satisfaction on their faces.

No wonder the sheets were rolled up. Hell, they'd probably worn holes in them and the mattress too.

But... Had he really seen that? Why hadn't they asked him to join in? After all, it was supposed to be a three-for-all.

No, three's a crowd.

The bottom line was: Carter couldn't remember and that made him an idiot and a loser.

The very bottom line? If the images were reality, not the blurred imaginings of an alcohol stupor, Jack Donohue was a dead man.

Cash had something up his sleeve.

Gemma couldn't put her finger on it, but he was acting...nervous. Which set her on edge. Cash was the most unflappable man she'd known. Well, he was even-keeled outside of the bedroom, at any rate.

She still hadn't seen or heard from Carter McKay. Maybe she should double-check to make sure Cash hadn't killed him for the stunt Carter pulled.

Macie hadn't been around so Gemma knew Cash's anxiety didn't have anything to do with his daughter.

Trevor? Why would seeing his old rodeo pal make him nervous? Hadn't Cash invited Trevor to stay at the Bar 9? Cash wasn't embarrassed to be working here, was he?

No. She noticed he'd taken pride in whipping the ranch into shape.

So, that meant his edginess had something to do with her. Fear settled in her chest. Was he leaving?

Don't be ridiculous. His daughter is here. He doesn't have anywhere else to go. He likes the Bar 9. He likes you.

If he liked her so much maybe he could make love to her

just one time with the damn lights on?

Shit. She could mope around all afternoon. Or she could do any one of the fifty jobs waiting to be finished at the Bar 9.

∾

Trevor said, "I thought I'd stop up and say hi to her first, get a bite to eat before I came back here to the ranch and..."

Cash grunted. Part of him didn't want to think about it.

"She doesn't know?"

"No. I told you it's a surprise."

"What if it's a surprise she don't want?"

"She does."

"Yeah? What if she says no?"

Cash tipped his head back and studied Trevor. "Will it bother you if she sends you packin'?"

He thought about it and said, "Probably not."

"You know this doesn't go beyond us, right?"

Trevor sighed. "I keep more damn secrets than you can shake a stick at, Cash."

"Good. Then you know what to do?"

"Be a sad day in my life when I don't."

∾

Carter didn't see Jack's rental car in the parking lot of the Last Chance Diner.

So who was the guy Macie was chatting up at the counter?

Maybe Jack had left his car at Macie's camper. And had spent all day hanging out with her. Talking to her, doing normal couple shit he hadn't had time for lately.

Seething, Carter stormed inside.

The place was deserted. Good. Less witnesses for the bloodshed.

The man had his hand on Macie's arm. She was smiling at him. *Smiling.*

He couldn't wait to plow his fist into the bastard's face.

"Get your hand off her, Jack, or I'll break it so you never draw another goddamn thing."

Macie looked up at him, horrified. "Carter?"

"Stay out of this, Macie. This is between Jack and me."

"But—"

"Turn around, coward. I won't sucker punch you, like you sucker punched me. 'Cause I wanna see teeth fly when I belt you in the mouth for tryin' to steal my girl."

Jack eased the stool around slowly.

Carter braced himself and cocked his fist.

But the man facing him wasn't Jack Donohue. It was his brother Colby's friend, Trevor Glanzer.

"Trevor? What the hell are you doin' here?"

"Plannin' on kickin' your butt as soon as I finish my pie. What is wrong with you, Carter? It ain't like you to pick fights."

Carter ignored the question and glanced at Macie. "Where's Jack?"

"How should I know? He's *your* friend."

"Because last night..." Damn. Could he be wrong? Could he really be that paranoid?

Yes, when it came to Macie all rationality vanished.

Because he loved her.

Wildly.

Out-of-his-freakin'-mind-all-or-nothing-kind-of-love.

Without taking his gaze from Macie, Carter said, "Trevor. Step outside for a minute."

Trevor mumbled something and slipped out the door.

"Please fill in the fuzzy details."

Macie's eyes narrowed. "After you passed out, Jack passed on the real reason you'd asked him here, and I passed on being any part of it."

"Really?"

"No. I went *Wahoo!* and screwed his brains out while you

were sacked out in the lawn chair."

The feeling of relief nearly buckled his knees. "So you didn't, I mean, you don't want that?"

"A ménage? I was kidding about multiple cowboys, Carter."

"You were?"

"That's not something I'm interested in trying at this point in my life." Those all-knowing hazel eyes clouded. "Hey. Did you just call me your *girl?*"

"Yes, you are my girl." *My everything.*

"I am not a *girl*, Carter McKay."

"Girl, woman, whatever, you're mine and I was ready to kill my best friend for makin' a move on you."

"He didn't."

"Lucky for him." Carter stalked her, until her back was against the cement wall. "Kiss me and make me all better, darlin'. Your sweet, hot kisses heal my damn foolish pride."

Macie whispered, "You are such a dumbass," and lifted her lips to his for the sweetest kiss on the planet.

When Carter could feel his heart beating again, he picked Macie up and threw her over his shoulder. He yelled, "Velma? Macie's takin' a sick day. She's feelin' a mite poorly."

Velma poked her head through the doorway and grinned. "That's fine. Just make sure she's here tomorrow."

"She'll be here bright and early with bells on."

She sighed. "Definitely better than dinner theater."

As Carter carted Macie outside, she said, "Trevor? Umm. Tell my dad I won't be home tonight."

"*All* night," Carter added and tossed her in his truck.

Macie expected Carter to play grab-ass with her on the way to his place. But he was strangely subdued. He parked and looked at her.

"Stay here until I come getcha, okay?"

She nodded. After ten minutes passed, she couldn't stand waiting any longer. She snuck inside the darkened trailer and heard him thumping around in his bedroom.

"Carter?"

"I thought I told you—"

"Yeah, I know. I don't listen very well." Macie paused in the doorway and watched him wrestling with a set of silky peach-colored sheets. Which, by the looks of it, were a size too small, which was probably the reason they wouldn't fit on the bed. "What are you doing?"

"Screwing this up, apparently." Disgusted, he tossed the sheets aside. "I wanted it to be perfect." A sound, half sigh/half laugh, rumbled from his chest. He scrubbed his hands over the stubble on his face. "But there ain't moonlight, hell, it ain't even night. I don't have candles, or soft music, unless you count Faith Hill. No flowers. Or champagne. Now I can't even get the damn sheets on the bed. And to top it off, I have a wicked hangover. Some romantic setting, huh?"

"Why are you setting a scene? I don't need all that for you to seduce me."

Carter looked at her. Her breath stalled in her lungs. Those blue, blue eyes held everything she'd ever wanted and he was looking at her. Offering it to her.

"It's not about seduction. It's about love. I love you, Macie. Really, really love you and I've never said that to another girl—woman—in my whole life. And I wanted it to be perfect when I told you—"

His words were cut off when she launched herself at him and kissed him. When Carter realized she was crying, he pulled back.

"Hey. What's this?"

Macie couldn't answer. She buried her face in his neck and sobbed. He hugged her tightly until she calmed down. She finally looked up at him. "I really, really love you too, Carter, and I've never said that to anyone either."

"I could be a gentleman and tell you that you didn't have to say it back to me just 'cause I said it first." He grinned. "But we both know I ain't really a gentleman and hot damn, am I ever glad to hear it."

"So what happens now?" *Do we ride off into the sunset together? Start picking out china patterns?*

Romantic nonsense, Macie Blue.

"We'll figure it out as we go." Carter pushed her on the bed and she squealed at the wicked, sweet, hot look of forever in his eyes. "For now, we've got a free afternoon and a whole box of condoms. That's as good as any place to start."

Chapter Thirty-Four

"He's here for *what?*" Gemma knew her voice was a shade shy of hysterical.

Cash gazed at her coolly. "You don't have to pretend with me, Gem, I know you. Heck, you told me you were interested in tryin' it just earlier this week."

"We were in bed! That doesn't count."

"Which is why it *does* count. Plus, I overheard you last summer, talkin' with Channing 'bout it, and how long your curiosity has been piqued. Trevor is here to satisfy it."

"Trevor. You asked Trevor if he wanted to be part of a threesome? With me? And you?" Gemma shook her head, even as her blood raced. "Cash, why would you do that?"

"Because you want it. And *I* want to give you something *he* never did."

He. Meaning her late husband, Steve.

Was this really happening? She and Steve talked about a threesome in vague generalities throughout their marriage, more along the lines of...a fantasy fuck. Gemma had a thing for country singer Chris Ledoux and Steve teased her that if the opportunity arose, he'd watch Chris doin' her, then he'd join in. Around that time in the conversation, Steve would explicitly detail what it'd be like to see another man sliding his cock up Gemma's ass while he fucked her pussy. It made them both hot. Then they'd head to bed, screw, and laugh it off afterward.

Except...Gemma had always wondered what it'd feel like to have two sets of male hands on her. Two men's mouths kissing, licking, and teasing her hot spots. Two cocks filling her holes in a variety of ways. Her softer body sandwiched between strong,

256

muscular, passionate masculine ones as they penetrated her. As they focused solely on her sexual pleasure.

She'd never been dissatisfied in her sexual life with Steve. After he'd died, her sex drive died too. She couldn't get beyond the grief to think about one man touching her, let alone two men.

Now that she'd moved on, Cash more than satisfied her sexual desires; he understood them. Which is why he'd gone to so much trouble to set this up. What might seem like bizarre, scandalous behavior to others was actually incredibly...sweet. A loving gesture from a man she suspected hadn't taken a lot of chances in his life to showcase his sweet, thoughtful side.

But Cash also realized in order for her to enjoy this fantasy, she'd have to be comfortable with the third player. He'd have to be a man she knew—and was attracted to. Trevor Glanzer fit the bill, a good-looking cowboy who'd literally been trying to charm the pants off her for two years. The fact Trevor traveled here, willing to make both her and Cash happy, if only for one night, appealed to the wild woman in her. She'd been too scared to take the opportunity when it'd been offered to her in her younger years.

Well, she was older and wiser. No way was she letting the chance pass her by again.

A delicious shiver of anticipation rolled through her.

"Okay. But three things first."

"Yeah?"

"No blindfold. Leave your hair unbraided. And the lights stay on."

A slow, sexy smile lit up Cash's face. "Whatever you want, Gem, tonight is for you. Trevor and I will be right back."

❧

"Carter?"

He softly kissed Macie's lips and tucked the covers under her chin. "Ssh. It's okay."

"Where are you going?"

"Out to the barn to work. I can't seem to get to sleep." He brushed his mouth over her forehead. "Sorry to wake you. Go back to sleep. You won't even know I'm gone."

"Mmm. Okay. Love you."

Carter's heart nearly burst out of his chest. "Love you too, darlin'."

He whistled as he headed outside. He knew exactly what his paintings had been missing these last few weeks. Risky, but he'd toss the whole works he'd already done and start over.

No wonder artists talked about love being the best inspiration; it was true.

He could finally show the world what Macie meant to him. Who she was to him and who he was to her. How she looked at him with love. Love he'd been searching for his entire adult life.

Trevor grinned at her. "Been waitin' for this day for a long time, precious Gem-stone."

"Yeah? Well, I am a little nervous, so be kind, okay?"

Trevor moseyed over and cupped her face in his big hands. Warm, full lips pressed hers before his tongue snaked inside.

Gemma jumped when she felt Cash move in behind her. "Easy." His fingers curled into her hips and he nuzzled his face in her hair.

Trevor licked and nipped at her mouth and pulled back with a sigh. "Kind? Huh-uh. I wanna fuck you like an animal. I'm gonna show you the dark side of lust." His lips came down on hers and he leisurely unbuttoned her blouse. Cash peeled it down her trembling arms. Then Cash unhooked her bra and her breasts tumbled into Trevor's hands.

Gemma's head rested on Cash's shoulder, his long hair drifted across her bared skin in an erotic tease as Trevor tongued her nipples. Cash breathed heavily in her ear, slowly sliding his hands down to unsnap her jeans.

A flash of heat speared between her legs and she moaned.

"I love the sound of a woman's pleasure. It's gonna be a

long night. We aren't even to the good stuff yet," Trevor said, kissing a path to where her jeans gapped. He inhaled. "Mmm. Love the smell of wet pussy. Help me take her jeans down, Cash."

Cash tugged and her pants slithered down her legs.

"Let's get you warmed up." Trevor's first two fingers slipped over her mound and into her sex. Deep. He added another finger, wiggled and pumped, filling the room with the juicy sucking sound of her excitement.

Gemma widened her stance and tipped her neck to the side giving Cash better access.

Trevor withdrew his hand and finger-painted up her torso, following the line with his mouth. He wiped the wetness on her nipples and sucked it off, moaning his enjoyment.

"Cash, finger fuck her while I eat these delicious tits."

"Gladly." Cash ground his cock into her ass as his hand moved between her thighs. He whispered, "You're wet. This is makin' you hot."

"Yes."

"Good. You wanna get off fast? Or have me draw it out?"

"Fast. Please."

"I knew you'd say that." He plunged three fingers inside her pussy, then brought those some three wet fingers up to her mound. He opened the hood of skin covering her clit with his two outside fingers, while the middle one stroked the small button. Tapped it. Rubbed it fast, the way he knew she liked it.

Between Trevor sucking and biting her nipples, and Cash's expert attention to her clit, she couldn't hold back. The pulsing started and she came with a startled gasp.

After the throbbing slowed, Gemma opened her eyes. Trevor grinned at her. "Good warm up?"

"Great warm up."

His hand traced the lines of her collarbones and up the center of her throat. He brushed his fingers across her lips. "Open up. Suck your juices off my fingers." Then he slid all three into her mouth. "That's it. I wanna see you enjoying your sweet cream."

She sucked, tasting herself on Trevor's rough knuckles.

259

She lapped at his fingers, trying to discern the salty taste of his skin from her musk.

"That's sexy as hell." He eased them out and said, "Cash? Your turn."

Then Cash's fingers slipped inside her mouth. She licked his thick digits, rolling them over her eager tongue, removing all traces of her taste. Suddenly Cash pulled his fingers out and smashed his mouth to hers, vigorously sucking her own juices off her tongue. Bringing the flavor into his mouth and swallowing it.

Gemma's head swam in a burst of pleasure.

While Cash kissed her, Trevor licked a path up to her ear. He kneaded her breasts, plumping them together. He whispered, "I want to fuck your tits. Grease them up and straddle your face so you can suck my balls while I'm sliding my cock here." His finger demonstrated. "It'll be hard and fast. I'd come all over your breasts and your belly. Then I'd start all over again."

Gemma shivered from the erotic whispers in her ear and the kiss assaulting her mouth. She broke away with a gasp.

Trevor chuckled. "I think she's ready for more. Want me to show you something fun?"

"Yes."

"Cash, strip. Both of you get on the bed."

As they disrobed and stood side by side, Gemma was amazed at how different Cash and Trevor's bodies were. The lighter tone of Trevor's skin compared to the reddish-golden hue of Cash's. The hair sprinkled on their thighs and arms, and the thick nest of curls between their legs. The sizes and shapes of their cocks—not that she could complain on either front. Still, she felt a little distressed the first time she'd seen Cash completely naked was in front of another man. But her distress was short-lived when four rough-skinned male hands caressed her everywhere.

"On your hands and knees, Gem-stone." Trevor paused and looked at Cash. "You sittin' on the fence this go-round or are you ridin'?"

Cash smiled. A bit cockily. "Oh. I'm ridin'."

"Good." Trevor focuses his attention on Gemma. "Get on

your knees at the head of the bed."

Gemma complied, trying to slow the beating of her heart and the slight fear laced with curiosity.

"Where are you gonna be?" Cash said.

"At the foot." Trevor's callused fingers raked the sole of her foot. Then meandered up her calves and the backs of her thighs, tapping the inside of her legs for her to widen her stance. "Or should I say, at the rear."

A long, wet tongue swiped up from Gemma's pussy to her anus. She gasped, turning to see Trevor standing behind her. He said, "Suck him, while I suck you. I assume you ain't opposed to a little ass play, since I'm gonna be in it soon?"

"No. Oh GOD."

Then Trevor was rimming her hole with his tongue, wiggling it inside, tickling the knot of nerves while his fingers delved into her wetness and slipped higher to masterfully stroke her clit.

Hands were on her head. Cash's cock was in her face. He growled, "Take it all."

Gemma opened and sucked him to the root. He began to thrust into her throat. She closed her eyes and just let herself feel the hot, kinky, overwhelming sensations of animal lust, the taboo experiences she'd only dared imagine.

Trevor canted her hips, licking and sucking everywhere between her thighs, making her wet and swollen with need.

Cash tugged on her hair and said, "It's fuckin' sexy watchin' my dick disappear into that hot mouth. Knowin' what he's doin' to you."

She hummed her response. The vibration sent Cash over the edge. His cock pulsed on her tongue, semen burst in her mouth and she swallowed as much as she could.

Trevor quit playing with her ass and concentrated his attention on her clit. The orgasm blindsided her—fast, intense spasms. She moaned, rocking back onto Trevor's mouth. Even as the throbbing eased, she heard the rip of a condom package, and felt cool gel on her puckered opening.

He pressed her upper body to the mattress. "Do you know how many times I've jerked off, thinkin' about rammin' my cock up this perfect cowgirl ass?" His fingers peeled her cheeks apart. The head of his cock brushed a slick circle around the entrance and pushed past the ring of muscles in one quick movement.

Gemma stiffened up.

"Jesus. You feel like heaven, Gem." Trevor pulled out an inch at a time and delved back in just as slowly. Over and over. Gently, but yet, knowing how far he could push for her maximum pleasure.

Cash scooted against the headboard. His hands slid under her to play with her nipples. He murmured, "You're fine. You look beautiful, all stretched out, with your ass in the air. Givin' him what all the cowboys on the circuit have been dreamin' 'bout."

She tilted her head up and locked her gaze to Cash's. "You too?"

"Me too. I wanted to fuck you every way possible. Buried balls deep in your sassy little butt was high on my list of ways. But this?" His gaze strayed to Trevor pounding into her ass. "This never..." He closed his eyes and twisted her nipples, skating close to that edge of pain. "Touch yourself. I wanna hear you come while he's fucking you."

Gemma didn't know if she could come again so soon. She found her clit and rubbed, concentrating on the feel of Cash's fingers. The clasp of her anus around Trevor's cock. A small orgasm broke free and she held her breath.

Trevor said, "I have a serious thing for ass-fuckin' but I ain't gonna last much longer. Damn. You are hot and tight and all slicked up. Feelin' those muscles clampin' down. Harder. Like that. Feels un-fucking-believable...shit. I'm done." Four thrusts and Trevor threw back his head and was shuddering behind her.

Time slowed. The room was cool and humid. And quiet beneath the sounds of labored breathing. Trevor went to clean himself up and Gemma lifted her body up and looked at Cash.

His back rested against the headboard. The unbound black hair hung over his shoulders. His legs were spread in a V and his cock was soft against the mattress. He clutched a bottle of water. Without opening his eyes, he said, "Want some?"

"Sure."

As she drank a few drops spilled onto his smooth, hairless chest. She watched as the droplets slowly slid down the curved muscles of his pecs. Her tongue darted out and lapped. Mmm. Wet and salty.

"Gemma."

"I never get to see you," she whispered, lest Trevor hear. "Let me look." His nipples were a deep brown, a complement to the reddish-tan skin surrounding them. Her fingers traced the puckered scars, old white ones and new pink ones, bisecting his ribs and upper abdomen. His lower belly had a slight pudge, which Gemma found unbelievably sexy. Her thumbs swept across his narrow hipbones and his stomach trembled beneath her touch. More scars.

She ignored his crotch and her fingertips moved down, over the fresh bruises on his thighs. Even at this angle she could see Cash was bowlegged—another endearing trait. Knobby, scarred knees. Gouges marred his thin calves down to his ankles. She ended the sweeping caress at his long, narrow feet. Ugly feet. All cowboys, especially rodeo cowboys, had hideously mangled toes and callused feet. Gemma stroked all these spots hungrily, her eyes drinking him in. "You are all rugged beauty and strength, Cash. Every part is...so you. Why do you hide this from me?"

"Gemma, you humble me. That's why—"

Trevor sauntered back in and rubbed his hands together. "Who's up for a Gemma sandwich?"

Right then, Gemma wanted the ménage fantasy to end. It seemed...selfish now. Like one of those "life experiences" Macie's mother had been determined to check off. She'd much prefer to make love with Cash, the man she loved, skin to skin, heart to heart, looking in his beautiful all-knowing eyes. That was her fantasy now. And she'd fulfill it herself. As soon as possible.

But she'd finish this for them both first.

"I am," Gemma said, leaning forward to kiss Cash. To touch him. To heat him back up. Didn't take much for his cock to stir in her hand.

Trevor trailed kisses down her spine. A warm sweetness that caused gooseflesh to break out and her desire to return with a surprisingly bitter edge.

Cash's hard kiss belied the soft touches on the front of her body; her breasts, her stomach, between her legs. Trevor kissed and caressed her back, and was rubbing his hard cock against her butt crack.

The ache rebuilt. Her body tingled, inside and out. Her pussy was drenched, needy. Already deliciously used. Her head spun and she wanted to know if the reality of two men buried inside her lived up to her years of imagination.

She retreated from the hunger of Cash's mouth and said, "I'm ready."

Trevor continued to touch her, his mouth moving across her lower back. "On the bed, or standin' up?"

"Umm..."

"Standin' up we'll both be able to get into you at once."

"Okay."

She stood alone, arms folded over her chest as condoms were rolled on.

Trevor stepped in front of her, smoothing his hands over her body, leaving sucking kisses on her neck as he lifted her right leg, placing her foot on the bed, forcing her wide stance. "Easier access," he muttered against her chest.

Cash's hot body pressed into hers from behind and he licked the slope of her shoulder to her nape.

Hard hands groped and petted and caressed her everywhere. Two hot mouths kissing her skin. Trading off to kiss her mouth. The bite of teeth. The trill of warm lips. Heated breath. Licking tongues. The scent of sweat and salt and latex and need. Trevor's rigid cock slipped up her thigh. Cash tilted her hips, opening her cheeks, poising his cockhead at her entrance.

Then a hard thrust and they were both inside her. She gasped.

Trevor withdrew and plunged in again. He waited, and Cash did the same.

Her ass was stretched, full, and then empty. Her cunt was trying to expel Trevor's cock and keep it in. She had no control. She began to panic.

Cash whispered, "Relax. Let go. Just feel. This is a one-time-only deal. Let us fuck you. Feel us both in you. You're perfect, Gemma. Hot and tight. Beautiful. Sexy. Mine." He kissed the side of her neck in the spot that drove her wild. Trevor followed suit, dragging his mouth on the opposite side of her throat.

In. Out. The pain of fullness gave way to pleasure and she lost herself in pure sensation of touch. Deep inside her. Fingers stroking her clit. Cash whispering in her ear. He groaned and Trevor stopped moving, holding Gemma's hips while Cash thrust hard and climaxed. While Cash's head sagged on her shoulder, Trevor pumped his hips and took his own release.

With sweaty male bodies plastered to her, and two cocks inside her, Gemma had no choice but to stay still and wait for them to catch their breath.

Finally, Cash said, "She didn't come, Trev."

"No, it's okay, I'm fine."

"It's not fine."

"We gotcha."

Trevor suckled her nipples, Cash's thumb flicked her clit and he sank his teeth into the curve of her neck, they both thrust hard at the same time.

That's all she needed. An orgasm rippled through her, her internal muscles clamped down, she felt the throbbing in her clit, her womb, her anus...everywhere.

After she stopped shaking, Trevor kissed her forehead. "Thanks, Gem-stone. I hope it's what you had in mind. I sure as hell had fun. You are one sexy woman." He pulled out of her body, and left the room.

Cash slowly eased out of her. "You okay?"

She wrapped her arms over her chest and withheld a shiver. "Yeah."

"Was it everything you imagined, sweets?"

"Yes. It was. Thank you."

"I'll clean up in the downstairs bathroom and see to Trevor." He kissed the back of her head. "I'll be up in a little bit. Don't wait up. I know you're probably tired."

Cash skirted her and she watched his firm naked perfect

cowboy ass as he strode out the bedroom door.

Oh. She was tired all right. Sick and tired of whatever was going on with Cash. She'd get to the bottom of it. But to do it, she'd have to be on top.

"Ain't you gonna stick around tonight?" Cash asked Trevor.

"Nope. I'm wired. I might as well hit the road."

"Where you headed?"

"Livingston."

The bug zapper by the machine shed made a loud crackling noise.

Cash sighed. "Am I supposed to thank you?"

"It was my pleasure, Cash. But I gotta be honest, havin' a horndog reputation across five states ain't the best for my ego these days."

"You love it. You ain't the type for settlin' down."

A surprisingly wistful look crossed Trevor's face. "Yeah. Well. You never know about me. I might just disappear off the face of the earth someday and settle where no one can find me."

"That why you're goin' to Montana?"

"No. I'm doin' some stupid thing for my dad. Don't want to get into it." Trevor shifted his weight against the pickup. "Maybe it ain't none of my business, but did something happen between you and Gemma when we took that short break?"

The muscles in Cash's gut tightened. "Why?"

"I sensed a change in her. Kinda like she was wantin' to back out."

Cash didn't know what to say. He'd felt it too. Part of him wanted to squirrel Gemma away, let her look her fill at him, and not let Trevor touch her again. But he'd managed to keep focused on her pleasure, fulfilling her fantasy, not his sudden displeasure with the situation.

"At any rate, she didn't. I hope it won't be weird the next time we run into each other. You are gonna do right by her, ain't ya?"

"Yep."

"She got no problem havin' an instant family with Macie?"

Lord, Cash could only hope they'd be a family. A real family. All of them. "Doesn't appear to."

"Good. Give that sweet Macie a kiss from me." Trevor climbed in his truck. "Keep in touch with me, you ol' ornery Indian. Miss your ugly mug."

"Speakin' of keepin' in touch...you hear much from Edgard?"

Trevor's grin died. "Haven't talked to him since he left last year."

After they'd been roping and traveling partners for a couple of years? That was weird. With forced cheer, Cash said, "He's probably hooked up with some little senorita and is stayin' out of trouble, eh?"

Trevor snorted and looked away. "Doubtful. Take care."

Cash checked Macie's camper, even though he knew she wasn't there. He checked the horses before he headed inside. Yeah. He was stalling. He'd be in a better place to deal with the aftermath of this tomorrow.

When he finally crawled into bed beside Gemma, she was already sound asleep.

Or so he thought.

Two hours later Cash woke up handcuffed to the headboard.

Chapter Thirty-Five

A naked Gemma sat on Cash's chest looking sexy. Smug.

And a little mean.

"What the hell do you think you're doin'?"

"I warned you. I want my wicked way with you, Cash. With the lights on. You wouldn't oblige me so I'm takin' what I want, just like *you* would."

Stall stall stall. "The lights were on last night when Trevor was here."

"Newsflash, cowboy. It's still night. And that doesn't count." She leaned forward, making her nipples within licking distance. "I want to look in your eyes when I'm making love to you. Would that be so bad?"

"Gemma."

"Cash," she mocked.

Damn. He closed his eyes.

"That's cheating."

"Fine. Do what you will. I'm helpless anyway."

"Don't sound so thrilled by the prospect of me touching you."

A beat passed. Nothing happened. Then he heard *snip snip.* Naturally, his curious eyes opened.

Gemma held a pair of scissors. Right next to his groin.

"Jesus. You're gonna castrate me?" His frantic gaze zoomed to the corroded steel blades. "With rusty scissors?"

"Would you rather I shut off the lights and did it in the *dark*?"

"Gemma!"

"Relax. I'm cutting off your boxers."

"Oh."

She stroked him through the cotton material.

"If you're lookin' to...release me, umm, there is a hole in the front for that."

"I know."

Every time she moved, those damn pretty tits swayed enticingly and he couldn't keep his eyes off them. Just a little closer...

Cash licked his lips.

Her saucy smile disappeared. An all-knowing feminine look glinted in her eyes. "But guess what? I've decided I don't care if you get off. You can watch *me* get off." She tossed the scissors to the floor and straddled his pelvis on her knees so his dick bumped into her ass.

Cash clenched his butt cheeks together.

Lord she looked beautiful. With her tousled blonde hair. Her pink lips swollen from their kisses. Tan lines criss-crossing her arms from slaving outdoors. The smattering of cinnamon-colored freckles across her chest. The curve of her ribs flaring into hips a man could sink his hands into. Her long legs, especially the strong muscles in her thighs from spending her life astride a horse. The bright red nail polish on her dainty feet—about her only concession to her femininity. He loved every square inch of her. He stared hungrily at her.

Not that she was paying attention to him.

Gemma flattened her palms on her belly and slid them up her ribcage. She arched. Her fingers fluttered higher. Then those ivory breasts were cupped in her hands and she strummed the pink tips with her thumbs until they drew into hard tips. She moaned.

His hips lifted slightly.

"That feels good. Mmm. But do you know what would feel better?"

My lips?

"This." Watching his face, she sucked her fingers into her mouth. "Mmm." She kept sucking, letting him get a flash of that naughty pink tongue.

Oh, he knew what damage that tongue could do. Bring a man to his knees with one wicked swipe.

Gemma eased her wet fingers out of her mouth, smiled, then used them to twist her right nipple. The fingers of her other hand glided down her stomach to the thatch of golden curls. The tip of her middle finger dipped down into her slit. Played around with the opening to her pussy and her ass as she rocked her hips forward, letting him see everything, letting him see how she pleasured herself. She pushed two fingers in deep.

His cock jerked hard.

Her moan was only slightly sexier than the moist sucking sounds of her fingers moving in and out of her pussy.

Then her fingers returned, glistening with her juices, to rub her clit.

Cash groaned. He couldn't tear his eyes away from this woman who held nothing back. In bed or out.

Her hips undulated and she said, "Oh, yes," as she touched herself like he wasn't here.

Screw that. He *was* here.

"Gemma. You're killin' me. You proved your point. Let me touch you."

And then she was in his face. "Why should I? You won't let me touch *you*. In fact, I don't even get to see you naked. It's been nearly three months you've spent in my bed."

"You can touch me right now."

She rolled her eyes. "So I had to ask myself: Am I that disgusting that you can't stand to look at my body when you make love to me?"

His jaw dropped. "Jesus. No!"

"Is it because I'm too old?"

"No."

"If it's not the body, then is it my face?"

"For Christsake, no!"

"Then it must be you."

His pulse pounded.

"You're not overly scarred, or tattooed, or ashamed of the

size of your big dick either. So, why is it, Cash Big Crow, that it always has to be so damn dark between us?"

Silence.

"I will leave you handcuffed here all night and all day if you don't answer. I might even stretch it out to two days. You know I don't make idle threats. Call this *my* pre-emptive strike."

He probably deserved that. "Gemma, sweets, please."

"No sweet-talkin', no bullshit. Tell me what in tarnation is goin' on with you and why we are always in the dark."

"Because I don't want you to know. I don't want you to see..." He squeezed his lids hard. But he knew it wouldn't do any good.

"See what? Please. Cash. Look. At. Me."

Cash opened his eyes. "See that I love you."

Gemma didn't speak.

"I've been in love with you for two years. From the first moment I saw you at the Ardmore Rodeo. You were perfect; a horsewoman who loved the land, who loved her stock, who was loyal to her friends. A sexy cowgirl who was smart, and smart-mouthed and could hold her own with rodeo cowboys and queens alike. But you were still grievin' for your husband and it broke my goddamn heart. So I bided my time, actin' like your friend, when in fact, I've been a lovesick fool for you for years, Gem, waitin' and hopin' you'd notice me. Give me a chance.

"Last year I thought you were finally gonna take a chance. But you weren't ready to move on. I didn't know if you'd ever be ready. 'Bout killed me to let you go. But I did. When you came to me, offerin' me a job, offerin' me the dream of bein' with you every day... I'm such a selfish bastard. I knew if I didn't claim everything I wanted from you up front, you'd give me scraps and I'd probably take them. But I found my pride and demanded all or nothin'. It floored me when you said yes."

"I wouldn't have asked you, or said yes to you if I hadn't wanted you. All of you." She smirked. "I'm a little stubborn in case you hadn't noticed. But you aren't answering my question. Why the darkness?"

"I hid your eyes that first night because I didn't want you to regret bein' with me, especially when I sorta forced your hand. And I sure as hell didn't want you to look down at me when we were both naked for the first time, and remember back to the last time a man had made love to you, and wish I was Steve."

She didn't move.

"Then I heard you cryin' afterward. It hurt like a son of a bitch. I didn't mean for it to go this far—with the blindfold, the darkness, and the funky sexual positions. But I knew I'd never be able to hide how I feel when I look in your eyes as I'm lovin' you. I wanted to wait until there might be a chance it didn't scare you and...you might love me back some day."

Gemma opened her mouth.

"Let me finish. Bein' naked, in body and soul, that's when I can't blame my goofy face every time I look at you, on the sun, or dirt, or gas fumes. That's when you can see that you are everything to me. It's like my fantasy come true, lettin' me touch your body, be a part of your life, givin' me a place to live, getting to do work I love. Acceptin' my daughter and my past."

"I see all that in your eyes, Cash. But you were so busy hiding from me, that if you would've bothered to look, you'd see the same exact thing in mine."

He swallowed hard. "I'm thirty-eight years old and I've never been in love. Made me wonder if I knew how to love." He didn't bother to hide his need or fear from her. "Will you teach me?"

"Yes. But you know more than you think."

"Uncuff me. Gemma, let me hold you. Please."

Gemma unfastened the handcuffs. Cash rolled her to her back and crawled on top of her. He didn't move. He just gazed into her pale blue eyes, eyes shining with love. For him. Damn humbling.

"Can I stay right here and look my fill, since I've been denyin' myself the pleasure?"

"It's the *only* pleasure you've denied yourself."

"True." He smiled. "Will you give me the pleasure of becomin' my wife?"

"Cash—"

"It'll be a bumpy road. Some people ain't gonna like the fact you married an Indian. They'll think I married you to get my hands on your ranch."

"The joke's on them, because we both know you want to marry me to get your big red hands on my body."

He grinned. "You are one horny widowed lady."

She smacked his ass. Hard.

His eyes narrowed. "You will pay for that later. Dearly. Anyway, as for family issues that might be a problem once we're hitched. I have a grown daughter I'm finally learnin' to be a father to after two decades. I'd like to think the worst is behind Macie and me, but it might not be. Are you okay with that?"

"Plus, there is a difference in our ages."

"Why the hell does that matter?"

"It doesn't. That's what I'm trying to tell you."

"What? That none of the issues we'll be facin' as husband and wife will matter?"

"No, they matter, but will you at least let me say *yes* to marrying you before you start laying out all our future problems?"

Cash froze. "You didn't say yes yet?"

"Nope. Ask me again." Gemma slid her arms around his neck. "Ask me as you're making love to me. Lookin' in my eyes."

"Whatever the lady wants. I'm never turnin' the lights off again."

"Be a little hard to sleep."

"There won't be a whole lot of sleepin' goin' on tonight."

Chapter Thirty-Six

Two weeks later...

The dappled gray filly pranced inside the training arena. She'd trot up to the fence, but the second Macie held her hand out to touch her, the high-spirited horse would whinny and race away.

"Pretty, ain't she?"

"Gorgeous. She seems to have a mind of her own."

"Like all good fillies do."

Macie laughed. "What's her name?"

Pause.

"You can name her whatever you want since she's yours."

"Mine?"

Her dad said, "Yep."

Hoofbeats faded as the horse galloped to the other side of the fence.

"You bought me a horse?"

"Yeah."

Macie squealed and threw her arms around his neck. "Omigod, I think I'm gonna cry."

He squeezed back. "She's young, and you're gonna have to work with her a lot before you can ride her. But if you train her right from the start, she'll always mind you, and she won't let you down."

"My first horse. Yay! I feel like an eight-year-old girl. Dad, thank you, thank you, thank you! I'll ride her, and pet her, and feed her, and take her for walks everyday, and she'll be my best friend..."

"You are such a smarty-pants."

"How cool is that? Pretty soon I'll be clip-clopping along on my very own horse, shootin' varmints with my new rifle."

"You bought her a rifle too?" Gemma asked.

They both turned around. Her dad's face lit up like the bug zapper. He wrapped his arm around Gemma's shoulders and kissed her temple. "Well, yeah. She needed her own gun out here in the wild wild West."

Macie watched her father and Gemma mooning over each other. They were so deliriously happy; she didn't begrudge them a bit of it. It spilled onto her. And rather than his relationship with Gemma driving a wedge between her and her father, it seemed to strengthen their bond.

Happy. Were she and Carter happy?

Despite the fact she and Carter lobbed the "L" word back and forth, things hadn't changed much in the last two weeks. He'd locked himself in the barn to finish up the final pieces for his show and she'd worked mega hours at the diner. They hadn't talked about what would happen after his show was over. They hadn't talked at all about her deciding to take Velma's offer to help run the diner. Carter had been so...obsessed with his work that he hadn't asked about hers. It shouldn't have bothered her, but it did.

It means your job in a small time diner isn't as important as his big art show.

Macie hoped with the diner closing for a little over a week they'd get to eke out time. If not, well, she did have a horse to train. She couldn't wait to tell him. After giving her father another hug, she drove to Carter's place.

Although his truck was there, he wasn't in the trailer. She hesitated at the barn door. He was protective of his space and she never ventured in uninvited after that first day. She yelled, "Carter?"

Silence.

"Carter? Are you in here?"

No answer.

She slipped inside. It wasn't the same pigsty she'd

remembered from last time when he'd given her the erotic painting lesson. No jars of mineral spirits or rolls of canvas, sections of thin boards or mysterious pieces of machinery covered the ground.

Damn dark in here though.

Macie reached for the light. Once her eyes adjusted, she found herself looking at paintings of herself. Everywhere. But not only was she buck-assed naked in the pictures, she was lost in the throes of passion. Or just looking lost. Each one focused on a different (naked!) part of her body. The disturbing part wasn't that the pictures were just...parts. They were parts of a whole person. Of her. Showcasing her expressions. Her moods. Her secret thoughts. It was all there, on her face. Atop her naked body.

Tears stung her eyes. This is what he'd been creating? Pornographic images of her? No wonder he'd acted so secretive.

She wasn't a prude. She'd seen art exhibits with nudes. No doubt the pictures were excellent. But that was a catch-22 because she couldn't pretend it wasn't her plastered on canvas. Her heart, her soul and—good heavens were those her *thighs*?— spread wide for the world to see.

Surely he didn't plan on exhibiting these in his show. He couldn't be that thoughtless, could he?

The barn door opened. Macie stood her ground even when she wanted to flee.

Carter trudged in. He stopped and looked at her, then at the paintings she'd seen, then back at her. "I didn't want you to see them like this."

"When were you going to show me?"

No answer.

"What? You were just going to spring these on me at your showing?"

"Yes."

Her stomach roiled. "Too bad. You can't show them."

"Macie—"

"You cannot display those pictures of me, Carter. I won't let you."

"*Let* me? It's a done deal. I have a show in two weeks."

"Postpone it until you can make something else."

Carter laughed softly. "Right. I don't have time."

"Make time."

"Come on, Macie. Be reasonable."

"Reasonable? I'm naked in them. What does me being naked have to do with Western art?"

"Oh, so people in the West don't get naked?"

"You know what I mean. Aren't there supposed to be sculptures of horses or cowboys riding through sagebrush?"

"I've already fulfilled those requirements in other mediums and other pieces."

"So you don't need to show these."

"Yes, I do. What's the big deal? You agreed to pose for me."

"Not like that! I told you no naked pictures."

"I thought you were kidding. You know, like you were kidding about wanting a cowboy ménage?"

"Not the same thing, Carter. I specifically said no nudes, several times, remember?"

Carter frowned.

"I'd never agree to this. Ever. Not even half-naked. Especially not..." Completely exposed. Had he been gauging her facial expressions while they'd been making love so he could reproduce them on canvas? Was that all she'd been to him? A muse he could fuck and use?

He stared at her blandly.

"Don't do this."

"Do what? Show the world how much I love you? How much I love every part of you? That's what the pictures are, Macie. Love."

"That is not love. That is porn!"

Carter sighed and raked his fingers through his curls. "I was afraid this might happen."

"What? That I'd freak out about strangers seeing my bare body painted in every conceivable position?"

"No, that you wouldn't understand."

Macie wanted to scream. Instead, she snapped, "I wouldn't

understand? Because I don't have a fucking Masters of Fine Arts that I can't see I'm utterly naked?"

"Stop actin' like a child. It's art. It's *my* art. And to put it crudely, darlin', I don't give a shit if you like it or not. This collection of stylized portraitures are the best I've ever done and I'll be damn proud to display them at the gallery."

Hollowness replaced her earlier joy. "Is that all I am now? A collection of portraitures to you?"

"See? You're confusin' you with the pictures."

"Same thing."

"No, *you* aren't a thing. These pictures are an extension of you. How can you not see that?"

"How can you not see how wrong this is?" She swallowed with difficulty because her mouth was bone dry. "Please. I'm begging you."

A muscle in his jaw flexed.

"Carter. Please. Don't show them."

"Macie. Stop."

"Don't display these."

He looked away.

"If you loved me you wouldn't do this."

Carter's hard gaze boomeranged to hers. "If you loved *me* you wouldn't ask me not to showcase my best work."

Macie wondered if he could hear her heart breaking in the silence. Without another word, she turned and walked out.

And this time, he didn't chase her down.

Luckily her father was gone when she returned to the Bar 9. She suspected the pictures—or Carter McKay—wouldn't live to see another day when he found out.

Just imagining her dad, or anyone else, looking at those paintings made her stomach hurt. She didn't remember ever feeling so alone. So helpless. So literally heartsick. Lord, she needed someone to talk to. Since her best pal Kat was hours away in Denver, she tracked down Gemma and poured out the whole story.

After the tears settled, Gemma assured her she hadn't acted like a child; Carter had stepped over the line. Besides soothing her and listening without judgment, Gemma didn't have any advice, beyond offering to run interference with Macie's dad if Macie needed to get away to think things through.

So with a week's vacation looming, rather than mope around the Bar 9, Macie packed her bags and did what she did best: ran.

Chapter Thirty-Seven

Two days later...

"The foundry in Gillette, Wyoming, called me in Denver to ask why you hadn't picked up your statues. They've been sitting there two weeks? Which means they're not finished. And here's where, as your agent, I remind you of the major showing you have in *less* than two weeks."

Carter scowled. He knew better to answer his cell when his agent called and he was in such a vile mood.

"What is going on, Carter?"

"Nothin' I can't handle. Look. I was just on my way to Gillette—" a total lie, "—to pick them up. They won't need a lot of polishin' so they are essentially done."

"My advice is to get them on a truck as soon as possible. What else is the gallery waiting for?"

"I shipped the major pieces last month. I'm finishin' up some portraits, but I ain't shippin' those directly."

"Why not?"

"Because I want to hang them myself."

Buck swore. "No way. That was not in the contract. The gallery will have an absolute fit."

"Tough shit."

"You do not get a say in how anything is exhibited, McKay, least of all paintings. Your job was to finish the art work, theirs is to display it."

"Then get the contract changed. Ain't that your job?"

Silence on the receiver. "My job is to look out for my client.

280

Which I'm doing, by telling you not to push the issue on this, because you are wrong. Get the paintings packed up. Either ship them by next Friday or I'll have the gallery send a truck for them. And the cost of that, my friend, will come out of your pocket, not mine." Buck hung up.

"Fuck!" Carter threw his cell phone against the wall. It cracked in two pieces and plastic shards scattered everywhere. Like he cared. Like anyone had called him.

Jesus. The last couple days had been a fucking nightmare. After his fight with Macie, he'd needed a day to cool off. When he'd swung by the diner around the time she usually clocked out, he saw the faded sign on the front door: Closed until further notice.

Why hadn't she told him?

Who said she didn't? Maybe you didn't hear because you haven't really listened to her in the past few weeks.

Talk about being a self-centered asshole. Dammit. This art show had sucked the life out of him. Had it sucked the soul and the conscience right out of him too?

Yes.

Regardless. He needed to talk to her to set the record straight. To make her understand.

Carter didn't bother calling Macie's cell phone; he knew she wouldn't answer. He'd called the Bar 9, in the guise of asking Gemma about Macie, but Gemma was curt with him. And vague.

Why?

Because Macie was gone?

No. She wouldn't just leave without saying goodbye.

Would she?

Sure she would. Cash and Gemma were getting married soon. Summer was ending. Macie couldn't live in the camper forever, and he knew she valued her independence too much to move into the main house. She probably felt like a third wheel. And with the diner closed, maybe she'd figured it was time to hit the road.

Or maybe someone encouraged her to hit the road.

Red rage built inside him. He wanted to hit something, but

it sure as hell wasn't the road.

Carter burned rubber getting to the Bar 9.

ॐ

Cash Big Crow was leaning on the fence when Carter's truck screeched to a stop.

He jumped from the cab. Four angry steps later he loomed over Macie's father. "Where is she?"

"Haven't we been through this once before, McKay?"

"Where is she?"

"If she wanted you to know, you would."

"You sent her away, didn't you?"

Cash faced him. "Don't you come here, accusin' me of something, when *you* are the one who chased her away."

Carter took a threatening step closer. "I did not."

"What did you do to her?"

"Nothin'! It was a stupid misunderstandin'."

"Explain it to me then."

"It ain't my fault *she* freaked out about—"

"About what?"

He paused and said nastily, "If she wanted you to know, you would."

"Don't you pull that smartass shit on me, son. I ain't in the mood. You came to me so you'd better start talkin'."

"Fine. Macie saw a couple of the pictures I painted of her. She didn't like them, and then she forbid me from displaying them at the showing. I told her tough, they were goin' up. It pissed her off and she stormed out. I ain't seen her since and I need to talk to her."

Cash glared at him. "It more than pissed her off. Accordin' to Gemma, Macie left here in tears."

Left? "Where'd she go?"

"Tell me 'bout these pictures that upset her so badly." Comprehension dawned on Cash's face. His eyes filled with rage. "Only one kind of pictures that'd make her cry."

Carter didn't look away.

"You painted nudie shots of her?"

"*Nudie*? The correct term is nude."

"Did she consent to that?"

"She posed for me voluntarily."

"But she didn't volunteer to pose for you naked, did she? That's why she's so goddamn upset."

"I don't see the big deal—"

Carter didn't see the punch Cash aimed at his jaw until it landed. He staggered back. Rather than taking a swing, Carter rushed Cash and they hit the dirt in a tangle of flying fists.

Cash kneed him in the stomach. Carter rolled and his elbow connected with the side of Cash's head. Cash flipped over and ground Carter's face into the gravel. Carter reared up and head butted Cash in the jaw. That knocked Cash back and Carter followed up with a hard right jab to Cash's ribs. Cash kicked Carter's knee, knocking him flat before Cash pulled back and punched Carter square in the eye.

Grunts, sweat, dirt, blood fueled their rage. Neither one backed down. Seemed like the fight lasted an hour, but it'd probably only been a minute when Gemma's voice boomed, "Break it up! Both of you!"

Cash took advantage of Carter's distraction and threw a right cross that clacked Carter's teeth together. Blood burst from his lip. Enraged, Carter swung high, his fist grazing Cash's eyebrow.

Then they were both sputtering and soaking wet.

Gemma aimed the hose at them until they moved apart. Still coughing, spitting, bleeding, trying to find a way to get another lick in.

"I said knock it off! Jesus. What is wrong with you two?"

Cash glared through the blood dripping in his eye. Carter dabbed at his bloody mouth and swollen lip.

"Carter, why are you here?"

He didn't answer.

"Let me guess, Macie."

He grunted.

"Haven't you done enough damage to her without pounding on her father too?"

"He took the first swing."

"And I'll take the last one, you—"

"Cash. Enough."

Silence.

Gemma sighed. "Carter. I think it's time you pack up your stuff and get back home."

Even through the throbbing in his ear, Carter knew she didn't mean home to the trailer. Why did the thought of leaving the Bar 9 make his head hurt worse and make it harder to breathe? "You ain't gonna let me explain, are you?"

"I don't need to hear your excuses. You took advantage of Macie and I ain't gonna stand for it."

"It's not what you think. I love her."

"You've got a piss-poor way of showin' it."

"You know, this is bullshit." Carter staggered to his feet. "None of you have even *seen* the damn pictures. They are a tribute to her. And you're—" he pointed at Cash, "—actin' just as immature about this as she did. Yes, they are nudes. So what? Macie didn't get her way with me by forcin' my hand, so she ran away, like I suspect she always does. You're frustrated that she left you too, so you're takin' it out on me. I did nothin' wrong but create beautiful art of the beautiful woman I love for the world to see."

Gemma helped Cash stand. She swiped the blood from his face and murmured in his ear.

Cash looked at Carter. "You're right, you aren't anything like your brothers. The McKays I know have honor." He limped up the porch steps.

Talk about a sucker punch.

"Cash shouldn't have taken a swing at you. But you shouldn't have expected any less from him either."

He waited.

"Macie asked me to keep the truth from him on what you'd done to make her leave."

"Is she comin' back?"

Gemma stared at him. "What do you care? You got what you wanted."

"That ain't fair."

"Why are you doin' this?"

"What's the big deal? They're just pictures."

"Then put them in your bedroom. Or in your studio. Not on a public wall in an art gallery."

"But they're good pictures."

"I imagine they are. What you can't see, Carter, is that this isn't only about Macie being naked. Maybe we are hicks, and we don't understand your art, but we do understand that you do *not* exploit the person you love. Ever. You protect them. You go out of your *way* to shelter them, not to expose them."

"I love her."

"That's not love. You took everything she freely gave you and used it against her to make yourself look good. And then had the balls to make her feel small for questioning *your* right to do it."

"But see—"

"I see by the stubborn set to your jaw that you're digging in your heels and won't listen to reason. And you think we're acting childish? Macie is hurting, Cash is hurting, hell, I'm hurting. You're hurting everyone around you and the only one who thinks what you are doin' is right, is you.

"Don't bother to clean up the trailer before you leave. I'm givin' you two days to clear out."

Gemma turned on her heel and hustled in the house.

Carter stared at the slamming door, staggered by their accusations, before he limped to his truck. Had he just lost everything he never thought he'd find? To hell with Macie and her father, and Gemma too. Everyone in the whole fucking world could go straight to hell. No one understood him. No one ever had and it was apparent no one ever would.

He snagged the bottle of whiskey from the passenger seat and chugged a mouthful of liquid fire. Maybe he'd discover the answers to his questions in the bottom of a bottle.

෨

Four days later Carter was still half-drunk from his four-day bender.

He was sprawled on the floor in the barn contemplating studying the back of his eyelids when the door opened and a splinter of light gouged his retinas.

"Jesus, it stinks in here."

"Yeah, like your barn don't stink, Cord."

"I'm just sayin'..."

Bootsteps shuffled, kicking up dirt and hay dust.

"Christ. *He's* what stinks."

"Think he's dead?"

"Roll him over."

"I ain't touchin' him."

"Colt, you are such a pussy."

Carter grunted. "I ain't dead." He managed to roll on his back. He opened his eyes and squinted. The McKay Posse—Colby, Colt and Cord glared down at him.

"What the fuck are you guys doin' here?"

"Thinkin' about killin' you now that we know you ain't worm food," Colby snapped off.

No mistaking it. His brothers were livid.

"Ma wouldn't let you." In the tense air Carter's voice sounded rusty as old nails.

"Don't bet on it. She was worried sick. No one could reach you on your cell. Your agent called their house. Then your buddy Jack called. The last straw was when Gemma called mad as hell because you were supposed to have cleared out. Instead, she found you passed out in the barn. Ma was halfway down the driveway with the shotgun before Dad stopped her."

"Shit."

Colt hunkered down. "You're lucky Keely distracted Dad while we were leavin' this mornin' and he ain't here. Jesus. What's wrong with your face?"

"Got into a fight."

"Yeah, we sort of figured that," Cord said. "Why is Gemma throwin' you off the Bar 9?"

Carter slowly sat up. "Because Cash Big Crow looks about as bad as I do."

"You took after Cash? I thought you had more brains than that, college boy."

"He took the first swing but I probably deserved it. Probably deserved way more."

"Cord, grab his other arm," Colby said.

The two of them hauled Carter upright. Pain slammed into his head. Sorrow into his soul. How had he fallen so far so fast? This time last week he'd been on top of the world. Now everyone knew he'd crashed and burned.

"I'm fine. You guys can go now. I'm sure you've got more important shit to do than babysit me for Mom."

Talk about sounding like a whiny prick. Carter shook off his brothers' hands and their help.

"Mom ain't the only reason we're here," Cord scoffed.

"Yeah. You might be a total shithead, but you're still a McKay. And you know we take care of our own, bro, no matter what," Colby said.

Carter bit back the urge to bawl. His brothers were pissed off and sporting the gruff attitude they'd inherited from their father, but they were still here. If he'd been wrong about them, what else had he been wrong about?

Everything.

Still, if they saw one grateful tear sliding down his bruised cheek, they'd cheerfully punch him in the face and give him something to really cry about.

He sighed.

"Jesus. Don't breathe on me," Colt complained. "You reek, Carter. How long's it been since you showered or changed your clothes?"

Carter tipped his chin down and looked. Huh. He still had on the same bloodied shirt and dirty jeans he'd worn when Cash handed him his ass. And he'd worn it for a couple of days before that when Macie walked out on him. "Probably a week."

"Man, that's just nasty." Colt walked to the other side of the barn.

"You been sittin' in here for four days mopin' over her?"

"I've been busy workin'."

"Workin' on two bottles of Jim Beam it looks like," Cord said.

"Don't you judge me, asshole. If you knew the hell I've been through—"

Cord's cruel laugh cut him off. "You don't wanna get into a pissin' match with me on that one, boy."

"I ain't a boy."

"Then stop actin' like one and be a man."

"Fuck off, Cord. You think you're the only one in the family who's been kicked in the goddamn balls by love?"

"Come talk to me about love after it castrates you."

"Enough." Colby shoved his hat back and scratched his forehead. "We're takin' you home. What of this artsy fartsy stuff are we haulin' back to the ranch?"

"I'm not leavin' here. This is where I live now."

Colt's bootsteps stopped.

"The hell you are," Colby retorted. "Gemma's throwin' you out."

"And you're helpin' her?"

"You need some distance and perspective."

"No. I need her."

"Holy shit." Colt whistled. "Who is she? Look at those tits. Them babies are definitely real. Man, I could suck on those nipples for hours. How come you're not doin' more raunchy pictures like—"

Carter stalked to where Colt stood, grabbed him by the shirtfront and shoved him hard. "Don't you talk about her like that. Don't you fuckin' *look* at her like that or I will rip your fuckin' head off."

Colt shoved back. "If you didn't want no one lookin' at it, why'd you paint it? You shouldn't have left it right there for everyone to see. What's the big deal?"

What's the big deal?

Hadn't he posed that same question to Macie? And Cash? And Gemma?

The big deal was he didn't want *anyone* else looking at these pictures of Macie.

Ever.

The truth slammed into him like a Wyoming coal train.

Jesus Christ. How had he ever thought he could stand by and let other men ogle naked pictures of the woman he loved?

Then why *had* he painted them?

Because he could. Because he was cocky. Because he wanted everyone to know he—Carter, the quiet, laid-back, invisible McKay—was worthy of that kind of intense love from a woman like Macie.

It sickened him to think he'd been so focused on showing the world and his family how special his art was, that he'd lost sight of how special *Macie* was. How special what they had together was.

Carter's gaze connected with the picture. This was *his* Macie. How he saw her. It didn't matter that she was naked in body; she was naked in spirit too. She didn't show those sides of herself to everyone. Just to him. And he didn't want—he had no right—to share it. He didn't need to immortalize what she was on canvas when he could have the flesh and blood version looking back at him just like that every damn day.

He stumbled backward over an old milking stool and landed on his butt. He couldn't speak because he wanted to throw up.

"Carter? You okay, bud?"

"I have to get rid of them."

His brothers exchanged a look. Cord said, "Get rid of what?"

"The pictures of Macie." He pointed to a stack of frames against the far wall. "There are more like that."

"More?"

"They were gonna be part of my show. The biggest part."

"You're fuckin' kiddin', right?"

His bleary-eyed gaze zoomed to Colby. "No."

Colby stared at him in silence for several seconds. "There are things between a man and woman that should stay private, and I ain't just talkin' about sex. Lines you don't cross. Stuff you don't share with nobody."

"I didn't get it until now."

"At least you figured it out before you put up them pictures. I see they didn't teach you everything in college."

"I know it's stupid, but I'm just so crazy in love with her I wanted everyone to know it. To see how lucky I am. To brag that this...perfect woman is mine. That she picked *me*. That she loves *me*."

"What do you care that the whole world knows that?" Colt said. "Jeez, Carter, the only important thing is *you* know."

Colby and Cord both gave Colt an odd look.

"I-I have to get rid of them. Burn them. But I don't know if I can. Because it is her, lookin' at me, and it'd be like I was destroyin' her or a part of her..."

Cord's gaze hooked his. For once no accusation or condescension burned in his eyes. Just compassion. "I'll do it."

Carter nodded. "Thanks. I have to make this right. I don't even know where to start."

"A shower would be good," Colt suggested

"Then I'm thinking you need to eat a helping of crow." Colby grinned and smacked Carter on the back. Hard. "A big helping of *Big Crow*."

Carter groaned. "No. Anything but that."

"Look at it this way, at least your face ain't gonna look any worse when he gets through with you this time."

Chapter Thirty-Eight

Gemma sagged against Cash as they watched Carter McKay's pickup zip down the gravel road. "You okay?"

"Yeah."

His arms tightened around her but he said nothing for several minutes. Finally, he kissed the top of her head. "I'm glad Macie wasn't wrong in fallin' for him. I'd hate to think..."

She waited for a response that was a long time in coming. "Hate to think what?" she prompted.

"That my daughter would believe all men she allowed in her life would let her down at some point. God knows I did."

"Cash, you're working on changing that. Macie knows you're trying, that's why she's sticking around. Even before Carter showed up full of apologies, you and I both knew Macie wasn't goin' nowhere. She wants to be in your life. She *wants* to count on you. We both know that kinda trust ain't gonna happen overnight. Nothin' worthwhile ever does."

He sighed. "I hope they can work it out. My girl deserves a chance at happiness."

"Speaking of chances... I was a little surprised you didn't bust Carter's chops and gave him a second chance."

"Takes a big man to admit he was wrong. Takes a bigger man to apologize and swear to make it right. Besides, where would any of us be without second chances, eh?"

Gemma knew the smartest thing she'd done was taking a chance with her heart, and getting a second chance at love. "Every day you give me a new reason to love you, Cash."

"I still think I got the better end of the deal. You see the best in situations and people, not the worst. How you saw beyond a vagabond rodeo Indian cowboy with ties to nothin' and no one—"

Gemma spun in his arms. "I saw a good man with a good heart. I still see that." She kissed his chin. "Neither one of us is perfect. We've both been rode hard by life; we've got a lot of miles on us. But we ain't used up yet."

"Thank God. The way I look at it, we have a good forty or fifty years left together." He waggled his eyebrows beneath his Stetson. "So, purty boss lady, you wanna mess around a little before we start chores?"

"Always. But there is one thing I want to talk to you about."

"Sounds serious."

"It is. I want to stop using condoms. I don't like the damn things."

Cash went utterly still before he leaned down and locked his gaze to hers. "What are you sayin', Gem?"

"If I get pregnant, then I get pregnant. If I don't, it wasn't meant to be. I know I'm old and the risks are huge, but I kinda feel like this might be a second chance for both of us."

"You humble me, *winyan*." He placed one hand on her belly and one on her heart. He closed his eyes and pressed his forehead to hers. "I love you."

"I love you too. Now take me to bed or I'm gonna fire you for slacking on the job."

Chapter Thirty-Nine

The next evening...

"It's my last night here and I don't want to be a wallflower at some street dance."

"Macie, you promised. Come on, it'll be fun."

"Fun for who? I won't know anyone." A dance was the dead last place she'd ever see Carter McKay. Not that she'd be looking for him or anything.

"You'll know me." Amy Jo inserted her contact and blinked. "Keely always ditches me at these things anyway, so it'll be nice for me not to sit by myself for a change."

"You sure you won't ditch me the second you catch sight of Cord McKay? Especially when he sees you all tramped up?"

"He wouldn't look twice at me if I rode into town buck-ass nekkid on the back of a purple longhorn bull." Amy Jo snorted. "The only reason Cord would talk to me is to ask me if I'd babysit Ky."

"And you'd ditch me in a heartbeat to do it."

"Nope. As much as I love that little guy, my babysitting days are over. I'm officially a college coed so I'd better start acting like one."

"Been watching *Girls Gone Wild* DVDs for some ideas, Miss Amy Jo?"

"No. I've been watching Keely McKay for years, which is better." She grinned. "And you're supposed to be calling me AJ, remember?"

"My mistake, AJ." Macie studied Amy Jo—AJ—as she applied eyeliner. AJ was dead wrong if she thought any man could overlook her. With her white-blonde hair, enormous gray eyes, pouty red lips and long legs, she looked every inch a cool, sleek Scandinavian model—not at all like the Wyoming cowgirl in pigtails and dirty jeans that Macie had met just last month.

AJ adjusted her black silk bustier. "What are you wearing?"

Macie glanced down at her white eyelet camisole shirt and faded jean skirt. "What's wrong with this?"

"Nothing. Oops we're gonna be late." Her smile seemed strained. "Let's go. I'll drive."

"But I thought I'd drive so if I want to leave—"

"Huh-uh. You're riding with me. Or I can call Keely. You choose. But I believe she said something about making an entrance on a Harley."

"That was just plain cold, AJ."

She spun the keys on her finger. "This is gonna be so great."

Macie froze. A strange feeling rippled through her. "What?"

"You'll see. Let's go find us some cowboys to tame, girlfriend."

Two blocks of Main Street were cordoned off. Macie and AJ wove through pickups and four-wheel drive vehicles lining the side street. Shouts sounded above the bass line of the Western song blasting from the loudspeakers.

Macie was having a hard time keeping up with AJ's long-legged strides, mostly because she was dragging her feet. She wanted to go home.

When she'd left the Bar 9 last week, she had no destination in mind. She'd ended up at Kat's apartment in Denver. While she'd been wallowing in ice cream, margaritas and Kat's pierogis, Amy Jo Foster had called her. She and Keely McKay were headed for Denver to finalize a few last minute things and had a couple of questions on the metro-Denver area.

Neither Keely nor AJ asked why Macie was in Colorado instead of Wyoming. Neither asked about Carter. Instead, they'd spent a few days together. She showed them around the city. Tagged along while they picked out furnishings for their apartment. When AJ heard about Macie's new horse, she asked her to hang out and ride horses at the Foster ranch. Macie admitted the week went by faster than she imagined. The days did anyway. The nights were long, and the only time she allowed herself to cry over Carter McKay.

Right now, she just wanted to hop in her Escape and drive back to Canyon River and try to rebuild her life. She missed her dad. She missed Gemma. She missed Velma and the diner. She missed the ranch. She missed Carter something fierce.

Damn.

Don't think of him. Think of how next week, he'll be plastering naked pictures of you in Jackson Hole.

It made her ache. She wasn't wrong about her ultimatum to Carter, but it'd never hurt so bad to be right.

AJ stopped abruptly. "Damn."

"What?"

"I have to go to the bathroom."

"Now?"

"Right now." AJ started up the sidewalk to a small white building, with the words *Community Center* centered above the door. The windows were dark.

"AJ, I don't think there's anyone in there. The door is probably locked."

"Hah. Nothing is ever locked around here. Come on."

Macie followed her inside. The interior door creaked. The main room was pitch black so she followed the sound of AJ's high-heeled boots clicking on the tile. Then the lights were flipped on. She blinked.

And saw him.

She blinked again.

Carter McKay was still standing in front of her.

"Macie. You're here."

She whirled around and saw AJ slipping out the door. Traitor. Her heart pounded like a bass drum when she faced him again.

Carter looked bad. Why did that made her feel good?

Why did her eyes drink him in like nectar anyway?

"I'm sorry."

Macie waited, letting him know that a simple, "I'm sorry" or "I missed you" wouldn't be enough this time.

"I didn't mean to hurt you."

"You did." Her gaze zoomed across the scabs and bruises covering his face. "Looks like someone put the hurt on you."

Carter rubbed his jaw. "Well, your dad has a wicked right cross, darlin'."

"You got into a fistfight with my dad?"

"Yep. And he still didn't knock any sense into me."

Why hadn't her father told her that he and Carter exchanged blows? "Is he okay?"

"He looks about the same as I do."

"When did this happen?"

"Last week. When I came lookin' for you."

"Why did you come looking for me?"

"I was gonna demand you quit bein' so stupid and childish and fall in line with my way of thinkin'. Then Cash told me you were gone, and I figured you were gone for good. And I...completely lost it, Macie. I lost my ever-lovin' mind.

"I accused him of stuff; he accused me of stuff. It was ugly. In retrospect it was one of the most embarrassin' moments of my life. Although, at the time I was mad as hell and bleedin' inside and out, and I thought you were all wrong." Carter took a deep breath. "Turns out *I* was wrong."

She waited.

"But I was hurt by you, too. Not only by your leavin', but because I wanted you to like the pictures. There was no ulterior motive when I started paintin' you. I really did create them from my heart. And I was so damn excited from a professional perspective that I'd captured the pure essence of you. I was so busy pattin' myself on the back, tellin' myself you'd come around and see the pictures the way I did...that I lost sight of the fact I'd lost *you*."

Macie didn't move outwardly, yet inwardly a small kernel of

hope grew.

"I'd rather have the real you than just a half dozen static images of you lookin' at me like you used to. After I sobered up—"

"Sobered up?"

"Yeah, I kinda went on a bender after you left, and your dad and I rolled around in the dirt, and then Gemma kicked me off the Bar 9. My life was pretty much shit. My brothers showed up and showed me the error of my ways. Not with their fists for once, which my body is thankin' them for profusely. Turns out I was wrong about them too."

Carter finally looked her in the eye. "I destroyed the pictures, Macie. Not because you wanted me to. Because the thought of anyone ever seein' you like that, not only naked, but with your heart and soul wide open, tears my heart and soul clean out of my body. The right to share that or show it doesn't belong to anyone but you. I hope I haven't destroyed my chances of ever getting to see it again."

"And your art show?"

"Still happening in three days. Turns out I have more than enough pieces without the pictures of you."

They stayed in place, watching one another.

"Macie. Talk to me. I love you."

She studied him. "Why do you love me?"

"What?"

"You told me you loved me, but why?"

Carter stared at her, taken aback.

"Why?"

"Because you're brave." When she opened her mouth to protest, he held up his hand. "Don't bring up your fear of storms, darlin'. I'm talkin' about you bein' brave when it comes to livin' your life.

"You're a fighter. It'd be easy for you to say, 'My father neglected me my entire childhood, so screw him.' Instead you're here, fightin' to have a real relationship with him.

"Because you're accepting. You don't try to change people. You accept your dad for who he is *now*. And his feelin's for Gemma never made you seriously question his feelin's for you.

Mostly, the accepting thing gets to me because you get me, the real me and accept me for who I am. You've taught me to accept myself. I've never thought I was worthy of the kind of love you've given me. And I want to spend the rest of my life lovin' you, givin' it back, times ten."

When she still didn't say anything he added, "And because you make the best goddamn pie I've ever tasted."

Macie had never been so scared or so hopeful or so paralyzed by emotion in her life.

Carter began to walk toward her. "Be brave, Macie. Fight for me. Love me. Accept what I'm offerin' you. Take a chance on me."

"Carter—" He seemed upset she hadn't thrown herself into his arms. She put one hand on his chest, stopping him.

"Please." His eyes searched her face. "Oh, my sweet darlin', why do you have that horrified look?"

She whispered, "Because the person you described? That's not me. I'm not brave. The thought of putting down roots scares me to death. Most of my life I've run instead of staying to fight because I've never had anything worth fighting for. I accept you, the real you, but will you accept me? The real me? The unsure, fly-by-the-seat-of-my-pants person I feel like inside everyday?"

"Macie. Didn't I just tell you—"

"Listen to me, Carter McKay. I don't have huge ambitions besides living my life happy. I like working in a diner. I don't aspire to be a polished woman hanging off your arm at big, fancy art shows."

Those blue, blue eyes flared anger. "I'm sorry, did I ever say I wanted or expected anything from you besides what you are?"

"No, but—"

"Did I say, 'Macie, go to cookin' school' or 'Study this book on the influence of cubism on 20th century art'? Hell, what kind of ambitions do you think I have? Last time I checked, darlin', I lived in a crappy rented trailer in nowhere Wyoming, and my income is close to poverty level.

"I've acted more immature in the last two weeks than you have in your whole life—and why the hell am I tellin' you this?" He tossed up his hands. "I'm supposed to be sellin' you on spendin' your life with me, not encouragin' you to run, though, now, it probably sounds like you should get as far away from me as possible."

And then she knew. When Carter didn't offer her flowery promises, sweet words and romantic bullshit about the perfect life they'd have together as they rode off into the sunset, she knew they'd be okay. They'd make it work. She just had to be brave and fight and take a chance on him. On them.

Macie stood on tiptoe and got right in his face. "I'll admit, your lines have improved since the first time I met you, cowboy. But if you ever use them on another woman, I'll kick your butt worse than my dad or your brothers ever thought of."

Then she threw her arms around him and kissed him.

"Thank you. Oh, Macie darlin', I love you. I love you so damn much." He peppered her face with kisses. "I'm so sorry I hurt you. So sorry. Thank God I didn't lose you. Thank God."

Carter didn't let go of her for the longest time.

"No more nude pictures of me ever, Carter. Promise me."

"I promise." He smiled down at her. "Marry me."

Her heart leapt into her throat. "Shouldn't we wait and live together first?"

"No. I want my ring on your finger. I want to start the rest of our life out right. No running away when the going gets tough, for either of us. We stick together for better for worse, forever." His eyes turned serious. "Besides, I already asked your dad if I could marry you."

"Did he say we're too young to settle down?"

"He said age was just a number and there are no age restrictions on when you might find true love. But most importantly, he said *yes*."

How had she gotten so lucky to have not one, but two good men in her life?

"Wanna go meet the rest of the McKay family before we head home to the Bar 9?"

Home. That sounded nice. "They're here?"

"Yep. They fell all over themselves to be here when I told them I was takin' my girl dancin'."

"You don't dance."

Carter twirled her in a clumsy circle and tromped on her toe. Then he stopped and cradled her face in his hands. "Macie, with you in my life, I can probably fly."

Tears spilled down her cheeks. "You are such a dumbass, Carter McKay. But you're my dumbass and I love you."

And they raced outside to dance together under the Wyoming stars, young, hopeful and wildly in love.

About the Author

To learn more about Lorelei James, please visit www.loreleijames.com. Send an email to lorelei@loreleijames.com or join her Yahoo! group to join in the fun with other readers as well as Lorelei! http://groups.yahoo.com/group/LoreleiJamesGang.

To stop a blackmailer and achieve her dreams, she only had to do one thing: seduce the enemy.

Sneak Peek: Watch Me
© 2007 Shelley Bradley

Shanna York was set to achieve her glittering ballroom dreams and become a dance champion—until her dance partner gets tangled up in scandal and blackmail. With the clock ticking and all her ambitions at stake, the last thing she needs is the gorgeous owner of a sex club tempting her with the forbidden.

Or maybe that's the very thing she needs...

Alejandro Diaz has sizzled for Shanna since he set eyes on her months ago. Her repeated rebuffs will make her surrender that much sweeter. She's ambitious and driven...but so is he. When she asks for his assistance to ensnare a voyeuristic blackmailer with a video fetish, he doesn't hesitate to help her stage a bedroom trap. But neither is prepared to face scorching, endless passion, the blackmailer's real identity—or the undeniable love that grows between them.

See Show Me *by Jaci Burton for the second story in the Sneak Peek Duet.*

Available now in ebook and print from Samhain Publishing.

Enjoy the following excerpt from Sneak Peek: Watch Men...

"Men are watching you, wanting you."

He grabbed her thigh, spun her around to face him, then placed that thigh over his hip. They rested nearly hip to hip again. As he leaned back slightly, he forced her chest against his. Still, she could not break his stare.

"You like it," he whispered.

She opened her mouth to deny it, but Alejandro's gaze stopped her, warning her before she could do anything foolish, like lie.

"I know you do."

The intensity of his stare, the way in which he'd dug past her icy defenses, seemed to see the real her, and guessed her dirty secret... He was a walking wet dream.

He was her worst nightmare.

He swayed with the music in the opposite direction, bringing her body with him. With a gentle caress of her cheek, he directed her gaze back to his—all while making it look like a part of the dance.

"You know you do," he murmured. "You love knowing that most every man in the room right now would kill to have your body against his and have a front-row seat of that smoldering sensuality you keep wrapped in ice suddenly melting in a pool at his feet."

His words made her shake. *Oh, no. No!* "Stop."

He performed an open step, then brought her back for a box. "Their eyes cling to you as you lure them in with the sway of your hips to the music and your femininity. Their gazes caress your breasts as your chest lifts with every move and breath. They watch the sleek movements of those gorgeous thighs and wish they were between them."

A glance around proved he was totally right. Easily a dozen men were openly watching her and Alejandro dance, their gazes ranging from more than mildly interested to sizzling with heat. Desire vibrated deep inside her, pulsing under her clit. How wet could she get before it stained the front of her thin costume?

And how had Alejandro known what turned her on?

Most people had only seen the driven dancer who yearned to win and find some way to make her family proud. No one else had seen the woman inside who used dance to express the sexuality she otherwise repressed. No one.

This man had seen her hidden sensuality in the blink of an eye. He'd all but mocked her icy reserve. He looked at her as if he could see past it, all the way to the fear and emptiness that fed her ambition.

Thankfully, the music ended.

"Thank you for an interesting evening, Mr. Diaz. Perhaps our paths will cross again." Not if she could help it.

Still, he didn't let go, continued to stare at her with that sultry hint of a smile as the music began again. "The evening is not over. I bought all of your dances tonight, for the whole night."

Shanna stared at him, wide eyed and stunned. Panicked. He'd bought *all* of her dances? She swallowed. That was bad. Very bad. Just being in his arms and hearing his words made her feel vulnerable in a way she didn't like and would not accept.

And she was stuck with him for the next three hours? Lord, she was in so much trouble.

"Why?"

"I enjoy watching you being watched and the way it arouses you. I love knowing that so many men in the room are fantasizing about slaking their lust with you—"

"You can't know what other men are thinking," she protested.

"But I can. It is exactly what I'm thinking. It is even more delicious because I alone am holding you in my arms."

Oh, God. Oh, God. "This conversation is inappropriate."

"Honesty disturbs you?"

"I'm not...I—I don't get aroused knowing that men are watching me."

"Really?"

He urged her into a cross again. No sooner than she turned to step into the next box, he pushed against her hand, sending her spinning to face the wall. Then he was behind her, hands on her swaying hips, his mouth hovering just over her sensitive neck in a darkened corner of the ballroom.

Shanna shivered as he exhaled, quivered as he gripped her hips.

Then he reached around to place his hand flat on her stomach again...but he aimed high, flattening his palm on the upper swells of her chest and smoothing his way down.

"Hard nipples," he commented. "Little edible, want-to-suck-them-in-my-mouth nipples."

She hissed in a breath, and opened her mouth to stop him, tell him to get lost...but he kept tantalizing her as he caressed his way south, down her ribs, over her stomach, until his fingers brushed the front of her costume right over her sex. He lingered. Shame and arousal crashed inside her. She closed her eyes. Her thong was about to overflow.

"You're always wet when you dance in public...like now, aren't you?"

At his touch, his words, pleasure spiked, hitting her full force, like a blast from a raging fire. She sucked in a breath. Damn it, why did he have to be right?

If he could figure that much out after just a few minutes with her, Shanna knew he'd dig deeper, quickly, into her soul, unless she put distance between them now.

"Stop," she demanded in her best ice-queen voice.

"Answer me, *querida*."

"No."

He danced her to face him again as one song segued into the next, this one a waltz.

"Do not be embarrassed. Your arousal turns me on. It's one of the reasons I chose not to give up when you rebuffed me at the Bartolino event. I want that arousal," he whispered in her ear, making her shiver. "I want it in my hands, my mouth, all around my cock when I fuck you and you wonder exactly who is watching us."

His words hit her like lava, sizzling her skin, charring her resistance and sanity. No one had ever talked to her like that. Between her brothers and the bitchiness she wore like armor, no one had dared.

God, even without uttering a word, Alejandro was stunning. When he talked like that, he didn't just turn her on; he turned her inside out.

Alejandro was dangerous to her career and her focus. She could see getting lost in such a man and the smoldering promise of spectacular sex—which she'd never experienced—in his hazel eyes.

"That's enough," she forced herself to say.

"We haven't started. I think about undressing you under soft lights, your back to my front and letting my hand smooth your dress from your lush curves. I ache to let your perfect hard nipples brush the inside of my palms before I roll them between my fingers. I fantasize about feeling my way lower, down to that soft, wet pussy, and grazing your hard clit. And stroking it until you come. I obsess about bending you over and filling you with my cock—all while you know hot eyes, strangers' eyes, touch you."

Desire pulsed, flared with every mental image he created. She could *see* herself naked, flushed, writhing under his hands or as he impaled her. She could feel herself dissolving at the thought of orgasming for him—and a roomful of aroused men.

*Recipe for Margarita Day: Take one shy woman, toss in three
determined alphas, mix liberally with sizzling sex,
add a dash of intrigue, and watch the steam rise.*

Margarita Day

© 2007 Nicole Austin and TK Winters

Stand alone sequel to Mimosa Night.

Jodi Matthews is the consummate gamer. One crazy night
she let her hair down, stripped off her clothes, and anted up for
a night of poker and wild fantasy sex. Now she has three alpha
players hot to win her hand.

Conner is a walking wet dream ready to share his vision of
the future. Wiz, a high roller looking for a cherished pet to
adorn his arm, while John's an average Joe who can turn Jodi
inside out with a simple look.

No matter what card she chooses, Jodi risks losing
something. The life she loves working as a Vegas dealer or some
close friends. Maybe both.

From champagne and diamonds to mysterious parties and
private jets, Jodi must accept herself and what her heart's
always known. The Smut Squad is there, ready and willing to
fortify her courage and orchestrate a daring hunt for the
ultimate stakes.

The only thing is—this is no game, and the jackpot will be
even better than her wildest dreams.

Available now in ebook and print from Samhain Publishing.

Enjoy the following excerpt from Margarita Day...

John slid his hands across his chest and abdomen, stopping only when reaching his erection. "Look what you do to me, Jodi." His strong fingers grasped both jeans and underwear. Rising higher on his knees, he shimmied his hips and peeled the clothing away, his parted thighs stopping the descent. His cock jutted straight and proud from a nest of dark curls. Clear liquid on the crown gleamed in the soft light from the bedside lamp.

Jodi watched in fascination as pre-come seeped from the slit and trailed across the thick head of his cock. Her back arched, hips tilting upward. She needed to have his shaft buried so deep inside her pussy she wouldn't know where she ended and he began. She needed to be held in his strong arms, feel his body moving above her, and have him slam into her wet channel until all the fear and confusion disappeared in a blazing glory of sensation.

She sat up and unclasped her bra, letting her breasts fall free. She cupped a heavy globe in each small hand, lifting them in offering.

"Oh, yeah. Hold them just like that, baby." John wet one finger with his pre-come, and traced a glittering path around one dark areola. Jodi watched the circle pebble, and the nipple grow long and hard under his light touch. He lowered his head, blocking her view of his tongue rasping across the peak, licking up his own salty essence before drawing her nipple into the warmth of his mouth.

She writhed beneath him, breasts thrust upward in response to the tugging of his lips. John's hands replaced hers to squeeze and knead. Teeth nipped at her sensitive bud, followed by his tongue laving away the slight sting. He sucked as much of her soft flesh into his mouth as he could, his moans of enjoyment vibrating through her flesh and paving a hot path through her belly straight to her clit.

Jodi wanted to give as much pleasure as she was receiving. She moved her freed hands between them and grasped his hard shaft, pumping once, twice, squeezing her fist around the throbbing length. Damn, his hard cock felt incredible in her palm. The heat pouring off the thick column penetrated her skin and ignited every nerve. She idly rubbed her thumb over an engorged vein, the steady beat of his blood starting a matching pulsation in her clitoris.

John's head came up, back straightening, hips thrusting his cock in reaction to the confining clasp of her hands. "Now, Jodi. I need you now." Rolling off the bed, he toed off his boots and finished stripping in one quick motion. He reached out, grabbed her ankle and tugged her toward the edge of the mattress.

"John," she complained, wanting him to stop dragging her all over the bed and get busy already.

"Keep your sweet ass right here, baby, and spread those pretty legs wide for me."

Before Jodi had time to respond or even comply, her panties were off, legs pushed open and his fingers had parted her swollen labia. Cool air followed by hot breath sent shivers rocketing through her body. She thrust her hips upward, seeking the source of the teasing warmth. A totally masculine, satisfied chuckle sounded through the dim room.

Her leg muscles bunched and she once more thrust upward, wet pussy making contact with smiling lips. This time she heard a whispered curse before he sucked her clit into his hot mouth and his tongue teased her hard bud.

"Yes," she cried out. "Yes! Like that...oh God, just like that, John!" Her hips bucked and ground against his mouth while he sucked and licked her clit. His tongue flicked along the sensitive tissues, delving into her dripping channel. Jodi felt her leg muscles tighten, toes flexing on the edge of the bed as her ass pushed high above the mattress.

John's hands shifted to clasp her soft cheeks firmly, keeping his mouth sealed against her clit as spasm after spasm rushed through her body. A high-pitched keen pierced the air in rhythm with her blistering orgasm.

"I can't wait anymore, honey." Pushing her farther onto the bed, his hard body came over the top of hers, knees spreading her legs, and in one long thrust his hard cock slammed into her pussy until it was seated deep inside.

"Christ, Jodi...I wanted this to be special," he gasped. "To take my time." He pulled his hard shaft back, increment by slow increment. "I wanted to romance you." His steel rod drove deep into her core. White-hot shards of sensation raced through her body.

John's breath rasped in her ear, every muscle in his back knotted beneath her grasping hands as he pulled his cock back with painstaking precision. The slow pace was maddening. "Slip the clothes from your body piece..." he panted, "...by piece." His neck corded with strain. "Carry you to the Jacuzzi..." His head fell back between his shoulders, and he labored to get each word out. "Hold you in the hot...water...whisper of days...to..."

His hips flexed, and his cock drove forward, a hammer pounding a steel spike home in one long percussive impact. Jodi's back arched, tight as a drawn bow, and her vagina contracted around his shaft. Damn, one more hard stroke, one more thrust against her cervix and her world would go up in flames of glory. "Unh...John, please!" He slowly pulled back to begin again.

"Share sips of champagne." Each word was emphasized by the hammering of his cock. "Share dreams...give you time to know the real me." Tremors raced through his taut muscles. Bracing his upper body on his elbows, John rose and all motion ceased. He looked directly into her eyes, smoothing back the damp locks of hair from her face.

"Marry me, Jodi. Please. Come share my life with me. I promise you moonlit walks. Nights spent in the warm ocean water, our bodies moving as one. Roses, chocolates, champagne. Enough excitement to last a lifetime."

The heartfelt words made her throat tighten around a thick lump of emotion. He finally gave in to desire and began to move in a steady rhythm. Jodi wrapped her legs around his hips, her fingers grasping his head to draw his mouth closer. Their lips met and she mumbled against them.

John pulled back, hope shining in his eyes.

"What, baby?"

"Margaritas. I hate champagne. Now shut up and fuck me, you fool."

GREAT CHEAP FUN

Discover eBooks!

THE FASTEST WAY TO GET THE HOTTEST NAMES

Get your favorite authors on your favorite reader, long before they're out in print! Ebooks from Samhain go wherever you go, and work with whatever you carry—Palm, PDF, Mobi, and more.

Samhain
Publishing, Ltd

WWW.SAMHAINPUBLISHING.COM